PREDATOR™

IF IT BLEEDS

ALL-NEW TALES FROM THE EXPANDED PREDATOR UNIVERSE

PREDATOR™

IF IT BLEEDS

EDITED BY **BRYAN THOMAS SCHMIDT**

TITAN BOOKS

PREDATOR™: IF IT BLEEDS
Print edition ISBN: 9781785655401
E-book edition ISBN: 9781785655418

Published by Titan Books
A division of Titan Publishing Group Ltd
144 Southwark Street, London SE1 0UP

First edition: October 2017
10 9 8 7 6 5 4 3 2 1

A CIP catalogue record for this title is available from the British Library.

Printed and bound in the United States.

Did you enjoy this book?
We love to hear from our readers. Please email us at
readerfeedback@titanemail.com or write to us at
Reader Feedback at the above address.
TITAN BOOKS.COM

For Kevin Peter Hall, the original Predator...
and
Jonathan Maberry, for friendship

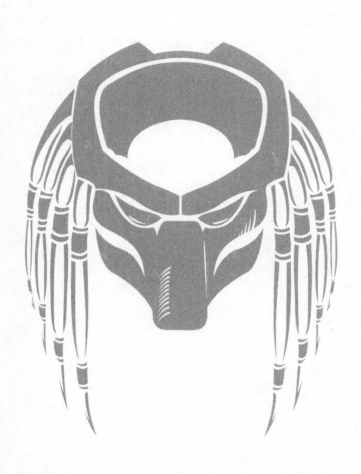

CONTENTS

INTRODUCTION

BY BRYAN THOMAS SCHMIDT

In June 1987, Twentieth Century Fox launched a new science fiction thriller franchise about alien hunters coming to Earth to hunt humans—*Predator* was born. A vehicle for rising star Arnold Schwarzenegger, who had already starred in such iconic roles as Conan and the Terminator, the film netted six times its budget and a franchise was born. Soon a sequel was in the works as well as a comic book line from Dark Horse Comics. Eventually there would be novels, crossovers with Fox's popular Alien franchise and more films to come, all aimed at satisfying the growing enthusiastic fanbase.

The stories in this volume are intended to celebrate the franchise's 30th anniversary as fans anticipate future developments featuring the Predators. We have worked from prior materials, including the previous three *Predator* films, the Dark Horse Comics, and various novels, and sequels or prequels to those are among the stories included here. Previous contributors to the universe, such as Tim Lebbon, Kevin J. Anderson, Steve Perry, S. D. Perry, and John Shirley, have all returned with new stories for us, plus we have new stories and new authors, as well—including some great adventures that document the intergalactic hunters' activities throughout human history, beyond even the future or our own contemporary age.

There are sixteen action-packed new adventures here stretching from future societies to the Vikings, ancient samurais, and even the American Civil War. And historical figures as well as familiar characters make appearances in many of them. The goal here was fun adventures that give fans what we have come to expect and love about *Predator* stories: lots of action, interesting twists and tactics, and human ingenuity vs. alien intellect and superior technology.

As a *Predator* fan myself, it was a blast putting this together. And so I hope my fellow fans will have an equal blast reading it. For me, one reason I love *Predator* is the sophisticated culture, language, strategies, and ethics the hunters choose to live by which make them far more interesting and even challenging than many alien opponents we often see. And the novels, comics, and films have all helped to expand that mythos in interesting ways. These stories do as well.

Whatever the case, this book celebrates both the past and the future of this exciting fictional universe. We hope it evokes old memories and makes new ones as we look forward to exciting new chapters in our favorite saga. If we write it, they will come.

If it bleeds, we can kill it.

Bryan Thomas Schmidt, Ottawa, KS, January 2017

"IF IT BLEEDS, WE CAN KILL IT"

—Dutch Schaefer, Predator (1987)

DEVIL DOGS

BY TIM LEBBON

Halley knows that this is a dream, but still the pain bites in, stabbing into her back as the dropship spins and rolls, out of control and plummeting toward the planet below. In reality the ship was pulled from its dive and they landed safely. But in this dream she is the only passenger, and she is loose in the dropship's belly. With each twist she's thrown against the bulkheads, with every turn she bounces from floor and ceiling, limbs snapping and ribcage cracking with the impacts, skull crumpling. It's her back that gives her the most pain. And it's the face of her mother she sees in her final moment, both sad and angry at the decision her daughter has made.

"If you go into space, you'll die there."

Halley snapped awake. She was sweating and panting in her narrow cot, bedding twisted around her limbs. She reached for the bottle beside her bed and popped two more phrail pills. She'd already taken six before going to bed. It was ironic that being addicted to painkillers brought her more pain than anything in life before.

She sat up and held her head, trying to blink away that final image of her sad mother. Her words had followed Halley into space, through the Colonial Marine academy, and into the dropship accident when she'd smashed the disc in her back. Being prescribed phrail had eased the back pain but introduced her to agonies of another kind. And her mother's sadness haunted her still.

The comm unit beside her bed buzzed. She jumped. It was silent in here, alone with the dregs of her nightmares. Sometimes she wished that holding a high rank didn't mean isolation from the rest of her troops.

"Captain Halley, you're wanted in Command."

"Who wants me?" she asked.

A slight, telling pause.

"The Major and someone else."

Halley pushed two hands through her knotted hair. "On my way." The comm hissed off and she stood, staring into the mirror over her small sink. She looked like shit. Three minutes to sort that out.

———

They gave Halley a Sleek-class destroyer for the mission, the *Doyle*. She knew the pilot, Corporal Jane Hanning, but the four marines were unknown to her. She'd requested that she choose her own troops, but the Major had told her that time was short, and that the team was being assembled even as she was being briefed. Her one comfort was that they were all from 39th Spaceborne, more widely known as the DevilDogs. She knew that anyone from her regiment would be a good marine.

The briefing was truly brief. She knew hardly anything, other than it being a rescue mission of some kind. The mission wasn't logged, and there was no flight or call number. Hanning would be sent coordinates once they were a thousand kilometers out from Charon Station, and everything else would be relayed en route.

The civilian passenger meant it was far from normal.

"So what's your story?" she asked the man beside her. They were each strapped into control seats on the flight deck. The *Doyle* had room in her hold for up to fifty troops, but with only seven of them on board, Halley had insisted they all sit up front. The big sergeant, Tew, acted as co-pilot to Hanning, seated to her left. At the comms station sat Rogers, the small French woman with the burn across her cheek. Next to her was Shearman, one of the tallest men Halley had ever seen, brash and confident but with too many battle scars to count. Behind them, seated close to the flight deck's rear bulkhead, Rosartz hummed a tune that bugged Halley because she was sure she knew it. Perhaps she'd get to ask her.

"I already told you my name," the man said.

"Kalien."

"Del to my friends."

"So what's your story, Kalien?"

"My story's nothing to do with your mission," he said. He tried to appear charming and calm, and give her the impression that this was actually her mission, not his.

15

But she could see through him. He was ex-military. There were no outward signs, but she recognized his bearing, his confidence, and the glint in his eyes. He'd seen things. Maybe he'd gone indie, but it wasn't like the Major to deal with mercenaries, no matter how highly sanctioned. Could be that he was a Company man now, ArmoTech perhaps. But she thought not. She'd met Company men and women before, and they oozed a particular smarm, and a derision for those in uniform, that was not easy to hide.

"So you're Section Seven." Akoko Halley hid a smile. Kalien's brief flash of anger was almost comical. "Hey, don't mind me," she said. "I'm just curious."

"Far as the rest of your unit knows, I'm a science observer," he said.

"You think all grunts are stupid?" she asked.

"Let's just wait until your orders come in, shall we?" Kalien unstrapped and pulled himself out of the seat, drifting across the flight deck to surprised glances from the Colonial Marines. They were still only minutes away from Charon Station, and grav wouldn't be turned on until they'd set coordinates and accelerated to cruising velocity.

Halley didn't worry about the man's safety. He knew what he was doing.

"Three minutes until thousand kilometer marker," Hanning said, glancing back at Kalien, then at Halley.

Halley nodded. "Hit it."

With the gentlest of vibrations the *Doyle* pulled away from Charon Station, the main Colonial Marine base in orbit around the Solar System.

"Oooh, that tingles," Shearman said, squirming in his seat.

"You're disgusting," Rogers said.

"Not what you said last night, mon ami."

Rogers gave him the finger over her shoulder. "For the record, Captain, Private Shearman has shared his privates with no one on this ship."

"Only in my dreams," Shearman said.

"Dream on," Hanning said from the pilot's seat.

Shearman threw Halley a feigned look of distress. "Captain, I'm being picked on."

"You look like you can take care of yourself," Halley said.

"I've had to save his ass more than once," Sergeant Tew said. "He might be big, but don't let that fool you, Captain. He faints at the sight of blood."

"Only my own," Shearman said.

Halley smiled. She enjoyed the banter, and as these troops were mostly strangers to her, it would be the best way to get to know them. The ship wasn't prepped for a long journey, so their destination must be only a couple of days away. Whatever waited there for them, she wanted to ensure that she and her squad were as tight as possible when they arrived.

She wished the Major had let her bring her own choice of marines. She guessed Kalien had something to do with that.

If he was really Section Seven, this was a Company mission. Section Seven were a group of ex-marines serving the Company's Thirteen, their main corporate board. Feared and disliked in equal measures, she'd never had any involvement with them. She wished that were still the case.

"Incoming transmission," Rogers said. Kalien pulled himself across to her station and took control of the comms unit. He paired his comm-implant and listened, head tilted. Appearing happy with the message, he flipped on the flight deck speakers.

Halley knew the voice she heard. Gerard Marshall, one of the Thirteen. She'd seen him in broadcasts and holos, but had never spoken to him before. He was very businesslike.

"Contact has been lost with the ArmoTech research station Trechman Two, ten billion kilometers beyond Pluto orbit. You're to proceed to the station, board, and investigate the cause of comm silence. My personal representative Del Kalien is your point of command, and Captain Halley is next in the chain. This is a military undertaking, but covered by Company jurisdiction. Del Kalien has final say on all decisions. Is that understood?"

"Crystal clear, sir," Halley said.

"Good. Any questions?"

"What's the Trechman Two's security designation?" Halley asked.

After a small pause, Marshall said, "Highest."

"And its purpose?"

"I told you, Captain, research and development."

"Military."

"ArmoTech, yes."

"So what are we likely to be facing?"

"Del Kalien has all the information you might need," Marshall said.

"And how many crew members are on board?" she asked.

"Crew members?" Marshall sounded almost surprised that she'd express a concern about the people they were going to rescue. Which made her suspect this wasn't a rescue mission at all.

"Thirty-two," Del Kalien said.

"Good luck," Marshall said.

"Thank you, sir."

The connection broke with a hiss, and Kalien pushed across to Hanning.

"Coordinates," he said, pressing his palmtop to the pilot's holo frame.

"How long?" Halley asked.

Hanning consulted the holo as a flight plan resolved. "If I pump us up to point-one, sixteen hours."

"Okay, let's roll," she said. "Once we're at point-one, grav on, then everyone to dining. We'll eat and get to know each other."

She unstrapped and pushed off, approaching Kalien.

"I need to know what we might be facing out there," she said.

"We'll know when we get there."

"And that's it?"

He shrugged.

"You fucking Company guys," she muttered so that no one else could hear.

He smiled. "What's for breakfast?"

As they approached the space station Trechman Two, Rogers hailed on open channels. There was no response. Two kilometers out Hanning put them into a slow orbit that matched the station's spin, and they gathered on the flight deck.

"Scans show hull integrity is intact," Rosartz said. "Life support is functioning, power's on."

"Any lifeboats been launched?" Halley asked.

"No," Shearman said. He was standing beside Rogers at the comm station. His quips and jokes had stopped now that they were geared up and ready to go. Halley liked that. She'd only been with this squad for half a solar day, but she could already tell that they would make a tight unit. Some had fought together before, and although no one had been upfront about it, she suspected they'd fought for Kalien.

Even so, she knew they were first and foremost marines. Working for the Company was just part of the job.

"And two transport ships are still docked," Shearman continued.

"Shall I take us in closer?" Hanning asked.

"No," Halley said. She was aware of Kalien's look of surprise but she continued staring through the windows, across the dark nothing of space to the dead space station. "I don't like it. No visiting ships apparent, and none of the station's vessels are missing. Send a drone."

"Roger that," Hanning said. She played her hands across the pilot's desk and a soft hiss sounded from elsewhere in the ship. They watched the drone flit toward the Trechman Two.

"We've got to get on board," Kalien said.

"If and when I've declared the place safe," Halley said.

"There's research on that station we need."

"Nice of you to tell us now that we're here," Halley said. "Please, be quiet. Now's the military part of this operation. Let us work."

Kalien did not reply. She thought she heard a heavy exhalation from Shearman that might have been a laugh. Halley kept her eyes on the drone.

"Screen down," Rosartz said. A holo-screen dropped and formed from the ceiling, drifting above the nav desk and increasing in size according to Rosartz's signal. The image flickered for a few seconds before resolving into an image from one of the drone's on-board cameras.

"Okay, give me a steady sweep anti-clockwise," Halley said. "Sensor suite on." As well as visual indicators, the drone would be checking for radiation leaks, atmosphere emission from damage to the hull, heat signatures, and other signs of damage or activity.

They watched in silence as the drone performed a full circuit of the Trechman Two. Hanning adjusted the controls and steered it around the structure in the opposite plane. Ten minutes later they'd all seen a full transmission of the space station's exterior. There was no sign of damage or trauma.

"So now are we going in?" Kalien asked.

"Wait a minute," Tew said. "Captain, can we swing by the central hub one more time?"

Halley nodded to Hanning. "What did you see, Sergeant?" she asked.

"Something…" He shook his head. He looked troubled, even scared.

"Sergeant Tew?"

"Just let me look."

They all checked out the screen as Hanning steered the drone for another pass.

"Closer to the windows. The third one along, then hold there."

A dark window reflected starlight.

"Lights," Tew whispered. A light speared on.

Tew cried out and stumbled back, and he'd have fallen if it weren't for Shearman holding him up. Rogers gasped and swore. Kalien drew in a sharp breath.

Teeth. Dappled wet skin. Tusks. The thing was back in the room, sitting almost motionless yet looking directly at the window. Watching them, watching it.

"*Yautja,*" Halley said. Of everything she'd been expecting to find here, this was the least likely.

"That's it," Tew said. "They're toast. We blow the station to hell and—"

"That's not gonna happen," Kalien said.

"You've got history," Halley said to the big sergeant, firm yet caring.

Tew only nodded.

"There's no ship," Hanning said.

"It didn't come here," Halley said. "It was brought. This is a research station, remember."

Kalien was frowning, staring at the image of the *Yautja* sitting in the darkness inside the Trechman Two, watching them.

"So what's the plan, Captain?" Rosartz asked.

"Stairway," Halley said.

"Huh?"

"'Stairway to Heaven.' The song you were humming earlier."

Rosartz beamed. "Damn, another fan of real music."

"The plan is, you do your military part of this operation," Kalien said. "You board the Trechman Two, retrieve the computer core, sweep for survivors, and kill that thing if and when it attacks."

"In that order?" Halley asked. "Survivors second?"

Kalien stared at her. His silence spoke volumes.

"Nuke it," Tew said. "There won't be survivors. Nuke it and get the fuck home."

"There's research on that station that—"

"Screw your research!" Tew said.

Kalien moved quickly. Tew was a good foot taller than him, but the civilian still lifted the marine and shoved him back against one of the flight deck chairs. It rattled in its mounting.

"Are you a marine?" Kalien asked.

Tew struggled in his grasp.

"Then be like a marine! Take orders and do your job. Or walk home." He let go and stepped away, straightening his clothes.

He could have killed Tew with one hand, Halley thought. She'd heard about some of the things Section Seven did. She didn't want to see them.

"We need a full structural plan of the station," Halley said. "Floor plans, service routing, location of the computer core."

Kalien held up his palmtop. Halley nodded at Hanning and he lobbed it her way.

"Now listen," she said. She felt a coolness descending, and behind that coolness was a driving need for a hit of phrail. Outwardly she presented a stony face, but inside she was quaking, nerves jangling as she anticipated the first hit.

When I get back, she thought. *When this is all done. That's my treat.*

"If you go into space, you'll die there." She almost heard her mother's voice out loud.

"Now listen," she said again. "There's six of us, fully armed, well trained, and six against one is—"

"About even odds," Tew said. "I've seen one of these things in action."

"Then you're useful to us," Halley said. "You all know the drill. You've all been instructed and trained to combat

Yautja." She looked to Kalien. "Will this one be weakened?"

"It'll likely have been drugged," he said. "But I can't guarantee you anything. Somehow it's escaped containment, so it's not easy to say what's happened in there."

"Plans are up," Hanning said, enlarging a 3-D image in the main holo frame.

"Right." Halley nodded. "We go in three by three. Two teams. Team one is Tew, Hanning, Rogers. Team two is me, Shearman, Rosartz. Kalien, you're staying here."

"Fine by me."

"Survivors. Computer core. Then out." She stared at Kalien, daring him to not put the search for survivors first. He looked ready to speak, but said nothing.

That coolness within her grew even colder. Ice around her heart. *Soon*, she thought. *When I'm back. Soon.*

"Let's arm up, then take us in," she said.

Hanning set an approach vector on autopilot, then they trooped down to the hold to prepare. As the long docking arm extended from the *Doyle* to the Trechman Two, Halley made her troops double-check each other's suits and weapons.

The nerves and fear were palpable.

She wished she'd popped one more phrail tab before suiting up.

There was still atmosphere. All life support systems were green. Nothing seemed out of the ordinary, other than the fact there were no people to be seen, and there was a *Yautja* loose somewhere on the station.

They all wore full combat suits with protective skin-masks and status readouts. The suits were flexible, but could also harden into armor. The combat rifles they carried could fire plasma bursts, laser sprays, micro-dot solid munitions, and explosive nano ordnance.

They should have felt confident.

"Stay on open channel," Halley said. "It knows we're here."

"No movement readings," Tew said. His voice was higher than usual, on edge.

"Don't trust your instruments," Halley said. "Eyes front. Okay, two teams head out." She watched Tew, Hanning, and Rogers break right, then led Rosartz and Shearman off to the left. Her team would reach the station's computer hub first, but on the way were several labs and the habitation pod.

She threw movement and heat feeds onto her visor, but always kept one eye focused ahead. She'd never confronted a *Yautja*, but she knew that they were born warriors, and their advances in tech often took surprising leaps. Their familiar invisibility suits were understood now, but no one could figure out how the beasts could sometimes evade motion and heat detectors.

"Sarge?"

"Clear," Tew said. His voice was smooth, almost in her ear.

"Stay cool," Halley said. She felt a pang at her choice of words. Someone had once told her she was cold, and the accusation bit hard. Phrail chilled her blood and numbed her senses. She'd hate to think it would leave her cold forever.

The silence was disconcerting. The stillness felt like the calm before the storm. Her heart hammered. Her suit gave a soft warning chime in her ear and fed her some calmer to settle her nerves.

They edged along corridors, checking every open and closed doorway, pausing at junctions and using suit drones to view around corners. They moved with caution but speed, aware that the longer they were on board, the more likely it was they'd make contact with the *Yautja*. It wasn't a large space station, but it was big enough to get lost in.

Halley hoped the *Yautja* was injured. Or perhaps it had seen them come aboard and had sloped away to hide, knowing when it was outnumbered.

Yeah, right, she thought. Everything she knew about *Yautja* told her that it would welcome such a challenge, not shy away from it.

"Lab on the right," Rosartz said.

The lab door was closed, but there was a large smear of blood around and on the handle. It was dried, flaky.

"Shearman," Halley said. She and Rosartz held back across the corridor, weapons aimed at the door, while Shearman pressed up against the wall and rested his hand on the handle. Halley prompted her suit to project a countdown onto their visors, and at zero he threw the door open.

Halley held her breath, finger squeezing the trigger. Nothing moved. But there were things inside the lab that had moved, once.

"Fuck me," Shearman breathed.

"Keep it down," Halley said. "Kalien, you getting this?"

"Yeah." His voice crackled in her earpiece, as if he was very far away. He might as well have been.

The lab was twenty meters square and filled with tables, pods, and sample storage cases. Some of the sample jars contained weird specimens—biological, mechanical, and strange mergings of the two. Blood was sprayed across almost every surface, and hanging from the ceiling were several bodies. They had once been human. They were badly mutilated, hanging by their feet from holes punched in the ceiling panels, spines torn out, bodies spewing insides to the floor and surfaces beneath them. Each swayed very slightly with the change of air pressure from the opened door.

"Six down," Rosartz said.

"Tew, anything?" Halley asked.

"Bodies," Tew said into her ear.

"How many?"

"Er... don't know. I'd guess... a dozen."

"Okay, we head to the computer hub," Halley said. "If we find survivors on the way—"

"There won't be any survivors," Kalien said.

"Radio silence from you, Kalien," she said. "Don't confuse the issue. This is a combat situation, and you're not involved."

They moved out, closing the door behind them. Halley wondered briefly about who those people were and what their families must be going through. *Best they don't know the truth,* she thought. *Company can tell them their loved ones died in an accident.*

"Movement!" Rosartz said. "Level two, zone four."

"Tew!" Halley said. "Got movement coming your way. Can you see—"

"Holy shit!" Hanning shouted. Then the shooting began.

Halley switched visual feed into her visor from her squads' bodycams, so she saw everything that happened next. Confusion, chaos, shooting, horror. And blood.

Hanning from Tew's point of view, sweeping her com-rifle up and around and unleashing a hail of laser fire, peppering the bulkhead and blasting electronics into a starscape of exploding points.

Rogers ducking down and rolling beneath the laser

burst, then rising and being pinned to the wall by something penetrating her chest. Her suit hardened into protective armor, but not fast enough. She opened her mouth to scream and blood filled her visor.

Tew staring, open-mouthed, terrified, as Hanning closed on him and passed by, shouting over her shoulder for him to hurry, focus on her, run so that—

Hanning's vision blurred as she was plucked from the floor and smashed into the ceiling. Her bodycam flickered, then focused again as she struck the ground. Above her, a shimmering shape manifested as if from nowhere. It stood astride her chest, raising one foot and bringing it down onto her face, again and again.

Her bodycam gave out.

Tew saw, and through his point of view, Halley saw as well. The *Yautja* was huge, head brushing the ceiling even as it stooped and stomped on Hanning. Sparks of white light sizzled across its armor. It wore bandages around its upper arms and wide thighs, and its traditional helmet was missing, revealing deep welts across its cheeks and around its throat. Tubes hung from these wounds. Its forehead was dotted with sensor points.

If it was sick, it didn't appear to care.

Tew raised his weapon, and at the last second Halley saw on his readout that he had selected plasma.

"Tew, no, you'll take out the entire—"

He fired. Halley's visor grew dark against the glare, and when she prompted it to access Tew's bodycam feed once more, there was only darkness. No vision. No sound. Nothing.

"We have to help!" Shearman said. "Level two, there's a staircase at the end of this corridor."

"They've gone," Halley said. It was not the first time she'd lost a marine on a mission, but it was the first time such a loss had felt so hopeless, so wasted. The *Yautja* had crushed the three of them, like grinding insects beneath its feet.

"The plasma blast must have killed it," Rosartz said. "Right, Captain?"

Halley wasn't listening. An alert was chiming in her suit, and the computer translated it from the Trechman Two's systems.

"Hull breach," she said. "Blast door on Level two, zone four has closed. Anything in there has been sucked out into space."

"No," Shearman said. "No."

"Let's get this finished," Halley said. "Computer core, back to the ship, then we'll blast this shithole into atoms."

"You sure our scientific advisor will like that?" Rosartz asked, dripping sarcasm.

"He can eat me," Halley said. "Stay sharp. Move out."

Every instinct was screaming at her to abandon the Trechman Two and get back to the *Doyle*. The whole place was compromised, with a dangerous alien on board and a hull breach. Even now she could feel a growing vibration through her feet as the superstructure strained under the tension. Fault lines would be spreading, pressures building, and internal blast doors were never designed to provide a permanent barrier between atmosphere and vacuum.

Time was ticking.

Halley led the other two past more closed doors. She knew they should be checking each room so that their retreat was covered, but they had no time. Now, they had to trust in speed to get the mission done.

She could mourn the loss of three marines and agonize over what she might have done differently later, when they were back aboard the *Doyle*. She'd have some questions for Kalien then, too. Like just what the fuck were they doing experimenting on a *Yautja*.

"Station's computer core ahead," Shearman said. "Security door sealed."

"Rosartz, get to it," Halley said.

Rosartz shouldered her rifle and got to work on the door mechanism, while Halley and Shearman covered the corridor in either direction. She tried to maintain her cool, but found that she was blinking rapidly, and sweat slicked between her face and visor. The suit removed it efficiently, but she was not handling this well.

Her vision was blurry. The distinction between her body inside the suit, and the outside, felt wide, as if the suit itself was much more than simply a thin layer of complex, hi-tech material. Halley felt apart from the action, and that would not do. Not now. Now, she had to be in the thick of it. Her two remaining marines depended on her.

"No movement," Shearman said.

"Yeah, nothing on sensors," she said. "It'll be coming, though."

"We're in," Rosartz said. The door whispered open and they backed inside, closing the door behind them. Rosartz keyed in a code and the door clunked locked.

"Kalien, we're in the computer core," Halley said.

"We need the hub and any backup devices," he said.

"We'll carry what we can without compromising our safety," she said.

"The *Yautja*'s still with the dead marines," he said. Halley froze, glancing at Rosartz and Shearman.

"But they must have been blasted out into space when the hull went. *All* of them."

"Just telling you what sensors are telling me. It must have survived, dragged their bodies to safety."

"Why?"

Kalien remained silent.

"I'll check," Halley said. "You two get what we came for." While they worked, she tried switching her feed back to the fallen marines' bodycams.

She gasped, then turned away so that Rosartz and Shearman could not see her reaction.

Viewed from Rogers' damaged camera, she saw the *Yautja* butchering Tew's corpse. She knew that the creatures often took trophies from the bodies of their victims, but to see it happening to someone she knew…

She switched off the feed. "We need to hurry," she said. "Done yet?"

Rosartz was prying a small unit apart with her combat knife, while Shearman loaded several circular objects into the belt around his waist. The backing sprung from the unit, and Rosartz reached inside and tore out an obsidian cube, about the size of her fist.

"We're done," she said. "Let's go."

As Halley approached the door, her suit warned her of movement on the other side. She glanced around the room and saw no other means of exit. She caught Shearman's eye. Nodded. Signaled to Rosartz.

Rosartz dropped the cube into a big pocket in her suit and aimed her palmtop at the door.

"As soon as it starts opening," Halley said. "Micro-dot.

Fill the corridor and blast it to shreds. On three." She started the countdown.

As the seconds ticked down, she frowned. The movement looked odd. Too small.

Reaching one, Rosartz signaled the door to open.

"Wait!" Halley said.

"Thank God—" a new voice said.

Shearman fired. A score of micro-dot munitions powered through the growing gap between door and frame, and Halley had a split second to see the woman standing beyond. Her white suit was grubby and stained with smears of dried blood. Her face was pale and drawn, as if she hadn't eaten or slept in days. On her collar, the familiar Company symbol.

Her eyes were wide with a terrible forlorn hope.

The munitions exploded and tore the woman apart. As the door was blown all the way open, the ceiling behind Halley smashed down and a heavy shape dropped to the floor.

She fell forward and rolled, coming up and bringing her rifle to bear.

The *Yautja* was already on its feet, heavy hand piercing Rosartz's stomach, holding her up in mid-air, blood dripping as her suit failed and peeled back. She was convulsing, com-rifle shaking in her right hand as she attempted to bring it to bear.

Shearman swung around, eyes wide in realization of what he'd done.

The *Yautja* threw Rosartz's ruptured body at the tall marine, pivoting on one leg as it did so, a movement almost balletic in its grace and simplicity. It spun around and brought its other leg up, catching Shearman in the stomach and dropping him. Rosartz fell on top of him.

32

They were out of Halley's sight, beyond the *Yautja* and a bank of computer cabinets.

Shearman screamed, and she couldn't tell whether it was fear or agony.

The *Yautja* stared right at her. She had never seen anything so alien, yet in its eyes was a calm, startling intelligence. It tilted its head as it looked at her, then crouched down and hissed, mouth open wide, fangs glistening and curved. The wounds on its throat shimmered with a bright green fluid that might have been blood, and the sensor pads across its face and head shamed Halley. The shame surprised her.

We did that, she thought. *Humans did that.*

She backed into the wall beside the door and lifted her gun, signaling the suit to switch the weapon to laser spray.

Behind the *Yautja*, Shearman stood. He was covered in blood. Some of it was Rosartz's, but he also had a terrible wound in his stomach where the *Yautja* had kicked him. His suit had hardened and was already applying med-packs to the wound, but Halley could see coils of what should have been inside poking out.

In his hand, Shearman held a plasma grenade.

Halley slid along the wall and fell backwards from the door. As she fell she fired down at the creature's feet. The shot struck the floor. The *Yautja* had already jumped at her.

Halley closed her eyes.

The suit darkened and hardened around the blast, but she still felt the white-hot shove of the plasma grenade's explosion. It tore her senses apart. The last thing she saw was a humanoid shadow leaping over her, ablaze, shrieking, thrashing.

And then there was night.

The pain bites in, scouring into her back as the dropship rolls and spins. This is a dream. Halley knows, but she can't pull herself out of it.

Every time the pain begins to spread, the phrail beats it back. It buffers her against the agony. It tortures her and makes her less than she could be, yet here and now it is saving her.

Here? Where? And now? What's now?

She struggles to open her eyes. She smells death, hears burning, feels a terrible warm wetness where her suit has been burnt away. Perhaps it's herself, insides turned out and the phrail giving her a few moments' grace between life and death.

"If you go into space, you'll die there."

It's not her mother's voice.

———

"...die... there," Halley said. Her teeth felt cold, lips hot and sticky with blood.

She opened her eyes.

The corridor ceiling and walls were deformed by the terrible plasma heat, still flowing in places as they cooled and reformed. She felt the heat on the air as she breathed, and around her where she lay.

She raised her head, looking into the computer hub. Fires roared. Black, greasy smoke rose from burning flesh, spiraling away as the station's emergency systems came into play. A sprinkler sputtered above her, spilling a trickle of water that hissed where it struck.

Halley sat up and reached for her gun. She'd fallen with it clasped to her side. Around her lay the scorched remains of the survivor they had killed.

Slowly, painfully, she got to her feet. Her suit was already addressing her wounds, and she felt the kiss of phrail entering her blood. It was in proper doses, small and targeted, not the heavy pills she took. Still it flushed through her system and reminded her of who and what she was—a captain in the Colonial Marines, and an addict.

She laughed. It came out as a croak.

Along the corridor were scorched patches surrounded by bright green splashes of *Yautja* blood.

"...in! Halley..."

A voice in her ear. For a moment she thought it was a surviving marine, but then she recognized Kalien.

"Halley... hear me?... happened to the..."

"Kalien," she said. "I'm coming back to the ship."

"Do you have it? Halley, do you have the computer hub?"

She glanced back into the computer room, at the merged remnants of cabinets and structure, and two melted marines. She shut him off.

Walking hurt. She looked down at her wounds and wished she hadn't, but her suit was maintaining her at a level of functionality for a while. It wouldn't last for long. She needed to get to the *Doyle*'s medical bay.

She knew that she'd probably never make it, but she had to try. She had to prove her mother wrong, one more time.

Phrail chilled her blood and numbed her wounds. She would not have been able to function without it. She walked without caring, turning corners and crossing junctions without checking what might be beyond. Her visor was still operational, but it hissed in and out of focus, its information only readable intermittently.

Reaching the airlock lobby, she looked behind her and

saw a trail of blood. She frowned. It wasn't all her own. Some of it was green.

The lobby was circular, and across from her, huddled against the wall, was the *Yautja*. It was shivering, curled into a ball at the base of the wall. Green blood poured from a dozen wounds. Burns wept all across its back, and many of its long hair-like tendrils had sizzled away, blackened nubs all that remained. One eye was gone, along with much of that side of its face.

It lifted its head to stare with its one remaining eye.

"Halley!" Kalien called. Halley frowned. She'd turned off the suit comm. Then she realized that she was hearing his voice for real, from past the open airlock doors and along the extended docking arm linking the Trechman Two to the docked *Doyle*. "Halley, do you have it? I can't let you on board until you do."

She looked toward the airlock entrance. The angle prevented her from seeing along the docking arm, but she knew what she would see. Kalien, standing there with a gun. They were expendable, and if he didn't get what he wanted, there was no way she was getting home.

Fine.

The *Yautja* turned from her and looked at the airlock door.

Halley slumped down against the wall and lowered her gun as the *Yautja* pulled itself upright. It must have been in terrible pain, but it made no sound. When it took its first faltering step toward the airlock, it left parts of itself behind.

"I'm coming," Halley said.

"You got what I want, Halley? It'll go well for you if you do. Promotion, rewards. You get what I want?"

36

"Yeah, Kalien," she shouted, and the *Yautja* paused beside the airlock entrance. "You'll get what you came for."

"Good. Come on through, then. I know you're injured. The med-pod is—"

The *Yautja* stepped into the airlock, and Halley heard heavy wet footsteps as it started to run.

"What the hell..." Kalien said, his voice just audible.

The alien roared. A laser pistol opened fire.

The man from Section Seven screamed.

With a grunt of pain, and another cool flush of phrail from the med-packs in her suit, Halley rose to her feet and pulled the plasma charge from her rifle. She primed it to blow, then linked it to her suit so that she could detonate remotely.

She lobbed it into the airlock, saw it tumble into the beginning of the docking arm, then slammed her hand on the airlock activation pad.

The doors slammed shut. She looked down the long docking arm, frowning, trying to make out what was happening in the *Doyle*'s airlock fifty meters away. She could not quite tell.

"Goodbye," she said, and she signaled the plasma charge to blow.

The thudding impact on the doors was heavy, but they held. The muffled blast was soon silenced by the sudden exposure to space, and when she looked through the viewing portal again, the docking arm was coming apart in a million pieces. Beyond, the *Doyle* was already drifting away from the Trechman Two, shoved by the sudden blast. Its open airlock door spewed air and debris, and then she saw two figures coughed out into space, locked in an awful, eternal embrace.

Halley rested her head on the airlock door and prompted

the suit to give her more phrail. But its supplies were used up.

She sank down to the floor. The pain would come in soon, and then she'd have to see if the station's med bay was still functioning. If it was, she might have a chance to make herself well enough to take one of the lifeboats and plot a course back toward home. If she sent a distress signal, a Colonial Marine rescue ship would come to pick her up. Her own DevilDogs would fly to her rescue.

Before that could happen, she had to get her story straight.

———

Halley knows that this is a dream, but the pain is assaulting her with wave after wave, burning into her very soul and chilling her to the core. The pain of injury is bad enough, the pain of addiction worse. In her dream rescue will never come, and she'll be resigned to existing forever in a state of perpetual, terrible need.

In reality, they will be here soon.

"If you go into space, you'll die there."

Maybe, Mother. But first I'm going to live.

STONEWALL'S LAST STAND

BY JEREMY ROBINSON

1

"If I look back and don't see your face looking the enemy in the eye, I will put a bullet in the back of your head myself." General Stonewall Jackson of the Confederate States looked over his men. They were lean and poorly dressed in patchwork gray uniforms. They carried an array of rifles, revolvers, and sabres. No two were alike, but the men *were* unified by the thing that bonds all soldiers—fear.

And that could be dangerous.

Disastrous.

A single man running in the wrong direction could undo an army. That was why Stonewall dealt with them in the harshest terms possible. Their enemy would be no less merciful, and Jackson wasn't about to let a bunch of Yankees take potshots at his soldiers. But he couldn't just make threats. He'd lose their respect. So he submitted to his own authority and declared, "Same goes for me. You see me running away from the enemy with fear in my eyes, it means I'm no longer your general." His index finger tapped his forehead. "Put a bullet. Right here."

He walked a few feet, eyes on the mud squelching up from under his boots. After several days of rain, the sun had returned with an unseasonable vengeance, pulling a good portion of that moisture back into the air, making it thick and sticky. There wasn't a part of his uniform that wasn't clinging to his body. He used the irritation to fuel his final words.

"Come morning we're going to give those Yanks a fight they won't soon forget. Next we speak, good ol' General Joseph Hooker's army will be retreating up the Potomac and straight into the Devil's asshole!"

The exhausted men rallied, letting out a rousing whoop. It spread through the ranks, a wave of sound rolling back through men who couldn't even hear the words. Didn't matter. His speech would be repeated in whispers throughout the night. Everyone would have their own version of the Devil's asshole speech. As long as they weren't thinking about their impending deaths.

"Now, eat well and sleep hard. We wake with the sun." Stonewall gave a wave of his hand and turned his back to glare at the dark woods separating his army from the open field, where many of these men would die. They had flanked Hooker's men. The plan laid out by General Lee was audacious, but perfect. But Stonewall wasn't about to commit his men to a battle without first seeing the battlefield for himself.

"Goose," he said, and the man was at his side a heartbeat later.

"We're ready, sir."

Goose knew the drill. He and his men were the best Stonewall had seen. Ruthless, skilled with both musket and blade, and sneaky. Before the war, he had little doubt that these were hard men. Criminals, most likely, and not just because they looked the part. They also protected their names, choosing nicknames for themselves. Including Goose. But on the field of battle, all men were equal, and the four gentlemen standing with Goose had more than made up for any past grievances.

Without another word, the six men strode toward the treeline, Goose by Stonewall's side, the others close behind, weapons at the ready. In the thick woods, Goose took the lead.

The spring's new leaf growth was already thick this far south, blocking what little light the stars provided. The moon, nowhere to be seen, had retreated like their enemies soon would. Goose paused, listening, his ears sharp. Wind shushed a course through the trees. It was followed by the hiss of falling water, shed from the shaken limbs. The rest of the night was still. Even the birds seemed to have fled.

There are killers in the forest, Stonewall thought. *The birds were wise to leave.*

"Lantern?" Goose asked.

"Just one," Stonewall said. "Keep the light small."

"Cotton," Goose said. The tall, wiry man slunk up next to them and crouched. After a few seconds of tinkering and a half-dozen whispered curses, a light flared, and then shrank down to almost nothing. But in the pitch-black night, it was plenty, and it would keep them from tripping over obstacles. Kept low, the light would be hard to spot, but a man falling on his face, that could be detected in any direction by anyone with a pair of ears.

"Remember..." Stonewall said, taking the lantern so the men could carry their weapons.

"We move in silence, observe the enemy and kill only when necessary," Goose said.

Stonewall couldn't see the man, but was sure he was showing his tooth-gapped grin.

"Or when fun," Cotton added and the others chuckled.

"Save that for the morning," Stonewall said, and then struck out into the forest's depths, eager to complete their mission, and if he was honest, hoping to drop a few Union soldiers before the night was over.

Twenty minutes later, he got his chance.

2

"I'm sweatier than the underside of Johnny Boy's momma's teat in mid-July," Cracker Jack whispered. He was the largest of Stonewall's recon team and said pretty much anything that came to mind, without fear of reprisal. Not because the others feared him—bullets paid no mind to muscles—but because this was how men such as these bonded.

"My momma's milk is the sweetest moonshine south of the Mason Dixie," Johnny Boy replied. He was Cracker Jack's opposite in every way. Short, fast, and sneaky. And while Cracker Jack was most likely to strangle an enemy barehanded, Johnny Boy could stick a man a dozen times and bleed him out in half the time. He was also shameless.

Stonewall winced at the image. He'd never met Johnny

Boy's mother, and reckoned he wouldn't want to, but his imagination never conjured a pleasant image whenever she and her various secretions came up in conversation. Johnny had a weasel's face and severely blemished skin. His mother was either a saint for copulating with a similarly built man, or equally unsightly.

"Quiet," Goose said.

At first, Stonewall thought Goose was just keeping the men in line. While on recon missions with this crew, Stonewall let his subordinate rein the men in. Kept their rebellious urges from targeting the general. But the stillness of Goose's body and the raised rifle in his hands meant he had actually heard something.

The men ducked down, breath held. Listening.

After a minute of nothing, Gator asked, "Sure you done heard sumptin'?" Gator had lived in the swamps of Florida. Didn't mind the heat, or the moisture. Seemed born and bred for it. Not much of anything scared him, not even, he claimed, "the twenty-foot gator I done killed with a hatchet." He wore the beast's long tooth around his neck as proof. Aside from his smell, Gator's weakness was his impatience.

He stood from their hiding place behind a thick mound of brush, shrugging his hairy arm out of Goose's cautionary grasp. He spun in a circle, eying the darkness. "Ain't nothin' out dere."

And then, a voice. "Momma's milk."

The garbled words were distant, but unmistakable. Someone had been close enough to hear their conversation and was now mocking them with the words.

Without needing to be ordered, the men readied their rifles and waited for orders. Stonewall gave Goose a nod and the man stood. "Two one two behind me. You know the drill."

Goose moved out from hiding, leaning forward, making himself a smaller target. Cotton and Cracker Jack followed, then Stonewall, and finally Johnny Boy and Gator. While Stonewall was willing to share the dangers of battle and recon with his men, he was no fool. His life and mind were far more important to the cause than those he served with. He would fight with them, but at times like this, any bullets flying toward them would most likely find another's body, before they found his.

"Low and tight," Goose said and then struck out toward the voice's source, guided by the oil lamp's paltry illumination. They were headed toward a trap, no doubt, but Stonewall needed to see what was hiding in these woods before he sent his army marching through it at first light.

The skill with which his men snuck through the darkness made him proud. The Yankees might know a handful of Confederate boys had ventured into the woods, but they'd never see them coming.

Goose paused to listen again, but it wasn't necessary. The Union men were announcing their presence with a boldly lit torch. There were three of them. All of them talking at once. Women in a kitchen, talking pies. But laced with fear and something worse, typically reserved for when a battle reached its end—desperation.

"Sumpin's got 'em all riled," Gator observed.

"Likely they know who we are by now," Cracker Jack said.

While Goose and his men had a reputation among the Confederate ranks, it was doubtful that reputation had reached the Union, primarily because when they encountered the enemy, they killed them.

Dead men don't tell stories.

"It ain't us," Goose said. "Listen."

In the silence that followed, the enemy's panicked voices slipped out of the night.

"I'm telling you, I looked right through 'im."

"His eyes glowed. The Devil himself lives in these woods."

"Wasn't the Devil. And it wasn't a beast." This voice remained calm. "It was a man. In the dark. Now, collect yourselves."

Just bits and pieces of conversation, but it was enough to start building a picture—one that Stonewall did not like. Not one little bit.

"You want us to believe a lone man slaughtered nine of our own without a single shot fired? Without a body left behind?"

These men had encountered an enemy in the woods, and it wasn't his men. That meant that the Union either had turncoat problems, which would be beneficial, or there was a band of lawless killers in the woods. That could be a problem, unless they joined *his* band of lawless killers. But the truth wouldn't be revealed until he questioned them.

"I want them alive," Stonewall said to disappointed faces.

"Damn," Cotton said.

"After they've opened their mouths, you can open their guts," Stonewall said. The rules of war said these men should be taken captive, alive, but they'd just be three more mouths taking food from his men. He pointed at Cotton, Johnny Boy, and Cracker Jack. "Flank them. When the light flares, well, you know what to do."

3

Explosive light filled the night, illuminating the surrounding forest with a suddenness that could wreak havoc with a man's vision. Combined with the sharp shattering sound of the lantern striking the ground, it was disorienting, so much so that Stonewall's eyes betrayed him. Despite being ready for the brilliant display, he saw a shadow dancing in the trees above, as though alive, and before the light lost its powers, he swore the shadow was looking back at him.

Stonewall's hand went to the revolver on his hip, but before he could drop it, a shrill scream pulled his attention back to the Union soldiers.

"Good Lord, it's come back for us!" Stonewall knew it was a man screaming, but it sounded closer to a coyote's shriek. The cry was followed by a cacophony of gunshots. An angry buzz stung his cheek and something heavy tackled him to the ground.

Remembering the living shadow, Stonewall struggled against the weight until Goose's voice was warm in his ear. "It's me, General."

A different kind of shouting followed the barrage. Men begging for mercy while others demanded submission. Stonewall noted the annoyance in Goose's voice as his subordinate helped him up. "Trying to remind yourself that you're not invincible?"

"I'm fine," Stonewall said, brushing the previous autumn's soggy fallen leaves from his jacket.

"You're bleeding." Goose poked Stonewall's cheek, the touch eliciting a hiss of pain. "Going to need a stitch or two."

Any other man who spoke to Stonewall in such a

manner would find himself on the frontlines of the coming day's battle, but Goose had earned the right. In the midst of this war, he was the closest thing Stonewall had to a friend. While he commiserated with esteemed men like Robert E. Lee, he couldn't just be himself. But Goose truly knew Stonewall. His fears about the war, his love for his wife Mary and for his newborn daughter Julia. He wanted little more than to be with them now, safe in their house, warm by a fire. It was why he fought with such ferocity. The sooner this war ended, the sooner he would return to them.

"The scar will suit me," Stonewall said, and then he turned his attention back to the small clearing, which had gone silent. He stepped past the fading light with Goose and Gator, the two men wary for trouble. They were miles from both Union and Confederate camps, but there was no telling who else lurked in the woods this night.

The three Union soldiers were on their knees, bleeding from fresh wounds, no doubt inflicted by Cotton, Johnny Boy, and Cracker Jack. The men had been savaged, but Stonewall was impressed his men hadn't killed one of them. Then again, most of their wounds appeared to be at least a few hours old, the blood dried and the bruises a deep purple.

Only one of the three looked up at his approach. The man was young, mustached, and wearing an officer's jacket. Their leader, and by the looks of him, a coward. His hands trembled. His eyes twitched. And then, eye contact. The man's face showed recognition, and then something Stonewall was not expecting—relief.

"S-Stonewall?" the man asked. "Thank God."

A Union soldier thanking the good Lord for the appearance of General Stonewall Jackson the night before a battle was set to be fought, or on any night for that matter, should have been unheard of. Yet here Stonewall stood, looking down at a bloodied Union man all but ready to kiss his feet, like he was Jesus Christ himself.

"Name and rank, son," Stonewall said.

"Captain Jason Ames, sir."

Sir, Stonewall noted. The respect wasn't just customary, it was sincere. But was that the fear talking or was it possible that his reputation as a cunning leader had earned the North's awe? If that was true, it boded well for the morning's confrontation. There was no weaker brew than an army steeped in fear.

"What are you doing out here, Captain Ames?" Stonewall asked.

Cotton drew a fist back, ready to clout the man, but Stonewall stopped him with a raised hand. He saw no resistance in the captain's eyes.

The captain searched the trees surrounding them. The two men with them hadn't stopped doing the same since Stonewall first looked upon them. Stonewall followed the man's gaze up to the branches. Where the shadows had danced. The lantern's spilled oil still burned, but the light was fading. They had just minutes before complete darkness returned.

"Captain Ames?" Goose prompted, keeping the conversation on track.

"S-same as you, I suppose. Scouting the—"

"Look at him," the man to Ames's right said. He was pointing at Stonewall, who hadn't yet looked away from the trees. "He's seen it, too."

Stonewall glared at the man. "Seen what?"

"Was a demon," the man said. "Lucifer himself."

The second nameless Union man added, "Bigger than the lot of you. Faster too. Glowing eyes. Killed nine men. We're all that's left."

"Ain't no surprise there," Johnny Boy said. "You Billy Yanks got about as much brains as you do—"

"Johnny," Stonewall said, silencing the man. Then, "Captain. You telling the same story?"

"It was a man," Ames said. "But he was alone. And big."

"And he killed *nine* of your men?" Stonewall's raised eyebrow revealed the statement was a question rather than a repetition of facts.

"Yes. Sir."

"And where are they? The bodies?"

"Taken," Ames said, eyes turning to the ground.

"Where?"

The captain turned his head upward. The trees were cloaked in darkness once more, the oil nearly burned out. Ames pointed up.

"No way it's jus' one man," Gator said. "I reckon we—"

A sound like a woodpecker pecking on a tree trunk thumped out of the canopy overhead. Ames and his men flinched at the sound. They'd clearly heard it before, and associated it with nothing good. "That him?"

Ames nodded. "We should leave."

"Only place you're going is a Confederate prison," Goose said.

There were few horrors on Earth that could compare to the deplorable conditions prisoners of war faced in the South. Starvation was rampant. The only thing that stopped its slow degradation of a man was cannibalism. These men had to know as much. Conditions in the North couldn't be any better. But Ames and his men seemed almost eager to meet this fate.

When a second woodpecker beat out a rhythm just above their heads, Stonewall's entire crew reacted, raising rifles toward the darkness above.

"Can't see shit," Cotton said.

"Ain't notin' up dare," Gator added, but he kept his rifle raised.

Goose began stomping out the last of the flames covering the ground behind them.

"Stop," Ames said. "All you're doing is blinding us."

Goose kept stomping. "A man can't shoot what he can't see."

"He..." Ames shook his head. "...sees just fine in the dark."

"Doesn't sound like a man to me," Stonewall noted, one hand on his holstered revolver, the other on his sheathed sabre. "Goose, light another lamp."

"Are you taking us back?" one of the Union men asked, his voice full of hope.

But Stonewall shook his head. "Not yet. We still have a mission to complete."

"We'll tell you everything you want to know," the second Union soldier said.

"Ain't no way to know if you're telling the truth," Goose said.

All three men seemed to melt from the inside out.

"Aww," Cracker Jack said. "Maybe we can convince ol' Johnny Boy's mom to wet nurse 'em back to—"

A crunch of leaves and twigs, at ground level, slipped out of the dark woods. Rifles shifted toward the sound.

Stonewall's men were putting on a good show, but he could sense they were spooked. Hell, *he* was spooked. But no one was leaving this forest until he knew what kind of danger awaited his army.

"Show yourself!" Goose shouted. He raised his rifle and looked back to Stonewall, who gave a nod. "Near as I can tell you've done us a favor. Come out now, and we can part ways as friends. You make me wait any longer than a count of five... well... I think what's comin' is pretty self-explanatory."

Gator, Johnny Boy, and Cracker Jack stood on either side of Goose, a regular firing squad. Cotton stood behind their prisoners, no doubt hoping the men would attempt to flee.

Stonewall counted down in his head. When he reached zero, Goose followed through on his promise, firing toward the sound's source. The others did likewise, shooting and reloading, again and again, striking trees and brush, but failing to elicit a shout of human pain.

"Hold," Goose said, lowering his rifle. He turned toward Johnny Boy. "Go see."

To his credit, Johnny Boy snuck away, disappearing into the woods. He would soon return with news of their failure, or success.

Stonewall flinched when something bumped into the back of his leg. He looked down to see Ames, shuffling backward, a look of abject horror carved into his face. "Cotton," Stonewall said, about to chew the man out, but then he turned around.

Cotton stood at an angle, dangling over one of the Union men. What looked like a harpoon jutted out from his chest, through the Union soldier's head and into the earth. As the life leaked out of him, Cotton's eyes met Stonewall's, pleading.

"Goose," Stonewall said, drew his pistol and shot Cotton in the forehead.

The moment his men spun around and caught sight of the horror, the harpoon withdrew, tugging the Union man's head against Cotton's chest.

Goose aimed his weapon at the pair of dead men. "What in tarnation…"

"Dare a line out da back," Gator said. "Somebody goin' fishin'."

As though to prove Gator's point, the pair of dead men were yanked forward, and then up. Into the trees. Where the shadows danced, and where someone continued the hunt he had begun with Ames's men.

4

"Bejabbers!" Cracker Jack shouted, as the skewered men flew up into the night. He spoke over the top of his raised rifle, looking for a target but finding nothing. Whatever had killed and taken the men was impossible to see, but it could be heard, crashing through the branches, moving away. "What kinda man could pull two heavy fellas up into the trees like that?"

"That's what I've been telling you!" the nameless Union man shouted, his voice cracking with panic. "It's the Devil himself, swooping down on us like a roaring lion. Eating our souls!" When he leapt to his feet and bolted, no one stopped him, and Stonewall didn't ask them to. Ames had all the intel he needed, and the runner was clearly a coward who would be of no use in the fight that was surely to come.

But when the man shrieked, and then gurgled in pain, all eyes turned toward him. He stumbled backward out of the dark, hands on his throat, blood oozing from between his fingers.

Cracker Jack and Gator raised their weapons and would have opened fire had it not been for Stonewall's raised hand and shout. "Hold!"

A moment after the command, Johnny Boy stepped into the clearing, wiping his blade clean on the bleeding man's arm. The Union soldier then succumbed to his slit neck, fell to his knees and then on his face. When Johnny Boy looked up, he saw the looks in his comrades' eyes. Then he froze. "What did I miss? Where's Cotton?"

"Up dare," Gator said, nodding his head up. "In dem trees."

"General," Goose said, doing his best to hide his fear. "Your orders?"

The only reason Goose would be asking for new orders was if he truly believed Stonewall's last orders—to reconnoiter the enemy camp—to be folly. Given Cotton's sudden demise and strange disappearance, Stonewall had come to agree with Ames. They were being hunted, but not by the Devil. By men. And men could be killed.

Stonewall pointed to Ames. "Give him a weapon."

Goose looked stunned and then complied, returning the man's belt, which held a holstered pistol and a sabre.

"Fight with us tonight," Stonewall said, "and if you survive, you have my word that you will be returned to your men unharmed, following the morning's battle."

After Ames had tightened the belt, he accepted a rifle with a nod. "I'm with you."

"Actually," Stonewall said. "We're with you. Lead the way."

Ames's eyes went wide. "T-to the Union encampment?"

"That is why we're here, and the cause for which my man gave his life. I intend to see it through, no matter the cost."

"Even if it's your own life?" Ames asked.

"This war is going to kill me sooner or later, and I'll be damned if it happens while I'm running from a fight." As he spoke the words, Stonewall's stomach soured. He didn't want to die. Had a wife and newborn daughter to live for. And he loved them more than a man at war could admit without going AWOL. But he wasn't a coward, and if he died fighting the enemy, then at least his wife and child would be proud of him. He pointed north. "Now... after you."

Gator took the lead with Ames, holding a torch that blazed brightly in the night. If darkness didn't hinder the men attacking them, he wasn't about to face them blind. Goose walked beside Stonewall, while Johnny Boy and Cracker Jack brought up the rear.

They walked just ten minutes in silence before Gator took hold of Ames and yanked him to a stop. "Smell sumpin'." He raised his nose to the air. Sniffed. "Dead men."

"Is this the way you came?" Goose asked. "Where your men died?"

Ames shook his head.

"Proceed," Stonewall said. "Slowly."

Gator crept forward just another twenty feet, Ames hanging back a few steps, and then he stopped again. "Body up ahead."

The group tightened and proceeded together. The details were hard to make out in the dancing firelight, but they resolved with each step closer. Two bodies hung upside down, dangling from the trees above, naked of clothing... and skin.

Their heads and spines had been torn away. Fluids tapped a rhythm on the forest floor, leaking from the opened bodies.

"Holee shee-it," Cracker Jack said.

"That Cotton?" Johnny Boy asked, tapping his rifle's muzzle against the open wound in the corpse's chest, right where Cotton had been run through.

Cracker Jack gave a nod. "Looks like it."

Stonewall knew what the others were thinking, because he had the very same questions. How could their heads and spines be ripped out? How could two men be stripped of their clothing and skin inside of ten minutes and hung, directly in their path? It didn't seem possible.

It didn't seem human.

The woodpecker returned, taunting them from the trees. Leaves shook overhead. From another direction, the voice: "Momma's milk." More shaking leaves. With every new sound, the group shifted their aim, waiting for a target.

He's playing with us, Stonewall thought. He glanced at Ames, who passed him a look that said, *You should have listened to me.*

Stonewall didn't argue.

A sound like wood crackling in a fire was followed by a whoosh that Stonewall heard, and felt. Something sailed past him and struck Cracker Jack. The big man was lifted off the ground and slapped against Cotton's corpse. As Cracker Jack's voice rose up in a scream, a crisscross of lines appeared on his face, squeezing the side of his head, and then cutting into it. Blood erupted from the conjoined wounds. His clothing fell away, small squares of neatly cut fabric revealing the same crisscross wounds all over his body. He was ensnared by a tightening net, squeezing his body against Cotton's.

As Cracker Jack's scream reached fever pitch, Stonewall drew his pistol once more and shot the man in the head. "I am getting tired of shootin' my own men," he shouted. "Show yourself, like a man. I want to know who's killing me before I die."

Stonewall had no intention of dying, but he couldn't very well fight someone he couldn't see. He hoped the taunt would do the trick.

It didn't, but then Johnny Boy whispered, "See him. His eyes at least. Watchin' us." He raised his rifle, looking over the sights, then he turned hard left and fired. The rifle's report was followed by an angry roar. The sound of it made Stonewall doubt his resolve once more. The roar, like the physical feats they'd seen performed that night, wasn't nearly human.

5

"Got that sombitch!" Johnny Boy shouted, as the branches overhead shook. Then he flinched, raised a hand to his cheek and smeared his fingers across it. They came away wet and luminous green, like he'd smeared firefly guts across his skin. "What the fu—?"

Johnny Boy's confusion—and body—were cut short by a spinning metal disc. It came and went in a whoosh, leaving the stricken man still and silent. Then he fell to his knees, and the impact loosened his severed head. Blood seeped from the wound and allowed the head to slide free and thump to the ground in time with his body.

Gator, unfazed by the recent violence, crouched down by Johnny Boy's still confused face. He didn't even flinch when Johnny Boy blinked. He just swiped his finger through the green smear. Smelled it. Tasted it. "Dat blood."

Stonewall slowly drew his pistol. He'd lost three men in under twenty minutes. Johnny Boy had managed to wound their adversary, but the bright green blood confirmed what Ames's men believed, and what Stonewall had begun to fear. They weren't being hunted by a man, or even by a group of men. It was that Devil himself that'd come for Stonewall Jackson. "Lord Jesus," he said, praying aloud as he did before every battle, "see us through this trial. Give us the strength of Samson and wisdom of Solomon. Guide us through these woods to safety and spare our lives. Your will be—"

Stonewall stopped. He finished every prayer the same way, 'Your will be done.' But God's will was a tricky thing. It might be for the greater good, far outside the grasp of mortal men, but it didn't always line up with human desires, even those of good Christians. So, instead, he said, "Please don't let the Devil kill me. Amen."

Finished with the prayer, he realized his compatriots were staring at him, Goose whispering his name. His real name. "Thomas." Nothing more needed to be said. It was time to go. Goose just needed a direction.

Stonewall turned to Ames. "Closer to the Union lines?"

Ames gave a nod. "By a few miles."

"I have your word that we will be returned safely to the Confederacy come first light?"

A second nod. "On my life."

"Lead the way. Fast as you can."

They ran through the night, guided by Ames's sense of direction and a lone torch. Just ten minutes on, Stonewall's lungs begged for respite, but he didn't believe, not for a moment, that the hunter had given up—certainly not after being wounded.

Ames stopped, hands on knees, chest heaving as he caught his breath. Before Stonewall could smack some sense into the man and get him moving again, the hunter bellowed in pain. The roar sounded similar to a man having a bullet pried from his body. It was wasting no time tending to the wound. He had little doubt it would pick up their trail soon enough, but at least the noise spurred Ames back to running.

After another ten minutes, their pace slowed considerably, but they didn't stop. Stonewall felt a surge of hope. The forest up ahead was framed by a dull light. A clearing. The Union forces wouldn't be too far beyond.

Gator must have seen this, too, because he picked up the pace and said, "Almost dare!"

He hit full speed in five steps. Then came to an abrupt halt, as though he'd run into a wall... that wasn't there.

Tiny streaks of what looked like lightning crackled from the point of impact, moving up and down, revealing an immense and inhuman form.

Gator fell back, rolled head over heels, and returned to his feet in a crouch. He looked up at their revealed enemy: "Is a gator man." He drew a long knife from his hip. "Like me."

The fearless alligator hunter lunged, blade swinging in a wide arc. The Devil reached out and caught Gator's face in its palm, but the man managed to complete his strike, swiping the knife across its midsection. The blade didn't sink deeply enough to eviscerate the beast, but it drew more luminous blood.

Whether or not the creature had even noticed the wound, Stonewall couldn't tell. While much of its reptilian-skinned body was exposed, it also wore a strange kind of armor, which included a sinister-looking helmet, or at least, what Stonewall hoped was a helmet. He had never seen or imagined anything so horrible in all his life, but he wasn't yet hopeless. This creature could be injured, and that meant—he hoped—that it could be killed.

With a shout muffled by the creature's large, clawed hand wrapped around his head, Gator drew his knife back, preparing to thrust it into the thing's gullet. But he never got the chance. The beast twisted its arm, spinning Gator's head 180 degrees, cracking his neck.

At the sound of Gator's snapping vertebrae, Goose opened fire, first with his rifle, and then his revolver. Every fired bullet was a perfect headshot. Had he been aiming at a man, there would be little left of his head. But this creature was far from a man, and its silver helmet deflected the barrage, showing only slight dents in the metal.

Goose saved his last round. "It's like shooting an iron plate."

The creature turned its glowing eyes toward Goose, as though merely annoyed by his assault. The woodpecker growl made Stonewall's hair stand on end. It was the only part of his body able to move. Then the creature's shoulder came to life, as a strange, third appendage, like a malformed arm made of metal, snapped into place. A triangle of red lines cut through the dark, emerging from the side of the creature's helmet, creating red spots on Goose's chest.

Goose took aim at the creature's torso and pulled the trigger just as a burst of bright blue light exploded from its shoulder.

Stonewall flinched away from the light, and the heat it threw off. He looked back in time to see Goose thrown against a tree, his body scorched. The creature stood still, looking down at its wrist, where a crackle of orange light revealed the damage caused by Goose's final shot.

"Sir," Goose groaned, reaching up. The front side of his clothes were burned away. His skin was red hot, cracked, bleeding and steaming, like a roast pig. "Give me... your pistol. And go."

Stonewall didn't want to leave the man. He'd rather put him out of his misery first, as he had done for Cotton and Cracker Jack. But Goose might be able to buy him precious seconds. He looked up at the sound of rustling leaves. Ames was beating a hasty retreat toward the forest's edge. Stonewall didn't know if the man was a coward, or just smart, but he decided it didn't matter. Running was the only sound option left. He handed his pistol to Goose, who winced, as his raw fingers wrapped around the pistol.

"Go," Goose said, teeth grinding. "Make it back... to your family."

Those final words propelled Stonewall after Ames without another word. He followed the faint orange light of Ames's torch, hoping the man knew where he was going. The clearing loomed brighter ahead.

And then a gunshot rang out.

It was followed by three more.

Two more shots, Stonewall thought. *He has two more.*

But the only sound that followed was a gut-wrenching scream that somehow seemed louder than the pistol reports. Stonewall stumbled to a stop at the forest's edge, torn between living and loyalty to the man he had left behind.

Then the Devil screamed at him from the dark woods, and Stonewall sprinted away, running into an open clearing, miles across, where his army would fight, kill, and die the very next morning. And where he suspected he might do the same, before the sun could rise.

6

Out of breath and more afraid than he would ever admit, Stonewall stumbled to a stop in the field's core. He was surrounded by tall yellowed grass, undulating in the night's breeze. The stars blazed overhead. Had he been with Mary and Julia, his thoughts would have been on the beauty of the Lord's creation. Instead, all he could think about was the Devil, set loose to torment him. Like the Biblical Job, but more personal.

He stood in front of the only sign of Ames he had seen since the man fled the forest. The man's torch stood upright in the field, like a beacon. And it had drawn Stonewall straight toward it, expecting to find Ames resting, or waiting in ambush. But all he found was the torch, casting a thirty foot ring of orange.

He was about to curse Ames when he heard a shushing behind him. Someone, or something, was moving through the grass. He turned slowly, having little doubt about who had followed him into the clearing.

The Devil emerged from the darkness, standing tall and bold. Luminous blood leached out of its sliced stomach and from two fresh bullet wounds, one in its thigh and one in its shoulder. Neither seemed to slow the creature down or cause any discomfort. Either shot might kill a man on the battlefield, from blood loss perhaps, but more likely from infection. He didn't think either would be a problem for the beast.

Stonewall drew his second pistol. "What are you?"

Three red dots hummed from the creature's helmet. The weapon on its shoulder targeted him.

The result of a shootout with this creature only had one potential outcome, Stonewall realized. Goose was a better, and faster, shot than Stonewall, and he hadn't been able to put this creature down. If Stonewall pulled the trigger, his fate would match Goose's.

Stonewall lifted his sidearm out, and then released it, letting it fall to the grass.

The monster cocked its head to the side, and then relaxed. The three red lights flickered off. With a clucking growl, the Devil unclipped its armor and shed the weapon mounted to its shoulder. Then it loosened the helmet and peeled it away with a hiss of fog.

Stonewall took a step back, as the helmet lowered.

Then four more when he saw its face, stopping only when the torch's heat licked up his back.

"Lucifer," Stonewall said. "In the flesh..." He drew his sabre, the long, polished blade glowing orange in the firelight. Gathering his courage, Stonewall shouted, "In the name of Jesus Christ, I command you to—"

The creature leaned forward, opened its muscular arms wide and bellowed. The hot stinking breath clouded around Stonewall, somehow both hotter and more humid than the thick early summer air.

With a metallic zing, two jagged blades extended from the creature's right forearm. It reached behind its back with its left hand and withdrew a razor-sharp disc, its fingers looped through five holes. Stonewall recognized this as the weapon that had severed Johnny Boy's head. It still held a thin coating of his blood.

The monster hunched in an attack position and began circling. Stonewall spun in a slow circle. His blade was longer than the creature's, but its long arms still gave it a longer reach. And he couldn't outmuscle it. But perhaps he could outsmart it? The way he saw it, his only hope was to make it strike first, hopefully dodge the blow, leaving the creature overextended and vulnerable. It was the same tactic that guaranteed victory against the Union during the upcoming battle, but would it work against a predator such as this?

After a few moments, the creature stood upright again, its horrible mandibles twitching as its eyes looked Stonewall up and down.

It's reassessing me, Stonewall thought. *It knows I'm trying to outthink it.*

With a flick of its wrist, the Devil sent the metal disc soaring off into the dark. The only evidence it hadn't flown away was the whirring of its blade through the air. The weapon was circling them. When the sound grew suddenly louder, Stonewall ducked with a shout. The blade soared past overhead.

It's controlling the weapon, Stonewall realized. *As long as I'm not fighting, I'm vulnerable. It's forcing me to engage.*

So he did.

Stifling the urge to let out a battle cry, Stonewall lunged forward, stabbing out with the sabre, hoping to sink the blade into the Devil's chest. But the strike was parried by the creature's bare hand.

Stonewall swung the blade, adding desperate fury to the strike. The sword sparked off the monster's armored wrist. He swung again, aiming low for the femoral artery, but he had no idea if the creature could even bleed out. The top half-inch of metal tugged through thick hide, leaving a two-inch slice.

Encouraged by the small victory, Stonewall raised the sabre over his head and hacked down, aiming for the Devil's shoulder. The sword came to a jarring stop that nearly pulled the weapon from his hands. The demon had caught the sabre between the two blades extending from its wrists. With a quick twist, the sabre was sheared into three pieces and yanked from Stonewall's hand.

He stumbled back away from the predator. His heel rolled on something hard and he fell to his backside.

Looking down, he saw his pistol resting between his legs. He snatched it up and began a slow crawl backward, away from the torch, and the monster it lit in hellish orange light.

Then a voice rolled over the open field. It was faint, but recognizable as Ames, and clear as the sky above. "Grapeshot!"

Stonewall's eyes widened. Grapeshot was composed of metal balls, the size of large grapes. When fired from a cannon, they could devastate an advancing infantry or cavalry. With a sudden clarity, Stonewall understood the torch's purpose. In the dead of night, it was a target, working in the same way as the creature's red-dotted triangle.

Backing up further, Stonewall adjusted his course, drawing the creature into the fire's light. Cast in the monster's shadow, Stonewall waited. The creature stopped again, peering first at Stonewall, and then the flame behind it.

It knows, Stonewall thought. *It's going to move.*

He raised the pistol and fired. The bullet struck the creature's side, snapping its attention back to him. He aimed higher, but heard the familiar whirring blade swooping in from the right. He flopped down onto his back, just as the blade cut through the space where his head had been. He raised his hand to fire again, but the boom that filled the night was much more powerful than his pistol could manage.

Luminous green burst into the night, covering Stonewall from head to toe.

He wiped his eyes clean. The Devil stood above him, its body ravaged by grapeshot, its head shredded into two halves. Stonewall rolled to the side, narrowly avoiding its falling body.

As he stood, a voice.

"You need to go!" Ames, on horseback, was carrying a canister of liquid.

The young captain slid off the horse and handed Stonewall the reins. "I made you a promise I intend to keep. Now go!"

"We can't let anyone know about this," Stonewall said. "No one will fight if they think the Devil makes his home here."

"Taking care of it," Ames said, sloshing liquid onto the body.

Recognizing the smell of kerosene and the sound of approaching men, Stonewall climbed atop the horse. "If we meet upon the battlefield, I will not hesitate."

Ames smiled, picking up the torch. "Then I will do my best to avoid you."

As the Devil's body was turned into an inferno, Stonewall kicked the horse into action and rode into the night, taking a direct course through the forest where his men had died. He rode without ceasing, feeling the Devil's claws reaching for him in the dark. He didn't slow down upon reaching the far side, or when the Confederate lines came into view, or even when he heard men shouting for him to stop.

What stopped him was a bullet, fired from his own men.

Stonewall lay in the grass, looking up at the sky, thinking of his wife and daughter, listening as his men shouted about the glowing green man, and he watched as a streak of light rose up out of the forest and winked up into the stars.

———

Thomas 'Stonewall' Jackson died May 10, 1863, from an infection caused by a bullet put in him by his own men, upon returning from a reconnaissance mission. The exact reason his men fired on him remains a mystery.

REMATCH

BY STEVE PERRY

Something is wrong.

The old sense hadn't been active much, only a twinge now and then, since the disaster in Alaska nine years back, but it was here, now, as strong as it ever had been.

Something is wrong. Danger! Death!

Sloane didn't pause, he kept moving, took the turn that circled the big oak, where the old deer path veered into the woods. Birds chirped, but he didn't hear anything else save his own breathing and soft footfalls.

Somebody was out there.

Who? The bikers? From the meth lab set up in the old RV parked by the pond deeper into the forest?

Nope, not them. Those clowns tromped through the woods like a herd of rhinos; you could hear them a mile away. They were stupid-dangerous, but, no, not them.

It was an overcast Oregon summer morning, and he was still a little stiff—these days, it sometimes took twenty or thirty minutes before he worked the kinks out. Back in his heyday, he'd slogged through the jungles of Vietnam carrying a full backpack, extra ammo, his rifle and scope, fifty, sixty pounds of crap, and he could come out of a dead sleep, ruck up, walk ten miles without blinking, set the sight, and center-punch Charlie from five hundred meters with a cold shot. He'd been good at his job. Long gone, those times. Had a birthday coming up, with a big number in the front and a zero following that, and he'd lost a step or two…

Somebody was watching him. He knew it.

He didn't want them to know he had any idea they were.

The path descended a little, weaving into the scrub fir and alder. Usually the mosquitoes weren't bad this time of morning, and he had planned to get five miles in and be back before Mary got up.

Not now. Now, he needed to cut his walk short and get home, where he had resources.

It had been a long time since he felt the need to carry a gun. He had a pocket knife, a little ZT tactical folder clipped inside his jeans pocket, but it wasn't a serious weapon, it had a three-inch blade. As a forest ranger in Denali, he had slung rifles that could hit hard enough to stop a charging brown bear the size of a small pick-up truck. Necessary there, not here.

These days, he saw squirrels or rabbits, and there didn't seem to be any bears locally, not even the little black ones you could shoo away by waving your hat.

He was good enough in the woods that he should have

been able to spot a casual stalker, and he couldn't, but he knew they were there.

Bad. And he knew why.

They were back. The killer aliens who had stalked him and Mary back in Alaska. The ones whose mysterious presence had been hushed up by the government, even though they had killed more than a couple of people.

And if they were here? It was because they had come looking for him. Too much of a coincidence otherwise. He had killed some of them, and they had tracked him down, years later, to repay him for it. No discernible reason to believe it, but that's what it was.

Every step he took, he expected one of those energy-bolts the predators used, waited for it to spike and burn a fist-sized hole through him. Be dead before he hit the ground.

He made the short loop and headed home. They didn't shoot.

Why?

The hairs on the back of his neck settled as he left the woods and headed toward the house, the sense of being watched fading.

It was them, but they didn't kill him.

Why not?

Mary was up, dressed in her old blue flannel nightgown, scrambling eggs in the black skillet. Still gorgeous at fifty-five, best thing that had ever happened to him, despite how they'd met. Her dead brother, the killed bears, the creatures...

He walked past the kitchen, straight to the junk room's gun safe. He twirled the dial, opened the heavy door, and pulled out his MegaBeast, the short-barreled custom in .610 GNR, and loaded it. One round, falling-block, based on the Ruger #1.

Only one round, but a solid hit would stop a charging elephant dead in its tracks. Punch a hole through a brick wall.

From the kitchen, Mary said, "Babe? What is it?"

He pulled the BFR from the safe and loaded that, too: five rounds of .500 Max. He felt better. He could hit back now.

Mary came down the hall. "Sloane? What?"

"They're back," he said.

"Oh, shit!" she said.

No need for him to say who.

———

Nakande chirred absently to himself.

<What?> Vagouti said.

<This is the Sniper? He is old, he moves slowly. Not even armed. Two of us? A *child* could take him.>

<Looks can be deceiving. You know what he did. It is why we hunt together.>

He nodded. Yes, yes. It was well known and often told, the story. A hunter of Hunters, the ooman. Fragments of recordings had been sent back to the ship when it happened, enough to tell the tale. But—look at him. He dodders. The victory would be hollow, the trophy meaningless. All the interstellar travel, for... *this*?

<I would stretch a little,> she said.

He looked at her.

<The wheeled house, with the great stink. They are all armed and young.>

He nodded again. <It would be good to stretch.>

"What are we going to do? Call the law?"

Sloane shook his head. "And tell them what? More of the alien space critters who look like Wonder Wart-Hog and who killed a bunch of bears and people in Alaska nine years ago have come to call? They'd lock us up. If they could get here in time."

"The feds know about them."

"Yeah, but which feds? And how long would it take for them to put a black ops team on the ground here? I don't think we can wait."

She dressed, put on her jeans, laced her boots, shrugged into a flannel shirt.

"We run," he said. "Pack the truck and go, far away and fast."

"How did they find us?"

He shook his head. "I don't know. They have spaceships, they have superior technology—doesn't matter, they tracked us down."

"You think they came to kill us?"

"I do. I don't know why they didn't take me out in the forest."

"You were unarmed. That wouldn't be sporting, would it?"

He looked at her. Of course. The predators took on giant brown bears using only their blades. No real hunter would get any joy from shooting a sitting duck. They wanted prey who could fight back. He had demonstrated that well enough.

"Okay, here's the deal. We grab the go-bags. When we get to Portland, I'll drop you off, you get a room, and I will—"

"No," she said. "You aren't going to draw them away

from me. We live together. If we die, then we die together."

"Mary—"

"Not open for discussion, Sloane."

He grinned. Well. Never any question she was as good as they came, far too good for him.

She said, "If it took them nine years to find us, maybe we can throw them off our trail longer, now that we know they are looking. New names, new place."

"Sounds like a plan," he said.

But when they went to open the pick-up, all four of the tires were flat, shredded, and that vehicle wasn't going anywhere.

"Well, shit," he said.

———

Harvey banged his shoulder on the frame of the fucking RV as he went out the door. Again.

"Fuck," he said, without any particular anger. Happened all the time: narrow-ass door, and him being six-six and two seventy-five.

He scratched at his bare chest; the new "88" tat itched. Fucking tattoo artist musta had a dirty needle; thing was more'n two weeks old and it still itched. Ought to be worth a discount when he got the next one.

He walked to the big Douglas fir tree, unzipped his crusted jeans, and pissed on the bark. Damned toilet in the RV was stopped up again. Martin was supposed to have fixed it, but Martin liked his own product too much and was stoned most of the time.

From behind him: "I need a new valve. To fix the crapper."

Speak of the devil.

"What, I'm your mother? Go and fucking get one," Harvey said.

"Money, dude, I ain't got no cash."

"Look in the drawer next to the sink, right where it always is. Should be plenty."

"Oh, yeah, right."

Harvey shook his head, tucked his package away and zipped up, turned to look.

Martin was on the skinny side, all the crystal, but he was still buffed. Liked to hit the iron, habit he'd picked up in the joint, and he was passing strong, but getting mush-brained—

Chirrr.

"What was that? Sounds like a giant fucking squirrel."

Harvey looked around. He pulled the cocked-and-locked .45 tucked into his back pocket, thumbed the safety off.

"Wadn't no squirrel," he said. "We got company."

Martin reached inside the doorway and came out with the Savage 12-gauge pump. He said, "Hey, Beau! Wake up!"

From inside, Beau said, "What?"

"Visitors!"

Martin stepped down, shotgun pointed ahead of him. After a second, Beau emerged, buck naked, hairier than Bigfoot, carrying an Uzi. "What? Cops?"

"I don't think so," Harvey said. "They would have been all over us by now. Might be some competition lookin' for free product."

"I'll give 'em some free buckshot," Martin said. He laughed.

Harvey was looking right at Martin when there was a flash, a loud sizzle, and a hole just... *appeared* in the middle of Martin's gut—!

PREDATOR: IF IT BLEEDS

"Motherfucker!" He pointed the .45 at the woods and cranked off rounds, as Beau started to hose the trees with his Uzi on full-auto—

Beau screamed, and Harvey looked over to see Beau's arm get blown off—!

———

Sloane heard the gunfire, a distant echo. Pistol. Full-auto subgun. Two shooters.

"The bikers," he said. "We need to get out of the house. We know the woods better than the aliens. We'll use the ghillie suits."

Mary nodded.

———

In his unit cruising, Mac got the call from Loretta. "Mac? We got a report of shots fired out toward Crown Pond."

"Copy that, dispatch. Bikers are probably target shooting again."

"You want me to get Charlie and Arnie to meet you there?"

"Nah. The bikers know better than to screw with us. I'll check it out. If I need help, I'll call you."

"Be careful, Mac. They are probably drugged-up. No telling what they might do."

"I hear you."

———

<Little sport here,> Nakande said. <Target practice.>

<They were inept,> his mate said. She shrugged. <But they were what was available. Better than nothing.>

<We didn't come all this way to slaughter such poor prey.>

<The day is yet young,> she said. <Shall we go find the Sniper?>

<Yes. And with hope he still has some of his former skill.>

He didn't believe it, though. Sad.

Been a long time since he'd worn a ghillie suit but it was like riding a bicycle. Still smelled like moldy canvas overlaid with cat pee.

He smiled at Mary as she zipped up her suit.

"Are you laughing at me?"

"A little bit, yeah. You're cute. Well, you would be if I could see you."

She grinned back at him.

"Which rifle you want?" He was taking the Beast and the BFR. Extra ammo. A big sheath knife. He wished he had some grenades. A rocket-launcher. A tactical nuke.

"The Winchester .308."

"Sidearm?"

"No. Anything big enough to stop one of them would probably break my wrist."

"Ah, you are tougher than you look."

She glanced down at the suit. "Right now, I look silly."

"Well, yeah. A little bit. Silly ghillie."

Mac could smell the burned meat when he rolled up on the trailer, and he saw the bodies quick enough.

Jesus Christ!

"Loretta. Send Charlie and Arnie. Call Sheriff Perkins. Call the state police and tell them to get a SWAT team out here."

"Mac?"

"I got three biker corpses, look like they were killed by death rays. We got big trouble here."

Vagouti said, <The dwelling is quiet.>

Nakande nodded. <Yes.>

<I see no signs of life. I cannot hear them.>

<The vehicle is disabled. They cannot have left.>

She stared at him. <And how did we come to be here? Do you think their *legs* are disabled, too?>

He shook his head. She had a barbed tongue, his mate, and never did she let him forget it. Fortunately, she had other virtues. An excellent Hunter, she was.

<I will go look,> she said.

<I can do that,> he said.

<One would think so. Nonetheless, I will go.>

He shrugged. Not worth the argument.

It wasn't long before she returned. <They are gone.>

<Well. They are on foot. Probably armed. We can hunt them. More sport that way.>

<Yes.>

"Sloane, do we have a plan?"

He nodded. "Yeah. We work our way through the forest, to the bikers' RV. They have a truck, and motorcycles. We will borrow a ride."

"You think they're dead?"

"Bet on it."

"After that?"

"One step at a time. If we hear pursuit, we'll take cover and knock 'em over."

"If we can see them."

"There's that. But, we did it before."

"We barely survived."

"Barely is better than not at all."

———

Mac should have waited for backup, but the place was as still as a tomb, and whoever had slaughtered the three bikers had to be long gone.

He unracked the shotgun and chambered a round. Not that doing so made him feel a whole lot better—he saw a .45 pistol, an Uzi, and a 12-gauge pump next to the dead men, and enough expended brass to see they had gotten off more than a few rounds. Somebody had killed them anyway.

In the damp ground near the biggest one's body, there was a footprint. It had a pebbled pattern to the sole, and when he put his boot next to it? Jesus, he wore a twelve, and that print was almost twice as long, and easily twice as wide.

Good Lord! The big biker's boot prints were all over, he had to be pushing three hundred pounds, and this print was way deeper. How big a man would that be? Seven feet? Four hundred pounds?

Bigfoot, armed with a weapon that punched a fist-sized hole through and through, same size front and back of the body?

"Loretta, where is that SWAT team?"

"On the way from statie base, forty-five minutes ETA. Charlie and Arnie should be there in ten."

"Turn our guys around. I don't want them showing up here and getting ambushed. The bikers got slaughtered by somebody with way more firepower than we have. I'm gonna move my unit and find a spot to lay low. Tell the staties to call me on tach-three when they get close."

"Copy that, Mac. What is going on out there?"

"Wish to hell I knew. But it's bad."

"Hear that?"

He looked at Mary. "What?"

"Listen."

He strained his ears. Yes. A faint noise, behind them, toward their house. Not really close, but not that far away.

"I should have gotten those hearing aids," he said.

"Remember that you said that later."

If there is a later.

"They are behind us. Or maybe it's just one. We need to get off-trail and hunker down."

"They have that stealth gear."

"Yeah. But it's not perfect. If you know what to look for, you can see it. My eyes haven't fogged over that much. Come on."

<We should proceed with more caution.>

<For an old ooman and his untrained mate?>

<Remember the story.>

<I am Nakande, who has stalked and slain *kiande*

amedha in single-combat! I am not cowed by a *story*!>

For once, Vagouti kept her silence, which was good, because he was not going to be warned off by his mate in this matter! Two old oomans, one step from the grave? Bah!

<They cannot be far,> he said. <I will spike the male. You can have the female.>

Again, she held her voice. Which was as it should be.

―――――

Sloane hadn't fired a weapon outside the Tricounty Gun Club in years, and even then, not as often as he should. The Beast wasn't a tack-driver at distance, but they were only fifty meters off the trail where it narrowed, and he could make that shot blindfolded.

He hoped.

He slowed his breathing, soft-focused his vision, taking in the trail. His weapon was ready. He was ready.

As soon as he fired, Mary would also shoot. All she had to do was line up on the twisted trunk of the little madrone tree and fire, because, if he saw the air blur, that's where he was going to take the creature.

As soon as they fired, they would roll and scrabble, in case anybody managed to figure out where the shots came from.

There was no talking now, no distractions. Only waiting. Time passed slowly, slowly…

"I see it," he whispered. "In three… two… now—"

He squeezed the trigger, sights lined up on the rippling air in front of the madrone—

Mary's Winchester roared.

"Go!"

PREDATOR: IF IT BLEEDS

They rolled, heard an unearthly scream, and a bolt of energy blasted the spot three meters behind them—

"Go, go, go!"

Either they missed, which Sloane didn't think likely, or there was at least one other out there.

Damn!

Vagouti knelt by Nakande. He was still alive, but he wouldn't be for long. He had been hit twice by projectile weapons, rifle pellets, one through the lungs, the other near the hip.

His voice was full of fluid. <You... were... right,> he managed to say, before a hard cough wracked him. He brought up bright green blood. <I underestimated the ooman—>

He coughed again and offered his death rattle, just like that.

Gone.

She grieved, but only for a moment. She deactivated his self-destruct. At this range, it would kill the oomans, but she wanted to live long enough to do that herself.

Yes, indeed.

Mac heard the shots, one much louder than the other. Big boom, high-caliber rifles. Who was shooting at whom?

There wasn't anybody else out this way, middle of nowhere, except for the senior couple who'd bought the McGee place a few years back. The old boy had guns; Mac had seen him at the range a couple times. Retired forest ranger or something, white hair, skin like old rawhide.

He didn't hold out much hope for them, they were

shooting. Not if three heavily armed bikers couldn't survive against them. Whoever *they* were.

Shit. He should wait for the SWAT team, but if somebody was in trouble out there? He had to check it out. That's what they paid him to do.

Well, shit…

———

Sloane and Mary moved as quickly as they could through the forest. Their pursuer would be looking for another ambush now, and he'd have superior weapons to clear out any suspicious spots. Speed was what mattered. If they could make it to the bikers' RV, get their truck or even a bike running, they could leave it behind. It probably had transportation somewhere, but an open road with the pedal to the metal was better than beating your way through the woods on foot.

"Sloane?"

"He'll be moving slower now, he doesn't know if we'll take another shot. Be a mistake for him to risk it."

"You hope."

"What I would do, and he's a hunter going after prey that just seriously wounded or killed his buddy. We should be able to stay ahead of him."

———

Vagouti mourned Nakande even as she was angry with him. His dying breath he had admitted it. He'd dismissed the ooman as serious prey because he was old. Age took strength and speed, but it didn't always take skill. Firing a weapon with which you had practiced ten thousand times? A squeeze of one digit, no strength or speed needed for that.

She would not make the same mistake. They were running for the wheeled house that stank, where the other, less-skilled oomans had died. It made sense—there had been transportation there, and they would think to outrun her that way.

Her mandible twitched.

It was a risk, but it made sense: Trying to follow them through the forest was not the best action.

Best would be to arrive where they were going before they did, and have them walk into her line of fire.

Though maybe she would use her blades. It would be more satisfying that way.

Mac stayed off the trail, working his way through the brush carefully. Concealment wasn't cover, but if they didn't see him, they'd have a harder time zapping him with their lasers or whatever. He moved deliberately, not trying to hurry. Either the old couple had killed the bad guys or they had been killed; there hadn't been any more firing, save those two shots. Likely whatever had happened was a done deal, and really, when he thought about it, he should wait for the SWAT team, but, no. On the off chance somebody still needed his help, he had to go look.

Sloane slowed down.

"What?"

He took a deep breath, let half of it out. "Thinking here.

If the creature behind us killed the bikers, then they know about the place."

"So? Oh. Wait."

"Yeah. They would know about the truck and bikes there."

"You think they shredded tires there, too?"

"If they knew the bikers were dead and they expected to catch us at home, maybe not."

"Then what?"

"They know we are running, and the nearest quick escape would be the bikers' truck or motorcycles."

"Yeah? And?"

"If I were tracking us and I thought I knew where we were headed? Moving slowly to keep from getting shot would be relatively safe, but circling around and moving fast to get there ahead of us? That would be my preference."

"Crap."

"If they have hunted people before, they have figured out how we think; that's the first thing you do with dangerous prey. You make it play your game."

"I am guessing that it might not be in our best interests to walk up to the bikers' place without great care. Well, maybe—what's that?"

He listened. "Somebody ahead of us, coming this way. Off-trail."

"The monster?"

"I don't know. Not making as much noise as I would think. Let's hunker down. Maybe it will step in front of our guns again."

Mac had worked up a pretty good sweat. The trees shaded him, but the marine layer was burning off, it was getting warmer—probably hit ninety today—and he was wishing he had brought a water bottle or a canteen.

There was a stream not far, and if he wanted to risk getting sick from sipping water full of beaver and duck crap, he could get a drink. Should have brought his filter straw, back in the unit's trunk.

Should have brought the Marines and the Air Force, while I'm thinking about it.

He looked at his intended path ahead. Mostly trees and bushes and blackberry brambles.

He stepped into a small clearing.

———

"Don't shoot," Sloane whispered. "It's a deputy."

Mary said, "I'm not blind, I can see that."

"Let's see if we can warn him without him blasting the trees."

He started whistling the alien theme from *Close Encounters of the Third Kind.*

"Really, Sloane?"

"Who's there?! Sheriff's office! Come out with your hands up!"

"Deputy, this is Sloane and Mary. We bought the old McGee place. You saw me at the shooting range."

"Come out where I can see you! Put your weapons down!"

"Deputy, we really have to hurry this up. There's somebody else in the woods and they are killers."

"I saw the bikers. Come out!"

"We are wearing ghillie suits. We stand up, we are going to look like bushes. Our weapons are down. Don't shoot us."

"Slow and easy."

They did that. Sloane already had his head cover shoved back, as did Mary.

"Jesus! How did I miss you?"

"We didn't want you to see us."

"What the fuck is going on here?"

"Step a little closer, we don't want to be yelling at each other."

"SWAT is on the way."

"We'll need them," Sloane said.

"Why did you whistle that tune?"

"To make you wonder just that, and not spray the woods with your shotgun."

"Ah."

———

Mac said, "You are fucking kidding me!"

"No. We ran into these things in Alaska, almost a decade back. The feds know about them. There was a big explosion afterward, wiped out the evidence. They are back."

"You're crazy." But he thought about the footprint. Bigger than any man's he'd ever seen.

"You ever see anybody killed like those bikers?"

"No, but maybe it's some kind of black ops thing. A rival gang, maybe."

"Does it really matter, if they are killing people?" Mary said.

He looked at her.

"Where did you park your car?"

"Couple hundred yards from the camper. Off the logging road."

"Good, maybe we can get there without it—or them—seeing us. You can take us in; we can talk about it somewhere safer than here."

"I'll need your guns."

"No. If that thing pops up, you probably won't see it, it's got some kind of electronic camouflage, and we need to tag it before it does us. Three shooters are better than one."

Mac considered it.

"We need to get moving, Deputy."

"Mac. Call me 'Mac.'"

"If it is ahead of us or behind us, either way, we can't stay here."

———

Vagouti arrived, and a quick scout of the area revealed that, save for the dead ones, she was alone.

Good.

She used her wrist-blades to disable the vehicles, a four-wheeled one and three two-wheelers. Slashed the tires on the wheeled house, too. Should have done that earlier.

She found a perfect place where she could watch the dwelling, then decided it was too perfect. Were she in the oomans' minds, she would note that spot upon arrival.

There was a second location, not as good, but sufficient. She went there. Even enstealthed, they had killed Nakande. How? It did not matter, only that it had happened. She had to assume they might spot her unless she had complete cover. Nakande had made a fatal error. She would not. She must control her rage. Her mate was gone, and a foolish gesture on her part might gain her similar results. The old ooman and his mate seemed no less deadly than the stories.

———

Sloane said, "We're thinking that it—or they—will probably have beaten us to the RV and set up there. Can we get to your car without being seen if they are there?"

"Yeah, we need to circle to the east, through the gully. Harder going that way."

"Beats the other option."

"Yeah."

———

Vagouti settled, calmed her breathing, and waited. A Hunter had to be patient. Nakande had been a good Hunter and fighter, but patience had not been high on his list of virtues. He was strong and fast, and that had been enough. Until now.

She would spike them. Skewering and carving would have been more satisfying, but she was not going to underestimate them. All the *Yautja* who had done so thus far, including her mate, had died for so doing. Quick and clean, take the skull, and go home, where she would have to explain to her young why their sire was not with her.

He made a mistake, she would say. *Learn from this.*

———

The gully was more or less dry, but fairly steep descending and climbing. The RV was a hundred or so meters to the west, not visible through the thick forest. With luck, they would climb out, work their way down the dirt road to the deputy's cruiser, and get the hell away before their stalkers knew they were gone.

Sloane and Mary had never spoken of what happened in Alaska to anyone, but that cat was out of the bag, now.

Whoever in the federal government was in charge of alien clean-up would have to come and do some work here, but that was something to worry about later. First, they needed to get clear.

They climbed the slope up the other side of the gully. Come the October rains, this would be a river, but that wasn't something he needed to worry about either.

Almost at the top, Mac grabbed a dry sapling for support and the wrist-thick bole snapped off just below his hand.

Made a loud *crack!* in the quiet morning.

"Shit—!" Mac said. He caught at a low branch on a big fir tree and stopped his slide down the slope.

Sloane held a finger to his lips for silence.

They listened. He was trusting Mary's and Mac's ears more than his own, but he held his breath, straining to hear…

Nothing.

It was a long way off, maybe the sound hadn't carried.

"Go," he said. "Quickly."

———

Vagouti heard the noise from the forest. Not close, not that far. A branch breaking, she knew the sound; she'd heard more than one large prey animal fleeing her make such sounds.

They were circling the dwelling. They sought to come in from an unexpected direction, because they suspected a trap. This was the mark of prey who was also a hunter. Smart.

She considered her strategy and tactics. She could easily

change her position and find a better vantage to cover that arc of the perimeter.

Or, she could go to meet them, when they didn't expect her.

Surprise might still exist there, but no longer here, not as much. They might not know exactly where she was, but they would be alert. Two of them, both armed? They would separate as they arrived, and if she lanced one, the other would have a target. That is what she would do in their place.

She needed them together.

She stood.

Mac said, "The cruiser is just around the turn ahead."

Sloane nodded. "Why don't you give me the keys, I'll go get it, bring it back. No point in all three of us getting closer than we need."

The deputy frowned. "I'll do that. My car."

Sloane said, "We'll cover you."

Vagouti smelled the vehicle before she saw it, the odor of burned petroleum distillates they used for fuel hanging thick in the air.

She frowned. There had been no vehicle there before when she had scouted the area. Someone had arrived since.

There were others.

That was where the Sniper was going, not where the dead oomans were. He meant to flee.

She saw the automobile. Recognized it. It was one of their law enforcement vehicles, they had a particular appearance.

More armed prey. How many?

She edged closer.

As Mac made his way toward the cruiser, Sloane said, "We need to separate. You stay here, I'm going across the road."

"Why?"

"Because if one of them is about, he'll have to shift his aim fast to get both of us. If you see a flash, shoot at the source."

Mary nodded. "Be careful, Sloane."

"I will. Stay low and concealed."

An armed ooman approached the vehicle.

She couldn't spike him, the others would mark her. She might be able to get them all, but that was not the wise choice. There were at least three, perhaps more.

If their intent was to flee in the vehicle, as it seemed it was? All she had to do was wait until they were all inside, unable to shoot back or dodge; then she could spike the automobile and be done with it.

Not as sporting as she would have it, but she would have the head of the ooman who slew her mate. And who, at a far remove, could criticize her for it? One against multiple? All armed? And as deadly as they came?

She crept back a bit, looking for a better angle. The vehicle would be departing along the dirt path away from her. The others must be farther along that way, waiting for the ride to come to them. You couldn't spike a target if you didn't know where it was. Again, they were behaving as a Hunter would behave.

She had taken dangerous prey on a dozen planets. She would take these as well.

She needed a better vantage point. She looked around.

Mac unlocked the car's door and opened it. Took in the surroundings.

Nothing.

He put the shotgun into the rack.

He slid onto the seat and cranked the unit. Did a U-turn and started down the road, slow and easy, didn't want to raise dust or make more noise than he had to.

Sloane saw the deputy's car roll slowly toward his position. He looked past it, into the woods.

So far, so good.

But—he had that feeling of being watched again.

Were he the alien predator, if he were there observing, how would he assess the situation? Three armed people. Dangerous to shoot, if there was only one of them.

Wait until everybody is in the car, then blow the car apart.

He nodded to himself.

The cruiser pulled to a stop.

"Get in," Mac called.

Line of sight, Sloane thought. *Where would I set up to hit the car?*

He had to assume they could see the car. And anybody who went to get into it.

"Mary. Crouch, and get into the back seat. I'm going to pretend to get into the front seat."

"Pretend?"

"If I squat low and open the door, then close it, they might not see what I did. Depends on the angle they have."

"Did you see something?"

"No. But they are there."

"You sure about this?"

"Yeah."

———

Mac said, "What are you doing?"

"I think we have a watcher. Give me five seconds after I close the door to get back to concealment, then stomp it, kick some dust up, and zig-zag."

There was a short pause. "Okay."

Sloane watched Mary creep toward the car's rear door. She opened it and hopped in.

Sloane took a deep breath and moved in a low crouch, duck-walked to the passenger-side front door. He opened it, then shut it quickly.

Either they see me or not. If they do, they won't take the shot. If not?

He scooted back into the brush and dropped prone.

Three... two... one...

Mac tromped on the gas pedal and the tires threw up dirt and dust. The car fishtailed, got traction, and took off—

—Sloane scanned the road and woods, looking, looking—

———

Vagouti targeted the vehicle. It spewed dust, obscuring her vision, but they were all inside—now was the time—

———

Nothing, Sloane didn't see that shimmer he was looking for. Maybe he was wrong—

—a cone fell from the big Douglas fir tree across the road. He saw it drop, followed the line back up—

You were a challenge, Sniper. I offer respect, but in the end, the Yautja are better Hunters. Death comes for you—

In the tree! It's in the tree! Where—?!

Had to be that thick branch, five meters up. Nothing smaller would support the thing's weight.

He couldn't see it. No blur. Shit!

Close to the trunk, squatting on the branch, leaning against the bole. Had to be.

No time. If it was going to shoot, he had to beat it.

Sloane lined his sight up on what looked to be empty space and pressed the trigger—

Vagouti started to command the spike, and then felt a terrible, terrible pain in her left side. She fell—

Sloane heard the impact, felt the ground shake, and he had already drawn his revolver.

No death rays.

Was it just the one?

He waited, handgun pointed at where the invisible thing had hit the ground—

Vagouti couldn't breathe; the impact had knocked the air from her lungs. Blood gouted from the wounds, front and back. A rib was broken, the shock had wrecked her insides, but she wasn't dead yet.

She managed to climb to her feet.

The stealth confounder shut off, damaged by the fall. She became visible to the shooter. She knew roughly where he had to be. She sent a spike, low, because he would be prone—

The ground half a meter to Sloane's left erupted as the energy weapon dug a two-meter long trench deep into the earth.

Dirt and heat sprayed him.

He lined his revolver sights up, center of mass, and fired.

Sixty meters, not that hard a shot with this handgun.

The predator went down.

No other energy bolts came his way.

Just the one. More would be shooting.

He came up.

Behind him, Mary said, "Did you get it?"

"Yes."

Mac was just behind her. "Think there might be others?"

"No, I'd be dead."

The three of them walked to where the dying or dead alien lay sprawled on the fir needles.

It was smaller than the others. A young one? No, wait, it was a female...

She looked up at Sloane, said something in a truly foreign

language, laughed—sounded like a laugh—then coughed and died.

"Man," Mac said. "Look at that! Never seen anything like it!"

Sloane saw something. It was wearing a... watch? Flashing something.

Oh, hell!

"Get in the car, go, go!" Sloane said.

"What?"

"It has some kind of self-destruct device! It is going to blow up, a big explosion! Go!"

They ran.

———

They were half a mile away when the bomb went off, and the shockwave spun the car sideways on the road, as if shoved by a giant hand.

After a moment, when they realized they weren't going to die, Mac laughed nervously.

"I can't believe it. I can't believe any of that just happened."

Sloane looked at Mary, who smiled. Then he turned back to the deputy.

"After a couple times, it gets easier to believe," he said.

MAY BLOOD PAVE MY WAY HOME

BY WESTON OCHSE

CENTRAL MEXICO. 1916.

A gibbous moon lit the world with a specter of what it could have been. The light had been enough to push forward until their mounts were faltering. Dun-colored ground gave way to dark lumps, creosote and mesquite scrub indistinguishable from the men that slumbered. Lieutenant Providence Pope made his way through the field of sleeping soldiers, his bones aching from fourteen hours in the saddle. Everyone had slept where they'd fallen except him and Sunderson. They couldn't bed down until they were sure their men were taken care of and guards were set. Then afterwards, Sunderson wanted to huddle up and spread out his maps. Those damn maps. As if a map could tell him everything.

"Maps don't say nuthin' the land don't want you to

know," Husker John was always fond of saying. The big sergeant spoke the truth.

Pope had tried to convince Sunderson of this, but the man ignored him. They'd both learned the same curriculum, albeit four years apart, the lessons of the Civil War drilled into them in class after class at West Point. But this wasn't two pitched armies fighting each other. This wasn't Gettysburg nor was it the first or second Battle of Bull Run. Both Pope and Sunderson could quote line and verse the timelines of each of those battles, map them in a sandbox, then rattle off the mistakes each side had made. No, this was more like Indian fighting where one force chased the other until the other turned to fight, then turned once more and fled.

Ever since Pope had been assigned B Troop in the famed Buffalo Soldiers, chasing Comanches and Apaches along the border, he'd known that they had to learn new tactics. He'd turned to Buffalo Soldiers like Sergeant Major Husker John who'd been fighting in the all-black cavalry for twenty years or the old man Fitz Lee, who'd won a medal for bravery during the Battle of San Juan Hill in the old Cuban campaign. They were more knowledgeable about the act of war than any of the retired colonels and majors teaching back at West Point. And now here they were, exhausted, bedded down in a valley with high ground on all sides, selected specifically by Sunderson because it appeared to be a place where they could "bed down unseen." Damn Sunderson. The East Coaster was going to get them all killed.

"Lieutenant Pope, sir," came a rough voice off to his right. "You be wanting some coffee?"

Two soldiers sat beside a smoldering pile of ashes, the outward glow hidden by dirt and rocks. Each wore the cavalry blue uniforms with yellow piping. Dark blue for the top with copper buttons the Indians were fond of taking and a lighter blue for the pants, each leg tucked into scuffed and worn cavalry boots. They wore utility belts that carried a canteen and ammo for their Model 1896 Krag-Jørgensen carbines, which lay beside each of them. They each wore slouch hats, which differed from the Stetsons worn by Pope and Sunderson.

Pope strode over and squatted with them, holding out the dusty tin cup that usually hung at his waist for just such a moment. "Sure. Thanks." He glanced at the two but didn't recognize them.

"I'm Private Pile and this here is Private Steve," the one who'd offered coffee said.

"Steve, is that your whole name?" Pope asked, eyeing the dark man.

"Father's name was Steve. My momma wanted him to be remembered so I'm Steve Steve."

"Where you from?" Pope asked.

"Biloxi, suh."

"This your first mission, Private?"

"Yessuh," the man said, his head and eyes lowered.

Pope had seen that sort of behavior plenty. Fifty years after the abolition of slavery and still black folk were afraid of the white man. He knew there were places where times hadn't really changed, but he'd never been there. Born and raised in the Hudson Valley of New York, then an appointment to the U.S. Military Academy at West Point where he had black classmates, had given him a different view of the state of black and white in America. Being posted to an all-black military regiment whose honors and glory were world-renowned put an exclamation point on it.

"Well, Private, you're in a proud unit so hold your head high. No bowing and scraping here."

"I told him, El Tee Pope, but he wouldn't listen. I told him us Buffalo Soldiers was the most decorated cavalry in the entire West."

"Private Steve, let me say this. General Black Jack Pershing wants his soldiers to keep their heads up so that they can see the enemy. You can't see them from staring at the ground, do you get me?"

"Yes, suh," said Private Steve staring at the ground. Then he caught himself. A shadow of a grin flitted across his face. Then he looked at Pope for the first time. "I mean, yes, suh."

Pope patted him on the back. "Good man." Then he stood, pulled out his pocket watch and shook his head. "Gotta go see a man about some maps," he grumbled. Pope threw back the rest of his coffee, clipped his cup to his belt, then headed to the command tent, formulating as he went the latest argument he was going to make to try and persuade Captain Sunderson to listen to him. Then he saw movement out the corner of his right eye. He thought it was a man, but when he turned, there was no one there. Still, he watched as a bush moved, then another, then a tripod of rifles fell. He didn't see who it was, and there wasn't even a whisper of a wind, but it looked like the passage of a man.

He let out a cry, pulled his pistol from his belt, and ran to the fallen rifles.

Men leaped from their positions, grabbing at their weapons, looking around. The whole camp awoke and they searched for an hour, until it was clear that no one was there. Still, he had the guard doubled, just in case.

"You seeing ghosts, Pope?" sneered Captain Sunderson,

when it was all said and done. He was commander of A Troop, the leader of their reconnaissance party, a prima donna and a horse's ass.

But Pope had seen what he'd seen. He just didn't know what it was. "Better safe than sorry," he mumbled, then squatted down to watch Sunderson play at his maps.

They were ten days into what was left of the Punitive Expedition—where General Black Jack Pershing took nearly ten thousand men into Mexico to retaliate against Pancho Villa for his attacks on United States sovereign soil. Things hadn't gone well from the start. Pancho Villa had turned out to be a virtual ghost. Then after the Battle of Carrizal, a messenger had arrived, informing the general that he and the army were being recalled. Not only was the Mexican government at odds with the idea that nearly ten thousand United States soldiers were five hundred miles deep in their country chasing after Pancho Villa and his army, but President Wilson wanted the 10th Cavalry Regiment heading east for a boat to send them to the war in Europe.

Pope remembered the moment well. He'd been in the general's tent and had felt the full-on power of an angry glower. Pope had done what Private Steve had done, his gaze seeking solace somewhere near the ground. The general's words were directed at President Woodrow Wilson, and no one in the tent would ever dare relay them or even say them aloud for fear of being dispatched by a line of seven soldiers with rifles.

"Scouts have Villa moving west," Sunderson began, pointing at the map. "Make sense that they're heading to Guanajuato," pronouncing the J.

Pope sighed. "There's no evidence Villa's anywhere near Guanajuato," he said, pronouncing the word correctly, replacing the J-sound with an H-sound. "I know. I know. Your recon has it that we are, but they're as… as…"

"Go ahead and say what you mean, Lieutenant," Sunderson said in his patronizing Virginia drawl. "We both know I haven't seen combat until this expedition."

"I didn't mean it like that, sir," Pope said in frustration. "It's just that I know what it's like to chase Comanches. They have a certain way of moving through a country. I can't pinpoint exactly how I know, but by God, sir, we're chasing Indians, not Villa."

"And the recon boys from the Motorcycle Squad, they don't matter?"

The Punitive Expedition had been the first time the U.S. military had used motorcycles in battle. They'd been mainly used for reconnaissance and message delivery. Pershing had given their hundred-man element two motorcycles.

"I'm surprised they can see anything as loud as those machines can get. Comanches can hear them coming a mile away. And let's face it, they have zero experience chasing Comanches."

"Just like me."

"You said it, sir."

"Fine, Pope. I've heard your arguments for the last ten days. Let me ask you this, what would you do if you were in command?"

"I'd split our forces into two. Your men know more about chasing Indians than fifty West Point grads. I learned that lesson the hard way when I arrived to take command." He pointed to their place on the map. "Problem as I see it is that we're currently huddled in this valley. If I was Comanche, I'd be holed up here and—"

The tent flap opened, and Husker John shoved his head inside. His wiry hair was cut into a Mohawk. An ugly mass of scars twisted the right side of his head where he'd almost been scalped.

Sunderson frowned. "What are you doing interrupting us, boy?"

Husker John ignored the remark, his eyes on Pope. "We gotta problem, suh. Sentries to the west and south are gone."

"What do you mean gone?" Sunderson asked.

"Just that, suh. Gone."

"Are the men prepared?" Pope asked.

"Yes, suh. Word is spreading. They'll be ready."

Sunderson grabbed Pope's shoulder. "What are you talking about? I didn't hear any alarm."

"This is Indian country, sir. We don't sound alarms in cases like these. What I did earlier was different. I thought someone was in our camp. In fact, there might have been someone. Your men know what to do. The Comanches think they have us at a surprise, but we know better." Pope made to stand, then paused. "You need to trust your men, sir."

Then he left, heading straight for the center of his troop. He kept his eyes down, but noted the many shadows that dotted the sides of the hills surrounding them. He kneeled by Husker John. "Have the men prepare to fire."

Husker John gave the low call of an owl. As it echoed across the valley, the Buffalo Soldiers of B and A troops slowly rolled onto their bellies and aimed into the darkness. They'd practiced this maneuver before and had used it effectively against a Comanche attack just south of Agua Prieta last year.

"Fire," Pope whispered.

Husker John screeched like the owl of its name and a

hundred rifles fired—grazing fire only a foot off the ground.

Screams split the night as Comanche warriors who'd been crawling toward their location were suddenly struck by bullets fired along the ground.

"Fire," Pope shouted and pulled out his pistol. "Fire at will."

Those Comanches who'd stood to flee were shot down. The cacophony of firing was intense as rifles from both sides fired, filling the air with dark, blinding smoke, making it even harder to see in the wan moonlight.

Then Pope saw movement toward B Troop's flag. The strangest looking Comanche he'd ever seen seemed to pop into existence. The Comanche wore strange armor and had even stranger hair. As the Comanche began reaching for the flag, Pope leveled his pistol, took aim down the eight-inch barrel, and shot the warrior in the back.

The warrior spun, his hair whipping around behind him. He held a strange pistol in his hand.

Pope fired again, catching the warrior in the chest, knocking him back a step.

The warrior fired, the bullet expanding improbably into a net.

Pope dove to his right, the net brushing his shoulder but passing over him.

It caught Private Steve on the head and Pope watched in horror as the net contracted, the mesh biting into skin until blood shot free. But he didn't have time to watch it all. He turned and fired, unloading the last four bullets of his pistol into the strange warrior. At first, he didn't think that his bullets had any effect, but then the warrior staggered, and as he did, he flashed in and out of existence.

Pope surged to his feet, but before he could even take a step, Husker John plowed past him and tackled the strange warrior. Husker John grabbed a stone from the ground and with two hands, brought it down on the warrior's head once, then twice.

Pope turned to get his bearings. His men were kneeling and prone, firing at moving shadows. He saw several of his men go down and cursed every time. He loaded his pistol with steady hands, remembering fleetingly his first Indian fight and how terrified he'd been. The memory made him look toward A Troop where Sunderson's men were gathered en masse around him, as if they were a Roman legion forming a cohort block. Their rate of fire was impressive, but they made even better targets. Then Pope understood. He'd had his men surround him as human shields. Fucking Sunderson.

Three of Sunderson's men went down. Then three more right after. Pope watched as one of the men seemed to be pulled into the air and thrown, the body crashing to the ground in an awkward twisting of limbs.

One of the motorcycles exploded, lighting the night.

Someone opened with their sole Model 1895 ten-barreled Gatling gun.

Horses screamed.

Pope scrambled over to Husker John and saw the Comanche for the first time up close.

Husker John glanced up with big eyes. "What kind of Comanche is this, suh?"

"None I've ever seen."

The Comanche wore armor of a sort. It felt like metal, but was softer. It also seemed to have a mask of some kind over its face. This was no Comanche. This was a completely different Indian all together.

Pope snatched the warrior's pistol from where it had fallen on the ground. He expected it to be heavy, but it was amazingly light.

Suddenly a Comanche broke through the lines and ran toward them.

Pope raised the pistol and fired. A net grew out of thin air and caught the Comanche on the head, knocking him back and slamming him to the ground.

The strange warrior stirred.

"*M-di mar'ct*," it said, the alien words coming from beneath the mask. Then it repeated. "*M-di mar'ct*."

"Doesn't sound Comanche," Husker John said.

"It's because this isn't a Comanche." Pope stood, now a gun in each hand. "I don't know what he is."

Another of the strange warriors blinked into existence. This one was taller and held a long spear with a wicked-looking end. The warrior moved incredibly fast, dodging bullets, slashing down the men of B Troop with the ease of a farmer slashing wheat. It became apparent to Pope that the warrior was heading his way. He felt a moment of fear take him as he watched the effortlessness with which the warrior was cutting down his men.

Pope backed a few steps and knelt beside the downed warrior. He holstered his pistol, then pressed the side of the strange warrior's gun to its head.

"Husker John, get behind me," Pope said. He watched as the new warrior cut down three more of his men then skidded to a stop, the long rectangular blade of the spear stopping inches from Pope's face. "Drop your weapon or I'll kill him."

Pope didn't know if the other understood him. He just had to hope it did.

"Drop your weapon or I'll kill him," the warrior said in return.

Pope blinked in confusion as he heard his own words said back to him.

"Who are you?" Pope asked.

"Who are you?" the warrior asked back in his voice.

The warrior was taller than the one they had on the ground. He wore the skeletal remains of what looked like a bear claw on a dark chain around his neck. His dark armor reminded Pope of pictures he'd seen of knights during the Crusades, but this one was articulated to allow for easy movement. His head was covered by the same mask as the one Pope had at the end of the pistol.

Pope noted that most of the firing had stopped.

"Is it the devil, El Tee Pope?" Husker John whispered.

Pope shook his head as he looked at his left hand that was holding the warrior in a sitting position. "The devil don't bleed." His hand was coated in a luminous green substance and he thought to himself, if the devil could bleed, wouldn't it be green?

"I'm not playing around," he said to the standing warrior. "Who are you and why are you here?"

The warrior's head turned slightly as if he were regarding a new thing. Then he said in an accent Pope didn't recognize, "We are *Yautja*," pronouncing the word like *Ya-OOT-ja*. "We fight with Comanches." The cadence of the words was unnatural.

"Comanches are our enemy," Pope said flatly. "Does that make you our enemy as well?"

The *Yautja* turned its head again as if it were listening to something. "*Ooman k'v var ooman,*" it said. Then in English it translated, "Humans hunting humans." Then came the sound of clicking from inside the mask.

Pope considered the statement and said, "We hunt them because they hunt us. We hunt first so that they will not hunt last."

The *Yautja* lowered its spear, then spun it several times until the blade was pointed down.

Shouts came from behind the *Yautja*.

Pope lowered the pistol. Several of his men were gathering behind the *Yautja*, weapons raised. A crazy idea came to Pope, one that had to be acted on at once. He stood, pulling the wounded *Yautja* to its feet. "Here. Take him. I don't know how to heal him."

The *Yautja* hesitated a moment, then stepped forward and took the weight of the smaller *Yautja* whose back glowed with smears of green luminescent blood. Now that Pope was standing he noted that the *Yautja* was head and shoulders again taller than he was.

"Lieutenant Pope, what do you have there?" came Sunderson's voice.

"Go. Now," Pope said, jerking his head to his left. Then loudly he said, "Do not harm these two. Let them go free on my command."

The *Yautja* held the smaller warrior in its arms and began to walk away.

"Lieutenant Pope, what are you doing?"

"Letting them take their wounded."

"What? I've never heard of such a thing. Belay that order and fire at will."

"Do not fire!" Pope shouted.

The men looked nervously from Sunderson to Pope, but listened to the white officer who'd been with them the longest.

"I've had about enough of this," Sunderson said in exasperation. He drew his pistol and fired it into the back of the retreating *Yautja*.

The giant warrior halted. He turned his head slightly and a piece of metal the size of a small plate flew from him to embed in Sunderson's chest.

Sunderson gasped and let his pistol fall from his hand. He dropped clumsily to his knees and coughed blood.

Pope ran to him.

A metal disc was sticking half out of Sunderson's chest.

Pope touched it and could feel it vibrate beneath his fingers. He watched in awe as the disc worked its way backwards, then flew back to the *Yautja*, who somehow caught it and then disappeared with the wounded warrior as if they'd never been there at all.

Buffalo Soldiers all around began to whisper and curse. Several got down on their knees to pray. Still more stood, unable to move, staring at the spot where the *Yautja* had just been.

Sunderson drew one last ragged breath and then collapsed, dead.

The rest of the night found Pope directing his men in parties of five to collect the dead and clear the battlefield. A triage area had been set aside to help the wounded. They set new sentries, this time doubling them. Pope believed they'd do well against the Comanches, but probably wouldn't have a chance with the *Yautja*, especially the big one with the spear. It wasn't until shortly before dawn that he had enough time to sit down and think. Private Pile brought him some much-needed coffee. He mentioned that Private Steve hadn't made it, but then Pope already knew that. Too many good soldiers had died that day. He'd reviewed their losses on the tally sheet Husker John had provided. Of the hundred men who'd entered the valley, sixty-five remained alive and of that number, thirty-nine were unscathed. Pope surmised that half of their number of dead had been killed by the *Yautja*.

Husker John sat heavily beside him. "We going back now, suh?"

Pope nodded. "That's the plan. Enough of us died last night."

"What was it for? Who was they?"

"*Yautja* is what it called itself. I don't know what they are."

"The men are calling it a demon. Do you think it could be a demon, suh?"

Pope sipped his coffee, which was the only thing keeping him awake. Exhaustion made him feel weighted down. "I don't know what a demon is, Husker John. Is it a demon? It could be, but I'm not so sure. It had a way about it."

"It bled green, suh," Husker John said in a hushed tone.

"The important thing was that it bled," Pope said, and then exhaustion clamped down on everything and sent him into darkness.

When next he woke, Corporal Motes was shaking him awake.

Pope blinked at the brightness of the day. The sun was high enough in the sky for it to be late morning. He'd dreamed of a girl he'd once courted from a wealthy Hudson Valley family. She had luxurious blonde hair and left the smell of lilacs and orange in her wake. Then he sat up straight and looked around, shedding the last vestiges of his walk with a pretty girl.

"Suh, Sergeant Major wanted me to wake you."

Pope wiped his face as if he could wipe away the tiredness and got to his feet. He tucked in his shirt that had come loose and adjusted his pants.

Corporal Motes had been with the unit for ten years and was a seasoned soldier. A ragged scar cut his left cheek, puckering his high yellow skin. Because of the scar, it always looked like Motes was smiling, but Pope knew otherwise. Motes' entire family had been killed by the Klan back in Kentucky and he'd come out west to forge a new life. Husker John had told Pope that not a night went by where Motes wasn't staring into the sky, what he was thinking about no mystery to any man that knew him.

"What's going on?" Pope asked. He leaned down and picked up his tin cup. Cold stale coffee stirred in the bottom. He considered it, then brought it to his lips and drank it. Cold as it was, it was still something that could speed him to wake.

Motes pointed toward the east end of camp. "We have a visitor, suh."

"Who is it, Corporal?"

"An old muleskinner sent by the Comanches. Says he has something to tell you, but he'll only tell you."

"Sentries still out?"

"All out and watching. Was the motorcycle what saw the muleskinner and brought him."

111

Pope smiled. The Comanches probably knew the motorcycle routes and told the muleskinner where to go.

"Thank you, Corporal." He turned to go, then turned back. "You and the men eat yet?"

"We had us some tack and water, suh."

"Think you could scrounge me up some?" Pope asked. The last thing he wanted to eat was hardtack. The small square crackers tasted like dust. But an army on the move didn't always have the luxury of real rations, so he'd eat it, and pretend half-heartedly that it was something better. Maybe a cookie made by that girl he'd met at West Point. Damned if he could remember her name, just her smell and the feel of her hair in his fingers. He knew he should know, she'd been special to him, but when he'd come out fighting, he'd shoved all the memories of everything good into a deep dark hole to protect them. Why this one was surfacing now, he didn't know.

"Oh, yes, suh," Corporal Motes said, nodding. Then he took off jogging.

Lieutenant Pope made his way to where Sergeant Major Husker John was detaining the muleskinner, who was on his knees. The man was a half-breed and going on sixty. His gray hair was bundled up behind him Indian style, but a few wisps blew free in the breeze. His face was pocked from disease. His eyes had a reedy film over them.

"What's this?" Pope asked.

Husker John shifted his considerable weight to his right foot and shoved the muleskinner with his left foot, knocking him onto his back. "Man says he has a message for you, suh."

"Did he do anything to offend you, Sergeant Major?" Pope asked.

"Yes, suh. He's half Indian, suh," Husker John said in his baritone.

"That's as good a reason to hate a man as any, I suppose. Especially in these parts. Out with it then. What message do you have for me?"

The muleskinner glanced fearfully at Husker John, then said, "Comanches sent me. Said they have a thing they want you to know... sumthin' you have to do."

"Out with it then," Pope urged, wondering where Motes had got to.

"The *nanisuwukaitu*... they demand you fight. They say your fight with them is undone."

"And who are these *nani whako*?"

"They call them *Ya-OOT-ja* but they are spirits. None can stand before them and they can walk the spirit plane. It's where they go when they disappear."

Pope raised an eyebrow. "Is that so. What do they want with us?"

"They say that four of them will fight four of your best warriors."

"Then what?"

"All of your men can go free."

"But they're free now."

"No," the muleskinner said, glancing around, fear owning the features of his face. "You're not. The *nanisuwukaitu* are all around us. They're just in spirit form."

The idea that they were surrounded by an invisible army of *Yautja* left Pope cold. He turned slowly, examining the shadows. Three times a *Yautja* made itself briefly appear then disappear, like it was making itself known. Each time it happened, a bolt of fear shot through Pope's gut.

"My men go free if we win or lose?" Pope asked.

The muleskinner glanced wildly behind him. "That's what they said."

"And how do I know they'll keep their word?"

"They have a strange honor, sir. That's how they came to us. They fought our best. We lost, but that didn't stop them from joining us... helping us. They've been with us almost six months now."

"So four of my people fight four of their... *Ya-OOT-ja*."

"That's right. The *nanisuwukaitu* love to fight. They don't drink. They don't play games. They fight."

Pope turned to his sergeant major. "What do you think?"

"I think we should skin this muleskinner and send him back to his mother, suh." He took off his slouch hat and rubbed his hand through his wiry hair, then put the hat back on, making sure the bill was centered. "But if we have a way of saving the men, then we needs to be doing that."

"There is that." Pope shook his head. He didn't like the idea of it, but he feared he had no other choice. "Go and tell them we'll oblige. Where and when?"

"You can tell them yourself." The muleskinner pointed further east. "They's waiting for you in the next valley. Just send four and they will, too."

Pope turned to Husker John. "Let the man go. We have to plan."

Pope knew that he couldn't send any man to do what he wouldn't do. That's not what leadership was, so he was the first of the four. His mother had named him Providence so he'd have a lucky life. It had worked out so far and it might carry him through the day. Husker John also insisted on coming. Pope was relieved to hear it, because there was no other he thought could stand a chance. As fate would have it, Motes arrived as they were discussing who next to ask and he volunteered himself. Motes was a fine enough soldier and they were unlikely to get anyone better, so they accepted him to their doomed group.

Pope left the pair to get ready and went to find Conroy, who was a classic Irishman who'd fight at the color of the sky being blue. He was one of the only other white men in the troop now that Sunderson was dead, assigned to them as part of the motorcycle unit. In the end he took very little convincing and Pope soon had his four dead men.

Pope, Motes, and Husker John each carried a rifle and a pistol. They also each had a skinning knife and hatchet they'd plucked from the bodies of dead Apaches. Conroy carried a breech-loading sawed-off shotgun, a pistol, a spear, and a knife. He also brought his motorcycle and drove it along beside their horses, which had become accustomed to the rackety machines during the long expedition.

"Let's run down what we know about them," Pope said as they walked. Then he laughed as he realized, "We don't really know anything, do we?"

"They come in different sizes, suh," Motes said.

"That they do. They also have different weapons. That may be based on size, but it could also be based on rank."

"So you think these *Ya-OOT-jas* have a rank system?" Conroy asked.

"They're warriors... maybe even soldiers. They have to have a ranking system. It's why I let the big fella take the wounded *Yautja*. Never leave a man behind, right?"

"Makes sense I suppose," Conroy said. "So how's the fight going down? Who do I get to hit first?"

Pope raised an eyebrow. "I'm not exactly sure but I'll tell you what, as soon as I know, you'll know."

Conroy snorted. "Spoken like a privileged West Pointie."

Turned out that the next valley was five miles away. It also wasn't much of a valley—a box canyon, really, ending in a cul-de-sac of rocks the size of rail cars. The flat space was probably sixty by sixty feet and covered in dirt and dry grass. He'd seen this on a map, but the map didn't show the impressive sizes of the rocks, or how they rose like giant stacked blocks into a three-sided wall. They tied the horses to a scrap of mesquite where Pope thought they'd be well out of the way. Conroy parked the motorcycle beside the horses.

Then all four moved to the center of the space and waited.

...for exactly ten seconds and then four *Yautja* appeared twenty feet from them.

More *Yautja* appeared on the rocks.

Pope hoped that they were merely spectators and that they hadn't walked into one immense trap.

By appearances, the *Yautja* matched the Buffalo Soldiers in size. One large hulking warrior stood out among three warriors closer to human size. It was as if the *Yautja* selected the size specifically to match that of the humans. Interesting, thought Pope. If his observation was true, it spoke to a fairness of fight that left him hopeful that the *Yautja* would keep their bargain.

A fifth *Yautja* appeared—this one he recognized as the giant warrior from the previous night's combat. He stepped between both groups, then turned to the Buffalo Soldiers.

"Four fight, then done," it said, its accent and cadence still peculiar to Pope's ears.

"Weapons?" Pope asked.

"Two only."

"They have armor, suh?" Husker John noted.

"Good catch." Then to the *Yautja*, Pope said, "If this is to be a fair fight, your warriors should remove their armor."

The *Yautja* cocked its head.

The other four, who had been standing impressively, suddenly were looking at each other. Was it worry? Pope hoped so.

"If no armor, then none of your loud weapons."

Pope thought for a moment, trying to parse what a loud weapon was. Then he got it. The pistols and rifles. Perhaps the *Yautja* armor provided a modicum of protection from their bullets; without it, they'd surely fall victim. It was a fair offer.

Speaking to the *Yautja*, Pope said, "That's a deal. But one more thing." He made a circle with his hands and then made to throw it. "No using that disc you shot into Sunderson."

The *Yautja* cocked its head once more, then made a series of clicking sounds from beneath the mask. "These *Yautja* do not use this weapon. They are not ready for it."

Pope nodded.

"To the death then?" he asked, hoping it wasn't.

"To the death."

"Excellent," Pope said, meaning anything but. He backed his men away and they began to remove their hats and shirts. They deposited their weapons in a pile.

Corporal Motes was the first to notice the other *Yautja*, who were removing their weapons and their masks. When he saw their faces, his eyes shot wide and his mouth hung open. "Jesus, Mary, and Joseph. What are they?"

The Buffalo Soldiers turned and fell in a state of awe as

they saw what lay beneath the masks. Pope identified the wondrous protrusions from the face as some sort of mandibles, like from a gigantic insect. Each one ended in a tooth or a claw or a talon. Whichever, they looked sharp and deadly.

Suddenly all four *Yautja* began clicking their mandibles together. Their shoulders shook slightly. Then Pope realized, they were laughing at the Buffalo Soldiers' reactions.

Pope turned to his men. "So now we know they wear masks to hide their ugly mugs. Right now, they are laughing at your reactions... your fear. Each of you have faced down Comanches and Apaches. Each of you have been up close and personal with someone who wanted you dead. This is no different. The *Yautja* are just a different type of Indian to us. That's all. Pure and simple. Most of all remember that they can bleed just like you or me. If they can bleed, they can die. Do you understand?"

Both Conroy and Husker John nodded, but Motes looked doubtful.

Pope grabbed him and shook him. "Motes. Did you hear me?"

Motes nodded slowly, then his nodding picked up speed. "I hear you, suh."

Pope thought for a moment against saying what he was about to say, but then dove in. "Listen, you were never able to get back at the Klan for what they did to your family."

Motes turned to stare at him as hatred bled the fear away from his eyes.

"Look at the *Yautja*."

Motes turned to stare at them.

"These are the Klan. These would kill your family all over again. You couldn't hurt the Klan, but you can hurt these warriors. Do you understand? Do you understand me, Corporal Motes?"

Motes shrugged off Pope's hands and said, "Yes, I understand, suh," his voice mean and ready.

"Then let's go."

Pope and his men turned and took a few steps forward.

"We're ready," he said.

The giant *Yautja* beckoned one of the human-sized warriors forward. This one's skin was mottled with greens and browns. Its face was fierce in the way a demon's would be. For the Buffalo Soldiers, these might as well be demons, but they still bled and they still could die, so they had a chance.

Pope started forward to meet it, but Motes pushed him back and strode to the center.

Like the rest of them, Motes wore his pants tucked into his boots, a white undershirt, and suspenders. He held a hatchet in his right hand and a skinning knife in his left. Pope couldn't see his face, but the soldier's head was held high.

His opponent raised its shoulders and flared its mandibles. It wore twin metal claws on each hand.

Pope waited for a signal to start, but there was none. The *Yautja* just charged. Motes stepped his left foot back and waited.

His opponent swung both of its arms, but Motes dove under them, bringing his hatchet around and cutting a slice from the *Yautja*'s thigh.

His opponent tumbled.

Motes controlled his roll, then rose elegantly to his feet.

Pope felt a surge of elation as his hope for their survival went from nothing to something.

The *Yautja* got to its feet and spun. Instead of charging

this time, it stalked Motes, but the Buffalo Soldier stood his ground. When the *Yautja* swung at him this time, he backed away, let his opponent miss, then lunged with his knife.

The *Yautja* kicked out with one of its legs, knocking the knife away.

Motes paused to stare at the weapon as it flew through the air and it was his downfall.

The *Yautja* brought its other hand around and swiped away Motes' windpipe. Blood spurted wildly as Motes fell to his knees. The warrior brought a metal-clawed hand down on top of the skull, embedding the claws in the bone. Then it raked its other hand once more against the neck, separating the head from the body.

The victorious *Yautja* turned to its fellow warriors and let out an unearthly shriek as it held its bloody trophy high.

Pope's elation almost died with Motes, but he knew that they had a chance. It was just that Motes had made a deadly mistake.

Husker John strode forward, grabbed Mote's body and brought it back. Blood dripped down the back of his undershirt, but he didn't take any notice of it. He gently lay the remains of the dead corporal on the ground, then got up and turned.

"Let me do it," Conroy said. "Let me fight next."

Pope put a hand on Husker John's chest and said, "Go ahead, Conroy. Kill the son of a bitch."

Instead of heading to the center, Conroy went to his motorcycle, kicked it to life, then drove slowly toward the center. He had a spear in his right hand.

Another human-sized *Yautja* moved to the center; this one wore metal claws as well.

Conroy gunned his motorcycle toward his opponent, who easily stepped aside. Then Conroy stopped, gunned the engine without moving, which caused the back tire to spin madly, eating through the grass and dirt until it was showering the *Yautja* in the face. Conroy took off, traveled for twenty feet, spun the motorcycle one hundred and eighty degrees, and gunned it again.

Pope had seen nothing like it. It was as if Conroy were using the motorcycle like a horse.

The *Yautja* was wiping at its face with the backs of its hands, trying to get the dirt out of its eyes and mouth when Conroy's spear entered its chest and pushed through. Instead of continuing on the motorcycle, Conroy held onto the spear and let the machine continue without him. It wobbled a bit, ran about a dozen yards, then hit a giant rock, fell over and died. Conroy drove the *Yautja* to the ground, pinning it there with the spear. Then he pulled a skinning knife from his belt and began to furiously stab the warrior, his hand rising and falling over and over.

Husker John pumped a fist in the air.

But Pope held his breath.

Then it happened.

The *Yautja*, probably with the last of its strength, brought its right arm around and embedded the claws in the side of Conroy's face.

Conroy screamed with equal parts surprise and anger, then the *Yautja* pulled him down into an embrace.

Then nothing, as both of them died.

"Damn it all," Husker John said. After a few moments, he retrieved Conroy's body and weapons and laid him beside Motes.

"My turn," growled Husker John.

He picked up Conroy's spear, the tip still slick with the *Yautja*'s luminescent green blood.

"No, let me," Pope said, preparing to step forward.

"No, suh. I don't want to see any more of us die, so I'm a goin'." And with that, he stepped forward into the bloodied dirt in the center of the box canyon.

The hulking *Yautja* raised its arms in the air. Its mandibles clacked together feverishly. It held the same long spear that Pope had seen wielded before, the blade wide, long and curiously curved. The warrior stepped forward.

Husker John began to jog, then to run at his opponent. He was within five yards when he reared back and threw the spear at the *Yautja*. The warrior brought its own spear around and swept the missile out of the way. But that left it open. It tried to bring the spear back around, but Husker John was already upon it. The Buffalo Soldier grabbed the *Yautja*'s neck, spun around behind it, pulled out his skinning knife, then cut the neck down to bone. Husker John held his opponent by the face, grabbing hold of one of the mandibles. They flared briefly, then sagged as luminescent green life spurted free from the enemy warrior.

Husker John let it fall to the ground, then strode back to where Pope waited, mouth agape, then grinning from ear to ear. "You did it! You won!"

"Yeah, but the others didn't and now I gots to see you die, too."

Pope grew somber. "I'm not going to die. My name is Providence Pope and God has something else in store for me." He grabbed his hatchet and strode to the center. He glanced around and saw that everyone was staring at him intently like he was an insect of interesting origin. He shook his head. "That fucking Sunderson following his damned maps. Had he just listened to me, we'd be back at the border, my men sneaking tequila, and me getting a decent night's sleep." He glanced at his opponent who had the same clawed hand attachments as the first two, which meant that they'd be fighting close. He'd planned for this and he hoped his plan would work.

He hefted the hatchet, finding the balance, then stepped forward in a tactical crouch.

Then was stunned when one of the blades from an upraised *Yautja* fist flew toward him. Pope tried to duck, but the blade stuck just below his left shoulder and mere inches above his heart. Had he not tried to get out of the way, he'd have been as dead as Motes and Conroy. The pain was excruciating, causing him to fall to a knee.

"Get up, suh!"

Husker John's voice focused him and Pope pushed back to his feet.

His opponent strode forward sure and confident.

Pope swung his hatchet from right to left, then looped the return, bringing the hatchet down, then up, all in one smooth move.

The *Yautja* dodged out of the way, then lunged, swiping with its right hand, which now only held one metal claw.

Pope met that claw with his hatchet and instantaneously realized he'd made a grave error.

The *Yautja* hooked the hatchet and jerked it out of Pope's hand, leaving it outstretched and empty.

Then a memory flashed hard through his mind of the Hudson Valley girl, smelling of lilacs and orange. He saw her hand outstretched as he left on a train three years ago, heading west to fight Indians. Her name was Charlotte and she'd been the love of his life.

Then he was back to the real world in an instant.

"Charlotte," he whispered.

His opponent raked a hand toward him.

Pope ducked under it, grabbed the netgun from where it was attached to his belt behind his back, then brought it up to the *Yautja*'s face and pulled the trigger. The net launched, carrying the warrior backwards, wrapping and then digging into its face. It fell onto its back and tried to pull it off with one hand. It aimed its left hand toward Pope and fired both claws. Pope ducked, letting them sail overhead. Then he was on a knee next to the warrior. Pope pulled the blade from where it was lodged in his shoulder, almost fainting from pain, reversed it, then plunged it into one of the *Yautja*'s eyes.

Then he fell over.

A moment later, he was picked up and held at arm's length by Husker John whose face was alight with victory. "You did it, suh! You won!"

Pope's elation was dampened by the incredible pain. "I told you I wasn't going to die today," he managed to say.

Husker John carried him back to their area and began patching him up. He packed magnesium in the wound and had it wrapped before the tall *Yautja* came over. Husker John got up and spoke with him at length, just out of Pope's earshot.

It was only later as he was leading two horses, carrying the bodies of Motes and Conroy, that Pope thought about what Husker John had eventually told him.

"As much as I hate these warriors, I respect them.

They've asked me to join them. They say they want to learn from me. I'm an old man, suh. I've done all I can for the Buffalo Soldiers, so I think I'm going to take them up on their offer. Fact is that life is too short not to seek out something you want. I've been wanting a change, and this seems right for me."

And with that, Husker John stayed behind. Pope would tell everyone that he was dead and his body was unrecoverable. They'd understand. They'd weep. Then they'd lick their wounds and return to New Mexico. And then Pope would leave them there. His commission was up and he had leave saved. He figured he'd take the time to go visit the girl he'd left in the past and see if she wasn't someone who was going to be part of his future. Whatever his decision, he was never going to forget his brave soldiers, the magnificence of Husker John, and the strange warriors who'd allowed his men their lives, just so they could test themselves on a few of America's finest cavalrymen—the Buffalo Soldiers.

STORM BLOOD

BY PETER J. WACKS
AND DAVID BOOP

NEW ORLEANS; NATIONAL GUARD FIRETEAM
05:21 AUGUST 29, 2005

Rain sleeted through the predawn sky, slicing sideways through the air. Icy stings peppered Sergeant Lejeune's exposed skin—what little wasn't protected by her National Guard uniform. The boiling black eyewall of Hurricane Katrina was a malevolent force, watching her, even though it was eighty miles away over the Gulf.

"Get the boy!" she shouted over the gale, carefully advancing through ankle-deep water. She re-clipped the anemometer to her vest. A woman on the hood of the wrecked jeep was mangled, impaled by a shattered tree branch.

Normally, Lejeune would never have left someone behind, but hell was coming and those were her orders. Though it tore into her soul, she had to choose getting her fireteam, and this child, to safety. Lejeune whispered a prayer for the dying as she fought her way back to the Humvee.

She climbed into the shotgun seat as the team got the survivor out of the hurricane. "We gotta move. We should've been to the Superdome half an hour ago... and the radio's out. Great."

Private "Inigo" Jones—nicknamed after drunkenly stumbling around barracks insisting on finding the six-fingered man—hit the gas. "We're lucky we could even dig out of that collapse, Sergeant. Not our fault we're behind." The Humvee lurched forward.

"I get that. But," Lejeune patted the anemometer, "winds have gone up fifteen miles per hour over the last hour. Water's up by a couple of inches..."

"Check it out—kid's got a video-camera," Tito Mendoza interrupted from the back seat as he pried a camera from the unconscious child's hand, working around the backpack the kid clutched with his other arm. He passed it to Lejeune.

Something pulled at Lejeune. She should help Inigo spot, but there was something... *off*. Her gut said to figure out what was up with this kid.

She made up her mind.

"I need you guys to be my eyes and ears while I check this out. Get us to the French Quarter, Inigo. Nevaeh, help him spot. Tito, help the kid. Get him warm. We *have* to find somewhere to shelter."

The reply was a chorused, "Yes, Sarge."

Lejeune looked over the Hi8 camera. She opened the flip

screen and pressed rewind for a second before hitting play. The tiny speakers burst with static.

———

RECORDING TIMESTAMP: 19:42:03 AUG 28/2005

The vibrant green flora of the bayou filled the frame. A Kalashnikov fired in the background. The camera bounced. Someone's leg shifted in and out of view with each squelching footfall. The view swung up, revealing a bald man, wearing camo, floating four feet in the air. Blood flowed from his back, coating a shimmering distortion in the air. The camera, catching the sight of more dead, panned away as his body was flung to the side.

"Yee haw!" sounded in the background as another Kalashnikov fired.

A loud snarl overpowered the second assault rifle—a basso growl so menacing it reached past the logic centers of the brain straight to the primal animal inside that screamed "run!"

"What? What the fu... No, it ca—"

Pistol shots sounded. The camera swung around and caught a gray wolf-shaped shadow as it vanished into the bayou.

"Ro, don't stop filming. Don't let the kid put it down! I'll get you a head start. Don't let us have died for nothing. This is it—what we all wanted—proof! They'll be legends!"

The camera swung up, revealing a young man with a hipster 5 o'clock shadow. Blood poured down his face from a gouge in his scalp. He looked at her one last time, resignation all over his face. "I'll be... well, I've already got what I wanted... that look in your eyes right now."

"Jason…" The camera bounced around as whoever held it started to run again, briefly showing the dreadlocked black woman Lejeune had seen dead on the Jeep. The woman had the drawl of Haitian Creole, audible in the single spoken word.

Again, the camera found the hipster as he stood, rain coating his blood-streaked hair. He raised the gun.

"Boy, are you going to look good on film," Jason said as he fired. Sparks jumped in midair, hitting something the camera couldn't see.

Whatever was said after was drowned out by the unmistakable thrumming of an airboat's fan firing to life. As the camera retreated two blades ripped out of Jason's back, then everything was too far away to be seen. The video panned across the swampy bayou, until the Creole woman was once more in frame.

She glanced back from the driver's seat, dreadlocks whipping in the wind. "Turn that thing off, Frankie."

NEW ORLEANS; NATIONAL GUARD FIRETEAM
05:34 AUGUST 29, 2005

Sergeant Lejeune snapped the camera closed.

"It's a hoax. Some film project or something," Tito said.

"Invisible men? Giant wolves?" Nevaeh Khanna made the sign of the cross. She and her husband had escaped religious persecution in Afghanistan in their early twenties, coming to America and taking new names. Her husband became a pacifist, but Nevaeh, wanting to help protect their new home, joined the Guard. "I thought such things were just myths."

"I saw some freaky shit down in Nogales, like demon worshipping and whatnot, but not no actual demons. Gotta be a hoax." Tito waved a hand, brushing off the idea.

Nevaeh, hands shaking, pulled a small cross from under her uniform, kissing it.

Inigo shook his head. "There hasn't been enough time since that timestamp for someone to go all Hollywood on it..."

"Focus on driving, PFC," Lejeune snapped as she hit rewind. Who would bother to put together such an elaborate hoax in the middle of a watery hell-on-earth? The tape clicked and she hit play again, starting from the beginning.

RECORDING TIMESTAMP: 14:11:52 AUG 28/2005

The camera focused on a G4 laptop being held by the bald man in camo. "Got the camera ready for our reaction shots?"

A voice off screen said, "Yeah, just hit play."

The bald man pressed the spacebar. A slate appeared on the laptop's screen. It read:

Cryptozoid Crackdown
s2e5"Running with the Rou"

What followed was typical faux-reality show opening credits, action sequences that implied danger, and scantily clad women.

I'm Darren.

And I'm the Maestro. Y'all know us from rocking out to HairForce!

When the band broke up, Darren and I stayed tight because of our mutual love of the supernatural.

Now we hunt creatures of legend; the kind only two dedicated rockers—like us—have the guts to find.

We still "Rock Till the World is Awake," but now we travel the world seeking out impossible creatures and dangerous ladies.

Taking the music world by storm is nothing compared to rocking the very fabric of reality. We will prove these monsters exist, even if we have to climb the highest mountains...

Or cross the thickest swamps, because this is a...

Cryptozoid Crackdown!

The camera frame jerked up to catch the reactions of two men—one bald, the other mulleted, both looking like they hadn't let go of the 1980s—perched on the front of an airboat that sped across the waterways of southern Louisiana.

"Fuckin' A, man!" Darren said. "You really captured my essence, Jace."

"Finally earning your keep," Maestro echoed. "Only took a year."

"Dude, we were number one in twelve markets last year. Cut me some slack," the off-camera voice responded.

Maestro pointed a finger at him. "Yeah, well, we won't stay on top if we have these last-minute shoots in backwater swamps."

"Would you rather me pull the second unit and start over next week when this storm blows over?"

"I'd rather it was Ro behind the camera and not you," Darren interjected. "She's the tits when it comes to B-roll."

Jason panned over to see the driver's reaction. She just rolled her eyes.

They continued to banter, so Lejeune fast-forwarded until she saw the camp; it was a bloody mess of carnage and intestines, staining the watery greens of the bayou. HairForce's front men were in frame again.

Maestro called out in an angry whisper, "Keep the boy quiet and pick up the damn camera. It could be here any moment." He was armed and looking half-crazed and scared witless.

The camera shuffled as someone put it on the ground, still focused on Darren and Maestro.

"Hey there," Ro said quietly, off frame. "How are you feeling?"

"What happened?" a child asked, raspy-voiced.

"Drink."

There was the sound of sputtering.

"What's your name?"

"Franklin. Frankie, after my da."

Jason joined them, leaning in conspiratorially and blocking part of the shot. "Do you remember anything, Frankie?"

The boy spoke haltingly with a thick Cajun accent, words broken by sniffles. "I came with Da. Someone hired him to run around... My da is the best rougarou actor in the parish..." he choked up.

"It's okay, Frankie. We're here to keep you safe."

"Somethin' kuh..." Frankie fought to get the word out. "...killed him."

"What?" Darren called over his shoulder in a hushed but excited voice. "What killed him? Tell me it was a real rougarou!"

The camera focused on Frankie. He was covered in the ochre mud of the camp site, and tears cut clean trails down his cheeks. He shook his head. "Something else."

NEW ORLEANS; NATIONAL GUARD FIRETEAM
05:52 AUGUST 29, 2005

Sergeant Lejeune stopped the recording, silently daring anyone to speak.

Inigo didn't have the brains to stay silent. "I'm telling you that wasn't faked. If it was, it woul—" Something impacted the passenger door and the Humvee skidded. It caught a curb and the rising winds outside helped it jump. The sturdy vehicle smashed into a lamppost already bowing under the hurricane's relentless assault. The thirty-foot pole crashed into the façade of a French Quarter barbeque shop.

NEW ORLEANS; ROMILLY SIBIAN
05:53 AUGUST 29, 2005

Romilly's eyes snapped open. She gasped in lungsful of air. The... *thing* stood over her, the weird shimmering effect sputtering with sparks as the torrential rain hit it. It jabbed at its forearm and became fully visible. The hood of the Jeep bit into her shoulder blades.

How was she still alive?

Why was she still alive?

This thing had taken Darren, Maestro, and Jason to pieces in seconds. She fought to find words around intense pain in her right shoulder. "I got no beef with you... Only interested in the boy. You know? The *boy*."

The thing made a sound halfway between hissing and clicking, moving its face close, studying her, mimicking the word. "Boooyyyy. *Ki'Sei, lou-dte kale.*"

It radiated warmth absent from the hurricane, a stark

contrast that she could feel across her body.

She was careful to stay still under its scrutiny. "I'm Ro." She was at a loss for what else to say so she mimicked it. *"Ki'Sei?"* Whatever the creature's thought process, it seemed satisfied. The thing stood, towering over her, pointing toward the French Quarter. *"Dtai'kai-dte."* It thumped its own chest. *"Yautja…"*

She stood, shakily catching her balance in ankle-deep water. The snapped tree branch had left a deep gouge in her stomach and chest, and was imbedded in her shoulder. The blood seeping from the gash was washed away by rain faster than it came out.

Focus, Ro…

Shaking her head, she pointed in the opposite direction. "Airboat's back there a mile. I need it. This is only going to get worse." She pantomimed steering, then pointed at the angry sky.

The thing seemed to consider what she said, then pulled a small triangular object off its forearm and tossed it to her. The corner of the triangle pointing at the French Quarter flashed every few seconds. Why had it given her a tracking device? And why was it tracking Frankie? She looked up but it was gone.

Romilly took quick stock of her injuries. She had no clue how she was up and walking, or even alive. Luck had played a part in making injuries that looked deadly superficial… but her arm wasn't.

Gritting her teeth, she jerked out the branch-turned-stake. Her knees buckled. Her right arm tingled and pain butterflied from the hole in her shoulder. Unsheathing her boot-knife, Romilly reached into the Jeep, pulling the seatbelt to full extension. She had been an idiot not to use it before, but now it had a second shot at its job, just not the way originally intended.

She bit down on the belt and cut. After struggling she managed to slice the other end free. It worked as a makeshift sling, binding her bad arm to her chest and keeping pressure on the wounds.

Romilly pushed her dreads off her face. *Insanity. All of this.* She started miserably trudging toward the airboat.

NEW ORLEANS; NATIONAL GUARD FIRETEAM
05:55 AUGUST 29, 2005

The windshield was eclipsed by snarling fangs and matted fur. The gray beast from the video snarled and snapped its maw against the glass. Inigo slammed on the gas. "Ohshitohshitohshit..."

The beast, way too big to be a wolf, scrabbled for purchase, fighting the motion of the Humvee and the onslaught of Hurricane Katrina. Blue lightning arced by and the beast flinched, sliding off the vehicle, snarling as it got blown into the same shop as the lamppost.

The Humvee fought its way back into the storm.

Inigo glanced at Lejeune as he spoke over the cussing and prayer coming from the back seat. "I can't get over twenty in this. I don't think we'll be able to get away from that. Whattya want me to do, Sergeant?"

Lejeune squinted, reading streets signs through the storm. "I think... maybe it's after the kid? We need to keep him safe. Up a block and over, there's a supermarket."

Inigo nodded, squinting to focus through the

downpour overpowering the wipers.

Everyone in her fireteam had reacted much as she had—freaked out but holding it together. She glanced back. Tito was holding the unconscious kid in place, cussing up a storm under his breath in Spanish while Nevaeh prayed.

Lejeune reached back and snapped her fingers loudly. "Focus. I don't care what you just saw. We're going to a defensible position and we'll deal with that... *thing*, there."

Tito blinked. "*Pinche*—You kidding, Sarge? Why the hell ain't we headed to the Superdome?"

"Superdome's out. We don't have the time to get there. That thing *might* kill us, but if we try for the Superdome and the eyewall hits us, Katrina *will*. We go to ground."

Inigo spoke without taking focus off the worsening storm. "But, Sarge, there are like thousands of us there and only one of that thing. Isn't that worth the risk?"

"Yeah—it just near took out our Humvee. How are we supposed to stop that?" Tito was wide-eyed.

Lejeune clenched her jaw. "No arguments. We won't make it any more now than we would've ten minutes ago, let alone endangering thousands of civilians. So we find a way to stop it here. We're the Guard dammit, so we guard."

NEW ORLEANS; ROMILLY SIBIAN
05:59 AUGUST 29, 2005

The alien may have let her live, but Romilly wasn't so sure Katrina would grant her the same consideration... and she could see the maelstrom around the eye, still far off. The eyewall was deadly, but even the fringes of the 400-mile-wide hurricane were drowning the streets. *Just two minutes to catch my breath…* She found shelter in the lee of a bus and her mind drifted.

Jason looked at her, pleading. Romilly thought he was the only one worth anything in this whole damn shoot, even if he bought into all that Hollywood crap. The two hair-banders dreamt only of fame and glory. As often as not, glory got people dead in Romilly's experience.

Her grandma had always said the rougarou was real—that it was a messenger from God. One look at this campsite and the message was clear—stay the fuck away.

"*Camera, Ro. Get everything you can. If things go badly, grab the boy and go. Don't look back. Save him. Promise me.*" *Jason met her eye, begging.*

Romilly grunted. "I will."

She had given her word. She rubbed her arms furiously, warming up. Forcing herself back into the storm, Romilly fought Katrina for every inch, slogging through calf-deep water until her prize, the airboat, came into view. She limped forward until she was on the craft.

Romilly gunned the engine to life and sped onto the drowning streets of New Orleans, following the tracker toward the French Quarter.

———

NEW ORLEANS; NATIONAL GUARD FIRETEAM
06:17 AUGUST 29, 2005

"In there!" Lejeune pointed at the squat structure of the supermarket as the Humvee was buffeted from side to side, inching its way forward.

"Where do you wanna put the Humvee, Sarge? I don't think we can make it through this on foot."

"The way in is the way through, PFC. Take us through the front doors and park inside. Deep inside." Lejeune didn't see a safer way to get her team under cover.

"Isn't that just gonna let the storm in, Sarge?" Tito asked.

"It is. We'll have to deal with flooding, but that's a lot better than what's out here." She pointed toward the horizon. The sky went from brownish-gray to ugly black farther away from the city. "I'm pretty sure that's Katrina's eye. As much as this thing is a tank on wheels, we won't survive in this for long."

Inigo cut through the parking lot and smashed through the supermarket's plywood-covered glass doors. He let out a quiet "yee-haw" as they crashed into the store. He looked half-sheepish, half-delighted as he guided the vehicle through shelves, crushing canned goods and packaged foods under wheel before parking.

Lejeune gave Inigo a flat look. "Alright. Get out, do your best to fortify our entry point against the storm. Use bags of rice to build a levee; put as much heavy shit as you can behind it. I'll take care of the kid. Go, go, go."

Nevaeh, Tito, and Inigo piled out. Lejeune checked on the kid. He was breathing evenly, but was on fire to the touch. She climbed out of the Humvee and started tromping across the wet floor, gathering supplies. Her fireteam had already started shifting bags of rice to plug the hole.

NEW ORLEANS; ROMILLY SIBIAN
06:21 AUGUST 29, 2005

Romilly used the wind, slicing across the lightly flooded streets of the French Quarter, relying on the craft's belt to keep her seated, having learned the "belt-up" lesson. This area wasn't as flooded—only half a foot of water covered the street. Asphalt and pavement scraped the bottom of the airboat, but the winds channeling through the tight streets were pushing her just enough to help. She followed the tracker as it led her along the Mississippi's welling banks.

The ominous black of the storm felt just inches away. For all practical purposes, it was. Once the eyewall hit, winds would pick up from 60 mph to over 135. The sky would open and pour down liquid hell.

The light on the tracker shifted to her left and she juked the airboat. The bottom tore as she bounced off a dumpster. Riding an airboat was a lot like skipping stones—so long as she didn't slow down, the ripped bottom wouldn't matter. There was a supermarket in front of her, and the tracker pulsed a couple of times every second. If she was reading it right, that was her destination.

Pulling every ounce of juice out of the craft, she skipped across six-inch deep water in the parking lot. Graffitied plywood covered the outside of the giant glass windows, but the front entrance of the market was destroyed and open. Ro squinted. Shapes moved inside—it looked like they were stacking something in the missing doors.

No way could she slow down. The airboat was basically a giant fan on a board and would get blown away, with her on it, if she let off the acceleration. Hopefully they would see her, because she couldn't be heard over the storm. She aimed at the opening, her Haitian Creole roots at war whether to pray to Christ or to the Loa.

People inside the market jumped to the sides as the airboat rammed into the makeshift two-foot wall. Ro killed the engine and tucked into a ball, seat-belted down as the craft skipped up and the back of the fan smashed into the roof. It spun out to the side, sliding to a halt inside the store.

She shakily undid the belt and slid down. It took a moment for the world to stop spinning. As her vision focused she realized she was staring down the barrel of an M16A2.

Romilly froze.

From behind her came the spine-freezing *chunk-chunk* of a shotgun being cocked, the single most intimidating sound mankind had ever produced, and it did its job on her.

She slowly raised her good hand. "Not moving."

"Hold on." The man behind the M16A2 was Latino, barely in his twenties. He was at the ready and slowly backing up, putting a few more feet of distance between them. Careful with each step, he slid his foot back to make sure he didn't trip on unseen obstacles. "Ain't you the lady from the Jeep? The one with the kid and that crazy shit on the camera?"

"Frankie's the kid's name." Romilly nodded, her soaked dreads dripping water down her forehead, into her eyes. "Is he okay?"

"Right. Frankie. Weren't you dead?" The soldier looked confused, ignoring her question.

Romilly blinked. *How the hell do you answer that?* "Uh... no?"

"Right. You're standing here. Okay. How did you find us, then?"

Acutely aware of the alien tracker, and the explanation she would have to give to someone already not asking the brightest of questions, Romilly opted for a simpler route. "GPS tracker?"

His eyes narrowed over the sights of the rifle, but his reply froze in his throat as a woman, a sergeant by her insignia, walked up behind him.

"What are you doing here, ma'am? And why," she motioned to the airboat, words failing her, "this?"

Romilly scanned the store's interior. "Following the child. I couldn't park out there and didn't want to make a second hole. It was the least dangerous of several bad choices. Where's Frankie?"

The sergeant got her team moving, "Stand down. Fix that hole," then looked back to Romilly. "The child is in the back of the store, in our Humvee. First, start explaining what the hell was on your camera footage."

Romilly spoke. "This place... it isn't safe. There are two things killing people. One is a wolf-like creature; it's called a rougarou. The other is... it's crazy is what it is."

"We already crossed paths with the rougarou. And I saw the invisible man on the end clip. So, you have a werewolf and an invisible killer?"

Romilly shook her head. "A rougarou isn't a werewolf—werewolves are made-up urban legends. Legend says it's more like an intelligent giant wolf. And the invisible man... it isn't that. I don't know what the hell it *is*, other than nine feet tall. I think its name is *Yautja* or *Ki'Sei*. It isn't killing indiscriminately though. It had me dead to rights and let me go. I think, maybe, it's only killing things it sees as threats. Dunno..."

The sergeant watched her skeptically.

"Sorry I don't have more for you, but you've watched what's on that camera. Y'know about as much as me."

"You're Ro, right? Call me Lejeune; I'm not sure my team could handle hearing me referred to by my first name."

Romilly found herself liking this sergeant. "Lejeune it is. I'm Romilly, but yeah, call me Ro."

Both women spun in response to a loud crash.

NEW ORLEANS; NATIONAL GUARD FIRETEAM
06:32 AUGUST 29, 2005

Rain hammered through the smashed corner window, the plywood and glass lay scattered in jagged pieces across the tiled supermarket floor. A beast crouched in the wreckage, growling and snarling. Matted gray and white fur covered the bear-sized wolf. It had landed squarely between the three guardsmen.

Inigo was the first to react, bringing up his M16 to firing position, but still too slow. The motion attracted the attention of the rougarou. Fangs flashed as it snapped to the right, darting low, catching Inigo by the thigh. Blood spurted from its maw as it clamped onto his leg. Inigo screamed and his shots went wide, the M16 firing upwards as he fell back.

"*Madre de Dios...*" Tito froze in place, his assault rifle in the safe position.

Chunk-Chunk

Nevaeh didn't pause. She pulled the shotgun's trigger and the rougarou's shoulder exploded in a red mist. The beast yelped, never letting go of Inigo's leg.

Chunk-Chunk

She pulled the trigger again, this time hitting its neck. Inigo stopped screaming and his limp body slid around the floor as the creature savaged him. The rougarou wasn't going down. While the shotgun blasts were hurting it, the weapon just didn't have enough power to pierce the beast's thick hide. That didn't deter Nevaeh.

Chunk-Chunk

The floor ran red with blood, diluted by Katrina's rain howling in through the shattered window.

Chunk-Chunk

The rougarou finally let go of Inigo's limp form, tossing the guardsman's leg to the side with a final wrench of its deadly jaws. It spun on Nevaeh, snarling. Red dripped from its fangs. Lejeune and the Creole woman slid to a stop next to the shotgun-wielding guardswoman. Lejeune snapped her rifle up and started firing.

Chunk-Chunk

The blast hit the rougarou's leg, and it had finally had enough. It sprang to the side, smashing through another boarded window, vanishing back into the hurricane.

Lejeune sprinted to Inigo, crouching by him. "Tito. Get the damn medkit from the Humvee! Now." She placed two fingers against Inigo's throat and paled. "Fuck."

Rain and wind pummeled the inside of the store. Katrina had found an opening and was exploiting it. Cans rattled and water washed away the red. Lejeune looked up at Romilly and Nevaeh, her decision made for her. "We're leaving and finding somewhere more secure."

NEW ORLEANS; NATIONAL GUARD FIRETEAM
06:41 AUGUST 29, 2005

"Sarge, I dunno if we should really be smashing through the front doors of a church…" The wind buffeted the Humvee around and everyone held on for dear life.

"Can it, Tito. We're doing a hell of a lot less property

damage than the hurricane is, and I'll take us through every
front door and wall in New Orleans if it keeps us alive...
And technically, we're going through the back door." She
clutched the steering wheel in a death grip, gas pedal to the
floor as they fought the wind and the incline. The Humvee
won out, though. Its low center of gravity and heavy frame
had been designed for terrain and conditions even more
adverse than this, if such existed.

Trees along the levees guarding the French Quarter from
the Mississippi's raging flow bent under the hurricane's
wind. A couple of blocks in, everything dropped to below
sea level. Their best chance was to stick as close to the levees
as they could, so that if they did—God forbid—break, water
would flow past them instead of drowning them.

She hooked a sharp right on St. Peter Street and drove
through the center of Jackson Square to avoid the trees and
other flying detritus as Katrina intensified. Straight ahead
was the massive, and more importantly, solid structure of
St. Louis Cathedral. She swerved into Pirate Alley, taking
off both side mirrors as she squeezed the Humvee through
a too-tight space. The second she was through, she hooked
hard to the right, and the whole vehicle lurched.

Protected from the winds by the cathedral, she managed
to get the Humvee up to thirty before crashing into the
building's door. Had the door not been inset into a several
foot decorative wooden frame, they wouldn't have made it
in. Pews were crushed as the vehicle came to a halt.

"Out." She killed the ignition. "Secure that door, Nevaeh.
Tito, get the front doors, make sure they're barricaded!"

ST. LOUIS CATHEDRAL; ROMILLY SIBIAN
06:44 AUGUST 29, 2005

Frankie's eyes fluttered open. Romilly put her hand against his forehead. "Morning." He was running a severe fever.

His eyes darted around till they settled on his backpack. He weakly reached out and clutched it, struggling briefly to pull its weight into his embrace.

Frankie rolled away from her, arms wrapped around his backpack. His shoulders shook.

Romilly frowned. She tucked the blanket around him and spoke quietly. "Stay put in here, okay? It's dangerous outside."

"'Kay." He nodded but didn't look at her, hugging his pack.

Romilly slid out of the Humvee and looked around. The Guard fireteam had dropped flares as they worked, but the cathedral was still eerily dark. Shadows danced, gluttonously swallowing the flares' light, catching the eye with ghost motions. She shook her head, ignoring the tricks her mind was playing. Lejeune was at the back door with Nevaeh. Tito, having secured the front doors, which faced the levees, was walking toward her.

Everything slowed as Tito raised his rifle, pointing it at her. Romilly felt her head tilt. What was he… She dove to the side as her reflexes processed what her brain wouldn't.

"Get down!" he yelled as he sprinted forward and pulled the trigger.

STORM BLOOD

ST. LOUIS CATHEDRAL; NATIONAL GUARD FIRETEAM
06:44 AUGUST 29, 2005

Nevaeh didn't have a chance to react. There was a flash of gray in the doorway against an ugly brown sky outside, then the guardswoman was falling back, blood and intestines spilling from her eviscerated body. As she hit the floor, her corpse slid one way and her shotgun the other. Her cross lay in a pool of blood between them.

Lejeune snapped her rifle up, squeezing off a three-round burst.

The rougarou yelped as it lost an ear, then spun on her.

"Get down!" Tito yelled in the background, then started firing.

The rougarou crouched, snarling, slowly advancing.

Behind them, across the pews, a large stained-glass window exploded inwards in a concussive spray of flying shards and metal slivers. In the center, a humanoid shape, built to the same scale as the rougarou, flipped through the opening. It landed in a crouch on the altar. The wood cracked beneath its weight.

Water dripped from the *Yautja* as it raised its head.

Three red lights flickered on, tracing ghostly lines between the thing's shoulder and the rougarou. The lights tracked up until they rested on the entry the rougarou had burst through.

A high-pitched sound, like a record being scratched in reverse, echoed through the cathedral and a blue pulse shot out. The wall over the rear door exploded, masonry tumbling down, trapping the rougarou in the building.

"The fuck?" Tito spun around and fired. "Die, you Neanderthal-looking motherfucker!"

The *Yautja* leapt as the altar splintered under the gunfire. Lejeune, on the other side of the cathedral, never let up on the rougarou. Even with the collapse around the doorway, water poured into the cathedral, making her footing tricky. The rougarou snarled and launched itself at her.

Tito swung the M16A2 around, never letting off the trigger. The alien hunter landed wide of him, tucking into a roll, then launching itself low, right at the guardsman. Tito overcorrected his aim, sending a spray of bullets into the shadows.

The *Yautja* landed in front of him and slammed its fist into his chest, batting aside the assault rifle with its other hand. Twin blades punched through Tito's chest and he blinked in surprise. Blood poured down his back. Snatching a combat knife from his boot sheath, he stabbed at the alien's shoulder, scoring a deep gouge that bled green. The blade fell to the ground from Tito's lifeless fingers.

The *Yautja* tossed the corpse off its blades, then spread its arms wide, tilted its head back, and screamed a basso roar of challenge. It charged down the aisle between the pews.

Lejeune slipped in the rising water, falling to one knee but never letting off the trigger, as the rougarou bore down on her. There was one thing she hadn't tried yet…

Lejeune jerked one of two flashbang grenades off her harness, pulled the pin, and threw it at the beast's head. A fist smashed into her ribs, breaking them, and the world spun as she went ass-over-teakettle to the side. She felt more ribs break as she impacted the pews and her vision went bright white as the flashbang detonated. The back of her head cracked into another pew and pain overwhelmed her. Her stomach rebelled and she vomited, spewing bile over her own chest.

ST. LOUIS CATHEDRAL; ROMILLY SIBIAN
06:44 AUGUST 29, 2005

Romilly pushed herself up to her knees. The *Yautja* smacked Lejeune aside with casual disdain then charged the rougarou as a flashbang went off. Romilly stopped and took a deep breath, rubbing her eyes. Not thinking was stupid, and stupid got you killed. She looked around. The wolf-beast and the alien closed in on each other, the alien raining blows on the rougarou's head while the beast snapped its fearsome maw at the hunter.

Weapons were easy. Both Tito's and Lejeune's rifles were reachable, but neither of them had seemed to dent the two combatants. Her eye fell on the Humvee. Frankie's face was pressed against the glass and he had the camera open and filming from his vantage.

The Humvee...

Romilly sloshed through the rising water to the Humvee, but paused before opening the door. The alien was holding the rougarou by the neck, fighting to keep the beast off while hammering the hand wielding the twin blades into the beast's shoulder and chest. The problem was one of size. The rougarou outweighed the alien by a couple hundred pounds, and the blades just weren't penetrating far enough through its tough hide.

The rougarou snapped massive jaws over the alien's face, ripping the mask free. It savaged the piece, shaking its head back and forth. Romilly's eyes went wide. Whatever she had thought might be under that mask, the truth was far more alien. It had four mandibles, both upper and lower, and a wide serrated ridge making a V over a bony forehead.

Its skin was ivory with red markings.

The rougarou dropped the mask and snapped at the alien's face, scoring a deep gouge between its mandibles. Green blood spurted from the wound.

Romilly clenched her fist and forced herself into the Humvee. The keys were hanging from the ignition. "Frankie, get down!" she yelled as she gunned the vehicle.

Outside the Humvee, the *Yautja* slammed the blades into the rougarou's throat, though they just skipped off its tough hide. The beast clamped its jaws down over the alien's wrist and the thing howled as its back arched and its mandibles flared.

Romilly backed the Humvee away from the two, and Lejeune—an avenging angel covered in blood and bile—rose next to the retreating vehicle. She pulled a steel cable from the Humvee's winch and paused, nodding at Romilly as she clipped the hook to her vest.

Lejeune ran at the combatants and jumped on the rougarou's back. It released the alien to snap at her. She looped the cable around the beast's neck, losing skin from her palms as she caught it in a makeshift noose.

The *Yautja* hammered a fist down, the blades slicing through Lejeune's leg, pinning her to the wolf-beast.

In a moment of clarity, Romilly understood Lejeune's plan and hammered on the gas. The Humvee lurched forward as the guardswoman reached to her chest then threw the last flashbang in front of the rougarou from her perch on the beast's back. The beast flinched and sprang back to the rubble blocking the door.

Romilly sped through the fiery pews and slammed the grille of the Humvee into the rougarou. Rubble sprayed out of the church, immediately lost in the maelstrom of Katrina. The rougarou, Lejeune, and the alien hunter followed, caught by the howling gale, tumbling along the ground like a twisted kite. The weight of the three jerked the Humvee to the side as the winch cable pulled taut.

Romilly sprinted out of the cab to the front of the Humvee and hit the retract gear on the winch box. Barely visible through the hurricane, she watched as the alien jerked the cable off the rougarou and smashed its blades through the beast's eyes. Lejeune was blown to the side by the hurricane as the hunter's biceps bulged in effort. The *Yautja* tore the rougarou's skull and spine free of its carcass. The alien had trouble standing against the gale-force winds, but managed to hold up the trophy momentarily before being forced to plant its blades into the flagstones to anchor itself.

Lejeune's body bounced in the wind as Romilly reeled her in.

For a fleeting moment, the alien locked gazes with Romilly. It clicked its mandibles together as it held eye contact with her, then it was gone, vanishing into the hurricane.

Romilly finished pulling Lejeune in. Somehow, the sergeant was alive. Exhausted, Romilly tended to her wounds, praying to the Loa that they would all survive the night.

NEW ORLEANS, THE AFTERMATH; ROMILLY SIBIAN
AUG 30, 2005

Romilly hooked her arm through the hold-bar in the Coast Guard Dolphin's doorway, squinting against the sunlight's glare, as the rescue helicopter swung up and away from the cathedral. The Hi8 camera was tucked into the sling the emergency responders had put her mangled right arm into.

She stared into the watery grave of New Orleans, absently watching the reflection of the Dolphin below. The corpse of the rougarou would be lost in the devastation Katrina had left behind, just more decayed meat and bone by the time the flooding was cleared. Questions spun through her mind. *Why was the rougarou after the boy? What was that alien hunter? Have we only been bait, was that why it let us live?*

Romilly carefully held the camera, thinking about the footage. There were some things that were too dangerous for the world to know... some things that would get them all locked up in some government lab. She pulled out the tape and snapped it in half, dropping it into the flooded ruins.

"Some questions are better unanswered," she mumbled.

Frankie huddled in the corner of the rescue vehicle, clutching his backpack. Everything was a frenzy around keeping the army lady alive and no one was bothering to watch him. He unzipped his backpack and looked in, remembering.

"Hey, Frank?" The 2nd unit director called out to Frankie's dad. "Can you stop that yipping? I'm trying to get some establishing shots."

His dad looked at him sternly. "Give that thing to me, Junior."

Frankie handed the found puppy over and his dad stabbed its shoulder with a dart.

The animal went limp and Frankie's eyes went wide. "Da! You didn't have to kill it!"

"I didn't. I used a tranq dart. We'll figure out what to do with it later. Now, go set it someplace away fro—"

He was interrupted by screams and spun around. "Oh shit. Frankie! Hide in here!"

Frankie blinked back a tear and reached into his

backpack, stroking the ears of a battered puppy. Dried blood matted fur that stuck to an emaciated frame. It stared out at him, something more than just animal behind its eyes. "I told you when I rescued you in the bayou I'd save you," Frankie whispered.

The rougarou cub weakly raised its head and licked his palm.

LAST REPORT FROM THE KSS PSYCHOPOMP

BY JENNIFER BROZEK

"Outta my way! I gotta get to the bridge." Emery shoved his muscular bulk by the smaller, rounder engineer.

"Weren't you supposed to be there ten minutes ago?" Trina grinned after her shipmate as she followed. The captain had called an all-hands and everyone was on the move. "With legs like yours, you'd think you'd be faster. Or at least more capable."

"Screw off, woman. I was asleep."

"Like you were during netball last week?"

"We'll see who's laughing next week. You may move like a fish in zero G, but I got skill and power to back it up."

The two of them hurried down the hallway toward the bridge. Trina, third-in-command, wasn't needed there for more than advice and to fill in on scanner work. Emery was both the security chief and the second-in-command. On a small scout vessel like the *Psychopomp*, all crewmembers had more than one job. The two of them burst onto the bridge, one after another. They were the last of the bridge crew to make it.

"I put five on you eating your words." Trina threw herself into the scanner station chair, and began a cursory look at what was before them.

Emery settled into the weapons station and pulled up the latest data. "I'll see your five and add in the loser has to eat a raw fish."

"You and the eating strange things. You're going to regret those words."

"Both of you are going to regret everything if you don't stop measuring your egos and get to work." Captain Ahmed stood, his salt-and-pepper hair gleaming in the bridge lights. "Debris field coming into sight." He stared hard out the forward viewports.

"The first of the larger derelict ships should be in sight any moment," Kaida said as she navigated the scout vessel in. "At least, according to the coordinates you won, Captain."

Ahmed nodded. "Now we find out if I was cheated or not."

"Too late to do anything about it if you were." Trina eyed the scanner. "But I've got the edge of a large shadow at the limit of my ping."

The captain let out a soft sigh as the first of the larger debris fields came into sight. "Derelict battle cruiser. That'll pay for the whole trip. Kaida, eyes on obstacles, slow and easy. Emery, prep shields and grav-pulse to keep the big stuff from crushing us. Trina, monitor for other live ships. We don't want this find stolen out from under us."

A variety of grunts and acknowledgments erupted from the bridge crew as they focused on their jobs. The *Psychopomp* moved ever closer to the score of a lifetime. Minutes ticked by as the battle cruiser loomed large in the viewport. The ragged holes and scorch marks spoke of the battle that'd been fought here.

The bridge door slid open. "Any survivors?" Vito asked as he entered with Gunnar close behind.

When no one answered the medic or the behavioral psychologist turned first contact specialist/adventurer—a paying passenger, a rare thing these days—Trina glanced up at them. "No. Not yet." The two men were almost mirror opposites. Both were white. Vito had black hair and eyes with tanned skin while Gunnar had blond hair and ice blue eyes with pale white skin. They complemented each other. Rumor had it that Gunnar came on this scouting trip more for Vito than for the chance to make first contact with another species—not that that was really a possibility. Aliens didn't hang out in dead spaceships.

"It's my duty to remind you that there is no life salvage. All mariners, spacefaring and terrestrial, have a duty to save those in peril without expectation of a reward. Salvage law applies only to the saving of property."

This last bit was mimicked and mouthed by everyone on the bridge. Vito always said the same thing as they reached a potential salvage score. Still, he always took his cut of the loot when payday came.

"It's my duty to remind everyone that saving a person doesn't negate our salvage find." Captain Ahmed kept his eyes on the forward viewport. "I—" He froze. "Kaida, cease all forward momentum now." His voice was tight and intense. "Go dead."

When the captain had that tone of voice, no one disobeyed or bantered with him. He had seen something very wrong and was doing everything he could to save their lives. As Kaida cut all power except to the most vital ship systems, the bridge went dark, lit only by a scant number of glowing buttons and system readouts. Trina's radar system was the brightest light in the back side of the bridge.

No one said a word. Everyone stared forward, trying to understand the captain's sudden fear and caution.

"Holy Mother of God." Emery let out a slow breath.

Trina put a hand to her mouth as she saw what had frightened Captain Ahmed. Just on the other side of the battle cruiser was a scavenger ship. Shaped like a torpedo with a series of rotating rings around its core, the scavenger's ship looked like it'd been in battle as well… many battles. Its main ramming cone was pitted and scorched, but still intact. Trina could tell who understood the danger they were in based on the soft gasps and muttered prayers mixed with curses. Only Gunnar seemed unaware that they were seconds away from being blown to hell.

The bridge door opened and Zuri, the newest recruit, stepped in. Trina waved a hand to silence the woman, but she need not have. Zuri took one look at the growing torpedo in front of the *Psychopomp* and backpedaled until her shoulders hit the door again. She didn't say a word. Her eyes were very wide and white against her dark skin. She knew what it was. There was a story there that Trina would have to ask about if they survived this.

She focused back in on her scanner, watching for the smaller scavenger scouts and ripper crews. She didn't see anything.

"Movement?"

Kaida answered the captain's question with a slow shake of her head. She gripped her long black braid tight as she stared at her instruments. "Nothing. They haven't seen us."

"Thank the Light that scavengers have terrible boundary protocols. Plot a course out. I don't care what direction. Just away. We'll consider what to do once we're safe."

"Captain, there's *nothing* moving." Trina stared at her scanner. "I mean, the torpedo is lit up, but it's not moving. It's drifting like the rest of the stuff around us."

"She's right." Kaida adjusted the navigation controls to allow the ship to drift while keeping a safe distance from any damaging debris. "I don't see a powered ship in flight at all."

The bridge remained silent while the captain considered this. "Emergency beacons?"

"Four. The battle cruiser, two of the destroyers, and..." Trina looked up. "The torpedo cruiser. Based on the timestamp loops, the torpedo set off their emergency beacon six days ago, but it's weak. The rest... more than a year ago. The only reason I can read any of them is proximity."

The captain's face tightened into a smile. "All right. Keep the escape course locked in under the emergency nav. I want a single button push to get us out of here if needed." He took a breath. "If it's a trap, we'll find out. Light her back up and head toward the torpedo cruiser."

The brightness of the scout ship coming back to life made everyone wince. Zuri frowned. "Captain, why are we going to the pirate ship?"

Vito answered for him. "Looking for survivors."

"We're going to save pirates?"

"No." The captain answered for himself this time. "We're going to kill pirates and rescue prisoners. Otherwise, we're claiming this whole field and sending the coordinates back to Kosana headquarters. There's enough here to set all of us up with our own ships. Or to retire."

"No answer to our hail, Captain." Kaida threw a glance at Emery.

He caught it. "No movement in shields or weapons. She's alive, but drifting."

They could all see the name of the scavenger's vessel now, emblazoned on its side. Captain Ahmed clasped his hands behind his back. "We need to know what took out the good ship *Oxenham*. I don't see any fresh battle marks. Something happened here. Looks like we're going to have to board her to figure that out."

Emery, Trina, and Vito waited in the airlock with Zuri. All four of them were suited up even though Zuri was supposedly on standby. Trina knew different. She was the titular head of the boarding party, though each person had their own areas of expertise. She would assess the engines of the *Oxenham* and determine if she could still fly. If so, that was feather in the cap of this salvage claim.

"Travel as a group until we can determine the threat level." She nodded to Emery as she spoke. Emery nodded back. "After the threat level is determined to be null, we break up into teams. Vito and Emery, search for survivors. Zuri, you're with me. We head to CnC to determine the vessel's damage. Or if we need to, head to engineering."

Zuri straightened at this. "Yes, ma'am." She grinned at Trina as the men glanced at each other and shrugged.

"Emery, Zuri, get us aboard."

The two of them moved to the outer airlock door. The *Psychopomp* drifted alongside the *Oxenham* at one of its outer doors. Emery punched a series of buttons to release the umbilical tunnel. Zuri maneuvered the far end until it encompassed the other airlock completely. She sealed it against the side of the drifting vessel and engaged the locks. The two ships drifted together as the connecting tunnel hardened into a straight corridor.

As soon as the tunnel was pressurized and the *Psychopomp*'s airlock door opened, Emery took the lead and floated to the other airlock door. He had the control panel open and set the lockbreaker to work. Trina could tell it succeeded when the adjoined *Oxenham* airlock began its pressurizing cycle.

"We're going in, Captain."

"Acknowledged. Remember, scavengers are criminals and are to be shot on sight. Anyone who is a prisoner is to be given medical attention *in situ*. Once their status is confirmed, then they will be allowed to board the *Psychopomp*."

"Yes, sir." Trina shifted her attention to the boarding party. "You heard the captain. Weapons at the ready." No one said a word as all four of them pulled their weapons— blasters of different types—including the medic. He'd seen enough scavenger handiwork to know he didn't want to be subject to it.

Traveling from one vessel to the other was a matter of traversing the tunnel and re-engaging the airlocks on both ends. Emery and Zuri took the front as the *Oxenham's* outer airlock door unsealed and rolled open. The crew boarded the scavenger vessel and waited until the seals were in place.

The artificial gravity kicked in as soon as they boarded the *Oxenham*. As the inner airlock door cycled, Zuri peered through the dirty window. "I think someone's out there. I see a shape."

Emery motioned Vito and Trina to the sides of the small room while Zuri crouched. Emery pressed the unlock button. Everyone had their weapons trained on the opening door.

There was a person waiting for them and he was very, very dead.

Pinned to the inner hallway with a ragged piece of metal, the man had been dead for days. It was obvious enough that Vito didn't rush forward to attempt to help him. Instead, he shook his head. "Scavengers. You'd think they'd be a bit neater than this." He gestured to the dried pool of blood on the floor. "Unsanitary."

Trina moved into the corridor after Emery gave the all-clear. "This doesn't look like normal infighting. Scavengers are an undisciplined, unruly lot, but they aren't... this. They don't leave dead bodies in the corridor. All together. Head to the bridge. I want to know what happened here." She pulled up the standard torpedo-class cruiser schematic and sent it to everyone's HUDs. "We follow the path until we discover they've modified this ship in some unusual way."

With Emery in the lead and Zuri in the rear, the four of them moved through the silent ship. Vito chattered to cover his nervousness and to relay data to the *Psychopomp*. "Atmosphere is normal. Oxygen and the like. No measurable airborne toxins. Of course, these guys could've come across something new and exciting. Recommendation: EVA suits on for the duration unless we figure out it's safe."

"It's never safe on an enemy ship. Someone killed that guy." Emery kept his head on a swivel, looking for threats.

That killed the conversation until they reached the bridge. Along the way, signs of fighting—scorch marks on the walls and dried viscera on the floor—kept them vigilant. Still, nothing greeted them except the twinkling lights of a ship, active but unmanned. Several stations were stained with something that looked suspiciously like blood. Though, nothing looked damaged. If there had been a fight here, either it was over quickly or they'd been careful not to damage the ship's controls.

"Secure the area," Trina commanded as she moved to one of the monitoring stations and began a scan of the vessel. "The bridge no longer has control of the ship's propulsion. It's been rerouted to the main engineering room. The only thing we can do here is passive commands."

Vito moved to another station. "Ninety percent of the ship still contains an atmosphere. There is a breach in one of the holds. Scanning for life signs now."

"Zuri, on the door." Emery accessed the security station. "Something took out this ship."

Everyone winced as Emery's station suddenly erupted in a shouting man's voice. "It's the ghost! It's coming for me. It's killed almost everyone else. We can't stop it! Oh, God, someone help me!" The man's voice cut off in a scream and a gurgle.

"What the hell?" Trina met Emery's eyes. "What was that?"

"Final log of this... guy. I don't know what his position

was. But, you gotta see this. He wasn't kidding about a ghost."

Vito and Trina joined Emery at the security station. He replayed the final log without sound. They watched as a disheveled man shouted into the recorder then was yanked backwards by his neck. Something had looped itself around him and pulled him off screen.

Trina peered at the monitor. She replayed the last seconds of the recording and froze it. She pointed at a blur around the man's neck. "What's that?" She looked between Vito and Emery. Both of them shook their heads.

"Stealth armor?" Emery guessed. "Maybe. I've never seen anything like it."

The station Vito had been at beeped. Vito returned to it. "Besides us, two living people. They're together and not moving."

"Nothing else? Nothing moving in on us?"

"No."

Trina considered the situation. "Captain?"

"I'm here." His voice sounded tense.

"Recommend blowing all the hatches and depressurizing the ship. I'll need to go down to the main engineering room to get that kind of control."

Vito held up a hand. "Wait. There are two living people onboard. That will kill them."

Trina scowled at him. "At least one of them is a murderer."

Captain Ahmed broke in before it could become an argument. "Gunnar has pointed out that this might actually be a first contact situation. Exactly what he signed on for. He wants to come aboard and make contact."

Emery shook his head. "Bad idea. We need to get off this ship. Trina has the right idea."

"Not until we get to those people. If they're scavengers, we'll leave them, but if they're prisoners, we have a duty to assist. That recording was a call for help. Space-maritime law requires that we at least *attempt* to help." Vito crossed his arms. "We all signed a contract agreeing to this."

Everyone stared at each other until the captain sighed. "Fine. Gunnar and I will come aboard. Buddy system. No one goes alone. Emery with Trina to Engineering. Zuri with Vito to get to those people. If you see anything like a blur on that final log, shoot to kill."

Trina didn't like it. However, Captain Ahmed was the captain for a reason. "I'll send the two paths to your HUDs."

"We'll be headed toward the people. You just get the ship under your control."

"Yes, sir." Trina glanced at Emery.

He picked up her thread. "You heard the captain. Zuri, Vito… get to those people. See what there is to see. You'll meet up with the captain and Gunnar. Assume *everyone* is hostile until proven otherwise. Take all appropriate caution."

Zuri gestured for Vito to follow her. "Let's go."

Trina shifted to private comms. "This is wrong. I don't like it."

Emery shrugged. "Me neither. However, orders are orders. If all goes well, this is our last scouting run. Best to get it over with quickly."

"Still think we should evacuate the atmo now."

"Bloodthirsty woman." Emery's voice held no rancor. "You're right, of course. Survivors can only complicate things."

She glanced at him before heading toward the engineering room.

Vito and Zuri followed the path laid out for them. Zuri stalked ahead, her weapon ready to fire. She stopped Vito from moving ahead as they came to a body sprawled in the hallway. What was left of a body. She pointed to a thin wire. "Trap."

They followed the line of the wire until it disappeared. "What does it do?"

"Nothing good." Zuri furrowed her brow. "Don't be too curious. This one's dead. Step over and around it. We're concerned with the living."

Vito gave her a look before doing as he was told. He marked the spot on the electronic map with a danger sign.

Minutes later, they passed another trap. This one had been sprung. The dried viscera said that the victim did not get away, though they were nowhere to be seen. Vito grimaced. "Someone lost a limb."

"And someone took it with them." She stopped at the end of the hallway and nodded to the door. "Through there. Two living people." She shifted from private to open comms. "Coming up on the living people. Voice monitoring live."

Zuri didn't wait for a response. She thumbed the door open and stepped inside, weapon ready for all attackers. A moment later she whispered, "Holy gods."

Vito stepped into the room. He didn't throw up. His gorge rose. He forced it back down with the will that made him the doctor he was.

"Captain… are you getting this?" Zuri moved into the room… the lair… of god knows what. It had once been a conference room. Now it was an abattoir, decorated with bones—human bones—and makeshift weapons. All about them hung gruesome trophies. Human skulls, spinal cords strung up with sinew, and spiral decorations in bone and blood dangled from the walls. In the center of the room, three bodies hung. One was headless and flensed, hanging upside down. The other two, both human males, were tied to cross poles attached to the exposed ceiling rails.

"Are they alive?"

The captain's question spurred Vito into movement. He went to the first man in a pseudo military uniform of gray pants and shirt. All patches and identifying marks had been removed. Vito ran his medical scanner over the unmoving body. "This one's alive. Barely." He shifted to the second, younger man in the same generic military uniform. As he raised the scanner, the young man opened his eyes and jerked with a cry.

Vito jumped back. "Friend. We're friends."

"Ghost! The ghost." The young man flicked his eyes over Zuri's shoulder.

She didn't hesitate. Whirling with speed, Zuri opened fire on what looked like thin air. It would've been foolish if half her shots hadn't rebounded off of what looked like a shift in reality. The ghost advanced and a large blade pierced Zuri through the middle. She screamed, still firing and fighting a creature she couldn't quite see.

Vito did the only thing he could do as Zuri fought the monster. He ran. Zuri's death cries followed him until both her weapon and her voice were silenced. "Captain, it's not a ghost. It's stealth armor." He moved as fast as he could in the EVA suit. It wasn't meant for sprinting. "Survivors are pirates." He couldn't be certain, but he thought the ghost was hot on his heels. "Need help," he gasped. "Zuri's dead."

Engineering was a disaster. Someone had set it up as a last stand. Like the Alamo, it had fallen. Trina and Emery picked their way through the mess of debris. Shoving aside the leftover trash from rations, Trina accessed the engineer's station. "Where are the bodies?"

Emery shook his head. "Whatever broke in here took them with it." He put his back to her with his head and weapon on a constant survey of the surrounding area. "Just get control of the ship or figure out if it's operable."

Trina didn't answer him. She didn't need to. She was as nervous as he was. As her gloved fingers flew over the keyboard, she knew whoever had holed up in here had lasted for a couple of days. There were ration packets strewn about the place and she was pretty sure the bucket in the far corner of the room had been used for the result of those rations. "C'mon, *Oxenham*, give me your secrets."

She worked as fast as she could to get into the system. Just as she succeeded, the screams began.

Captain Ahmed and Gunnar moved through the ship at an unhurried pace. Gunnar peered about him with fascination. "These pirates—"

"Scavengers."

"These scavengers live on this cruiser and go about space, what, capturing and boarding ships? Then stealing whatever they want or need?"

The older man nodded. "That's about the size of it."

"What do they do with the crews?"

The two of them stopped at the trapped body. "If there

are any still alive after the ships are rammed, they kill them or make them slaves. The lucky ones get ransomed." Ahmed pointed at the thin metal wire that ran from the body and up the wall. "Don't touch this."

Gunnar nodded. "I've seen these before. Usually protecting something important in a tomb."

The two of them stepped over the body and paused as Zuri and Vito commed them. Ahmed scowled with concern as he eyed the video. "Are they alive?"

Gunnar shifted around, excited. "I've heard of this. There's a race of warriors who hunt—" He jerked away from the sight and sound of the sudden fight. "Vito?"

"Stay here, Gunnar. That's an order." Captain Ahmed put a hand on Gunnar's shoulder, pushing him back as he turned to head towards his medic.

The consultant ignored Ahmed and pushed past him at a run. "Vito!" The consultant had his blaster ready and ran toward the sound of weapons fire.

Vito ran down the long hallway as fast as he could. He didn't bother to look behind him. He wouldn't see anything if he did. His EVA helmet would obscure his view unless he turned all the way around and from what little he did see— Zuri impaled on a blade, lifted up by the blurry air as she fought and screamed—it would do him no good. Instead, he ran.

"Vito! I'm coming!"

It was Gunnar over the comms.

"No," he panted. "Get to the ship." He stopped talking as the end of the hallway came up on him fast. He had the choice of running into it or slowing down to take the corner. He didn't want to do either. In the end, he did neither. With a stutter-step to slow enough not to knock himself out when he rebounded, he prepared to take the corner.

An incredible force hit him from behind and he was slammed into the bulkhead. Banging his forehead against his front helmet plate, Vito moaned in surprise and pain. Everywhere there was stinging, cutting pain. He opened his eyes and found himself pinioned to the wall in a web of thin metal that slowly cut into him.

Movement down the hallway caught his eye…

———

Gunnar moved at speed. Despite what the crew of the *Psychopomp* thought of him, he was an experienced spacefarer and had done his share of EVA suit training. His was the best money could buy. Ghost or no ghost, he would help Vito. Then he'd make first contact. He rounded the corridor with Captain Ahmed on his heels, cursing at him in a dialect he didn't need to understand.

There, at the other end of the hall, Vito was caught against the wall in a net. This would not stand. He was helpless there. Not even struggling. "Vito, I'm here. I'll get you out of there."

"Run." Vito's voice was soft with pain. "Behind me. The ghost. Run."

Gunnar ignored this and holstered his blaster before unsheathing his knife. "No. I can help you." He got to Vito before he realized that his knife was useless.

The air blurred next to them.

Gunnar shouted a word at it. "*Mdi!*" He wasn't sure he'd gotten it right—if this was the creature he'd thought it was.

The blurred air solidified into a humanoid creature at least two meters tall. It had reptilian skin, a broad chest, clawed hands, and a huge head with dangling appendages. Most terrifying were its red eyes and mandible mouth. It was covered in armor, weapons, bones, and other unidentifiable things. It flared its lower mandibles.

Elation soared. He'd been right. "It's a Predator, Captain." Gunnar held out both hands, one with the knife and one open to keep the creature at bay. He didn't know where Ahmed was. It was only now that he realized that the captain wasn't at his side. "A secretive order of hunters—"

The Predator growled in a particular clicking noise before speaking softly. *"Nan-deThan-gaun."* With that, he put an end to the soft meat's prattle.

"You don't have it. Do what you can. Now."

"Yes, sir." Trina didn't like the tightness in the captain's voice. It said he was looking death in the face and didn't know if he'd survive.

Trina typed line after line of careful script, giving her control of the *Oxenham*. She was the new captain of the torpedo cruiser and had the highest permissions. In truth, she'd copied most of what the previous person—Shaw Doty—had done. There was no need to reinvent the wheel. This time, though, she linked control of the vessel to her wrist pad and to her voice.

Emery hovered behind her, looking as tense as she felt. "Have you got it?"

"I think so. *Oxenham*, vent the rear port atmo and open door Engineering 3B."

The entire cruiser shuttered and listed, causing the two of them to stumble to the side. Trina cursed under her breath. "Kaida, keep the *Psychopomp* synced with the *Oxenham*. Don't let that umbilical corridor break."

"On it. Don't do that again if you can help it."

"Roger that."

Emery eyed her as the two of them got their collective balance. "That was a dumbass move."

"Maybe. Maybe not. Now I know I have control." Trina felt heat run up the back of her neck. "Let's get out of here before that 'predator' ghost finds us."

Captain Ahmed stopped when he saw Vito pinned to the wall. He knew it was a trap. Instead, he aimed his weapon, looking for the blurred air, and switched his comms to crew only, cutting Gunnar from the conversation. "Vito is down. Gunnar is about to go. Trina, what's your status?"

"I'm in and getting control. I need just a couple..."

"You don't have it. Do what you can. Now."

"Yes, sir."

Ahmed didn't answer. He watched and listened as Gunnar ran to his death. Now the only thing the consultant was good for was information: who or what was the enemy?

The air blurred.

Gunnar shouted something.

The blurred air became a creature of whispered legend. Ahmed went cold with fear and determination. As soon as he got a good aim on it, he fired. It was too late. The blast

172

rebounded off the creature's shield. At the same time, the Predator sliced Gunnar from groin to sternum. Ahmed fired again as the Predator stabbed Vito in the side and pulled his own projectile weapon.

The ship rocked as it fired, causing the curved metal blade to miss.

Ahmed turned and ran. His mind moved faster than he did in the EVA suit. He knew he couldn't outrun the creature—his old mentor had whispered of these hunters when he was in his cups. *"If you run into one, run and don't look back. Don't try to save anyone if you want to save yourself. Run, Tariq. It's all you can do."* He had to outthink it. The booby-trapped body was his only salvation.

He unspooled the grappling hook from his belt. It was usually used to hook onto the outside of a space vessel. Now, it would either save his life or be part of his death. He bared his teeth in a fierce grin. He would fight for every second of life as he always had.

Ten meters away from the body, Ahmed waited in the open. If he was right, the Predator would reveal himself as he came in for the kill. The explosive under the dead man's body might be enough to hurt the monster and allow him and the rest of his crew to escape. He held the grappling cord in one hand and his blaster in the other.

The Predator came, snarling.

Ahmed yanked the cord attached to the tripwire and prayed the explosion would kill the monster.

He prayed in vain.

PREDATOR: IF IT BLEEDS

As the captain's curses and the sounds of fighting died away, Kaida broke in. *"Orders, Captain? ...Captain?"*

Trina jerked her head at Emery. "Answer her." The two of them had heard the explosion and the captain's dying words in a language neither of them knew. That put Emery in command whether he liked it or not.

He knew this as well as she did and scowled. "Orders are to stay put, Kaida. Don't leave your station. Be ready to evac on command." Emery shifted from foot to foot before taking off at an almost run. Trina could see him sweating inside the EVA suit despite the climate controls.

"But the captain..."

"Will be fine or is already dead. Man your post."

There was a pause then Kaida's voice came back tremulous with an underlying core of steel that promised pain. *"Yes, sir."*

Trina waited until the comms cut out before she said, "You didn't have to be so blunt." Her breath came in soft pants as she hurried to keep up with him.

"Yes, I did." He was one step in front of her. "You're my responsibility now. Your job is to get to the *Psychopomp* and get out of here."

She couldn't see his face, but she didn't like what he was implying. "What about you? What's your job?"

"Make sure you do yours or die trying."

They turned the corner to the hallway with the airlock attached to the *Psychopomp*. The other end held a limping monster. It roared its fury as Emery moved to meet it.

"Get ready for netball." It was the only warning Trina gave as she watched the Predator run at them. She cut the artificial gravity to the *Oxenham*.

Emery was ready. "Get to the *Psychopomp* now." He launched himself at his mortal enemy.

Trina did as she was ordered and opened the inner airlock door. She overrode the commands to open the door to the umbilical corridor between the two ships while keeping the inner airlock door open for Emery to get through. "C'mon, Emery. It's open." She pulled herself into the tunnel, moving fast through the weightlessness of it.

Emery's answer was a cry of pain and a whispered, "*Go!*"

Whirling as she grabbed one of the side handholds, she looked back at the open airlock. Against hope, she prayed for Emery to reappear. He did not. "*Psychopomp*, open airlock hatch 2D." Behind her, the airlock door unsealed and opened. Before her, the air blurred in the *Oxenham* airlock. "*Oxenham*! Emergency shut all airlock doors!" The *Oxenham* airlock inner and outer airlock doors rolled shut in a hurry.

Trina swung herself in the direction of the *Psychopomp*. "Kaida, emergency evac as soon as I'm in. Don't wait."

"What—?"

Trina slammed into the *Psychopomp* airlock and hit the emergency uncouple to the umbilical corridor. The airlock door cycled shut as the corridor detached. "Go, Kaida! Go! Evac!" Trina wasn't sure, but she thought she saw a blur in the tunnel between the two ships just before the *Psychopomp* jerked to the side and spun. As the ship's thrusters fired, she whispered, "*Oxenham*, self-destruct. Primary override Delta-Echo-Alpha-Delta. Now."

The last thing Trina did was order the measured drop of salvage claim beacons, leading back to the drifting space vessel graveyard. A couple of the beacons wouldn't be in perfect alignment after the *Oxenham* imploded, but it was close enough for the Kosana Salvage Company to find the salvage claim again. That was all that mattered.

That, and that both she and Kaida had survived.

Salvage beacons 1A through 1G at the above coordinates in outer rim section, Sector Kilo-Mike-Kilo, Quadrant 7429, have been dropped, claiming the entire find for the Kosana Salvage Company.

Anomaly: There was a live torpedo cruiser drifting in the midst of the wreckage with an SOS beacon lit. Per space-maritime law, the crew of the *Psychopomp* boarded the scavenger vessel. For unknown reasons, the skeleton crew of the pirate vessel had turned on each other, murdering one another and setting booby traps. There was also a wild animal loose on the ship. The animal killed crewmember Zuri Becker and Security Chief Emery Mazur. Booby traps killed civilian consultant Gunnar Larson, Medic Vito Cocci, and Captain Tariq Ahmed. Larson's booby trap set off the self-destruct on the torpedo cruiser. Due to this last, salvage beacons 1A, 1B, and 1C will be slightly out of alignment.

Salvage claim find reward to be split between Navigator Kaida Asari and Engineer Trina Gannon. Death benefits are due to the families of Zuri Becker, Vito Cocci, Emery Mazur, and Tariq Ahmed.

Witnessed by Kaida Asari, Navigator.
Witnessed by Trina Gannon, Engineer.

"You expect me to put my thumbprint to this?"

Trina didn't have to look at Kaida to know she'd been crying. "Yes. I do."

Kaida gazed at the ceiling of the *Psychopomp*. "Don't you think they're going to want proof?"

"I've already taken care of that. If the company cares enough to ask for proof, I can send them what I've packaged up." She'd already cobbled together a decent set of audios and visuals for the report, backing up her words. The rest she'd erased from every machine that kept track of these things.

"It's all a lie."

Trina turned the other woman to face her. "Do you want to tell them that a ghost murdered our crewmates?"

"Not a ghost. A Predator."

Trina shuddered. "I don't know what that is. I don't want to know. If you're smart, you're going to take your reward and settle down on a nice safe planet or space station. That's what I'm going to do. We're set for life. If you want to hunt these things, you're on your own. This was my last scouting run."

Kaida stared at her for a long moment then pressed her thumb to the screen. "You're right. We're done."

Trina pressed her own thumb to the screen before she sent off the final report from the Kosana Scout Ship *Psychopomp*. She prayed that nothing would follow them home.

SKELD'S KEEP

BY S. D. PERRY

820 AD

When Jarl the Sword's Son and the fighters returned from their successful travels—the monasteries across the sea had yielded many treasures—there was a story waiting at Jormungand's house. Three different messengers had come from the north weeks apart to carry the news.

The first item related that Skeld the Boarstooth had been killed by the warlord Asger the Spear, who had taken Skeld's lands as his own. There had been a great, bloody battle in the early fall, and Asger and his men had won.

The second story was that Asger had gone mad, and was burning the farms and villages near Skeld's Keep, slaughtering livestock and driving people into the wilderness.

The latest was that Asger was dead, and had been dead since the day he'd taken the Keep. It was Skeld and his council who were murdering everyone within reach; they had risen from their graves as draugar, as the long wet days of fall crept into the early days of winter. Now they roamed the borders of Skeld's lands and fed on any man that dared come close.

Jarl didn't believe in draugar—a monster story to tell children over the fires—but he believed that it would be just like the dishonorable Skeld to spread such a tale, to keep a weakness hidden. If he'd suffered heavy losses to Asger, he was vulnerable. Skeld was getting old, and Jarl the Sword's Son had more gray in his beard than red; if he meant to have his revenge on the Boarstooth—as honor dictated—what better time? The Keep boasted three fine long houses, stables, a high wall, and the sturdy stone watchtower that had given the place its name.

Jarl's Keep. He liked the sound. He would stock it with fighters and women and spend his late years making sons and drinking and watching over the villages that gathered round for his protection, making raids as it suited him. All that had to be done was for him to take it.

When the warriors had gathered to celebrate their successful return, Jarl stood up. Stelgar shouted at the drinking men to shut up and listen, for the Sword's Son would speak. The laughter and calling died quickly, drink-bright eyes turning toward Jarl. Jormungand the Skull was chieftain, but Jarl had been his best fighter and raider for long years. It was Jarl who trained the new fighters; it was Jarl who led them.

"I want to take Skeld's Keep," he said, loudly and clearly. "Skeld once said that I was no fighter, and he spat at my feet. I have waited many years."

There was a rumble of approval. The ordeal of waiting to take revenge was proof of good character.

"It is said that Skeld has become a draugr. I believe he has run out of fighters, and looks to frighten men away with stories."

"What's a draugr?" Ult called. Ult was from inland.

"Almar, will you speak of draugar?" Jarl asked.

Almar was strong, a good fighter, and was also the most superstitious man Jarl had ever met. He was full of lore and always carried charms and fetishes to battle. He stood reluctantly.

"There are times that when a willful man dies, he becomes a draugr," Almar said, his low voice a rumble in the warm lodge. "The draugar are not alive but stalk the living, eating their flesh and drinking their blood. They swell and grow tall, some as tall as giants, and can weigh as much as an ox. They carry no weapons, for each has the strength of ten. It is said they are hideous to behold, corpse-blue and stinking; it is said that a draugr spreads madness to all who hear its voice. It will attack every man or animal it sees until the flesh rots from its bones."

Someone made a joke about man-bones and there was another swell of laughter, but Jarl saw that Stelgar wasn't laughing; nor were Helta the Bowman or Ult or Thrain, all strong men, all top fighters. They looked interested.

"How are they killed?" Ult asked.

"They are already dead," Almar said. "They can't be killed. Burn them, or chop them to pieces. And burn the pieces, and throw the ashes into the sea. And that is all I know of draugar."

He sat down, nervously fingering one of the charms he wore on a string around his neck.

"We have just returned from a long journey," Jarl said. "I know some of you have business to tend to, wives to keep warm, and would not choose to travel again so soon... But I will speak to Jormungand on the morrow and leave the next, to put an end to Skeld the Boarstooth. If he is a draugr, I will burn him and claim the Keep. If he is a man, I will do the same. Are there those who will accompany me?"

Stelgar stood immediately. He was Jarl's closest ally and sworn brother since childhood. "Skeld has no honor. When he spat at your feet, he spat at mine. I will come."

Helta and Ult and Thrain stood. All were of Jarl's age, all had fought beside him for many years. Thoralf rose, still grinning.

"Sigrid will keep warm whether I'm here or not," the younger man said, to new laughter.

More men stood up to be counted: Rangvald the Hammer, Geir, Bjarke, Sten the Reckless, Egil... Seventeen in all, a mix of young and old, enough to drive a small knorr up the coast, enough to take the Keep if the stories about Skeld's losses were even close to accurate. A week on the sea would bring them to the borders of the Boarstooth's lands.

The chosen men settled down to feast and drink, their spirits high at the prospect of brave battle; there was no satisfaction to be had stealing from the Jesus-men, who died on their knees. Even those who wouldn't travel were excited, satisfied that the Sword's Son would have his revenge on the dishonorable Skeld.

Almar did not volunteer. He clutched at his talismans, his thick face a mask of worry.

In the warmth of the hovering ship, Tli'uukop and the three young Hunters watched the small vessel riding the coast, the men that drove it armed with primitive weapons, blades and bludgeons and spears, a few simple projectile devices. Tli'uukop—One Eye, to his students—was pleased. He had promised the young Hunters that the long trip would be worth their time, but after many days of watching men working in crop fields or pulling food from the sea, they'd grown impatient. The thick musk of their agitation was barely filtered by the ship's cyclers. One Eye had been about to announce that they would travel to fight the great white animals of teeth and talon instead when the ship informed them of the traveling men, detecting the forged metals they carried.

One Eye felt a growl of anticipation stir in his throat, and was immediately joined by his students. All three were recently Blooded, and all from prestigious lines. As Blooded, they were free to pursue their own Hunts, but additional training by an elite Hunter was considered an honor, and One Eye had come from a long line of great Hunters, elites and clan leaders. After an honorable retirement following the loss of his eye, he had chosen to teach, and found that he liked it. Taking Unblooded on their first outing wouldn't have suited him—Unblooded *Yautja* were tiresome creatures, vibrating with bloodlust and inexperience—but training a select few in the finer points of tracking and wrist blade was a different matter entirely.

"They're small," Shriek observed. Shriek was tall and angular, with thick mandibles. He was an excellent fighter but tended to rush to battle. He'd gotten his name for the distinctive sound of his victory cry.

"Primitive," Ta'roga said, dismissively. Ta'roga was a

prodigy with a fixed blade, but was far too sure of himself. "They wear skin, not armor."

As usual, Kata'nu said nothing. Of the three, One Eye thought Kata'nu the most promising. His physical skills were not as advanced as Shriek's or Ta'roga's, but the slight, nimble youth looked before he thought, and thought before he spoke.

"When I first saw them, I thought the same," One Eye said. "Too weak to fight, too small, too simple. But they think. They reason, and adapt. Experienced Hunters have been bested by them on a level field."

"When will we begin?" Shriek asked, too quickly.

"When they leave their vessel to cross the land, you will track them," One Eye said. "Study them; watch what they do. You will choose an appropriate target and engage at your best discretion."

"I will take a dozen trophies," Ta'roga trilled.

"Trophies are the result, not the reason," One Eye said, as he said often. "The Hunt is the practice of the Hunt. It's an experience, not a goal."

The students nodded but he doubted they heard him; the air was charged with their excitement, the scent like hot, thin oil. Even Kata'nu's measured gaze was eager.

One Eye sighed inwardly. They would succeed or they would fail, but either way, they *would* learn.

Seven days on the icy sea and they reached the small fishing village that marked the beginning of Skeld's lands. The dim sky spit new snow at them as they dragged the boat ashore. The village was deserted, although they found no bodies, no signs of violence—only clear evidence that the villagers had packed up and fled, heading north. An inconvenience; Jarl had planned to raid the village for supplies to see them inland, but the villagers had taken their food when they'd gone. The men ate the last of the dried herring and stale bread that they'd brought and slept in the drafty meeting house, taking turns at watch.

Skeld's Keep was two days from the shore. In the morning they started east, collecting squirrels and rabbits in the woods along the way, a winding climb into hills lightly dusted with snow. They passed a handful of small farms and found them as empty as the fishing village—dead fires and signs of hurried packing, footprints in the rotting wet leaves where the snow hadn't yet gathered. Some of the men laughed at first, joking about the fearful farmers running from draugar, but as the day wore on, the laughter fell away. The woods and snowy fields weren't only empty but silent, a watchful tension in the air that all could feel.

Helta, who had the best eyes, saw branches move without wind, thrice. Bjarke, Olav, and Haavid had heard steps beneath the barren trees. The information that they were watched, followed, was passed casually from man to man, and just as casually, Jarl slowed their pace, and put his hand on the hilt of his sword.

As the weak sun began to cast its long shadows, they saw smoke just south, thin and high above a stand of snow-flocked evergreen. They approached carefully; the scent of smoke was overwhelmed by the smells of shit and blood as they moved through the trees. Jarl drew his sword before stepping into the clearing.

It had been a pig farm. There were a dozen of the dead animals littering the ground in front of the smoking timbers of the farmhouse, the fences torn down around their blood-soaked bodies.

Jarl scanned the small clearing. Nothing moved but the thin smoke. The men spread out, their weapons and shields at the ready.

Jarl squatted next to one of the animals. Its eyes had been gouged out, its jaw broken and hanging open; its guts spilled from a ripped and ragged hole in its belly. A bloody, jagged rock next to the glass-eyed sow was clearly the weapon of its demise. Finger marks of dried blood decorated her spotted skin. Clear teeth marks—human teeth—marked her skinny flanks.

Jarl dipped his fingers into the pool of entrails. Cold, but not frozen, and no smell of rot. That, and the smoke... A day or two, no more.

"Here," Helta called softly. He and Geir were looking at something hidden by the heap of burnt wood.

Jarl nodded at Stelgar, and they went to see. The farmer and his family. There had been three sons, the youngest only a few years old. All of them—the farmer and his wife, their young—had been beaten to death. Broken bones poked through their ripped clothes, splinters and dirt marking each injury. Jarl saw more teeth marks, on the slender, milky limbs of the children. The woman's skirt was hiked up, her sex battered into pulp.

"Not a clean wound in sight," Stelgar said, and Jarl nodded. There were a number of bloody sticks and rocks around the pitiful family. There was no snow near the smoking ruins, and Jarl could see footprints on the ground. Four or five men, perhaps. One of them had been barefoot.

"Draugar," Geir said. A few of the others nodded, the

whispered word passing between them like a breeze.

"There are no such things as draugar," Jarl said. "These people haven't been eaten, they've been bitten. And beaten. By normal-sized men."

"Madmen," Geir said. "Almar said the draugar spread madness."

From the state of the farm and its inhabitants, Jarl couldn't argue against insanity. Still, he wouldn't put it past Skeld to create such a fiction.

He shrugged. "We'll know when we know."

Thoralf, standing over one of the slaughtered pigs, called out cheerfully, "So, pork for dinner, then?"

Most of the men chuckled, but no one lowered their weapons. Jarl nodded. They could salvage meat from the animals and use a cook fire near the smoking farmhouse, to keep themselves hidden from—

Skeld's soldiers? Cannibal madmen?

—from anyone watching. They would camp beneath the trees, though, and there would be no fire after dark. They needed their night eyes.

"We'll be at the Keep by noon tomorrow," Jarl said, firmly. Whatever answers there were to be had, he was sure they would find them there.

Ta'roga watched the men sleeping on the ground, rolled into their cloaks and grouped together for warmth. He sat with his back to a massive tree a hundred paces away, occasionally sneering at the three puny guards that slowly circled the camp. They couldn't see him.

He clicked his mandibles, pleased with himself. Shriek

and Kata'nu would burn with envy when they saw him take out the leader of the traveling men, the clear choice. Ta'roga would prefer to see them fight before he moved in, to confirm that the leader was the best, but he didn't plan to spend another day following these animals around. The legendary *man* was a short, pale flat-face who ate meat off the ground, nothing more.

One Eye had sent a message that there was a herd of them farther inland, the direction that these men traveled, too many to fight without tech—expressly forbidden in Hunts against primitives. There was a small pulse-beam emitter in Ta'roga's kit—One Eye had all of his students carry the failsafe—but the young Hunter couldn't imagine any circumstance that would require him to use it. When the world's star came into view again, Ta'roga would separate the leader out and dispatch it with a clean blow from the fixed blade on his dominant arm, the weapon as sharp as teeth, as strong as honor. The first trophy would be his.

Ta'roga's legs went numb from waiting for them to stir; he ignored the discomfort for a while, but after one of the circling guards—the tall one, that carried a bow—had passed him by, Ta'roga quietly shifted, stretching his legs out in front of him.

The guard, the tall one, had stopped walking—and now moved back in Ta'roga's direction, holding its bow in both hands, an arrow resting between the curved wood and the string.

It heard me.

Ta'roga didn't move. A minute passed, and then the man took off its head covering, a thick animal skin with metal stitched around the eyes, and set it gently on the ground before standing again, looking directly at the tree where Ta'roga sat. It moved closer, but didn't seem to be searching for anything. Rather, it turned its hairy face from side to side, slowly. Listening.

Ta'roga had never seen one so closely, and felt, for the first time, that perhaps One Eye was right to speak so respectfully of these creatures. It wasn't charging to attack, or shouting for help, or deciding to ignore the small sound; it was *thinking*. Presented with evidence by its senses, it was searching for the source of what it had heard.

Ta'roga's mask blocked the sound of his breathing, but his heart beat quickly. If this man found him because he'd acted foolishly, if there was a forced interaction, he would be shamed.

The man looked up into the branches, its long, thin hair ruffled by a frigid breeze. Then it took a step back, widening its point of view, scanning the trunks of the trees, finally looking at the ground.

It stepped closer again, lowering its center of gravity by bending its knees... and focused on Ta'roga's feet.

Ta'roga carefully looked down without moving his head, and saw the symmetrical depressions in the soft dirt beneath his boots. He tensed, ready to react. If he killed the man, here, he would ruin the Hunt, disgracing himself. He could try to lead the man away, claim that it was his plan, to gain a trophy... but if he moved he would be heard, possibly seen, and the man would attack.

The man's gaze ran over the ground... and then it straightened, its body relaxing. Since there was nothing visible to its eyes, it obviously thought that whatever had made the tracks was gone.

Ta'roga let out a slow breath as the man turned away. He was embarrassed, but if there was no disruption to the Hunt, no reason to—

The man had continued to turn and suddenly whipped around to face Ta'roga, its bow drawn, an arrow nocked. The man released and already had another arrow in place as the first drove deep into Ta'roga's inner right thigh.

The suit stunted the arrow's brief flight but the powerful hit pierced the thin armor, the metal arrowhead tearing deep. Ta'roga rolled to the side and onto his feet, shocked and furious with disbelief.

The man loosed a second time, the arrow *thunking* into the tree where his head had been a second before, and Ta'roga extended his arm, wrist blades snapping into place, stepping forward to cut the throat of the man—who leapt backwards and shot again. The arrow hit Ta'roga's chest plate and was deflected, but the sound of it had the other guards calling out, running toward the bowman. Most of the men were suddenly on their feet as if they'd only pretended to sleep, their weapons in hand.

The bowman shouted something—and was cut off mid-cry as its head was split in two. Ta'roga recognized Shriek by his height and the angle of the cut. The bowman collapsed, blood and brain running down its shoulders. Suddenly there were a dozen of the men upon them, raising swords and heavy bludgeons, more running over. Their eyes burned, their strange mouths set in lines.

Shriek cut the throat of the first to leap forward. Red blood spurted from the cut, steaming in the cold air, gouting across the arm of his suit. Another man brought its bludgeon down on the moving splash of red. Bone crunched and

Shriek fell backwards. Ta'roga spun, driving his wrist blades into the man's soft belly. Astoundingly, the man raised the bludgeon again, trying to attack even as the blood poured down its body, even as it died.

Ta'roga jerked his blades free and grabbed Shriek, pulling him back from the attacking men. The leader shouted something and the men circled, facing outwards, their weapons at the ready. They ignored the three who bled at their feet.

Combat through incompetence was not a Hunt. Ta'roga had failed. The only honorable choice was to turn off his camouflage and fight, to face death, but Ta'roga was not thinking about the Hunt or his honor; he only felt a profound dismay at the realization that he had so badly underestimated these creatures.

Shriek was backing away and Ta'roga backed away at his side. The men raised their weapons and started after them, showing their teeth, shouting in their incomprehensible tongue, loud and furious. After a few steps Shriek turned and ran, cradling his injured arm. Ta'roga clutched at the arrow in his thigh and ran after him, his humiliation complete.

———

They followed the sound of running steps but in seconds, the sounds were lost... and although there were a few strange green splashes to be seen, spattered and far apart, glowing like fire, those, too, dried up after only a short distance; beneath the shadows of trees, they could not track which way the invaders had gone. Jarl called a halt and the men returned to their camp, to investigate where the attack had taken place.

There were marks on the ground as of footprints, but too big and oddly shaped to be a man's. There was a small pool of the liquid green fire at the base of the big tree, next to where the three dead men lay.

Jarl counted Helta's arrows. There was one in the tree, a second on the ground, its tip bent. A third was missing.

Stelgar squatted by the green pool. He carefully touched it with his finger.

"What is it?" Bjarke asked.

Stelgar shrugged. "Helta is missing an arrow. He hit something."

"It is draugar," Geir said, nervously. "The draugar must bleed green!"

"Draugar don't use weapons," Stelgar said, and motioned at the dead men. Helta the Bowman's skull was cleft in twain. Thrain's throat was cleanly cut, and Sten the Reckless had been stabbed in the gut by dual swords. "They don't hide, either."

"There were two of them," Bjarke said, pointing out the strange prints, at the tree and just east of it. "One rested here. The other came this way."

"Helta heard something," Rangvald said. He had also been on watch, as had Thoralf. "I saw him take off his helmet, to better hear. He shot only a moment later."

"I saw something," Thoralf said. "The air moved, like shadows."

Geir looked around anxiously. "We are tracked by monsters."

"Grow some balls or fuck off to your mama's teat," Stelgar said, standing. "If they bleed, they can die. And if Helta heard them, so will we. We know to listen now. And we know to watch for shadows in the air. If they return, we will kill them."

Jarl nodded, along with most of the others. Stelgar was the voice of reason.

"Gather branches," Jarl said. "Keep in pairs and threes, with one to watch and listen. We will build a pyre for the fallen, and to warm ourselves for our journey to the Keep. From the tower we can hold off any foe."

The men nodded and broke away. Jarl gazed down at the dead men, at the two wet pieces of Helta's head, hanging from his broken neck. Stelgar nudged one with his boot. A powerful blow, to be sure, and it had come from almost directly above; Helta had been a tall man, too.

"Walking corpses and green-blooded giants we can't see," Stelgar said "You sure you want *this* Keep?"

Jarl laughed. "What better path to Valhöll? Any fool can be killed by *men*."

Stelgar laughed along with him, a full, bright sound in the cold air.

The arrow had to be cut out of Ta'roga's leg, leaving a good-sized hole in his suit. A tab of disinfectant and a skin-seal took care of him, but he did not meet his teacher's eye, as was appropriate. Shriek's forearm was broken in six places; he sleeved it himself and injected a painkiller, his head even lower than Ta'roga's.

One Eye wished he did not have to share in their shame, but he'd known their deficits and sent them to hunt men, anyway. A Hunter's code was strict, but early mistakes were tolerated as part of the learning process. They had been arrogant and reckless, as he might have expected; it was their decision to flee that was unacceptable. Bested and injured, they had run.

He looked coldly at the two shamed and silent *Yautja* in the medical bay. It would be within his rights to kill them, but there was his own culpability to consider; the last time One Eye had hunted this world, there had been no fighters quite like these.

A clicking from the ship called his attention. One Eye stepped to the console closest and raised a screen, running his claws down the lines of symbol. Kata'nu was accessing sensory information. Their travelers were crossing an open field, moments from the barrier to the village, or whatever it was. Kata'nu was south of the men, but close; he was counting the villagers and checking for forged metals behind the village wall. Kata'nu's patience, his lack of arrogance... these were the traits of a Hunter.

One Eye looked back at the disgraced *Yautja*, thinking. Ta'roga and Shriek might yet be given a chance to redeem themselves... either by exhibiting excellence, or by dying well. There would be no trophies, but they might erase their shame.

"The men you were hunting are about to enter a village, where there are four times their number," One Eye said. "A Hunter worthy of his blood might shed all of his weapons and stand without armor, without hiding, and face his prey with bare claws. A Hunter worthy of his blood might even win... and if he dies, he might die cleanly."

Ta'roga and Shriek were on their feet before he stopped talking.

"You will *not* disrupt Kata'nu's Hunt," One Eye said. "Get in his way and I will carry your heads to your fathers and tell them of your dishonor."

Ta'roga fastened his suit and started shucking its armored plates. With only one good arm, Shriek struggled to keep up, his blades clattering to the floor. One Eye watched their sincere, solemn preparations without comment. There was a chance that they might survive; even injured, both were technically proficient.

He would move the ship closer to Kata'nu's position, the better to clean up afterwards and to keep the two disgraced Hunters from charging in prematurely. And he had already decided, he would not be bringing any more of his students to the man's world. Hunting men was a skilled warrior's game.

———

Skeld's Keep sat against the low peak of an *iss fell*, at the top of long slopes where the snow was starting to build; the Sword's Son and his party walked through fields of bowed winter rye, past empty houses and empty farms. They saw signs of Asger's siege, dead men and rotting horses, and the remains of large fires where bodies had been burned, blackened bones sticking up from the snow. Stelgar pointed out drag marks through the crops, long lines of crushed rye and dead barley leading toward the Keep. The one house they stopped at had dried blood on the walls, and dried shit, and vomit, and torn clothing. What they didn't see was a single living person.

The snow was picking up as they finally climbed within sight of the Keep, thick flakes coming down. No one guarded the high wooden wall; the heavy gate was standing wide open. The tower of stone peered over the top, gray and empty, its windows like dead eyes.

A few hundred paces from the wall, Jarl turned to look at

his allies, his friends and brothers. He saw wariness but no fear. Whatever they were to face—hidden giants, madmen, draugar—these men would fight well.

"There seems no need for stealth," Jarl said. "We have come for the Keep and will have it. Stay within reach until we know what we face. And watch for shadows in the air."

"They should watch for us," Thoralf said, and everyone grinned, and Jarl's heart was full. What better feeling than to head into battle with skilled men, united against an unknown foe? They would win or they would die, and both had their rewards.

That was when a man screamed from behind the Keep's walls, his single hoarse cry joined by another, a third, a dozen, twice that, too many to count; the wordless shrieks of pain, or anger, or hunger, the sounds of lunacy and loss rose into the snowy sky like the howls of wolves.

"Odin owns you all!" Jarl cried, and they stormed the gate.

———

Disguised by the falling ice, Kata'nu closed the distance with his travelers as they hesitated outside of the opening in the wall. They carried themselves at the ready, clearly expecting conflict.

Inside the enclosure, men cried out, and the leader led his shouting travelers through the gate. Kata'nu followed them. He could see the heat signature of many men pouring out from the large structure farthest north, still crying as they ran toward the travelers. Most carried no weapons. Many moved unsteadily, falling and staggering.

Kata'nu veered away from the travelers, toward one of several massive heaps of dead herd animals, swollen with rot, dead men piled on top of them. The travelers circled up, facing outward, screaming like Unblooded at their first kill.

The men from the structure ran and stumbled into view… and Kata'nu could see that there was something wrong with them. More than half wore little or no clothing. Many shook as if from fever, and fell down, and were trampled by others. Their legs were striped with thin waste and they made strange faces as they shouted and called.

Sickness. Kata'nu checked his mask's filter read, as he had regularly since leaving the ship. The humidity was up, ice falling ever more heavily from the sky, but he didn't see—

There. A high concentration of organic material was in the air, some kind of alkaloid; the makeup was that of a fungal spore. The fields outside the village were cultivated, heavy with cereal grasses; had their crops become infected? Their meat? Had they ingested the spore, or was it carried on the air?

The first sick men had reached the travelers. Screaming, weaponless, they attacked, and the travelers stepped fearlessly into the fight. Kata'nu trilled and shifted on his feet, excited to watch the unfolding battle—until he realized that a number of the charging sick men had abruptly changed direction and were running toward him.

The people of the Keep shouted gibberish, their eyes wide and rolling, their hands mostly empty—but their obvious madness was a weapon in itself, as they charged unflinching into the swinging swords and axes of Jarl's men. Jarl saw soldiers of both Skeld and Asger among the villagers and farmers; whatever plague had come, it had taken all.

The first man to reach Jarl wore shit-stained breeches and nothing else. Jarl swung and slashed the man's throat. Steaming blood poured into the snow as the man collapsed, gurgling.

Three more attackers took his place. A naked woman with slack, hanging tits covered in bloody vomit screeched and clawed at him. Jarl gutted her, quickly, as a man wearing a stained cloak grabbed for Jarl's shield and a teenaged boy threw himself at Jarl's feet, scrabbling at his boots with rotten fingers.

"My father's boots!" the boy cried. "You stole them!"

Jarl slashed and hit, kicking, cursing as he stomped the mad boy's head. The man in the cloak fell backwards, clutching at his stomach as his entrails spilled through his fingers. Blood misted the falling snow.

He saw Stelgar, grinning, cutting the throat of a bloody man wearing a string of boar's teeth around his neck. Rangvald smashed his hammer into the skull of a wild-eyed farmer raving about ghosts, crushing in the side of another man's face on the upswing. Therin loosed a half-dozen arrows, men and women falling like the snow, more coming. Geir had stepped away from the group to better swing his staff; he went low and wiped out three men with a single blow, thigh bones cracking beneath the heavy wood, but the attackers came on, fearless in their insanity. Many hands grabbed at the staff, and as Geir fought to free it, a soldier wearing a cloak of Asger leapt on him, tearing at his throat with cold-blackened fingers.

Another woman ran at Jarl, screaming, blue with cold and brandishing a thin stick as though it were a sword. Jarl slammed his shield into her face and she went down, still screaming through a mouthful of bloody teeth.

"Look!"

Olav and Bjarke were both shouting, gesturing toward the wall as they fended off the encroaching mob. Jarl looked, and saw gathered snow hanging in the air, in the outline of a great man-shaped beast's giant, shaggy head and wide shoulders. A stream of deranged attackers threw themselves at the creature, the tops of their heads barely reaching its chest, which still looked somehow like falling snow. Jarl saw shining blades sweep out of the flickering air, saw the creature taking shape as steaming blood sprayed across its body.

"Giant at the wall!" Jarl called, as a fat man with a spear ran at him. Jarl got his shield up and ducked, swinging his blade at the man's legs. He hit hard enough to feel the bones breaking through the blade, the impact humming through his fingers. The man shrieked and fell.

Hot blood dripped from Jarl's beard. Some of the unarmed people were running in fear now, away from the battle, shouting nonsense, but the soldiers of the Keep were picking up weapons, some memory of skill returning. A number fell back from the direct attack, their mad eyes searching for openings.

"At least now we can see the fucker!" Stelgar shouted, sidestepping as an old man tripped over the hacked bodies that surrounded them, dropping his stick. Stelgar chopped into the man's face.

"Odin smiles upon us!" Thoralf called, and the men still standing laughed tightly. A soldier with an axe got to Olav, though the young fighter managed to take his killer with him by a final swing. Egil and Haavid were also dead.

Jarl and his men fought on, trying to keep an eye on the

slashing, silent giant as the bodies piled up, as their own number dwindled.

———

Kata'nu fought well, killing ten men in the space of a few heartbeats… But by then he was visible, dripping with man's blood, and the travelers, the skilled fighters, were edging toward him as their battle raged. One Eye had no doubt that Kata'nu would fight to his death… But *he* would lose his only promising Hunter.

"Go," he said, to the *Yautja* standing silently behind him, not looking away from the visual. "Redeem yourselves. Fight well."

They hurried to the lock, thanking him for his leave in respectful clatters. One Eye growled an acceptance of their gratitude, already divorced from concern for their fate. He watched Kata'nu move with the grace of youth, his form strong, his movements measured; he watched and was pleased.

———

Kata'nu spun and slashed, knocked men aside with crushing blows, well aware that he was likely to die if the attackers organized. And it was his own fault for not brushing the falling ice from his suit. For all of his care, he'd proved as foolish as the others.

He glanced at the travelers frequently, feeling an odd kinship with the men he'd followed to this place of sickness. More than half had fallen, overwhelmed by sheer numbers, but those standing continued their gleeful dance, slaying the howling villagers, as committed as any Hunter to victory or death.

A man had picked up a spear from one of the fallen travelers and rushed at Kata'nu, screaming, raising the weapon over its head. Kata'nu dropped to one knee and slashed open the man's gut with his wrist blades, but another with a sword took the opportunity to rush in from the side. The man swung, the tip of the metal blade slicing deeply across Kata'nu's shoulder.

Kata'nu pivoted, still on the ground, and drove his blades into the attacker's chest. He pulled back but the blades stuck, dragging the dying man in close. Frustrated, he shook his encumbered arm, using his other to strike at a man with a rock in his hands. Wet heat coursed from his bleeding shoulder.

Over the screams of the dying and the sick, Kata'nu heard voices calling out, drawing his attention. He shot a look at the leader and his second, followed their gazes—

—and saw Shriek and Ta'roga striding in through the open gate, weaponless, their camouflage turned off.

Distracted, Kata'nu didn't see the man with the axe until it was too late.

———

Jarl had formed a vague idea of what the giants looked like from the blood-splashed monster stabbing men not twenty paces away, but he still felt his eyes widen. These newcomers wore dark metal masks, shining and smooth and ominous; black beaded braids hung to either side. Each wore a thin gray covering that outlined their bulging physiques, muscles hewn and chiseled like the strongest man's.

No armor. No weapons.

Jarl glanced at the giant dressed in blood just as it fell to its knees, an axe in its guts. One down, and two to take its place.

"Giants at the gate!" Stelgar shouted, and the men tightened what was left of their defense. Stelgar's cry seemed to redirect the mad attackers. At the sight of the giants, the men of the Keep seemed driven to new heights of fury. They screamed and ran toward the two massive creatures, howling like animals, slashing each other in their frenzy to reach the new enemy.

One giant dropped into a crouch, opening its arms wide; the other, taller, stepped directly into the oncoming attackers, smashing faces and pounding heads. Bone snapped. Men went flying through the snow, broken and bleeding. The tall monster made its way to where Thoralf and Ult fought, back to back, and both men turned to face it. Thoralf rushed in low to slash at its massive legs. Ult spun away, coming around to thrust at the striding giant with his heavy sword.

Ult's blade pierced the giant's side, the cut deep. Glowing green poured from the wound. The monster swung around and grabbed Ult by his head, twisting and pulling—and tore it from Ult's body. Blood gouted into the air, Ult's headless corpse crumpling to the snow. The giant threw Ult's head at one of the Keep's raging soldiers, knocking him off his feet. Thoralf slashed at the monster's thighs and danced back, drawing more green blood.

The shorter, crouching giant tore at the half-dozen armed men who'd crashed into it, ripping arms from sockets, tossing them like sticks, but as more piled on and brutally hacked at the creature, it faltered. Bjarke rushed in and swung his axe, the curved blade opening a thick line of green on the crouching monster's back. It turned and slapped him hard enough to break his neck, dropping him. Therin loosed an arrow at the creature and more shining green blood poured from where it lodged in the thing's massive chest.

The giants were stumbling. The red snow at their feet was spattered with heavy splashes of green.

When the taller one turned its back, Jarl ran forward, his sword high, barely keeping his balance on the slippery bodies of dead and dying men. He reached the bleeding giant and brought his blade down and across, howling with joy.

His sword sank deep into the side of the monster's neck. Green sprayed across his face, hot and bitter, and the giant turned, and punched its fist into Jarl's chest. Jarl felt his sternum shatter like ice, and pain like heat shot through him and a terrible, crushing pressure squeezed his heart—but the giant was slain, the spurt of its terrible blood already slowing.

Jarl grinned, and died.

The battle seemed to die with Jarl the Sword's Son. Men still screamed, but they were the failing screams of the mortally wounded. The last of the armed madmen had gathered around the two dying giants, were expending their fury in thrusts and jabs at the strange beasts. Thoralf walked behind the crazed men, slashing their throats easily.

The third giant, the one that had hidden, was also down. Stelgar could only see a mass of green and red in the snow, unmoving. Across the blood-soaked yard, he saw the men and women who hadn't fought, a dozen or so, huddled together by the stables. They sang and cried and fell to their knees, weeping, shaking from cold or from whatever madness had cursed Skeld's Keep.

Cursed. Thoralf, Rangvald the Hammer, and Therin still

stood, scratched and bloodied but alive. Everyone else was dead. They had taken Skeld's Keep, but Stelgar didn't want it; no one would. They should set it on fire.

Stelgar directed the others to put the dying to rest and walked to where Jarl lay, and squatted next to him. Jarl stared up into the falling snow, not caring that it landed in his eyes. Stelgar was happy for Jarl, but also felt an emptiness. He would miss his brother.

"Stelgar!"

Stelgar looked up at the urgency in Thoralf's voice, saw Thoralf pointing at him, saw Rangvald and Therin both running toward him—

He turned his head. Behind him towered the giant dressed in blood, not dead after all.

Kata'nu woke up to One Eye clattering in his ear.

"You're not dead. Pressure patch the suit, inject a stim, and get up. Use the pulse-beam to ensure your safe return to the ship. This Hunt is over."

Kata'nu blinked at the read in his mask. The ship was close. The axe had gone deep, though, and he knelt in a puddle of his own blood, already crusting with ice. His head felt light, hollow.

He looked across the battle site and saw that the leader— his trophy—had fallen, his sword buried in Shriek's throat. Ta'roga was a pile of chopped meat a few paces away. One Eye was surely disgusted by how his students had performed, all bested by men. Many of the travelers had died… but they were also the last standing.

The leader's second had gone to kneel by the dead

warrior. There were three others who still lived. They walked among the field of fallen men and dispatched them with their swords.

Kata'nu crawled to his feet and staggered toward the second, holding his guts in with one cold arm. He wasn't sure what he meant to do, but he couldn't imagine cutting the brave men down with a pulse-beam. He had failed; they had not.

He stopped behind the second, swaying on his feet. He expected the pale man to stand up and kill him, but it only stood, staring up at him, its eyes moving back and forth. Curious, perhaps. Kata'nu slowly lifted his free claw and reached for his mask. The other three surviving travelers had run toward them but the second spoke in its strange tongue and they only stood by, their weapons ready.

Kata'nu wanted to express to the man that he, Kata'nu, son of Esch'ande, had learned from this Hunt. Whether or not the man understood was not the point. He unlatched his mask and pulled it free. The cold was like a slap and the air was foul, but he liked the feel against his fevered skin. He was alive. He looked at the man, wishing that he could read its face or understand its language.

He held his mask out. An offering. A trophy.

After a long moment, the man reached out and took it.

Kata'nu was glad.

———

The giant turned and staggered for the gate, stumbling, parts of it seeming to disappear into the snow. In seconds it was gone.

"What the fuck was that?" Rangvald said.

Stelgar held up the fine, heavy helmet, big enough to cradle a babe. "We beat him, that's what. He pays tribute to our dead."

He bent and placed the helmet on Jarl's chest. *I will see you in Asgard, brother.*

"We're leaving, and burning this cursed place to the ground," Stelgar said. "Get those people to start gathering wood."

Therin nodded somberly. "The Valkyries will see the smoke and come to lead our brave friends to Valhöll. Skeld's Keep will make a fine pyre."

"It's the least he can do, spitting on Jarl's feet like that," Thoralf said, and even Stelgar had to chuckle. It was a good joke.

INDIGENOUS SPECIES

BY KEVIN J. ANDERSON

1

The colony planet was named Hardscrabble, and that should have been his first clue. Filled with hope and determination, Jerrick and the other 150 colonists should never have believed the propaganda or the brochures from the colonization initiative.

But now they were stuck on this bleak planet, to live or die depending on their own grit and resourcefulness.

As he drove the mammoth combine farming vehicle across the rugged landscape, Jerrick made a sour face as he remembered the obviously doctored images in the database, but the young man's father, Davin, had been convinced. Davin was a dreamer, optimistic and—worse—charismatic. He had persuaded half of his extended family and a large group of friends to join him on the venture, and all of them believed that this unclaimed planet would be a new opportunity, a new home. No one had thought to wonder why no one else wanted Hardscrabble.

The combine's engine hummed and rumbled, and Jerrick guided the giant vehicle with ease and long familiarity. The huge treads rolled along the dirt roadway, taking him around the field patches of enhanced wheat and corn.

The colonization initiative had given their group a basic setup allotment with tools and supplies, preserved food, crop seeds, livestock embryos, prefabricated buildings, large agricultural equipment, and a sketchy survey database with meteorological recordings and a cursory biological summary obtained by automated satellites.

When they had arrived on Hardscrabble a year ago, the colonists found a bleak world with a temperate climate and breathable, though sour, air. Native plants provided oxygen, but the soil was not hospitable to Earth-based life-forms, requiring a great deal of fertilizer. Their herd animals could not digest the local species of grasses. Hardscrabble's insect and bird analogues were inedible, and often just a nuisance. None of the animal life could be considered game, and some indigenous creatures were deadly predators—as the colonists had discovered in the first year. A special plot of land had been designated as the settlement's own cemetery.

Many would have opted to jump aboard the next supply ship that arrived on Hardscrabble... except that no ship was coming. This was their world now, sink or swim.

As he drove along, Jerrick clenched his hand into a fist and slammed it down on the polymer control deck of the raised cab. The colonization initiative had lied to them. The 150 dreamers here were not afraid of hard work, and none of them expected this to be easy—but they had expected honesty.

Sometimes when he was alone in the giant machine, driving across the virgin landscape, Jerrick would let his anger and disappointment get the best of him. Yes, he had a temper and he knew it. His father kept telling him in a calm and patient voice that he was just a young man and had much to learn.

But Jerrick was determined, along with his fellow colonists. Beating the land into submission, they first planted a fast-growing genetically modified grass that soon covered the rolling hills, laying down a soil matrix and providing pastureland for the first ten cattle revived from stored embryos. Other fields of grain ripened quickly, increasing the stores. Step by step, they were gaining a foothold. The Hardscrabble colony would survive—just barely.

Jerrick drove the mammoth agricultural machine that could plow and fertilize the soil, plant crops, and later harvest them. The solar panels on the combine's roof soaked up energy from the overcast sky. On his regular rounds of the valley, he inspected the crops, the spreading pastureland. The ten head of cattle grazed peacefully on the well-defined fields of green grass in the rolling hills. Beyond the grassland lay darker, thickly forested hills that remained unexplored.

As he reached the rolling, grassy hills, he expected to see the cattle placidly grazing, as they did every day. The ten animals tended to stick together, given the limitations of the fertilized pastureland. He scanned for the locator pings on his control screen and frowned. No movement. When he topped a low rise and saw the discolorations on the grass, the splashes of red, the slumped brown shapes, he felt suddenly sick.

Swallowing hard, he accelerated the mammoth combine, rolling the treads across the uneven ground and not even noticing the vibrations. As he leaned forward to look through the slanted windscreen, he saw the fallen shapes.

The cattle, their bodies torn apart and shredded.

Jerrick wrenched the combine to a halt, sick and infuriated. Leaving the engine thrumming, he popped open the cab door, swung down to the tread, then leaped to the ground. He raced across the bloodstained grass, appalled by what he saw. Six of the cattle lay before him—or what remained of them. The smell of blood in the air was like a heavy mist of bitter iron. Jerrick gritted his teeth and narrowed his eyes as he tried to understand what he was seeing.

One of the cow's heads had been torn off and lay discarded, the big bovine eyes staring sightlessly, pink tongue lolling out of its mouth, red blood spattered everywhere in the grass. Its side had been raked open, ribs splintered, entrails pulled out like confetti. One of its hind legs had been ripped off and cast aside. The other five cattle were just as mangled, and Jerrick found it difficult to determine where one carcass ended and another began. He breathed in and out, his nostrils flaring, his blood boiling.

When he heard one of the cattle lowing from the other side of the grassy hill, Jerrick just reacted. He ran, thrashing through the grasses, nearly slipping on a sheen of blood and loose intestines. He reached the top of the rise, saw other dead carcasses strewn about, and gaped.

The last surviving cow bleated in terror as it tried to struggle away. Long red gashes marked its side.

But it couldn't escape the monster.

Jerrick recognized the horrific creature that had killed seven colonists last year, the most fearsome indigenous predator on Hardscrabble.

The gruzzly was like a nightmarish crossbreed of a dinosaur and a grizzly bear. Black, spiky fur covered the huge frame. Its pointed, scaly face was like a flattened crocodile's. It had a plated belly, and sharp spines covered its tail. The wide paws were tipped with claws the size of threshing rakes.

Before the giant beast could slaughter the last cow, Jerrick roared out a wordless challenge, hoping to distract the thing. The gruzzly stopped and looked up at him, focusing on new prey.

Despite his defiance, Jerrick nearly soiled himself. He instantly regretted that he had left his plasma rifle in the combine's cab.

Last year, the gruzzlies had unexpectedly come out of the nearby hills, massacring livestock as well as colonists, even though the taste of Earth animals—or people—was not appetizing to them. The native predators simply slaughtered their victims and left the bodies strewn about. Gruzzlies attacked anything that moved.

Now the huge beast reared up, turning to face Jerrick and leaving the wounded cow to limp away, still bleating in terror. The young man bolted, desperate to get away.

With an ear-splitting roar, the gruzzly bounded after him.

Sweating hard, Jerrick tumbled over the uneven grassy ground, tripping in the blood, springing back to his feet. He raced back toward the mammoth combine, either to take shelter in the cab, or preferably to get the plasma rifle.

Despite his panic, he kept thinking that those cattle

had been Hardscrabble's future! Jerrick wouldn't let some mindless monster kill them all and face no consequences.

As he ran, he could hear thundering footfalls ominously close behind him, the crackle of crushed grasses as if a great machine were barreling down on him. Jerrick put on a burst of speed, seeing the safety of the combine ahead.

But he wasn't close enough. He couldn't run fast enough.

He glanced over his shoulder to see the enormous beast right there, huffing, swinging back an enormous paw. Jerrick slipped on the bloody grass, stumbled over a loop of intestine, and fell forward—and that saved him. The paw would have raked across his shoulders and ripped out his spinal column. Instead, the glancing blow just knocked him sprawling on his face. He rolled, crawled toward the nearest carcass. He backed up against the dead mass, panting so hard that each lungful screamed in and out of his mouth.

The gruzzly lurched forward. Jerrick slumped, surrendering, knowing he couldn't outrun or fight the thing.

Then he saw a ripple in the air, like a ghostly silhouette of a large man. The shape seemed to be made out of air, water, and invisible motion. The gruzzly didn't see the three red dots on its scaled chest plate, like a targeting mark.

With a whistling roar, an energy burst ripped through the air. It came out of nowhere and struck the gruzzly, leaving a smoking crater of flesh and black blood. The big beast reeled backward, raised its paws and clawed at its wound. The hulking thing turned to find its attacker, but could see nothing.

Jerrick heard a rattling, clicking sound... an inhuman sound. The air shimmered again, and the camouflage faded to reveal an armored man standing there—no, it wasn't a man. It wore a strange metal mask with blank eye slits; tufts of hair dangled like tentacles fastened to its skull.

The strange hunter let out its clicking, clattering challenge again, like a growl made of rattlesnakes. The hunter was focused on the wounded gruzzly. He held a cylinder in his huge, clawed hand, then squeezed inset controls. Long pointed ends snapped out of each end of the cylinder to create a javelin. Cocking back a well-muscled arm, the hunter hurled the javelin, which spun through the air and plunged into the gruzzly's upper right chest with a crackle of blue lightning.

The big monster clawed at the high-tech weapon, snapped the metal shaft in half, then lumbered toward the barely seen hunter. The rippling mirror-like camouflage dropped away entirely, and Jerrick's strange savior let out another sound of clicking challenge. The hunter drew two long, wicked blades, holding one in each hand, as it stormed forward to face his opponent.

The injured gruzzly threw itself upon the mysterious hunter, who was a deft fighter. He slashed with the curved blades, drawing bloody designs on the beast's chest plate, and cut the thick, matted fur. The gruzzly snapped its powerful jaws, but the hunter drove a wicked blade beneath its scaled jaw and through its palate.

Bleeding from mortal wounds, the gruzzly thrashed, clawed, and struck the hunter aside, sending him tumbling into the grass. The hunter sprang back to his feet, close to where Jerrick lay frozen in amazement and terror. The stranger was at least nine feet tall and packed with muscles. From the lithe way he moved, the hunter did not seem at all human.

Bleeding, dying but not knowing it, the gruzzly attacked again. The masked hunter regained his feet, and another weapon popped up on his shoulder, spinning, acquiring a target. Three bright red dots appeared over the gruzzly's heart. Just as the monster spread its clawed arms wide to crush its opponent, a searing blast ripped through its chest, blowing a crater through the sternum and all the way out the back, leaving bent ribs and splintered vertebrae like a crown of bones and gore.

With a hissing, choking rumble, the gruzzly collapsed to the ground.

The alien hunter stepped back and regarded the carcass, letting out a long succession of clicking growls as he inspected the kill.

Jerrick kept panting, frozen in amazement as he slumped against the bloody cow carcass. He felt helpless, but oddly not afraid. He didn't know what this hunter was, but he had killed one of the fearsome gruzzlies, the bane of the Hardscrabble colony. The young man swallowed hard, but made no sound.

The alien hunter took out a long saber-like knife, which hummed and then glowed blue. Bending over the dead gruzzly, the hunter tilted up the reptilian snout, and then with a single sweep of the vibrating blue saber, he decapitated the kill. The energized blade cauterized the stump of the gruzzly's thick neck, and the head rolled away, almost three feet wide. Jerrick could only guess how heavy it was, yet the alien hunter lifted the trophy with one hand.

Hearing his involuntary gasp, the hunter slowly turned, still holding the gruzzly's head. For a long moment, he looked at the young man with unreadable eyes behind the metal mask. The hunter seemed to find him uninteresting, lying there weak and unarmed among the dead cattle.

Turning, the stranger stalked away with his trophy, using his free hand to tap controls on the armored suit. The mirror-like ripple swallowed him up in a blanket of camouflage, and Jerrick couldn't see him anymore...

Eventually, the young man got back to his feet, covered with blood, shaking. He looked around at the massacre. The gruzzlies were horrifying enough, but now he had just seen another predator on Hardscrabble that was far more deadly.

2

It was late afternoon by the time Jerrick drove the mammoth combine back to the colony settlement. The dull gray sky showed only intermittent patches of olive green.

Ahead, he saw the fenced village compound. The tall barrier wall of spiked tree trunks surrounded the huddled prefab buildings. Upon first arriving, the colonists never dreamed they would have to make a fortress of their little settlement, but after the previous year's gruzzly depredations, colony leader Davin had sent crews into the hills to cut down trees and use the long trunks as a primitive but effective stockade.

After that first year, the colonists realized they had been naïve to bring only a dozen plasma rifles, confident they would have a peaceful settlement—but that was predicated on a peaceful planet, without fierce gruzzlies that came out of the hills once a year. The stockade's defenses were medieval, but effective.

As he drove up to the tall gate, Jerrick could still feel the drying blood all over his hands and his clothes. He kept trying to process what he had seen. Their year-old cattle had been slaughtered, and the colonists would have to start from scratch with new embryos. All that vital food lost.

Even though it would be nightfall soon, his father might send out crews with big spotlights and plasma rifles to harvest the meat from the mutilated animals—if he could get any volunteers to go out after dark. But Jerrick knew the carcasses would be safe enough until tomorrow, since the other predators on Hardscrabble wouldn't eat the foul-tasting Earth meat.

As he rolled the mammoth combine through the open stockade gates, people came out to greet him, but as soon as he swung down from the cab, covered in blood and looking distraught, they knew something was wrong.

His father hurried up to him, his face filled with alarm, creases deepening in lines along his cheeks. "What is it?" He grabbed Jerrick's shoulders, holding him at arm's length. "What happened?"

The young man let out a long, shaking sigh. "The gruzzlies are back."

The colonists moaned and muttered amongst themselves. His father stepped back to inspect Jerrick, looking at all the blood. "Are you injured? Did it attack you?"

"The gruzzly killed all of our cattle. And yes, it attacked me… but I'm not hurt. There's… more."

He described the strange camouflaged hunter, the inhuman being with superior weapons, how it had killed the gruzzly and taken the head as a trophy.

More colonists gathered as the twilight set in. Jerrick told his story again, while Davin furrowed his brow and started recalculating. "Without the cattle grazing, all that fertile grassland is now wasted acreage. New embryos will take months to revive, and we don't have another crop in place on that pastureland." He shook his head. "This is not good."

"Not good?" Jerrick widened his eyes, alarmed. "Did you hear what I said, Father? *The gruzzlies are back!*"

Two broad-shouldered men closed the stockade doors behind the mammoth combine. While Davin seemed preoccupied with other concerns, Jerrick shouted to the other colonists. "Get our plasma rifles and set out a watch from the top of the stockade. We better be prepared."

Davin nodded. "Good idea, although last year this stockade was proof against the gruzzlies. They left us alone."

Jerrick scratched dried blood from his cheek and said quietly, "Maybe so, but the gruzzlies aren't the only threat I'm worried about."

As darkness closed in, sudden spears of fire erupted in the surrounding hills. The dark forests gushed flame and orange explosions. Jerrick pulled himself up to one of the watch platforms just above the stockade wall, staring into the gathering darkness.

Davin climbed up next to him. "What could that possibly be? It looks like a war zone."

"That other hunter, the way he killed the gruzzly… I've never seen anything so cold and deadly in my life. And what if there's more than one of them?"

Davin watched the string of explosions in the hills. Even though the blasts were far away, they could hear faint bestial roars in the sudden empty silence. "Maybe they're hunting and killing gruzzlies—and good luck to them."

"If that's what they're doing," Jerrick replied as he looked at the line of explosions. "Or maybe they're driving the gruzzlies down here into the valley where they can fight them."

3

Hardscrabble had never been a pleasant place, but now it was a battlefield, monsters against monsters. Explosions continued throughout the night; the roars of gruzzlies and the bright flares put the entire colony on edge. The people huddled inside the stockade, knowing that the sharpened log walls were only a suggestion of security. If either of the two deadly species put their minds to it, they could easily crash through the wooden wall.

Soft pink dawn suffused the landscape. Standing on the observation platform again, Jerrick used a pair of zoomlenses to scan across the carefully tended fields. He couldn't tear his eyes from the dark furrows that energy weapons had torn through the croplands. During the night, the orange glow of continued explosions had sickened him. Now at daybreak he saw that a section of their corn and wheat fields had been burned and trampled.

Three huge dead gruzzlies lay sprawled on the ground, also decapitated—their heads taken as trophies, their bodies discarded in the middle of the colony fields.

Huffing with the effort, his father climbed up beside him, keeping his silence. Without a word, Jerrick handed his father the zoomlenses. Davin stared ahead, going pale. "Our crops…"

Jerrick watched the smoke rising into the sky where it mingled with the gray overcast clouds. "We have to retrieve the dead cattle, process the meat so we at least get something out of it. Can't waste a scrap now."

Davin nodded, still staring through the lenses. "We should awaken more embryos right away. The pastureland is still good, even if the cattle are dead."

Anger swelled within Jerrick. "The pastureland? Father, our people can't even leave the stockade with those things out there!"

Davin lowered the lenses and glanced at his son. "Last year, the gruzzlies returned to the hills after a time. It'll take that long for the embryos to turn into calves anyway. We have to hope—and prepare."

"But those other things, those alien predators… they're just hunting the gruzzlies for sport."

Davin remained stubborn. "Then when the gruzzlies are gone, the hunters will leave too. We'll be fine."

Jerrick knew he could never penetrate the man's lofty and stubborn optimism. "Our people may very well starve," he muttered. "We had few enough advantages on this planet. We were barely holding on by our fingernails as it was." He shook his head. "And we can't send a distress beacon. It would take years before we get a response. The colonization initiative just abandoned us on Hardscrabble. By the time a scout ship comes to check on us—maybe in ten years?— they'll just find a ghost town."

"We'll survive," Davin said, hardening his voice. "*We will!* We have extra stores. We can spread out ponds of nutritionally dense algae and grow that, if we need to. It tastes like shit, but we can survive on it. And even with the burn damage, we'll salvage some of our crops."

"Only if those things go away," Jerrick insisted.

As if to challenge them, a shimmering ripple of a humanoid form sprinted across the fields, stepping over the flattened roadway that led up to the stockade. Jerrick caught the motion out of the corner of his eye, and he turned to study it, recognizing one of the alien predators in its camouflage disguise.

Letting his shimmering cloak dissipate, the imposing figure came up to stand before the stockade, glancing at them, assessing their defenses. This one looked different from the hunter Jerrick had faced the day before. He seemed to find their wooden walls laughably primitive. The flicker changed in a quicksilver blur, and the creature vanished entirely. Davin stared at the empty air in angry disgust, and it was clear that he shared his son's doubts about the colony's chances for survival.

The older man climbed down from the observation platform, while Jerrick used the zoomlenses to scan the landscape again, obsessed. He didn't want to move. Deep in the hills, the whistling explosions and flashes of fire continued intermittently, far away, but now the young man focused on another turmoil much closer at hand.

In the nearest field of swift-growing wheat, a huge and hairy gruzzly loomed out of the morning mist like a monstrous shadow. The dark fur on its left side was singed and scabbed, as if it had been injured by one of the hunters' energy weapons. The big beast stalked forward, snarling, sniffing.

Jerrick glimpsed the mirror flicker again as the armored alien predator made itself partially visible. The great gruzzly generally relied on its sense of smell and hearing, so the camouflage wouldn't be a perfect defense. The beast's black tongue flicked out of its reptilian snout, and it roared, sweeping its rake-like claws from side to side, looking for its target.

Facing off, the alien hunter dashed toward the gruzzly, then disappeared entirely as its camouflage locked in.

The wounded beast lumbered along, wading through the wheat field, destroying the precious stalks as it looked for the alien hunter it could sense nearby. Seemingly coming out of nowhere, a line of fire licked across the ground like a fire hose of flames. The hunter was intentionally burning the fields to madden the animal. The gruzzly stumbled away from the dark smoke and crackling flames.

The hunter set more of the crops aflame, boxing in the huge beast.

Jerrick watched, appalled. "That's our field! Damn you!"

The alien predator seemed not to care, using the flames to drive the gruzzly. The predator was a humanoid-shaped blur against the rising fire. The furry beast charged directly into the flames, somehow finding its enemy.

The predator blasted his prey with the flamethrower, but the heat rolled off the big animal's reptilian chest plate. Facing a real battle now, the hunter switched off his camouflage field and withdrew two long knives before throwing himself at the smoke-maddened gruzzly. The furry creature smacked him sideways, bowling the predator aside. The armored hunter rolled through the rising fires in the field, stumbled back to his feet, then lunged forward again with both knives extended. His snakelike hair tentacles writhed, and through his metal mask he let out a bellow that sounded just as primal as the gruzzly's.

They engaged. The hunter's sharp blades dipped into the gruzzly's body again and again like a stinging wasp. With massive arms, the beast clasped the hunter, wrapped around his body, and squeezed tight. Long claws struck sparks across the armor, damaging it.

Then the predator clamped a small self-adhering explosive to the gruzzly's back. With a brief, bright flare, the explosion blasted through the beast's vertebrae and into its chest cavity, incinerating its heart and spine. The huge monster collapsed, dead, while the predator reeled backward, barely able to keep his own footing. His shredded armor sparked with random energy pulses, and his body leaked runnels of acid-green blood. Though obviously wounded, the predator remained upright over his kill.

The dead grizzly lay twitching, smoking. The burning fields crackled around them.

Watching the carnage from his observation platform, Jerrick muttered, "Damn you."

Unexpectedly, he saw the stockade gate open below. He leaned over the sharpened wooden barrier. "What the hell?" A figure stepped out onto the wide, trampled road... a lone man carrying a plasma rifle.

His father!

Davin closed the gate behind him and marched down the road toward the burning wheat field, the dead grizzly, and the wounded predator. Out in the burning field, the hunter was preoccupied with decapitating his kill, sawing through the thick neck.

Jerrick shouted, "Father, come back here! What are you doing?"

Davin turned to him, held up his rifle, and called back to his son. "You're right—somebody has to fight for our colony." Though obviously determined, he looked very small. "If that predator is wounded, this might be our only opportunity to hurt one of them." Davin began to sprint ahead.

"Come back!" Jerrick called. What if the man's actions simply enraged the other alien hunters?

Some of his fellow colonists had climbed the corners of the stockade, looking out over the wall. Several others opened the stockade gate to watch. His father was foolishly convinced he was right, as always… and Jerrick knew the man wasn't always right.

As he approached the wounded predator hunched over the carcass of the gruzzly, Davin opened fire with the plasma rifle, but most of his shots went wild, striking the churned ground. One even hit the side of the fallen carcass, burning a new hole in the thick, furred pelt.

The muscular alien stood, dripping with dark gruzzly blood as well as his own bright green blood from his wounds.

Davin raised the plasma rifle and shot again. One of the energy blasts ricocheted off the predator's hip, striking sparks from the alien's armor, but not seeming to wound him. Transient spiderwebs of static flickered up and down the alien's body as the camouflage field flickered on, then faded again.

Emboldened, his father yelled bravely, stupidly. He shot four more times, missing repeatedly, until one blast struck the predator's shoulder and destroyed the popup energy gun mounted there.

The muscular hunter seemed angry rather than intimidated. He grasped at his belt and removed a metal cylinder, squeezing it. The long, pointed javelin ends extended and then locked into place with a *snick*.

Davin strode forward, firing indiscriminately, poorly. Though the colony leader was still far away, the predator cocked back his arm and hurled the whistling, crackling javelin.

Jerrick screamed, helpless. His father couldn't duck fast enough, though he managed to fire twice more—and missed both times. The energized javelin slid through his abdomen, piercing him smoothly.

Davin stopped in his tracks, staggered forward two more steps, then fell sideways.

Jerrick howled, unable to tear his eyes from the zoomlenses. "Noooo!"

Limping, the predator stalked forward, moving sluggishly from his own injuries. He stopped, looming over Davin's body.

Through the lenses, Jerrick could see his father grasp at the smooth, sharp end of the javelin, but couldn't get a grip with all the blood.

The predator grabbed his weapon and slid it back out. The pointed ends retracted into the handle.

Davin lay there, choking, already dead but not yet realizing it.

The predator turned his smooth metal mask toward the distant stockade where Jerrick stood screaming and shouting. After a moment of consideration, the predator bent down, slashed Davin's neck with his jagged blade. He grasped the colony leader's hair and peeled the head back, then with a brutal yank, he pulled off the head along with several vertebrae and the frayed ends of the man's spinal cord. The predator held up Davin's head like an unimpressive trophy, tucked it onto a clip at his side, then he retrieved the much larger head of the gruzzly. He carried both trophies as he limped off into the dissipating smoke and flames of the destroyed field.

4

Jerrick's grief transformed into a twisted knot of anger, injustice, and a need for revenge—but he knew it was a useless longing. He had no illusions about challenging either a giant gruzzly or an armored alien predator.

One of those hunters had killed his father, slaughtered him in full view of the colony settlement, torn off his head and kept it as a trophy. Davin had been trying to defend his home, but those evil hunters just wanted… sport.

And his father had fallen victim to that sport.

With the gate closed again, while the colonists huddled behind the scant protection of the stockade wall, the fire in the wheat field gradually burned itself out as the gray skies became more overcast, clouds thickening with disapproving storms. Jerrick, meanwhile, brewed enough of a storm inside him.

His father had told him repeatedly that until Jerrick could control his temper, until he could think of the bigger picture, the young man would not make a good colony leader. But now his fellow colonists were looking to him in that position. Maybe anger was what they needed. Davin had been too passive, too optimistic… too naïve. And now he was dead.

Looking at the mournful colonists, Jerrick breathed quickly, smelling bitter smoke in the air, possibly tainted with blood.

"We will bury him," Jerrick announced. "I'll go get his body myself, unless someone else wants to help." Five people volunteered, and more looked ready to join in, but he cut them off. It was risky enough as it was.

After Jerrick had scanned the territory with his zoomlenses, seeing no movement from either gruzzlies or predators, they opened the stockade gates. Under thick gray skies, he and the volunteers rushed down the dirt road, two of them carrying plasma rifles. Davin's rifle still lay on the ground near his body. Apparently, the predator hadn't felt any threat from it.

The enormous gruzzly carcass lay sprawled and bloody, its thick pelt and reptilian plates torn by the predator's attack. But Jerrick only had eyes for his father—or what remained of him. The man's head was gone, half the spinal column uprooted like some noxious weed. His familiar brown work shirt was now soaked in red. He remembered his father sitting at home by the warm glowlight, mending rips in the garment, adding patches, because the Hardscrabble colonists couldn't afford to waste good clothes. Now, the shirt was beyond repair, just as Davin was. There would be no fixing this.

Jerrick stared, feeling his stomach roil, his heart pound, his cheeks growing hot. Tears filled his eyes, but they didn't fall; instead, they seemed to turn to steam with his anger.

He picked up his father's feet; two of the other colonists took him by his sprawled arms. As they set off in a slow, somber procession, Jerrick scowled down at the weapon. He said to one of the other volunteers, "Take the rifle. We might need every possible defense."

If it came to all-out war, he doubted they could fight even one of the alien predators, and many of them had come to Hardscrabble for their grand hunt. Fortunately, the aliens seemed interested only in the gruzzlies—but that could change. The colonists could not rely on the protection of simple stockade walls or the barricaded doors of prefab colony homes. Jerrick knew of no other way to intimidate the predators into leaving them alone.

Anxious, he glanced around, listening for that threatening, clicking growl, looking for the mirror-shimmer in the air that camouflaged them. But he saw only drifting smoke and the remaining flickers of the burning field.

Reaching the barricaded settlement as the clouds

darkened and a late afternoon storm set in, Jerrick did not want to leave his father's body lying outside. Their cemetery, which displayed far too many graves already, was outside the wall in the unprotected area. Jerrick and his companions worked together swiftly to dig a resting place for the optimistic dreamer who had convinced them to come here. They used shovels and picks, taking turns with the heavy work while others stood guard with their plasma rifles.

When it was finished, Jerrick thought the empty hole looked like a cold and lonely mouth yawning open. He just stared at it before he nodded and bent down to pick up the headless body. With two others helping, they wrestled Davin into the grave and covered him up with dirt.

As the wind picked up and the sun dropped below the horizon, everyone went back inside the stockade to huddle with their loved ones, to hope against hope for some way to survive...

5

Jerrick had other ideas. He felt abused, beaten, but not defeated, and he would not simply cower. In his heart, he understood how foolish his plan was, how he might be putting the entire colony at risk if he failed.

He didn't care. He needed to do this.

As the storm gathered with greater force, Jerrick took one of the plasma rifles, checked that its charge was full, then opened the stockade gate. Telling no one, he climbed up into the mammoth combine machine and swung himself into the cab. He took a deep breath and touched the controls. Starting the engines, switching to full battery power, he activated the bright headlights.

Cones of illumination stabbed into the blustery blackness, showing Hardscrabble's bleak landscape, the burned and damaged crops, the wreckage of their hopes. Jerrick's anger grew hotter as he rolled the giant vehicle through the gate and outside. Behind him, he saw three colonists running after him, attracted by the noise. They waved their hands and shouted, but Jerrick didn't stop. At least they could close the gate behind him.

He drove on into the storm. The treads rumbled along the dirt road as the mammoth combine surged toward the grain fields. The lights of the big harvesting machine showed some patches of green that still remained. Not all of their wheat and corn had been burned and trampled by the gruzzlies and the alien hunters. If the outside threat went away, the colonists could replant immediately, try to survive on reduced rations until the settlement recovered.

But before worrying about the colony's long-term survival, he had to make sure they all made it through this night. He had to intimidate the predators enough to make them leave the people alone.

He widened the beams so he could scan the landscape beyond the fields. As he skirted the burned patches, he counted four dead gruzzlies scattered on the ground, all of them headless. The giant beasts had been driven from the hills, causing devastation to the delicate colony—but now they were killed in some sort of extraterrestrial big game hunt. And the colonists were caught in the crossfire.

Tonight, Jerrick intended to go hunting himself.

The windows in the cab rattled in the wind gusts and a splatter of rain as the big machine crawled across the landscape. He drove toward the pasture where the cattle had been slaughtered. Even after nearly two days, their mangled carcasses still lay untouched. On Earth, there would have been carrion birds and scavengers, but none of the indigenous Hardscrabble species could eat the Terran-based flesh.

As the mammoth combine rolled into the low hills, Jerrick played the broad spotlights across the grassy patch. Suddenly, he spotted an enormous, hulking form caught in the beams. His heart froze—this gruzzly was even more enormous than the one that had attacked him before, more gigantic than the ones the alien predators had killed in the fields. This one was huge, like the mother of her race.

Now, she bent over another carcass—a big gruzzly that lay slaughtered on the ground. In comparison to this huge monster, it looked like just a child.

A cub.

The massive mother gruzzly leaned over the decapitated carcass and rose up on massive hind legs, responding to the bright lights of the oncoming vehicle. She let out a roar so loud that the cab itself rattled. Instinctively, Jerrick glanced at the plasma rifle beside him on the seat, and knew that he could empty the entire charge and not stop this titanic animal.

But he did not intend to fight with a mere plasma rifle.

Jerrick operated the controls, swung down the armored clearing saws, the diamond-hardened blades designed to mow down forests for cropland. The blades hummed and squealed.

He jammed the accelerator, pushed the armored treads into charge mode. The combine rolled forward, and the mother gruzzly reared up, sweeping both paws at the big mechanical opponent, not backing down for an instant. The sawblades whirred and spun. Laser guidance lights flayed across the targeting zone ahead of the combine.

Jerrick gritted his teeth. These monsters had killed several colonists, massacred all ten of the cattle, ruined their chances for survival. It didn't matter whether or not the alien hunters were worse; both were his enemy, and Jerrick had to make his mark.

The gruzzly faced the oncoming vehicle, swung a huge paw and smacked at the spinning blade. The diamond-hardened teeth caught in its thick hide, cutting deep, but the monster's blow was strong enough to misalign the saw, bend its extended arms.

Responding quickly, Jerrick swung the second blade down and cut into the monster's shoulder, but the gruzzly retreated, ripping its flesh free. Its roar of pain rattled the night.

Bringing the engines to full power, Jerrick pushed the combine forward. He swung down the rotating thresher arm, a spinning cylinder designed to harvest crops and throw the plants into spinners and processers. The gruzzly grasped one of the rotating thresher plates, but caught its arm inside the unit. The cylindrical force was strong enough to break the monster's arm. The trapped gruzzly tried to break free and let out a maddened howl, but she was powerful enough to jam the thresher. Although the engines strained and groaned, they couldn't keep turning. The mother gruzzly tried to wrench her broken arm free.

"Die, damn you!" Jerrick snarled.

The gruzzly ripped herself loose, snapping the threshing cylinder, then staggered backward. Even in her pain, the injured monster turned toward another sound.

In the darkness and the blowing wind, Jerrick saw movement through the window of the cab. On the fringe of the broad spotlight cones, a rippling, mirrored figure appeared—a lithe and enormous predator. Standing on the killing field, the alien hunter launched a blue plasma bolt from its shoulder-mounted weapon. The blast seared through the blackness, striking the grizzly in the ribs and leaving a cauterized wound there.

The monster reeled and staggered, but Jerrick felt only indignant anger. He had struck first, gravely wounding the mother grizzly. He didn't know if his idea would work, but he knew he had to see this through.

Disengaging the mammoth combine's treads while the thresher and the clearing sawblades continued to stutter, he popped open the cab, grabbed the plasma rifle, and sprang all the way to the ground, bracing his boots in the grass.

"That's *my* kill, you bastard!" he shouted at the alien predator. "Leave it alone!"

He sprinted toward the dying grizzly, but even with such wounds, she could still cause a lot of damage. Out of the corner of his eye, he spotted the camouflage flicker and wondered why the alien predator was so afraid to show himself. Jerrick certainly wasn't.

He ran out into the open, yelling. He fired five direct blasts with the plasma rifle, and—unlike his father—he struck his target each time. One high-energy projectile after another hammered into the grizzly's chest. The enormous animal collapsed to the blood-soaked grasses with a loud *whuff!*

Jerrick approached the monster, showing no caution. One of the grizzly's arms had been nearly severed by the sawblade, the other mangled by the thresher cylinder. Her blood looked dark in the glare of lights from the harvesting machine.

Jerrick saw the mirrored camouflage of the alien predator also closing in on the dying beast—but he arrived first. Defiant, he stood over the monster, pointed his plasma rifle at the wounded gruzzly's throat, and blasted at point blank range.

When the giant creature lay dead on the grasses of what should have been peaceful pastureland for the colony's cattle, Jerrick held his plasma rifle in both hands, sweeping its barrel across the night, looking for the flickering hint of the alien hunter.

"This is mine," Jerrick shouted. "My kill—my *trophy*!" He placed a boot on the great gruzzly's furry carcass.

He swung the plasma rifle around, doubting it would save him if the alien predator decided to attack. He saw a flicker off to the right, and he stared defiantly. "*My kill!*"

The camouflage field flickered into traceries of static, then dissipated to reveal a tall and powerful humanoid figure. A smooth, eerily inhuman mask covered his face, and snake-like ropes of hair dangled from his skull down to his shoulders. Even though the eye holes were blank, Jerrick could read deep menace there, a simmering bloodlust. The predator might respond with fury, killing Jerrick for daring to intrude on the kill... but Jerrick didn't think so. The predator faced him, stared at him.

"My trophy," he said again in a lower voice.

Risking everything, Jerrick pointed his plasma rifle and fired twice more at the dead gruzzly's neck, severing its head. He tossed the plasma rifle aside, heard it clatter on the grass, then he bent down to grasp the dead monster's hideous head, and dragged it away from the rest of the body. He stood with his legs spread on either side of the cauterized neck. "My trophy."

He crossed his arms over his chest as he faced the predator.

The ominous alien stared at him, muscular arms at his sides.

After a long, tense moment, the predator bowed slightly in acknowledgement, then turned away. He activated his mirrored camouflage and stalked off into the night.

Jerrick nearly collapsed with terror and relief. He stood blinking in the whipping wind and intermittent rain, but otherwise the night remained silent—until off in the hills he heard a series of explosions as the team of predators kept hunting gruzzlies...

6

Rattling along, limping with mechanical damage, the mammoth combine rolled back to the settlement inside the stockade. Cradled in its harvesting scoop, the big machine carried the oversized gruzzly head—Jerrick's trophy. The dead monster stared out with glassy eyes as the combine rolled toward the gates.

Awed colonists swarmed out, both terrified and relieved. When they opened the stockade gate to see that Jerrick had brought back the head of a huge gruzzly, they recoiled. He stopped the vehicle just outside the defensive wall, swung the combine around, and worked the controls to set down the scoop. He deposited the head of the mother gruzzly on the ground.

Leaning out of the cab, he shouted to the colonists, "Leave it there as a warning to those predators! It's my trophy. Maybe the smell of death will even keep the gruzzlies away." He let out a bitter laugh. "They don't want to tangle with us."

Jerrick regarded Hardscrabble's greatest indigenous predator—but he had killed it, so maybe *he* was the greatest predator on this raw, unclaimed world. He saw fire rising in the distant hills and knew that the alien predators would keep hunting gruzzlies as those beasts retreated deeper into the wilderness.

Leaving the oversized head outside as a warning, Jerrick rolled the machine inside the stockade, and the colonists swung the gate shut behind him. He felt vindicated now. Victorious and, oddly, safe. He hoped the alien predators as well as the gruzzlies would give the human settlement a wide berth for now.

The desperate colonists would pick up the pieces, then figure out how to survive. For now, Jerrick wouldn't worry about what the next season would bring.

BLOOD AND SAND

By MIRA GRANT

LAST BRIDGE TOWNSHIP, MONTANA, 1933:
TWO NIGHTS AFTER THE STAR FELL DOWN

"Boy!"

The shout is furious: the shout is always furious. Tommy doesn't understand why they even have a rooster, since it's not like it ever gets to wake anyone up. Aunt Mary always takes care of *that*, shouting high and loud and angry even before the sun is in the sky. Boy! Why haven't the pigs been fed. Boy! Why hasn't the fire been lit. Boy! Where's that useless sister of yours; doesn't she know the morning's half-over already, and the chickens are still brooding on their eggs.

Boy, why are you here. Boy, why aren't you good enough. Boy.

She never yells at Annie the way she yells at him, and he supposes that might be better, except that Annie says it's not. Annie says there's something wrong with the way Aunt Mary looks at her, like she's a prize sow being fattened for the market, and they're both of them eleven years old, and they both know how to count. Ten boys their age, or near enough as to make no difference, on the farms within a solid day's ride. Some of those farms are doing fair well, especially when compared to their own rock fields and empty hoppers. Some of those farms might pay for a dutiful daughter-in-law.

No girls. It's like the gods of Montana know this is no place for girls. He said so to Annie once, when he was feeling particular blue, and she smacked him so hard his arm ached for a week.

"Girls aren't better nor worse'n boys," she'd said, voice hot and angry, as it so often was since they'd come to this awful place. "They're just different. Easier to sell without feeling guilty on it later." Then she'd been gone, off to do the mending for Aunt Mary—there's always mending for Aunt Mary; she takes it in from those same neighboring farms, and claims every straight stitch is Annie's, like that drives the bride price up just a little bit more.

"*Boy!*"

Tommy jerks himself out of his woolgathering with a start, suddenly terribly aware that he's committed the greatest sin in all Montana: he has made his Aunt Mary— Aunt Mary, who took him and his sister in when she didn't have to, didn't they know their mama had been worthless and their daddy even worse; Aunt Mary, who is the only person left to love them and isn't sure they're worth the bother—he has made her *call him twice*.

236

He pulls himself out of the cubby in the kitchen where he'd gone to think, and he runs toward the sound of her voice, swift as the cat his mama used to have, that big stupid orange thing with a purr like rocks grinding together. He never would have thought he could miss that cat, which was sometimes mean and left dead mice on his pillow while he slept, so that he'd roll over and see death as soon as he opened his eyes, but he does. He does, though. He misses that cat like anything, dead mice and all, because that cat was a part of *home*, and this?

This is not home.

His Aunt Mary is standing on the porch, searching the red-tinted horizon like she thinks he'd go running out *there*, out in the big, unfamiliar desert, where near anything could come to snatch him up and carry him away. The sun is down low enough in the sky that the light has gone all funny and forgiving, and for a heartbeat, she looks almost like his mama. Then she hears his footsteps and turns around, letting him see her face, the way the lines of it have pulled into something petulant and mean, and she doesn't look like his mama at all.

She's his mother's sister, though, the same as Annie is his, born on the same day, in the same bed, and sometimes that's enough to scare him halfway to the grave. If his mama's own sister, who she'd always spoken of fondly, can somehow turn into Aunt Mary, what's going to happen to him and Annie? Is one of them going to get spoiled and twisted, worn into something so petty it can't even find kindness for kin? And if that has to be—if that somehow can't be helped—is there any way to make sure he's the one who suffers?

Annie is good. Annie is maybe the only good thing left in his life. If one of them should be spared, it's her.

"Where the hell have you been, boy?" she demands.

There's no good answer here, not the truth and not a lie, so Tommy says nothing at all, merely looks down at his feet and waits to be told what's expected of him. Silence has been a hard habit to learn. He's done it, though. For his own sake, and for Annie's, he's done it.

"No matter," grumbles Aunt Mary, sounding almost sorry that he didn't challenge her authority. "Your uncle's been out in the cow pasture a good hour past when he told me he'd be home for supper. Go out and fetch him, and be quick about it."

Tommy looks up, naked fear in his eyes. Aunt Mary is frightening. Uncle Jack is *terrifying*. But the desert?

The desert is something altogether different. There's nothing out there under that painted sky that doesn't think a little boy would taste like heaven incarnate. Even the ground is treacherous, turning underfoot like a live thing, capricious and cruel. Tommy would sooner another session with the belt than go out to the desert.

"Mind me, boy, or I'll send your sister instead."

Annie might like that. Annie thinks the desert is beautiful, thinks the things that live there are worth admiring. Annie is wrong, but try telling her that. For a moment, Tommy is tempted to let Aunt Mary send her instead of him—but that's a temptation that ends with another funeral, another headstone with a family member's name written in the stone, where it can't ever be erased.

"I'll go, I'm sorry, I'll go," he says, and runs, almost tripping over his own feet in his urgency to show her what a good boy he can be, how well he can mind her. If she sees, she gives no sign, and when he reaches the edge of the light cast by their oilpaper windows and looks back, she isn't there anymore. It's only him, alone against the deepening dark.

No: not quite alone. There's a scuffle in the rocks and shrub off to his left, the sort of sound that could be the billy goat broken out of its pen again, or could be a coyote, lean and hungry and looking for a little boy to swallow down whole. Tommy gasps and turns—

—and Annie smiles at him bright as anything, pretty as a picture and unafraid of the desert. "Hi, Tommy," she says, and her voice, while cheerful, is pitched low to keep their aunt—who has ears like a bat sometimes—from hearing her. "Going walking? Mind if I come?"

"The desert's not any place for a girl," he whispers harshly back.

Annie shrugs, unconcerned. "It's not any place for a boy, neither, but there you are, and here I am, and I guess if we're together, it'll be a little more of a place for both of us."

"Why do you want to go to the stupid desert?"

"So I'm not alone with Aunt Mary," says Annie, and his heart breaks a little. Then, with the careless bluntness of sisters, she adds, "And I want to look for my star, and if you're with me, the cougars will have something to eat first."

"*Annie*," he hisses, and punches her in the shoulder while she giggles. "Go home."

"No," she says. She's as stubborn as the night is long— and here in the desert, the nights go on forever. "I want the star."

Tommy glares at her. Annie is unrepentant.

The star fell two days ago. It was like lightning running through the sky, so bright and blazing that it couldn't be real. For just a moment, as they watched it fall, it had been like

Mama had never died, like they were still in California, safe in their little house that had never been fancy, but had been *theirs*. It had been enough, and they had loved it.

Make a wish, my dearest ones, and see what you can see. That was what she'd always said, with her hands on their shoulders and her eyes on the sky. Make a wish, and maybe it would come true. So they had watched the star fall, and they'd made their wishes, and then Uncle Jack had come hollering for them to get their butts to bed, oil cost money, and the moment had passed.

Not for Annie. She'd been set on going out into the desert and finding that star ever since. She still is. Tommy can see how serious she is in the way she looks at him, the stubborn set of her chin and the narrowing of her eyes.

"You let me come, Thomas Warrington, or I'll scream so loud Aunt Mary will come running."

"She'll smack us both upside the head if you do that."

"Yeah, but I'll have earned it."

Tommy wants to argue, wants to stand here fighting her until the sun comes up or Uncle Jack comes back on his own, whichever one comes first. But he knows better. Maybe he didn't, when they first came to Montana, but he's a quick study, and he has to be the responsible one. It was the last thing his mama asked from him. He has to take *care* of her.

"Hush, then, and come on," he says. "We have to find Uncle Jack."

"And my star."

Lord, but she's stubborn. "And your star, but Uncle Jack first," he says.

"All right," says Annie, sweet and sly, and she slides her hand into his as they look toward the rapidly darkening vastness of the desert, which might as well go on forever. Side by side, they step over the border of their half-tamed farm, and into the wild desert that makes up the bulk of their family's land.

Walking in the desert isn't the same as walking in streets. Everything's loose here, ready to trip a body up and knock them down. Stones and gravel and great brown sticks, which don't make so much sense, since it's not like there's trees here for them to drop off of. Falling is even worse than it sounds, because half the desert seems designed to *hurt*. Cactus spines and scorpions, sharp rocks and rattlesnakes— nothing here knows how to be kind. Falling down doesn't just mean skinned knees and bruised elbows. It means pain, more than Tommy would ever have thought existed.

None of that stops Annie, though. She's roving ahead, far enough that if she hurts herself he'll have to run to catch up, looking under stones and scuffing in the gravel, still chasing after her star. Tommy more than half expects her to break her leg.

Even so, it's a shock when she stops and screams, the sound slicing through the night like a sawblade. All the blood in his body turns into ice in an instant, and he breaks into a run, racing to catch up to where she stands frozen, the remains of her scream held captive behind the wall of her left hand. Her right hand is pointing, jabbing at the air, and he turns to look, briefly unable to understand what he sees.

It's a cougar, or it was, once, one of those big tawny cats that prowl in the high bluffs. They had cougars in California too, even if he never saw one. They were more common here, their screams breaking the walls of night. They always sounded like they wanted nothing more than to fill their bellies with boy flesh, which was sweet and delicious when compared to the stringy things that called the desert home.

This cougar won't be screaming anymore. This cougar is recognizable only by the color of its pelt and the shape of its paws. The rest of the creature has been split open like some sort of ripe fruit, and its skull... its skull...

"Where's its head?" asks Tommy, looking to Annie with alarm, like he's afraid she has it tucked under her arm as a prize. She shakes her head, still silent. There are tears rolling down her cheeks, fat and sad. Annie's always loved cats. She even loved that stripy old thing Mama had, even though it scratched and spat whenever she got near. What happened to that cat, Tommy can't say. It didn't get sent to Montana, though.

Lucky cat.

"Annie?" This time his voice is soft, hesitant; he's not sure how scared she is. He can't leave her here, but he can't take her home either, not until he finds Uncle Jack. As soon as she followed him into the desert, she became an unsolvable problem.

"It's not fair." She lowers her hand. She's still crying, but she's angrier than she is upset. That should probably be a good thing. It will be, as long as she aims that angry at something that's not him. "It's just a kitty. No one should go killing kitties."

It's a kitty big enough to have eaten them both and gone looking for seconds: it's a killer with whiskers. Tommy's smart enough not to say any of that. He shakes his head and says, "I don't think fair counts for much out here."

"Tommy... what if whatever hurt the kitty is still hungry?"

That's a new problem, and not one he particularly wants. Tommy swallows hard. "Guess we'd better move then. We need to find Uncle Jack before Aunt Mary comes looking for *us*. I'm more scared of her than I am of anything that might not be anywhere nearby."

Annie wipes her cheeks with vicious swipes of her hand, and mutters darkly, "I hate them."

Those are forbidden, fighting words, and Tommy can't do anything but nod agreement and whisper, "So do I."

They walk side by side into the desert night, leaving the slaughtered cougar behind them, staying close together and not admitting why, exactly, they feel like that's a thing they ought to be doing. The desert sky grows brighter by the second as the stars come out, and the moon is so big it's like a balloon on a string, floating just out of reach.

They pass a snarl of rattlesnakes on a rock, none of them moving, all of them split open like the cougar, their fangs and rattles missing. "Wolves," says Tommy, and he doesn't believe it, and neither does Annie, but words have power, and so they walk on, through the endless desert night, heading for the distant line of wooden posts and barbed wire that marks the end of their land. They have more rocky field than livestock or capacity to farm, but Uncle Jack won't sell it on. Mama would have called him proud and senseless. Aunt Mary calls him forward-thinking, says Montana will be the next golden shore, just you wait for all those fools on the coast to realize that the real riches are in cattle farming and a sky that goes on the better part of forever.

Tommy thinks Uncle Jack isn't the only one who's senseless. But Aunt Mary is as trapped as they are, pinned down by a husband who won't give up his land. Worse, she's done what some animals in a trap will do: she's turned mean. She might not have been, in the beginning. It doesn't matter now. She's mean, and she's cruel, and she's as bad as their uncle, in her own way. Even if they had a way to escape, she wouldn't let them. She'd drag them back and holler to the heavens how the trap is the best place she's ever been, and she'd never let them go.

"I don't know where my star fell," says Annie.

Tommy thinks they've got bigger things to worry about, things with leather belts and heavy hands, things that would see her married before she was anywhere near a woman. He keeps them to himself. Some things are better unshared.

In the distance, something howls. It's not a wolf or a coyote; it's not a cougar. It sounds like the lion they heard once at the circus, captive jungle fury packed into a steel-barred cage, fur that smelled like a kind of heat even the desert has never known. It sounds like Annie's fallen star given flesh and thought and rage at the idea that the sky is no longer its domain.

It sounds like death.

They cleave together, two children clinging to each other underneath the desert stars. Tommy is shaking, and Annie is still as stone, like she used up all her tremors on the dead cougar. Finally, in a low voice, she asks, "Do you think Uncle Jack heard that?"

"I think the whole *state* heard that."

"Come on." Annie steps away from her brother, not letting go of his hand, and starts to tug him toward the boundary line. "Uncle Jack always has a gun when he goes to the fence. He wants to be ready for bandits. This sounds worse than bandits."

Tommy wants to argue, wants to tell her that running toward Uncle Jack isn't running toward safety, no matter what she thinks. But he wants an adult even more, wants someone who can make everything make sense, and so when she breaks into a run, he lets her pull him along with her. He doesn't fight.

He just wants this to be over.

Silence greets them at the boundary line—silence, and broken barbed wire all along one stretch of fence, snapped like fishing line when a fish that's too big catches hold of it. Annie stumbles to a stop, her feet suddenly leaden, her grip suddenly like a vise. Tommy digs his heels into the gravel, holding himself up, holding them *both* up.

"Annie?" His voice is too loud. It's like a shout against the dark line of the cliffs. The desert has always been frightening. For the first time, he's terrified.

"He's like the kitty," says Annie. She sounds much younger than she is, sounds like she used to when they were littles, still holding fast to their mother's hand. There's a note of wonder in her tone, like she can't quite make sense of what she's seeing. "How is he like the kitty?"

"What do you mean?" Tommy asks, but he doesn't move, doesn't strain to see. He doesn't want to know. Annie shouldn't be seeing this either—whatever it is isn't meant for her eyes—but he doesn't pull her back. One of them has to look. It's already too late for her.

Annie turns, her face pale and drawn, her eyes wide and dry. "His head's all gone," she says. She sounds more confused than anything else, as if this is something unthinkable. "How can he be alive when his head's all gone?"

She already knows the answer. Death is no stranger to either one of them: hasn't been since they were babies, when their father caught sick and didn't recover. Even then, death had remained a distant acquaintance until their mother—God rest her soul and all the angels keep her—had started coughing and not been able to stop, not until she'd stopped doing anything but getting slowly cold in her bed, not even breathing anymore. The undertaker had put her in a pine box and the priest had put her underground, and Annie and Tommy know better than anyone what death is. Uncle Jack is dead. Dead is all that's left for somebody whose head's all gone.

"We should go," whispers Tommy, but his feet stay rooted to the spot, because where *can* they go? To Aunt Mary, who will scream and wail and blame them for the death of the man she married, who maybe she'd loved before Montana had ground all the goodness out of both of them? Aunt Mary isn't a woman who stands idly by while the world does her wrong. She looks for people to blame. Tommy's pretty sure that her sister's unwanted orphans will be easy targets.

They could run away, just the two of them, fleeing deeper into the desert. It has to end somewhere, doesn't it? Their mama had always said that their pa came from a place called "Boston." That can't be any farther from Montana than California is, and the train got them from San Francisco to here in just three days. Maybe they can walk to Boston in four, or five. Not so many. It should still be possible, a goal that can be achieved if they make it past the mountains. They can go to every house in the city until they find their grandparents, and then they'll live happily ever after, far away from the desert, far away from men who haven't got any heads, far away from—

"My star!" Annie's voice is suddenly full of wonder, the body of their uncle clean forgotten as she takes off and runs. Tommy makes a wordless sound of protest as he turns to follow her, and then he sees it, flickering behind a rock in the desert ahead of them: a pale, heatless light, something that doesn't belong here. It should be burning in the sky, not down here, where ordinary people are trying to survive their ordinary lives.

"Annie!" he shouts. But she's faster than he is, she always has been. She ran into the world faster than he could, beating him by minutes, and she's beating him now, running across the desert as fast as hope and fear can carry him. Those two together are a heady brew, and she's standing by the stone before he can catch her.

The light is not coming from a star. The light is coming from a machine the like of which he's never seen before, a jagged crack running along one side of it, like it slammed too hard against the ground and hasn't yet been put back together right. It's so small that he could hold it in one hand, and bright enough that it takes a moment for Tommy to see the other source of light, the pale green glow that tips some of the stones, pools on some of the gravel. If it wasn't glowing—cold light, such a *cold* light—he'd call it blood. But it can't be that. It can't.

"Is this my star?" asks Annie, and reaches for the strange machine.

There's a clicking sound behind them, something like a rattlesnake and something like a spring winding underwater. It's wet. That's the only word that fits the sound: *wet*, meaty, almost. Bowels frozen with his fear, Tommy turns.

The thing behind them is a man. It has to be, because it stands on two legs, wears clothes, has hands like a man's hands and eyes like a man's eyes, almost. Close enough. Nothing else has eyes like that, so they must be a man's eyes.

But it has a face like a flower in the process of withering, a flower made of meat and bone and terror. It clicks at them, and that strange face pulses and rearranges itself, never still, never anything but vital and awful and alive, and Tommy damn near wets himself, because he knows what this is. It's the Devil his own self, come to haunt the desert, to hunt for bad kids.

It has something in one hand, something red and sticky and segmented like the curve of a spine, and Tommy doesn't want to see.

"Oh," says Annie softly. "That's where their heads went. The star took them."

It's such a small statement. It holds too much weight; it can't possibly keep from collapsing inward on itself. Tommy moans. The thing—the man—the *Devil* makes that clicking sound again.

Tommy doesn't decide so much as he just *does*, stepping between the Devil and his sister and spreading his arms as wide as he can. "You can't have her," he says, and his voice barely shakes at all. "She didn't do nothing to you, and you can't have her."

The Devil looks at him, and he'd swear he can see confusion in those amber, almost-human eyes. It clicks again. Tommy shakes his head.

"No," he says again. "She's mine. Kill me if you gotta, but you can't have her."

The Devil reaches out with one clawed hand. Tommy can hear Annie breathing fast and hard behind him, sounding like she's finally found the sense to be scared. *You didn't find it fast enough,* he thinks. If she hadn't wanted to come looking for her star, if she hadn't run away—

You can build a whole palace out of "if," but there won't be a single wall thick enough to block the wind.

That was what their mama always used to say. Tommy closes his eyes and waits to die.

The clicking sound gets louder as the Devil gets closer. Tommy feels something brush his cheek, the barest whisper of a sensation, like a bee buzzing a little too near on a summer's day. There's a soft, descending purr, and then, silence.

Silence, until Annie whispers, "I don't think he wants to hurt us, Tommy. He's just... just looking at you."

Tommy cracks open one eye. If Annie can stand to look at the Devil, he supposes he can too.

The Devil's still standing in the same place, looking at the pair of them with an unreadable expression in those awful eyes. Slowly, it raises its hand again, fingers spread, and gestures away from the mountains, back toward the farm.

"Tommy, I think it wants us to go."

Tommy frowns. This is the *Devil*. This is Satan, the trickster, the Lord of Hell, and they're just two innocent kids who couldn't win if they tried. Why isn't the Devil hurting them? They should already have their heads off and their blood on the sand, like the cougar, like the rattlesnakes, like Uncle Jack. They should be *dead*.

"Tommy, come on. Let's go."

What do all those things have in common that they don't? What makes those things the same, and them different?

PREDATOR: IF IT BLEEDS

"Tommy, please. I don't like this."

Cougars are dangerous, they're all teeth and claws and hunger. They're not mean, not like people can be mean, but oh, they'll hurt you bad if you let them, or if you surprise them, or if they're bored. Cougars are about the worst thing in the desert.

"Tommy."

Rattlesnakes too. Those are some of the worst snakes in the whole world. If they bite you, you're just as good as dead—that's what Uncle Jack said when they first came to live here, and Tommy believed him then. Still believes him now. Rattlesnakes aren't as bad as cougars, but they're still bad.

Annie whimpers, and doesn't say anything more.

Uncle Jack, now... Uncle Jack was worse than a cougar, because when a cougar hurt somebody, it didn't *mean* it. Cougars hurt people for food and territory, to protect themselves. Uncle Jack, though, he *meant* it. He liked it when people were afraid of him, when he saw the bruises on their bodies to prove that he'd been there, and Tommy wishes he could be sorry that Uncle Jack is dead now, but he's not, he's not, he can't be and he's not. Dead is dead and alive is alive, and Uncle Jack is dead and maybe they can be alive a little longer.

Maybe.

He looks at the Devil, standing there all terrible and strange, and suddenly he knows what's different about him and Annie; what makes them something to spare, and not something to slaughter. It's about the only thing that makes sense.

"Annie," he whispers, "I'm gonna need you to trust me, and I'm gonna need you to run."

"What?" There's a hitch in her voice, the kind of sound

that comes right before she breaks down and has one of her big cries. Tommy can't afford to let her get that far. She starts crying, they're never getting out of here together and alive.

Maybe they aren't anyway. What he's about to do takes a whole lot of brave and even more stupid. He's got plenty of the second—Aunt Mary tells him so every day—but he's not sure how much he's got of the first. If there's enough of it to save one of them, he hopes it's enough to save Annie. Whatever happens to him will be worth it, if he can just save her.

Please, let him save her.

"*Run!*" he shouts, and he grabs the Devil's machine, not letting go even when the jagged edges bite into his hands, and he runs. He runs like his heels are on fire and the only bucket of water left in the whole world is back at the house; he runs like his life depends on it. He runs like his *sister's* life depends on it.

Annie has always been faster than he is, and when she passes him, legs pumping like pistons and tears streaming down her cheeks, it's all he can do not to waste his breath on whooping. They're outrunning the Devil, him and his sister, running for the horizon. Running for their future.

He hears feet pounding the earth behind him, hears breathing that's too harsh and too fast to be human, and he doesn't look back. That would be a waste as much as whooping would. He needs to run like nothing on this world has ever run before. He needs to run like he *means* it.

He means it. Oh, how he means it.

The light from the farmhouse windows is visible ahead of them. The walk into the desert had seemed so long, but maybe it was never more than a few hundred yards; maybe it was fear that stretched the land out like a sheet, drawing it strange and tight and making it eternal. Panic and fear aren't the same, and it's panic that drives him now. Panic makes things shorter, smaller, narrower, like Aunt Mary and Uncle Jack have been doing to them since they came here. If they don't get away now, before the panic crushes them completely, they're never going to.

I love you, Annie, Tommy thinks fiercely, and runs even harder, toward the light that will change everything. One way or another, it will change everything.

———

Annie reaches the house first and runs on, heading for the barn, where her best hiding places are. Tommy doesn't waver. He hits the porch like thunder and slams the door open, revealing Aunt Mary sitting by the fireplace. She looks up, lowering her knitting, already preparing to scold him for banging the door like that. Then she stops, face drawing in and turning even meaner than usual.

"Where is your uncle, you stupid, worthless boy?" she demands. "Do I need to remind you that you're here at our sufferance?"

Tommy doesn't have the breath to answer her. He doesn't even try. All he can do is fling the machine at her as hard as he can. His arms aren't as strong as he'd like them to be: it lands on the floor at her feet, rolling to a stop.

"Why, you insolent—" she begins, even as she starts rising from her chair.

Tommy is still moving. He dives beneath the table, putting his hands above his head, closing his eyes as tight as he can.

He hears the Devil enter, claws scraping on wooden

floor. He hears the soft, purring click of the Devil's speech, and Aunt Mary's scream of terror and outrage and refusal. It's the first time he's felt like he understood her all the way down to the bone, because he knows that refusal, that denial that the world can possibly be this cruel.

He hears the shotgun she keeps next to the fireplace rack into place.

He hears her fire.

Then there's only screaming for a little while—screaming that doesn't last particularly long. Something warm and wet hits his cheek. He keeps his eyes closed, keeps them closed until he hears footsteps approaching, until something hits the floor in front of him.

Cautiously, Tommy cracks one eye open, and sees Aunt Mary's shotgun in front of him. He opens his other eye and lifts his head, and there's the Devil looking down at him, that strange meaty flower of a face pulsing as its petals open and close, open and close.

Everything is blood. Aunt Mary… isn't, anymore. What's left doesn't really look like her. Not at all.

The Devil clicks, and nudges the gun closer to Tommy with its foot. He shakes his head, pulling himself farther under the table.

"N-no," he says. "I'm not a danger. I'm not."

The Devil looks at him thoughtfully. Tommy looks back, and waits.

Finally, the Devil says, in a voice that is no man's, that sounds almost approving, "*Gahn'tha-cte*," and turns, and walks away.

Tommy stays where he is, and cries.

Annie finds him there, he doesn't know how much later. She puts her arms around him and pulls him out into the light, her tears falling on his cheek.

"It left," she says. "It took its machine and it left. Tommy, what did you *do*?"

He set them free. He led the Devil to Aunt Mary, and saw her judged for her sins, and now they're free. They can find some other family to live with, family that doesn't hit, that doesn't hurt. They can get out of this desert.

He killed her. As sure as if he'd been the one to hold the knife, he killed her. He's a sinner now, like her, like Uncle Jack, and when the Devil comes back—the Devil always comes back—he'll be fair game. He'll be something to be hunted.

For now, in this moment, he puts his arms around his sister, and he doesn't say any of those things. He holds her fast, and he says nothing at all.

TIN WARRIOR

BY JOHN SHIRLEY

The prisoner paced. It waited. Sometimes the prisoner lifted its head to sniff at the air. The smells were alien, yet becoming disgustingly familiar.

The cell was twenty paces by forty. There were soft places to stretch out but without frames under them; there was plumbing, designed to be impossible to pull out of the floor. The cell was resistant and seamless, so that nothing could be used as a weapon.

The electric lights dialed down automatically in the evening—was this a mock of night? But this dimness was nothing like the deep night of its own world.

The prisoner was reassured by the fact that these soft primates knew little about his world. They had worked long, so long, trying to understand the *Yautja* technology—what little they could find. They had tried to communicate, using a few words and phrases gleaned from some fool *Yautja* prisoner—some coward who had betrayed its people; a weakling who had died from a terrestrial disease, apparently.

But the prisoner had not responded to their feeble attempts to communicate. It told them nothing.

They had tried to weaken the prisoner's mind by drugging its food, with no result except that it had almost died.

The prisoner had recovered—but still, it was trapped.

No matter. They did not control it. Not in its mind, not in its inner life.

The prisoner felt sure its moment would come.

And it would make them suffer for their presumption. Many soft, pink-skinned heads would be added to its trophies.

"You up for this, Sarge?"

"Lieutenant Curson said I get a week's furlough after this," Nialls said, peering into the helmet, reaching in to adjust the radio mic. "You were there, you heard her. She said it's straight from Dault."

"What an officer says to us don't mean nothing," Corporal Ramirez said, as he squinted at the seams of Nialls' armor, going through the standard check. "Army gives and the Army takes away, Sarge. Big Green Machine rolls over you any damn time it wants to."

"I've logged three and a half months straight! More'n three months in a blackout base in the middle of the high desert! I'm due, Corporal. I'd wrestle the devil to get that leave."

Nialls put the helmet on, and Ramirez made some

unnecessary adjustments—the helmet was already perfectly in place, because it sealed itself. It was as if a ghost were doing it.

The heads-up display instantly lit up in response, with luminous green readouts alongside his shield mask. It probably wasn't as information-comprehensive as the *Yautja*'s own bio-mask, but the HUD had a lot of sensors, it had sharp zoom function, and, rear view scanning. And it fit well. Nialls had spent a lot of time testing in two other prototype armored suits. The Mark I and Mark II suits didn't do a third of what this new one did. They'd been bulky, clumsy. But the Mark III...

Nialls pulled on his left-hand gauntlet, thinking, *The Mark III fits like a glove.*

He figured what he had to do today couldn't be tougher than that last Mosul action in Iraq. He signed on for the armor-testing assignment so he could help develop new ways to keep his brother Rangers alive. Rangers and every other American in combat. The Mark III had the potential to do the job. Super lightweight composite materials made it easy to move in, and provided good ballistic protection. The nanotech cut down on weight and energy consumption, sped up responses. And the *Yautja* tech...

First time he'd seen the original tech, from a Predator scout ship shot down in this same desert, he'd felt a long, cold shiver go through him. The marl and gnarl of that gear— definitely not something designed by human beings. They'd retro-engineered a good deal of it; energy flow from the extraterrestrial's bio-mask, the alternative micro-circuiting of the wrist gauntlet—and especially, the plasma caster. It was a whole new edge, all right, to U.S. military power. But it had to be tested in the field...

And then that crazy son of a bitch General Dault hit the team with his big idea.

Sergeant Nialls couldn't upbraid a two-star general. So he finished his armor prep, went to full power and walked out, boots softly clanking, to the clean room, for a final inspection. Beyond the clean room were two sets of metal doors—and beyond those, the testing field...

Lieutenant Olivia Curson was just as fed up with the blackout base as Nialls was.

She'd met Nialls in the rec hall. They'd drunk a beer together, chatted, and she'd noticed how unfailingly respectful Nialls was—respectful but never obsequious. Of course, she outranked him. But that didn't stop some enlisted guys from leering at her after they had a couple of beers. Nialls never leered, never spoke condescendingly, never tried innuendo. And he met her eyes steadily when they spoke—his own eyes were sky blue.

They talked again when she was brought into armor testing, after she'd read his file—his military history intimidated her. She'd seen barely any combat—and he'd been steeped in it.

Then there was Speevis. *Captain* Speevis, who'd smuggled a fifth of Wild Turkey into the base. The booze was contraband, even for officers, on a blackout base, because a drunk man, off-duty or not, forgot what high security was all about. And he forgot how to behave around women officers, too, which was why she'd had to knee the captain in the groin when he waylaid her behind the mess hall. She'd cracked his nuts hard enough to make him yelp; he'd staggered away and barfed on a flagpole in front of a major. He claimed, later, she'd come on to him and kneed him when he turned her down.

But Nialls, passing by, had seen the whole thing. He stepped up on his own to testify for her; stood up in military court against a captain and General Dault—Ervin Dault, who just happened to be Speevis's drinking buddy.

Nialls had a silver cross, a bronze star, and three purple hearts. Every decent man at Area 57 looked up to him. So Speevis lost the case and got himself shipped to a radar base in the arctic.

Now she glanced at Dault: a paunchy, jowly middle-aged man in a perfectly ironed, excessively starched uniform. Dault cracked his knuckles, his tongue tracing the edges of his teeth.

What was Dault's real motivation, she wondered, in setting up this particular test? They'd already tested the suit a dozen ways, put it through incredible stresses. The enemy they were to test the suit against today, while formidable, was unarmed. The whole thing seemed like a pointless exercise to her—unless the point was retaliation aimed at Nialls for testifying against Speevis.

Across the field, just above the gate that would release the *Yautja*, two snipers stood on a platform just behind the curved wall. One of them was Cliff Javitz, another sycophant of General Dault's. Javitz had been caught by an IED, back in Afghanistan; he was missing his right ear and the right-hand section of his lower nose, fully exposing a nostril. Rumor had it his personality had changed after the IED, due to traumatic brain injury. He was as psychopathic a man as Olivia had ever met, though he did nothing he could be convicted for. The other sniper was Earl Smithson, a black man who rarely spoke. Presumably the snipers were there to protect Nialls from the *Yautja*, should the armor malfunction or the creature get the upper hand.

Below, the doors from the clean room opened, and they watched as Nialls stepped into the dull late afternoon sunlight of the acre-wide testing field. Nialls' movements in the armor weren't quite as free as a man in field cammies, but free enough.

Olivia wondered how far up in the chain of command Dault had gone to get approval for this. Maybe he hadn't gotten any, anywhere. Far as she knew, this *Yautja* was the only living extraterrestrial in custody. There was a whole exobiology team in this building studying the *Yautja* through hidden cameras, watching it exercising, eating, pacing, eliminating wastes; using DNA testing and remote body scans they'd worked out what to feed it, how its body worked. She knew the entire exo team was mad as hell about this little gladiatorial setup. Suppose the alien got badly injured, or killed? They had already dissected other dead *Yautja*s. They wanted this one alive…

But Dault had overruled them. He had always been an arrogant son of a bitch. And he insisted this fight was going to be part of their research on these interplanetary Predators. The *Yautja* wasn't likely to get killed, he said.

But from the reports Olivia had read, these things were fast and deadly. Suppose it slipped past Nialls' defenses and killed *him*?

Her heart thudded as she watched the gate open, and the *Yautja* showing itself in the passage opposite Nialls. At first it crouched in the shadows of the passage, its hooded yellow-red eyes and mandibles gleaming…

Felt different, facing this thing up close and personal, instead of seeing it through an unbreakable window. Its cold inhuman intelligence gave him chills.

Nialls had the plasma caster gripped in his right hand, the weapon hooked to a power source in his armor by a jointed metal tube, and it could be attached to a pivoter on his right shoulder, more or less like the *Yautja*. But they hadn't worked out the shoulder-based aiming as well as the *Yautja* had, and Nialls preferred to keep the weapon in his hand.

Then the Predator shuffled slowly out into the circular testing field, turning its head this way and that, the mane-like thick dangle of hair about its bald, mottled head waving a little with its motions. It was assessing, calculating, taking in the high, slick, inward slanting walls, the snipers, the gate closing behind Nialls—and then the *Yautja* stared directly at its adversary. It looked Nialls up and down. Then the Predator hunched down and spread its arms like an old-style wrestler, making low, glutinous clicking sounds deep in its throat.

Nialls did his own assessing. The thing was at least a head taller than he was. It had claws. But otherwise the *Yautja* was apparently unarmed. It did have some chest armor, and that net-like material over its limbs that would project its camouflage. Its muscles rippled powerfully under skin that looked like something he'd seen on a desert toad. It had some form of gauntlet, but no plasma caster.

How should he handle this? He didn't have orders to kill it—"just engage the alien," as Dault put it.

It's got no reason not to kill me if it can...

Then it opened its mouth—its jaws opening wide, showing the big fangs that pointed almost inwardly, the red-webbed mouth—and he was looking down the Predator's throat as it lunged roaring at him.

Nialls quickly sidestepped—and then realized the *Yautja* had only been feinting, pretending to be coming at him to see how quickly he reacted; see if he could be startled into freezing.

"That's not going to work, crab-face," he told it. The armor had responded well, enhancing his movements but not overdoing the enhancement.

It responded to his remark—Nialls had heard the creatures sometimes parroted human speech. *"Not going to work..."* came the mocking voice.

Nialls squared himself, trying to keep his head clear, his pulse down. *Focus and maybe get this over with early. Get it to accept defeat...*

He pointed the plasma caster, and fired.

Nialls hadn't aimed directly at the creature—not supposed to kill it. He aimed at the ground just in front of its clawed feet, to give it a warning and knock it back with a shockwave.

But by the time the blast hit the ground the *Yautja* wasn't there. It had switched on its active camouflage, was all but invisible—he caught a barely visible cubistic outline of it as, far faster than he'd given it credit for, the *Yautja* leapt over the plasma caster's blast trajectory, coming right at him, whipping metal spikes from its left-hand gauntlet at his helmet.

Nialls overreacted in his surprise, stumbled back, fell on his back—and then it was on him, its knees on his chest. It had triggered the long, barbed metal gougers from its left gauntlet. It *did* have a weapon—he could glimpse light reflecting from it, despite the electronic camouflage.

It slammed the heavy, barbed gougers at his faceplate; the transparent layers protecting his face held, but Nialls felt like his head was inside a ringing church bell. And he could sense the strain in the helmet. It slammed the gougers down again. Was that a crack in the corner of the faceplate?

Struggling to shove the creature off him, Nialls swung hard up at the *Yautja*'s head with his mailed left fist—but the *Yautja*, red-yellow eyes glowing with kill-lust, blocked it easily with the gauntlet. The blow somehow switched off its camouflage and he saw it all too well, roaring at him, its eyes bright with hate as it slammed his helmet again with the gougers.

The snipers were up there on the wall. Why didn't they at least wing the *Yautja*?

The *Yautja* raised its tautly muscled left fist, gathering its strength—preparing to smash his faceplate. Nialls was reluctant to disobey orders but he was going to have to shoot this thing off him. He aimed the plasma caster at it almost point blank but it grabbed the caster by the muzzle, used all its strength and its better positioning to turn the weapon— just as the caster fired—right where it wanted the plasma beam to go.

The top of the enclosing wall on the right shattered. A piece of shattered wall struck the alien, and its grip was loosened for a moment. Nialls got his right knee bent, braced his foot under his hip and used the whole force of the leg— his and the armor's force—to fling the alien away.

The *Yautja* roared as it was thrown back, and Nialls felt a wrenching in his suit. He lost the grip on his gun. He rolled, got quickly to his feet—and saw that the plasma caster was no longer in his hand.

The *Yautja* had it—had snapped its connective cable. It was crouching, aiming the caster at the sniper platform...

Neither sniper was in sight now.

It fired—blasting more of the upper wall away, then turned the weapon toward Nialls.

But he knew something the creature didn't. The human-engineered version of the caster was fed by the cable; it only stored one shot at a time in its load chamber. And the *Yautja* had used that shot. The gun failed to fire—and the alien tossed it away.

It slashed at Nialls with its gougers; he blocked the blow with his right hand, smashed at the thing with his left, caught it on the side of its head. Its luminous yellow-green blood spurted from a scalp wound. He circled it—and it rushed him, slashing. He jumped aside... but it had simply gotten him out of the way.

It jumped to the break in the wall and pulled itself over.

Nialls bounded after it, jumped—but it could jump higher than he could. He couldn't catch the lower edge of the break in the wall.

Cursing, he dropped back. Someone up there screamed. A gun fired. Then there was silence, except for the base's alarms going off...

Sitting on the table, Nialls held the helmet in his hand, looking it over, as Olivia came in.

"Scratch on the faceplate, but no crack," he told Ramirez. "It wouldn't have taken much more."

"Smithson is dead," Olivia told him, as Ramirez checked over the armor. "The first blast broke his collarbone, stunned him—then the thing killed him. Javitz is alive—he shot at it, but it was smoky in there, not a good place for a sniper rifle, and he missed. It ducked out a fire door and killed two sentries... just tore into them..."

She took a deep breath. Nialls nodded. "Thanks for letting me know, Lieutenant. I'm sorry about Smithson. He was a good soldier."

"It wasn't your fault," she said. "The alien breached the wall, not you."

"Lieutenant's right," Ramirez said, taking the helmet and looking it over. "No one thought the wall was that vulnerable. But it was old. That wall's thinner at the top, in that spot, to make room for the platform."

"Seems to me," Nialls said, "that weapon was powered up about double what it should've been for that situation." He felt tired, dispirited. Three good men dead so far...

"It was powered up to where the General told me it should be," Ramirez said. "I kinda wondered about it."

"You didn't tell me."

"I thought: more power, better for you, Sarge."

"Yeah. No one told me it had those gougers."

Olivia nodded sharply at that. "I was told it had no weapons."

"I kind of thought the snipers would've taken it out, when it was on top of me. That angle, they could have put a couple of fist-sized holes right through its head."

Olivia looked angrily at the door. "I had the same thought. Javitz says he was told not to fire unless the General gave him the order."

The door opened—maybe Olivia had been expecting someone.

General Dault. He looked pale, and a little scared. "Sergeant Nialls. That thing's just killed another sentry. Cooper shot at it, missed, and it gutted him. Took him a while to die."

Nialls winced inwardly. He should've kept that thing bottled up. But no one had told him it had a weapon—and he'd been told not to kill it with the plasma caster. Still—it was his job to knock the thing down and keep it under control.

Dault seemed ready to confirm what Nialls was thinking. "This is on you, Nialls. Put that helmet back on. Get a jeep and get out there."

"He hasn't got the caster!" Ramirez objected. "It'll take me a whole day to fix it!"

"Tough. He's got the armor. Everything else in it works. He can take a rifle."

Olivia shook her head. "Sir—what about an attack helicopter? We've got armored vehicles—"

"Negative. That thing is headed to town. It's dark out. And by the time we track it it's going to be out there with civilians around. We're not firing any rockets into any civilian towns, Lieutenant. No. This is on Nialls."

———

Javitz's head was throbbing, and the bandage was too damned tight, but he was already dressed by the time the General came to the infirmary.

"You good for duty, Javitz?" Dault asked.

Javitz saluted. "I am, sir. Just a crease on the head. Nothing I ain't had before."

"Requisition a rifle. We've got more to think about than just a runaway monster. What I'm hoping is, Nialls gets the thing's attention, gets it cornered. Then you put a round through its leg. We recapture it... I'll send a backup team; you can call them when it's down, they'll be right behind you. Then—we shut all this up. No one needs to know how this shitstorm got its start."

"Shut it up how, sir?"

"I'm counting on you, Javitz. I cannot trust Nialls, see. Or Olivia Curson. You saw what happened—Nialls testified against my man. Over a goddamn attempted rape accusation! That kind of disloyalty..." He shook his head. "Cannot trust him to keep his mouth shut. Anyway..." Dault went to the door, glanced out into the hall, looking both ways. He closed the door and came over to Javitz. Dault lowered his voice. "Nialls is going to get caught in the crossfire. You understand me?"

Javitz thought about it. It'd be good to have the General beholden to him. But this...

"Kind of a risk to me, General, if this comes out."

"You want a promotion, special privileges?"

"For a start."

Dault winced. Finally he said, "I can get you ten grand on top of it."

"And... the lieutenant?"

"I'll send her out to check on him. If the alien doesn't get her—you make it look like it did anyway."

Double the risk. But...

Promotion. Special privileges. Cash.

Opportunity like this didn't come along too often. A man had to grab it by the tail...

After a moment, Javitz nodded.

"I'll get 'er done, General. But—my rifle's not much use against that armor Nialls is wearing."

"That's right—it stands up to snipers, small arms fire of all kinds, grenade fragments, flamethrowers, mines, and most IEDs. But you think it'll protect him from a 30mm cannon? He'll be pulverized inside it. Second shot'll blow it open. I'm giving you a Stryker outfitted with a cannon."

"Those things have some kind of self-destruct in their gauntlet? I don't want to suck on a small nuke..."

"You don't think it would've used that by now if it had one? It was unconscious when we found it. We stripped that out of its gear." He sighed. "Only thing I gave back to it was the chest armor, its camouflage, and those spikes in its gauntlet. Mistake to let it have the active cammie..."

"Thirty millimeter. Only fired one once."

"It's pretty self-guided, these days. Just try not to use it on the alien. Not unless you have to. Only don't let that thing get clean away either. But make sure Nialls is dead. Slam him with the shell dead center. We'll say he just plain got in the way."

It was dark by the time they'd picked up the trail. Just Ramirez, driving the Humvee, and Nialls, suited up beside him.

"It's not headed for town, if the heat signature is right," Nialls said. He could see its tracks glowing red in his helmet's infrared scan mode. "It's changed directions."

"What the hell for? Those things are into taking trophies, right? More trophies in town." Ramirez winced, put his hand to his throat. "They take the head off, the skin off the skull..."

"There's a ranch out here. And there's Special Hangar Fourteen right past the ranch. I don't think it's going for any more trophies. It already took some. Security camera has it shoving the heads of three sentries in a duffel bag."

"Oh Christ. Cooper and Morris and Lapsky. I didn't know it..." He grimaced. "What's in Hangar Fourteen, anyway? Above my pay grade."

"T situation, I guess you've got a right to know. They found the alien out cold after its vehicle was shot down—built the hangar around ship. They keep trying to take it apart without detonating it. It's got armament—soon's they took the *Yautja* off, the ship started up some kind of defense protocol. Two techs got themselves fried by its plasma casters."

"So that's one time the rumors were true."

"Tracks are heading down that wash... right along the road there. Take the road for now."

———

Gage Binch had spent all afternoon clearing brush from the back acreage. He figured he could turn it into pasture. The acreage was right up against that tall fence topped with razor wire around the Army outpost. Outpost Fourteen. Gage doubted it was an outpost—it was a distance off, across a pretty wide stretch of asphalt; but he could see it well enough: a long squat gray metal building, with two fifty-foot-high metal roll-up doors. Place looked more like a hangar than an outpost. And those searchlights, those four sentry boxes—lot of security for some little outpost.

Plus the fact that the Army MPs told him he was not to even get near the fence.

Screw them. This was his land. This was a "don't tread

on me" situation. If he wanted to turn it to pasturage, that was his choice. He could hear his cattle mooing from the other side of the ranch house. Soon enough he'd be able to put the new bull in with some cows and get another herd started. And he'd put it right here in the new pasture.

He surveyed his work. Six of those little desert trees cut down, room to move his tractor in so he could push the rock out of the way, lay down some soil for the grass. There was the old oak tree, likely to fall down on its own next big wind. But he had to leave it: too close to that fence to mess with. And nearby the oak was a small fenced pasture where he kept the new Brahman bull—Gage could see it tramping up and down, shaking its big horned head. Something was spooking it, seemed like. Maybe the chainsaw noise.

But it was dark out. Time to go in, drink some Scotch. Have a talk with Regina. Of course, his wife had died on him, but he talked to the urn of her ashes all the same.

Maybe just cut that one snag... He had enough light with the electric lantern...

Gage tugged his goggles into place, switched on the chainsaw, held it firmly in both hands, and cut through the snag on the scrub tree.

Then a shadow cut off most of the light from his lantern.

He turned. There was a big man there—he couldn't see the guy's face. Just a mane of some kind, a gnarly bald head, those strange hands... a bloody duffel bag lying on the ground beside it.

"Who the holy fu—"

Then the guy vanished. Just sort of blinked out.

What the hell? Was he having a stroke? He thought he caught some motion from the corner of his eyes, turned—in time to get a big military trench knife shoved through his belly.

He stared down at it, stunned, exploding with pain, gurgling, the chainsaw still in his hands—

He tried to swing the chainsaw toward the knifer—but the chainsaw was taken from him, all too easily pried from his grip. Then it reversed, and came right at his throat...

"*Que mierda!*" Ramirez burst out. He stopped the Humvee, and its headlights lit up the bloody, decapitated head of a bull, a gray-black Brahman with thick, curving horns. The hulking head was stuck on a post to either side of the road leading up to the ranch house. Its jaws were open, lolling tongue dripping blood onto the gravel road. Its dead eyes were still shiny in the headlight glow.

Nialls' gut lurched at the sight. "Guess it didn't have room in that duffel for the bull's head—so it figured to scare us off."

"Yeah. It'd work on me, too, if I was out here alone, Sarge."

Ramirez accelerated slowly past the staring bull's head, peering at the cactus garden in front of the ranch house. "Damn thing could be anywhere out here with that camouflage."

Nialls switched on his infrared vision. Saw nothing but what appeared to be an owl sitting in a saguaro.

But there, to the right, maybe a trail of blood. Traces of footsteps. He switched to night vision instead. The dark landscape lit up in greens and yellows. No sign of the *Yautja*. "Pull up. Roll the windows down..."

Ramirez pulled up, the windows hummed down. "I hear something... like a... is that a chainsaw?"

"Yeah. Must be how it cut through that bull. He was

probably watching someone using it and…"

"And they're dead about now."

"Go slow, around to the right. There's a road to the back…"

They drove around the dark ranch house, Nialls considering cutting the headlights—and then they saw something big, bigger than the alien; shifting, falling—it was an oak tree tipping over onto the high razor-topped fence around the Hangar Fourteen compound. The big tree fell with a clinking crunch they could hear through the open windows. Ramirez picked up speed, drove toward it, bumping over cut shrubs and plant debris. Then Nialls spotted it, in pale gray outline. The *Yautja*, climbing up the slanting trunk of the fallen tree, which had fallen on the fence. It had cut down the tree with the rancher's chainsaw, giving it a way past the guards at the outer sentry box.

The *Yautja* was already running, now, across the asphalt, going into active camouflage, the canvas bag of trophies showing over one shoulder as if the bloody duffel were flying along alone.

"That thing is crazy smart," said Ramirez.

"We've got to get word to Fourteen—I'll have to go through Dault." Nialls spoke the code word that would voice-activate his radio, and heard its line crackle open. "Mark Three calling base, code twenty-three, connect me with General Dault." He waited. The line crackled with static. No response. "Maybe the damn helmet was damaged after all," Nialls said. "Try the Hummer's radio."

Ramirez picked up the mic, clicked the *on* button.

No response. He checked the dashboard radio unit. "Someone's cut the wires! This radio's dead, Sarge. We're in this alone."

"Maybe not alone," Nialls said. "I just spotted a drone flying over."

"Is it armed?"

"Just an observation drone. The General doesn't want to hear from us, seems like. But he wants to keep an eye on us. Let's jam through where the fence is down..."

There was just enough room to drive the Humvee through, following the *Yautja*. Nialls hoped the fallen razor wire wasn't going to wreck the Humvee's tires. But it kept on, rumbling over the broken fence and onto the asphalt.

"Some nervous nelly at the checkpoints might open fire on us," Ramirez said.

"Someone's got to have told them—"

That's when the cannon shell struck the Humvee. One second they were driving steadily toward the looming light-streaked hangar, the next was all fire and splintering glass and the world flipping sideways. The Humvee pitched over, Ramirez yelling wordlessly, falling down on Nialls. The Humvee rocked and settled on its right side. The windshield was partly smashed out in front of Nialls, smoke was thickening, and Ramirez was groaning. Nialls said, "Mark Three, full operation." Lights flickered inside his helmet. He reached up, pushed out the metal rooftop hatch, and wriggled through, then pulled Ramirez out by his collar, Ramirez shrieking in pain.

He got him out just as the Humvee lit up like a bonfire.

Carrying Ramirez in his arms, Nialls hurried away from the Humvee before the rest of the gas tank went up. Nialls turned, saw flame geysering, lighting the area around the burning wreck. It quickly died back, but there was no getting into that Humvee.

Which meant that Nialls had no weapon now—his assault rifle was in that burning Humvee. But then, his armor was itself a weapon. He could batter down a metal door with it—or an enemy's skull.

Ramirez went limp in Nialls' arms. He laid him gently on the ground, switched on a helmet light, and saw broken bones jutting up, pink and yellow, from the corporal's chest; a blankness was coming into his eyes as if the night around them were pooling in the sockets.

Ramirez was dead before Nialls straightened up.

In a cold fury now, Nialls looked around, spotted the Stryker, its lights off, swinging toward him, the cannon centering itself. Maybe forty yards off. That looked like a 30mm cannon swiveling toward him. A direct hit and his suit would crack open like a lobster shell under a hammer.

Nialls ran left, his boots clanking, the armored suit working overtime; then he zigged to the right. The cannon's muzzle tracked to compensate, and Nialls changed direction again, then leapt—as the shell hit the ground behind him, the shockwave lifting him, pitching him head over heels.

He came down on his back, dazed, ears ringing, but intact.

"You missed, you prick," he growled. He rolled over, saw the smoking blast crater in the asphalt. He got up, ran to the crater, flattened down and tried to recon the field.

Who the hell was in the Stryker? Dault? Naw. Too risky. Most likely Dault's bully boy, Javitz. Using a weapon that could be sure to bust through the Mark III armor in a direct hit.

Nialls switched on the infrared, hoping to pick up a body shape in the Stryker. No good, the Stryker's armor was too thick—but he picked up another figure, silhouetted in red: the *Yautja*, moving toward the armored vehicle from its rear. No mistaking that outline. It had ditched the chainsaw, still held the duffel bag, and there was something else in its hand. The distinct shape of a special forces issue combat knife. Long, partly serrated, vicious. What the Predator had used to take the heads from the sentries at the base.

The Stryker was moving, coming slowly, implacably toward Nialls, the cannon tracking—wanting that direct hit.

But then the infrared outline of the *Yautja* was hunched atop the armored car. It was going after whoever was in that vehicle. Why them, in particular? But maybe it was the Stryker it wanted.

Nialls switched on his night vision, saw the creature more clearly, a glowing white-gray shape tugging at a hatch. Figuring out how to open it. The hatch swung back. Driver had neglected to lock it.

The Stryker suddenly stopped as if the driver had realized someone was breaking in on him and wanted to deal with it…

Nialls jumped up, ran toward the Stryker, making sure he was angling to keep out of the cannon's current firing zone. He was aware of shapes moving beyond the Stryker's windshield—a flurry of movement.

Then a pair of headlights swung into his path and a car came straight at him.

He had no way to evade the car in time—but it stopped, brakes screeching. A moment, then Olivia Curson got partly out of it, waving for him. "Come on, Nialls, now!"

He rushed to the car, his boots clanking on the asphalt. He was aware of sentries in the distance, shouting from the front of Hangar Fourteen—flashlights, men shouting orders, other men arguing. Nialls stopped by the car.

Maybe he should remove his helmet, ID himself…

"Nialls—get in!" Olivia yelled, getting behind the wheel.

Nialls looked toward the Stryker—and then saw it had turned away from him. It was rumbling toward the hangar.

It knows how to drive it. Can it figure out how to fire the cannon?

Nialls reached the car, climbed in beside her, having to move the seat all the way back—there was barely room for him in his armor. "Turn this car around!" he shouted, not caring about rank right now.

She brought the car around, started toward the hangar— then had to jog the wheel, skidding to avoid a headless body lying on the asphalt. Nialls caught a glimpse of a sniper specialist insignia on the corpse's shoulder. Javitz.

Up ahead the Stryker was picking up speed, the big armored car going faster and faster, heading for the big doors of the hangar. The cannon remained silent—he guessed it didn't have time to figure out the firing interface.

"I think Dault's trying to kill you—maybe me too!" Olivia said, as she drove toward the hangar. Her voice was taut, her knuckles white on the steering wheel.

"Be a good guess. And the *Yautja*'s got hold of that Stryker…"

"Oh no, it couldn't—!"

"It did. Slow down! We're liable to catch some fire from our own people!"

She hit the brakes; the car fishtailed to a stop about twenty yards from the hangar—where men were firing, but not at them, at the onrushing Stryker. Nialls could see bullets sparking from the titanium sheathing. Then the Stryker plowed over two riflemen, and kept going, crunching head- on into the big metal doors, smashing partway through—then grinding to a halt. Stuck. Its wheels kept spinning in place.

"Pull over there, around the corner of the building. I'm going in the personnel door."

———

The front end of the vehicle had jammed partway through the big reinforced doors—still, the escapee was able to climb out the door on the right, then leap at the nearest onrushing primate, to bear him down before he could fire his weapon. Its blade flashed, slashed, and the primate soldier was jerking in death. The escapee picked up the automatic weapon, turned it to the men guarding the spacecraft, and squeezed the trigger, spraying awkwardly at the enemy across the brightly lit concrete floor. They scrambled for cover, though the clip was quickly empty, useless.

The escapee could see its landing craft, waiting, scarred but functional, in the middle of the hangar. But an enemy projectile struck the escapee in the right side; it ignored the pain, turned and vaulted over the front of the armored vehicle, dropping to cover. Then it reached through the shattered window, pulled out the well-stuffed bloody duffel bag.

Now...

The escapee growled to itself, switched on its active camouflage, and then sprinted, with projectiles banging and ricocheting around it, to the landing craft. The ramp was down, the door open—that much they had achieved. But after they had taken out their unconscious Yautja *prisoner the vessel went immediately into self-protection mode. It had been keeping the enemy at a distance ever since, tolerating scans and superficial observations but not allowing disassembly.*

Now that a Yautja *master was in sight again, the vessel lit up, as if in welcome. The landing craft's gun muzzles emerged and* fired plasma bursts at the primate creatures, burning two of them to bubbling ashes, driving the others away… By now, the landing craft would be contacting the cloaked mothership…

Indifferent to the pain of its wound, the escapee roared in joy and ran up to the ramp into its landing craft…

Thinking: What glorious trophies I have…

But it had one more duty to carry out before it could leave this wretched planet.

Using full armor power, Nialls smashed down the locked personnel door, ran into the blazingly lit hangar, switched off his night vision in time to see the Yautja running up the ramp into the alien vessel. The craft was about eighty feet long, fifty wide; it was shaped like the spade of a shovel, with intricate aft parts, and insectoid metal legs holding it over the floor.

The ramp was still down. If he could get to it, penetrate the vehicle, he could stop the Yautja from escaping. The Mark III might protect him from the ship's defenses—long enough.

And then he heard the helmet's computer speaking to him. "External control engaged."

"What?" His legs suddenly stopped moving—to be precise, the armor's legs stopped, so his own had to stop inside them. The armor was frozen in place. "What external control is that?"

"Origin unknown. Centered in the mechanism directly ahead."

The Yautja craft? Then Nialls remembered they'd copied some of Mark III's circuits directly from the Yautja's gear. It was responding to the alien's control wavelength. Stopping him where he was…

The ramp lifted up, folded into the craft. The underside began to glow. A fat burst of energy turned everything blue-white. Nialls felt a wave of heat. He heard the screams of men who couldn't get out of the way...

He was in a cloud of energy that threatened to burn through his armor.

The ceiling of the hangar exploded upward, the blowback clearing the air around the Mark III—and Nialls could see again.

He looked up, watching the *Yautja* craft levitating, its legs folding up under it, then arcing up, up on a pillar of energy. Gone.

The computer in his suit said, *"Control returned to primary user."*

Nialls felt the armor's limbs unlock. He felt a gush of cool, filtered air drawn in, cooling him down. Sweat running down his face, he turned and walked toward Olivia Curson who was bending over a soldier, trying to give him battlefield first aid...

Half an hour later they drove out past the long line of ambulances, back toward the blackout base. Nialls had removed his helmet and gauntlets, wiping sweat with the back of his hand. "Ramirez... he's dead."

She nodded. "He really looked up to you."

"Another guy I should've saved."

"You can't be blamed for a round from somebody else's cannon."

They didn't speak again till they were almost back at the blackout base.

She glanced at him. "What'll you do now?"

"Testify against Dault. You?"

"Same."

"After that?"

"Request relief from the Army. I'm done."

She stopped the car, on a shoulder, turned to him, took his hands in hers. "Look—I—"

The flash of blue light made them turn toward the base, squinting against the glare—just in time to see the administrative building explode. The building burned— Dault was sure to be burning with it. Then another flash of light, a red beam fired from high above, destroying the exo- team's building.

Nialls and Olivia watched, open-mouthed, as the *Yautja*'s spacecraft buzzed over the smoking wreckage, as if inspecting its handiwork... and came toward them. It seemed to hesitate above them, for a moment, and Nialls waited for the blast—it was too late to run. He hoped it'd be over quickly.

But then the craft backed away, hovered wobblingly— and shot up into the sky, vanishing into the thin cloud cover. Gone from this wretched planet...

After a long breathless moment, Olivia drove them back on the road, toward the base, to see if they could be of any help.

But up ahead a roadblock was being set up. MPs waved them away.

Silently, she turned the car around and they drove away from the blackout base. Fire trucks passed them, emergency crews in trucks from the external outposts.

"Why," he asked hoarsely, "didn't it blow us up, too?"

"My guess?" She cocked her head, thinking. "It seemed to know who you were. Someone worth fighting—the way a real warrior fights. Maybe another time. But not that way, from a distance. So… it was about respect."

Maybe, he thought. *Maybe so.* "Let's go into town," he said. "I want to get out of this suit. And then—I want a drink. Or three."

"Never was any doubt of that," she said, as she turned onto the main highway.

THREE SPARKS

BY LARRY CORREIA

They found the first bodies around noon, suspended from a branch high above them, arms dangling. Samurai? They could not tell. It was hard to know someone's social status after they had been skinned.

From the bloat and the stink, combined with the heat, Hiroto guessed they had been dead for three days. He had skinned a lot of game, so even in their sorry state he could tell that this oni was very skilled at butchery. Hiroto was impressed. There were no signs of rope. It would take an incredible amount of strength and balance to haul corpses all the way up there. He had seen great cats cache their kills in trees, but this felt different, as if staged for their benefit. Was it to send a message? Marking territory? He tried not to let his appreciation show. A regular porter should be frightened, so he tried to act that way.

The others, however, didn't have to act.

———

"Captain Nasu Hiroto, hero of the battle of Dan-no-ura, hero of the battle of Kurikara, master swordsman, and champion archer of the Minamoto clan. Some say the finest archer in our history, if not, second only to his father. Yet after the war, there would be no peace for him. No. Hiroto took one of *my* ships, and was carried about wherever the waves would take him, always searching for a new battle, for new beasts to slay. Over the years, I heard he was hunting tigers in the jungles of Tenjiku or great white bears in the desolate lands north of Joseon. It is widely believed Nasu Hiroto is the greatest hunter in the world."

There were some exaggerations there but Hiroto did not correct the shogun's inaccuracies. When the most powerful man in Nippon wanted to ramble, you let him. So Hiroto simply knelt and waited for Minamoto Yoritomo to pronounce his judgment.

"You were one of my most trusted warriors, Hiroto. Why did you leave? After our victory over the Taira clan, I would have given you great responsibilities."

"I left because you would have given me great responsibilities."

"Your life was mine to spend, Hiroto."

"Spending it teaching children how to use a bow would have been a waste. I am not trying to be facetious, my lord, but I would have died of boredom. I am not very good at peace."

"Then you picked a fortuitous time to return."

The castle was stifling. It was a miserable day in what had to be the hottest summer in generations. A servant was fanning the red-faced and sweating shogun. Nobody was fanning Hiroto. He did not rate a fan.

"I should have you executed for your disobedience, you impudent ronin bastard. Yet curiosity gets the better of me. After all these years you returned to Kamakura. Why?"

"I received word that the Shogunate has need of my services."

Minamoto Yoritomo chuckled. "I should have known that the Oni of Aokigahara would bring you out of hiding. Summer began with it murdering a score of my warriors, picking them off, one by one, and leaving them hanging from trees, skinned. Since then, samurai have been rushing there in order to defeat it and win my favor. All have failed. Witnesses whisper of an invisible demon, stronger than any man, which kills by spear, claw, or even bolts of lightning, before vanishing as quickly as it appeared."

"You can see how such stories would catch my interest, my lord."

"Sometimes, three glowing embers appear upon its chosen victim." The shogun held up three fingers, then put them against his forehead, fingertips making the points of a triangle. "Being marked by these fire kami are the only warning before it strikes. So many samurai have perished that they believe the oni cannot be defeated by a mortal hand. I seem to recall they said the same thing about the Great Sea Beast, before your father killed it with a single arrow through the eye."

"A truly heroic moment."

"I know. I was there. No man has ever equaled his feat...
including the man who has hunted every dangerous beast
beneath the sun. Hmmm... Perhaps if you were to defeat the
Oni of Aokigahara, you could finally match his legend?"

It might have been in his blood, but that wasn't why Hiroto
followed his path. The shogun may have been a brilliant general,
but he did not understand the compulsion to constantly seek
out new dangers. "You are wise, my lord, but what is one little
forest demon when compared to a mighty kaiju?"

"You could never resist a challenge, could you, Hiroto?"

He had never fought a demon before. "No, my lord. I
could not."

It was a few days' ride to Aokigahara, the dense forest to
the north of Mount Fuji. Despite the blistering sun, Hiroto
enjoyed seeing the land of his birth again. He felt eager and
alive. Each morning the mountain was a bit closer and so
was his next great challenge.

Unfortunately, he was not making the journey alone. The
Shogunate had sent a representative, a young warrior born
of high status, named Ashikaga Motokane, and his retinue of
five bodyguards. Though Hiroto had helped their lord rise
to power, that had been a long time ago. Now, the shogun's
samurai looked upon him as a dishonorable outcast, a wild
man, an anomaly in their orderly world.

Worst case scenario, Hiroto would use them as bait.

The map provided by the Shogunate had shown a small village
at the edge of the forest, so Hiroto had picked that as their

destination. Upon arrival it had proven even more pathetic than expected, simply a collection of rotten huts and stinking pig pens, yet it would provide a final opportunity to restock their provisions. Hiroto also hoped for first-hand information.

The villagers saw the warriors approaching and abandoned their fields to hide in their huts. That was not surprising. Villages like this were often menaced by one conquering army or another, and during times of peace there were always bandits. One farmer remained in the center of the village to greet them. That would be their appointed headman, the presenter of taxes and hospitality.

"The rest of you hang back for a moment. There is no need to spook them further." Of course the shogun's representative did not listen. When Hiroto dismounted and began walking into the village, Ashikaga Motokane followed, swaggering in the most intimidating way possible.

"I need to ask these farmers some questions."

"Why bother? They'll know nothing."

"You might be surprised."

Motokane looked upon the village with disgust. "They're beneath us. We're authorized to take whatever supplies we require. Let's do it and get on with it." It was no wonder the poor farmers saw little difference between bandits and samurai.

The headman had seen their banner bore the Shogunate's mon, and as they approached had already launched into a rapid speech telling them how wonderful they were, but that his poor village had paid its taxes, and for them to please have mercy because the terrible heat had caused their crops to wilt and their well to run dry, so on and so forth.

Hiroto didn't have patience for such frivolous things

when there were monsters about, so he cut the headman off. "I am Nasu Hiroto. We've come to kill the Oni of Aokigahara."

"You are not the first. The stories are true. Our land is cursed! It is a terrible scourge. We are so thankful more brave samurai have come to fight the demon." Only the headman didn't actually sound relieved, if anything he was annoyed. "Many of you have come through here this summer, eating our food, putting our men to work as guides—"

"Yes, I know." The village had probably seen a parade of warriors by this point, but he needed information. "Have you seen it yourself?"

"No, but I have felt it watching. Many have, though. Young Hagi saw it first, perched high in the trees, shaped like a man, but bigger, with a head like an ox. She thought it was an angry ghost and ran away. Old Genzo saw it too. He heard the thunder when it killed the first samurai. It put the three sparks on him too, but Genzo fled before more lightning came! Lucky it didn't chase him because it is swift as a horse!"

Any creature capable of effortlessly slaughtering samurai would have an easy time with a place this defenseless. "How many of your people has the demon killed?"

"Who cares?" Motokane said. "They're just peasants."

The headman looked nervously between the two imposing warriors, unsure whether he was still supposed to speak or not. Hiroto wished that Motokane would keep his idiot mouth shut. These farmers were probably as frightened by hungry soldiers as the demon plaguing their woods.

"I must know, how many of you have died?"

"It is hard to believe, but none, noble samurai. He has only attacked mighty warriors such as you. Our village has not been troubled by Three Sparks."

That name would suffice. "All of those men beheaded or skinned nearby, yet this Three Sparks has not harmed a single person in this humble village... Curious."

"Perhaps they're in league with the oni!" Motokane snarled. "Why else would it leave them be?"

The headman immediately threw himself into the dust and began begging for mercy, which with a hothead like Motokane was certainly the wisest thing possible. "No! Please! We would never! After the killing started some of us left offerings at the shrine to appease it at most!"

"You gave gifts to a demon that was killing my brothers?" Motokane bellowed as he reached for his sword.

Hiroto sighed. Clan officials always made his job more complicated. He wasn't going to get any answers if Motokane started slaughtering villages. "Please, calm yourself."

"The shogun will abide no treachery!"

"And I will not abide you interrupting me again." The official may have outranked him, but Hiroto was the one handpicked for this assignment, and his patience was wearing thin. "You said it yourself, peasants are beneath your notice. You and Three Sparks have that in common. Now walk away and let me finish."

Motokane was quarrelsome, but he wasn't stupid. Rank had privileges, but they were a long way from Kamakura. The young man gave the headman one last threatening glare, then let go of his sword and went back to join his troops. *Good.* Hiroto didn't particularly want to murder him, but he would if necessary, and then simply tell the shogun that the demon had gotten him. "Now where were we?"

"I'm sorry, great and noble—"

"Enough groveling, and stand already. I'm no tax

collector." He waited for the farmer to get up. "I'm simply a hunter, and you're going to tell me everything you know about this demon so that I can kill it."

———

It was hard to tell over the clanking and huffing of Motokane's bodyguards, but beyond them the forest was unnaturally quiet. The wind did not penetrate far into the Sea of Trees. There were no birds singing, no insects buzzing, just the occasional tap of collected humidity falling on leaves.

It was no wonder the place had been considered haunted even before an oni had moved in.

That morning the others had dressed for war. Motokane's retinue were wearing their armor and helmets, with bows strung, spears held high, and their swords at their sides. The shogun's finest looked like fearsome combatants, a worthy challenge for any demon.

Meanwhile, Hiroto lagged behind them, unarmed and stripped to the waist, with a bamboo pole balanced across his shoulder with a bundle hanging from each end. He had even gone and rolled about in the fields to complete the act. The other samurai thought he'd gone mad when he left his swords behind, but Hiroto looked and even smelled like a local farmer.

Hiroto tried to appear inconsequential, head down, tired and stumbling from rock to rock beneath his clumsy burden. He would be no threat, especially to a mighty oni. He was simply a porter, conscripted from the village to carry his betters' supplies because the forest was too rugged for their horses. The headman had told him that some of the other would-be demon hunters had done the same, and each time their porter had come running back alone, terrified, sometimes covered in blood, but alive.

In his experience, most beasts targeted the weakest prey. This oni was different. It attacked the strong. He would use that to his advantage.

———

They walked for hours. It was slow going across such rough terrain. Thick roots waited to trip them. Each warrior was drenched in sweat. The air felt heavy and smelled of moss. The soil was dark and littered with black volcanic rocks. Between the heat and the uneven ground, the samurai were surely regretting wearing their armor, but they were all too proud to show it. Each of them thought that they would be the one to take the trophy back to their lord, and they passed the time by boasting of what they would do with their reward.

Hiroto just kept his head down, appearing meek and subservient. He reasoned it did not do much good to use his eyes to hunt a creature which was supposedly invisible. Instead, he listened.

In a forest without sound, the faintest things became audible. The oni was quiet, but not as quiet as a tiger. In trees packed too tight for the wind to rustle through, the smallest movement was a clue. Occasionally he'd hear flesh scrape against bark, or the creak of a branch as weight settled on it. There was another sound beneath as well, barely audible, but unnatural, like the chittering of an insect combined with the slithering of a snake across sand. It made the hair on his arms stand up. All of that information would have been lost amongst the noise of a living place, but in the haunted stillness of Aokigahara, it told a story.

They were being followed.

It was somewhere above them and to the right. He tried not to let his excitement show.

———

"Over here," Kaneto called from the edge of a nearby stream. "There's another."

This body had been there for a few days, and was missing its head, but from his fine clothing and the broken katana lying in the water, he had clearly been a samurai. Motokane knelt next to the corpse and pointed at the emblem embroidered on the sleeve. "I recognize this from court. This is the personal mon of Hōjō Murashige!"

Hiroto had no idea who that was, but the Hōjō were a family of some importance. The corpse's identity seemed to shake the others.

"He was a fearsome swordsman," Zensuke whispered. "The best of us."

"It didn't just take his head. It ripped out his *spine*." Motokane stood up and glanced around nervously. A full day of nerves and stress had worn him thin. He suddenly raised his voice and bellowed, "Show yourself, demon! Show yourself so I can kill you like the wretched cowardly dog you are!"

Hiroto took a few steps away from the angry samurai. The peasants had spoken of it throwing lightning bolts, and he didn't think it wise to stand so close to the most tempting target. He listened, but if the demon was still watching, it was being especially quiet, or at least quiet enough he couldn't hear it over the shouting. So while Motokane continued to rant and threaten the trees, Hiroto looked for tracks. Signs always told a story.

The black ground was too hard to leave good prints, but the moss once smashed grew differently than what was around it. There were the marks of normal sandals, and then much larger footfalls, heavy enough to crush the moss flat. The two had fought back and forth for quite some time, covering a lot of distance. He examined a cut on a tree. From the height and angle, it had come from someone extremely tall. Deep cuts. *Incredible strength.* Twin blades... *An odd weapon.* There were other cuts in the bark. The oni had fought with a wild and ferocious style. Then he found the dried blood where the oni had finally struck true. He followed the trail. These rocks had been stained green. *Paint?* He touched it. No... it had the consistency of dried sap... *So oni bleed green. Curious.* The smell was completely alien. He spied something else lying on the rocks, something out of place. He picked it up.

And then Kaneto's chest exploded.

There was a *whoosh-crack* and a flash of light. Motokane's shouting was suddenly interrupted as the bodyguard's blood sprayed him in the face. Bits of meat and armor rained out of the sky, making ripples across the stream. Kaneto dropped to his knees, lifeless, and then flopped forward with a splash.

The wound on his chest must have been incredibly hot because it boiled the stream around it. Steam rose through the giant hole in Kaneto's back.

The samurai's reaction was near instant. Spears were lifted, arrows were nocked, only they had no target for their wrath.

"Where'd that come from?" Motokane shouted.

Hiroto had dropped his bundles, crouched behind a tangle of roots, and was listening carefully. The lightning strike had made his ears ring, but besides the warrior's heavy breathing, he caught a rapid series of *thumps* as the oni danced from tree to tree. It was pulling back to watch from a position of safety... toying with them.

That meant they had some time before the killing would resume. The odd item he had found was still clenched in his fist, so Hiroto opened his hand to study it. The thing was too big, it ended in an obsidian claw, and the exposed meat was bright green instead of decaying red, but from the joints and knuckles, it was clearly a finger.

So Hōjō Murashige must have challenged the oni to a duel, it had accepted, and lost a finger in the process... No wonder it preferred to attack from ambush.

"Why won't this damned thing come out and fight us like a proper warrior?" Motokane grumbled as they trudged through the forest.

"Because it isn't stupid," Hiroto muttered from the back of the line.

"What was that?" he demanded.

They were going back along the same trail they had come in on. Ostensibly to *find better ground to fight on*—or so the official declared. Hiroto assumed it was because Motokane had realized he was in over his head, but he didn't want to lose face by outright calling it a retreat.

Hiroto kept his voice down. It wasn't a low-born porter's place to offer tactical advice to samurai, but he did not feel that the demon was near enough to eavesdrop. "A clever hunter pits his strengths against his prey's weakness. He does not pit his weakness against his prey's strengths."

"Nonsense," Motokane spat. "He's just dishonest like

you! Now shut up and keep moving!"

They continued walking, but a few moments later the nearest samurai whispered to Hiroto, "What did you mean by that, hunter?"

"It knows we are strong in close combat. The Hōjō was a good swordsman. The demon fought him, katana against some odd manner of dual blade. It won, but left behind a finger. A costly mistake. It will not be so foolish to face one of us head on again."

"Ah... I see..." The samurai was carrying a tetsubo, a heavy war club, a fearsome weapon which wouldn't do him much good when the invisible oni returned and blasted them with lightning bolts from the tree tops. "Unfortunate."

Since Hiroto had assumed most of them would die poorly, he had not bothered to learn all their names, but this one did not seem as dense as the others. "What do they call you again?"

"Nobuo."

His attention had been elsewhere during the attack. "Did you see the fire kami mark your companion? The three sparks?"

"Yes, but I did not react in time. I saw light flickering on his breastplate, but the heat made me slow. At first I thought it was a trick of the eyes. Then it was too late. Kaneto's death is my fault."

He was still not sure what purpose the sparks served. "How long did they linger before the lightning struck?"

"They were already there when I looked over, for how long before that I don't know. Then only the space of a few heartbeats before I was nearly blinded by the flash."

"Hmmm..." At first he'd suspected the sparks held

some spiritual significance, but now... Nipponese archers trained to see their target then draw and release in one smooth movement, but the archers of the Song dynasty he had trained with always drew, then paused to sight down the shaft before release. "It sounds as if the demon uses the fire kami to *aim*. This knowledge may prove useful."

They continued on for a time in silence. Hiroto could not currently hear the demon stalking them. He assumed that was because it had waited for them to leave the stream, and now it was skinning and hanging Kaneto from a tree. He had been tempted to stay and wait in ambush, but Motokane had ordered his men to move out. Faced with the choice, Hiroto had decided that live bait was more valuable than dead.

"Hunter, another question."

"Please do not call me that. The oni might be listening."

"Apologies."

Hiroto sighed, because samurai apologized to low-born laborers *so very often*. "What is it, Nobuo?"

"We have seen this hunter's strengths. What are yours?"

"I am a fast learner."

———

The next attack came at sundown.

Hiroto saw a single leaf fall from a tree fifty paces to their side, then a few moments later a branch vibrated high in a tree thirty paces ahead. The blessing of Hachiman—god of warriors—was upon him, because if they were anywhere other than the unnatural stillness of Aokigahara, he would not have sensed it.

"The oni is here," he whispered.

Nobuo quietly repeated that to the next samurai in line,

who repeated it to Motokane, who immediately ruined any chance of an effective response by shouting, "Halt!"

Spears and arrows were readied. The warriors watched the thick undergrowth, wary. Hiroto acted the frightened porter and ducked behind a tree. Several tense seconds passed.

Three flickering sparks appeared on Zensuke's helmet.

"Look out!" Nobuo shouted as he hurled himself against his companion. As they collided there was another whip-crack of sound and a brilliant flash. The two samurai fell in a shower of sparks.

Hiroto had seen exactly where that bolt had come from. He quickly dumped the satchels from the bamboo shaft he'd been carrying. His real cargo had been hidden inside all along.

One of the samurai—he had not bothered to remember this one's name—launched an arrow into the branches. To his credit, he was close, yet not close enough. The oni must have felt rushed, because the three sparks did not linger this time, and the bolt struck the warrior low. The resulting blast still sent him flipping through the air. One of his legs flew in the opposite direction.

Careful not to cut himself on one of the specially prepared arrow heads, Hiroto retrieved his bow. He had it strung and had taken up one of his poisoned arrows before the crippled samurai landed.

The oni was hurling lightning down upon the samurai like he was Raijin the thunder god. Another warrior drew his katana and screamed a challenge, but the oni had learned the hard way what happens when you duel with a samurai, so it blew his arm off instead. As Motokane ran away a tree exploded next to him, and the official was lost from view in a cloud of splinters.

Hiroto had guessed right. The oni concentrated on the warriors and ignored the supposed peasant. Like him, it only enjoyed hunting dangerous game.

That had been a terrible mistake.

Focusing on the source of the lightning, Hiroto raised his bow and brought it down as he drew. The instant his thumb touched his jaw he let fly. The oni was still invisible, but its angry roar told him that he had struck true.

Yet Hiroto did not let up. He had once pierced a great northern bear six times and it had still retained the strength to charge him. Surely a demon would be tougher. In the blink of an eye he launched another arrow, and then another. This time when the oni moved, he saw it. Light seemed to twist and reflect, like staring into a diamond, and for the first time, he saw it was truly shaped as a man.

Another arrow went into its chest. The oni dropped from the tree. Hiroto could not see if it landed on its feet or its back. He would hope for the best and expect the worst.

Zensuke was screaming in pain. Because of Nobuo's quick reactions his sode had been hit instead of his helmet, but there was a glowing molten hole through the iron shoulder plate and the lacquer had caught on fire. Nobuo had taken out his tanto and was slicing through the cords before his friend cooked to death in his own armor.

He could only hide so many of his own arrows inside the bamboo pole, so he picked up Zensuke's quiver as he ran past them. "It is wounded. Follow when you can."

Hiroto leapt through the bushes, arrow nocked, ready to draw the instant he saw light bend. There were insects and lizards which could become the same color as the ground around them; apparently this oni's magic worked far better, but in a similar manner. Cautiously, he approached the spot where the oni had fallen.

There was more of the green blood splattered across the rocks. It turned out that when it was fresh, the oni's blood glowed like a smashed firefly. There was a lot of blood, but considering he thought he had struck it with four arrows, not enough. The light was fading quickly, which would make the glowing blood trail easier to follow.

The other samurai caught up a moment later. Nobuo had gotten Zensuke's burning armor removed in time, but the other samurai's shoulder was a bloody, charred mess. His right arm hung useless. He had to be in terrible pain, but he hid it behind a mask of grim determination, and carried his katana in his left hand.

"That's its blood?" Nobuo gestured with his war club. "Then we can track it!"

"Wait," Hiroto said as he knelt and picked up a broken arrow shaft. It was slick with the green slime. "I coated these arrow heads in a concentrated poison made from the venom of a jellyfish some pearl divers introduced me to. Its sting causes weakness, paralysis, and usually death. I do not know what it will do to a demon, but we will give the poison a moment to work."

Samurai considered poison a cowardly and dishonorable way to kill, but Nobuo and Zensuke did not protest. At this point they only wanted to survive. Surprisingly, Motokane found them a minute later. Hiroto wasn't surprised to see he was still alive—officials were more survivable than rats—but rather that he wasn't in the process of running back to Kamakura.

"Everyone else is dead."

Hiroto had assumed that by the way it had violently blasted their limbs off. He gave a noncommittal grunt in response to the news. It was time. Hiroto began following the spilled blood.

———

The poison did not kill it, but either it or the arrow wounds were having some effect. Earlier the demon had been effortlessly leaping from tree top to tree top. Now it was sticking to the ground, and from the relative strength of the glow, it felt like they were catching up.

The ghostly forest was eerie in the dark. There was a full moon, which was enough to keep them from breaking their necks, but not much beyond that. It made the trail extremely easy to follow… perhaps a little too easy. If he were wounded, and a hunting party was following his blood trail, he would use that to his advantage to set an ambush, or lead them straight into some prepared traps.

"Motokane, you should take the lead."

"What? Why?"

"From all this blood, the oni appears to be weakening and dying. It should be a man of your status who gets the honor of striking the killing blow on behalf of the shogun."

Sadly, Motokane wasn't that gullible. "I don't feel like catching the first lightning bolt, hunter. Nobuo! Follow that trail."

Like a good dutiful samurai, Nobuo did as he was told. That was a waste. Hiroto thought the lad had potential.

The trail led them steadily downhill. The footing was treacherous. Nobuo tried to listen for danger over the clumsy crashing and slipping of the exhausted samurai. The demon staying on solid ground rather than shifting branches made it harder to hear. He thought he caught the hissing insect noise a few times, but could not be sure.

Nobuo signaled for them to stop. "Hunter, come look at this."

He left Zensuke and Motokane and crept forward. Nobuo had followed the blood to a narrow path with stagnant pond water to both sides. Trudging through that mud would make for slow going. It was a splendid place for an ambush. When he reached him, Nobuo was pointing at something ahead. There was quite a bit of glowing firefly splatter on the land bridge, as if the demon had stopped for a bit. Even as keen as Hiroto's vision was it took him a moment to spot the danger. There was a tiny reflection of blood light against something metallic hidden among the roots.

It had to be some manner of trap. "Good eye."

But then Hiroto noticed something the less experienced warrior had not. After setting the trap, the blood continued across the land, and then turned sharply to the side as the demon had doubled back through the pond, where its dripping blood would be swallowed from view.

It was circling behind them.

When the trap was sprung—probably a snare or a spring noose—against the lead man, the sound would draw their attention forward, and then it would assault the rear. There were only four of them left. It could take half of them in one move. Hiroto grabbed Nobuo by one of the horns on his helmet, dragged him close, and whispered, "Count to thirty. Then set off the trap." He picked up a rock and shoved it toward him. "Throw this at it."

Then he began creeping back toward Zensuke and

Motokane. With luck, he would be in position to put an arrow into the demon as soon as it moved. As soon as he could make out the other two in the dark, he hunkered down, wiped the sweat from his eyes, and waited for Nobuo to finish his count.

There was a thunk as the rock was tossed... The whole forest erupted with yellow light.

That was most unexpected.

The demon hadn't set a normal trap. He had summoned the fires of Jigoku. Nobuo had been hurled through the air. Sparks were falling from the sky like rain. It was like being beneath an erupting volcano. Rocks big enough to split a skull crashed through the branches. Hiroto covered his head as fiery debris fell all around him.

Rather than fear, he felt a pang of jealousy. *If I had weapons such as this, there is nothing I could not hunt!*

Hiroto could barely see, but the three red dots climbing up his arm were clear as day, but he lost them as they crawled onto his chest. Instinctively, he flung his body to the side.

The tree he'd been leaning against came apart. Splinters pierced his skin.

He was the one who had hurt the oni so now he was its greatest threat. Somehow it had picked him out... The oni could see in the dark!

Hiroto rolled to his feet and ran, trying to put more trees between his body and the oni's fury. Lightning struck. Branches came crashing down. Rocks shattered into a million stinging pieces. Bushes burst into flame. Hiroto dove behind a boulder. When the boulder wasn't immediately cleaved in two, Hiroto risked a peek over the top.

The oni's trap had set some of the tree tops ablaze. It

was still using its magical trickery, somehow forcing the air to obscure its form, but that did not work so well near a flickering fire. It looked like pieces of broken glass, piled in the shape of a tall man, each bit reflecting the fire in slightly the wrong direction.

Zensuke had seen it, too. He lifted his katana in one hand and charged, screaming a battle cry. The light twisted around where the oni's head must be, facing the new threat. A refracting glow that could only be an arm rose, and two gleaming blades leapt from the end of it.

Hiroto rose, drew back the bow string, and let fly.

The arrow sped across the forest and disappeared into the demon's unnatural form. He heard it sink deep into flesh.

Dead center. A man would perish in seconds, but not this damnable oni. The pile of broken glass and flames remained standing. But everything had a weak spot. Like his father had taught him, *the arrow knows the way.* As it prepared to meet Zensuke, Hiroto nocked another arrow. The long bow creaked, power gathering in his hands. *Find the way.* Hiroto set the arrow free.

This time he had been focused on the arm. If it had no heart, then he would cripple its limbs.

The arrow sailed across the forest. It struck in a flash of blue.

Yet the arm still came down, slicing Zensuke in half.

As the samurai went sailing past both sides of the demon, Hiroto truly saw it for the first time. His last arrow had broken the evil spell! Gray beneath the fire and moon, it was truly a giant, easily two feet taller than the biggest samurai, with a too-large head made of shining metal, hair like a sadhu monk, and a body covered in a fisherman's net.

PREDATOR: IF IT BLEEDS

When it realized Hiroto was staring right at it, the oni reached for its wrist, clawed fingers dancing—probably casting a spell—only there was an arrow shaft blocking the way.

"Enough of your tricks, demon!" Hiroto shouted as he sent another arrow across the forest. That one punctured the demon's stomach. The next struck it in the leg.

The boulder in front of him disintegrated and Hiroto found himself hurled through the air. It turned out the demon didn't need to use the three sparks to aim its lightning after all, though it did help the accuracy.

He hit the ground so hard it knocked the wind out of him. Worse, he lost his bow. From the burning bushes he could see that he was near the edge of the pond. Twenty paces away, Nobuo was lying in the mud, breathing, but knocked unconscious, his helmet visibly dented by the demon's incredible trap.

The oni was coming. It had completely given up on stealth, and its heavy footfalls could be heard crashing against the rocks, getting closer and closer. He had no weapons. Nobuo's swords were too far away. His only hope was to hide and perhaps surprise it... He was an excellent fighter with just his hands, but his opponents weren't usually as big as a horse.

Gasping for breath, Hiroto crawled into the reeds. As he tried desperately to fill his lungs with air, he found himself wishing he had a hollow reed to breathe through. Now that would have been handy for hiding. As the demon got closer, he held his breath and sunk beneath the muck.

He was trying so very hard not to move to avoid ripples, not even daring to exhale because it would make bubbles.

Even with his eyes open he could see nothing through the thick silt, but he felt the water vibrate as the demon stomped right past him. Either it hadn't seen him, or it was going to finish off Nobuo first instead.

Hiroto's hand bumped into something. Wooden, but sanded smooth. His fingers drifted along it until it was touching the first embedded metal spike... Hachiman had smiled upon him once again.

As he slowly, painfully, silently lifted himself from the murk, he saw that the oni was looming over Nobuo. Arrow shafts were embedded across its body, each wound leaking green. The oni may have been an unnatural being, but its emotions were as clear as any performer telling a story with only a dance. The oni was *furious*. Nobuo wasn't the warrior who had filled its body with painful arrows! It lifted its arm blades to kill him anyway.

Hiroto had been trying to rise as quietly as possible, but something gave him away; maybe it was the pond water dripping from the spikes of Nobuo's war club, or the sucking sound of his body leaving the mud, but regardless, the oni heard. It spun about, braids whipping, drawing itself up, so that it towered overhead.

He never understood why it didn't strike him down in that moment, but the oni paused, just for a heartbeat, confused, as if Hiroto were the invisible one.

Hiroto smashed it with the tetsubo.

He'd been aiming for its metal head, but its sudden movement caused him to strike it in the shoulder instead. Glowing blood flew as flesh was pulverized.

The solid blow would have shattered human bones. The oni lurched to the side, but stayed upright. With a roar he hit it with another overhand strike. The pressure caused blood to squirt from the various arrow holes. Then Hiroto swung the heavy weapon in an arc, striking the oni's extended leg. Something snapped deep within and it went to its knees.

Except kneeling, it was still as tall as Hiroto. The twin blades lashed out. He blocked it with the tetsubo but the demon metal cut right through the wood as if it wasn't there and still retained the power to slice cleanly through his face.

It was the worst pain he had ever experienced, worst he had ever *imagined*. He fell. The blow had rattled his brain. The world was spinning. All Hiroto could do was hold on. But something else was wrong. Desperate, sick, he reached up, felt along the two burning cuts to the empty socket where his left eye had once been, and screamed.

Through his remaining eye, he watched the oni try to stand, but its broken leg buckled. In his life he had seen thousands of things die. Something about the way the oni was moving told him that it was done for. Hiroto would perish, smug in the knowledge that his killer would follow soon after. The oni began crawling toward him. Hiroto tried to stand, but his body would not cooperate, all he could do was scoot backwards.

"Hunter!" Nobuo had woken up. He was too far to get there in time, but he threw something.

It was a good thing Nobuo's sword was still sheathed, because it landed right in Hiroto's lap.

The oni was bearing down on him. It pulled back its fist, blades aimed at his heart. Hiroto drew and slashed in one smooth movement.

The katana went through half the demon's chest. Green blood flew across the forest in a long arc. The two of them remained there a moment, mangled face to metal face. The demon twitched. The twin blades slowly dropped. He twisted the blade free, and Three Sparks, the Oni of Aokigahara, was no more.

Hiroto was in terrible pain, but he laughed anyway. The summer of death was over. It had been a fine hunt.

As they limped out of the forest, they came upon Ashikaga Motokane, hiding inside the trunk of a hollow tree.

"You're still alive! Is it done?" the official asked as he slowly climbed out.

Hiroto's face was being held together with stitches and dried blood, and his newfound lack of depth perception was making him nauseous. He was not in the mood, so continued walking.

"Were you hiding in there all night?" Nobuo asked.

"Yes. And I was all alone! Because some bodyguard you are!"

Hiroto didn't even look back when he heard Nobuo's sword clear its sheath. There was a gurgle, and then the sound of a head bouncing down the rocks. The young samurai rejoined him a moment later, cleaning his katana on his filthy sleeve. "When we report to the shogun, it was a shame there were no other survivors."

"Yes, a terrible shame."

Nasu Hiroto knelt before the shogun. Their report had been delivered. The magnificent trophy he had presented to Minamoto Yoritomo was on the floor between them. Now they were alone. The shogun had dismissed everyone else from the room so that the two of them could speak privately.

"The eye patch suits you, Hiroto. What do you intend to do now?"

"If you aren't going to execute me for deserting all those years ago, then I'm unsure."

"When we last spoke, I came to understand something about you. Other samurai try their whole lives to make a mask that never shows fear, that declares they live for battle, hiding their true weakness beneath. For you, there is no mask. You only feel alive when you are hunting something capable of taking your life. Nothing else will do."

Hiroto nodded. The shogun was truly a wise man.

"Your report has inspired me. I think it has given me the answer to a problem which I have struggled with for the last few years." The shogun leaned forward and picked up the oni's mask. "We could learn much from the Oni of Aokigahara. Invisible. Calculating. Hiding in plain sight, then attacking with ruthless efficiency, leaving his enemies filled with dread… The ultimate assassin."

"To be stalked by such would bring nightmares to even the bravest samurai."

"Indeed. What if I offered you the opportunity to never be bored again? A hunt which never ends?"

"I am intrigued."

"The Shogunate has many enemies, dangerous men. Often politics make it so that I cannot deal with them directly. The oni has shown me the answer. I have need of invisible killers, inspired by this beast, who make its way theirs. Men who will engage in irregular warfare which most samurai would find distasteful." The shogun stared into the blank eyes of the mask. "In short, I require men who can fight like *demons*."

Hiroto was becoming excited. "Such an endeavor would have to be done with the utmost secrecy."

"They would be the hidden men, *shinobi-no-mono*, emulating the Oni of Aokigahara to bring ruin upon the enemies of Nippon. Would you build this organization for me, Nasu Hiroto?"

"It would be an honor."

The first ninja bowed to the first shogun.

THE PILOT

BY ANDREW MAYNE

She smiles over her shoulder at me as we head for the fence and the water just beyond. That was the smile that got me. Sure, watching her climb over the railing in those tight jean shorts didn't hurt. But it was that mischievous smile that never let me go. It's the last thing I think about before the blinding white light and the thought that this is how I'm going to die.

The next thing I'm aware of is a man in a commander's uniform sitting by my bedside, sipping a cup of tea. Also that it's really goddamn cold and I appear to be babbling on about how when I was eleven and accidentally glued my fingers to my model Spitfire I'd stayed up all night making.

The commander seems not very amused by my anecdote and the bald man next to him, wearing a thick gray coat and no military piping, has an even more frustrated look on his face.

"Captain Moore, the commander was asking about the radar on your plane. Do you know the estimated range?"

Ah, snap. Now I get it. It's coming back to me. I was doing a flyover of some tiny speck in the East Siberian Sea because a satellite picked up an infrared flash and we got a weird seismic signal.

At some point I must have got hit—which is really, really hard to do with an SR-71. Fact is, I think I may be the first. Well, crap. Although I don't remember getting hit—there was some kind of bright light and all my instruments decided to take the night off. After that... I'm not sure when I ejected, but I'm pretty sure my bird was on a trajectory that would have taken her into the Laptev Sea—making her a bit hard for the Ruskies to salvage. I hope.

I can't remember if I hit water or land, but from how sore everything feels, my money is on that I landed on the sharpest pile of rocks in all of Mother Russia.

The commander says something in Russian a little too quickly for me to understand. I know enough to get by and tell what their pilots are talking about when we pick up their chatter in the air—usually their fat wives in Minsk and their pretty girlfriends in Moscow—but not enough to make sense of rapid-fire conversation.

The bald man adjusts the IV drip and for the first time I notice the room around me. There's some medical equipment and strange-looking Soviet machinery, but it doesn't appear to be a hospital. The trusses and restraints remind me of the stuff in Grandpa's barn where he'd castrate bulls. It's all lit by gas lanterns—which just reminds me how weird Russia really is.

I glance at the IV and realize that the painkiller has been making me loopy and probably a bit talkative—which was the idea.

"The radar, Captain Moore, what is the operational range?" the bald man asks again. I realize that he's been speaking in perfect American English—okay, not quite perfect; he's got a bit of an East Coast affectation about it.

So this is the game: get old Billy here to start spilling his guts about the Blackbird. No, sir. Kelly Johnson himself would come out of retirement and take me to Grandpa's barn and do worse to me than these commies if I revealed any of her secrets.

"Did I tell you about the time Julie Conner and I decided to go take a skinny-dip in the reservoir?" It's my go-to happy thought and how I refuse to let them cage me in mentally.

The commander says something I'm pretty sure means, "Take away his painkillers and put him in a…" I think he meant "cell," but the word sounded a lot like kennel.

Clang clang… clang

Two clangs, a pause, followed by another clang means the guard with the fur cap is coming, according to the code I've worked up with the Chinese pilot at the other end of the metal pipe running through my cell.

They brought him in a few hours after me. He must have been doing an overflight in a JZ-8 and suffered the same malfunction I did.

From the looks of the burned-out light bulbs and the fact that I haven't seen a single working piece of electronics, I suspect that whatever took us down also affected the whole base—or "Agricultural Resource Institute" as it's listed on the maps.

Ping, as I've come to think of him over the last two days, must have been more banged up than I was. Despite that, he put up a bit of a fight from the commotion I could hear down the hall when they put him into his cell.

From the sound of gunfire I heard go off, it looks like Ping may have gotten hold of an AK-47. But after the beating they gave him, he'd hadn't made a whisper until I started banging my spoon on the metal pipe, seeing if anyone was at the other end.

I tried for a few hours with no response. Then sometime late at night—I think it was late at night—he responded. I don't have a watch or a window to tell me when—not that one would help much this far above the Arctic Circle.

The first response was a clang like the one I'd made. I tried tapping out a little Morse code, but evidently they didn't teach him that in flight school. So we had to get creative.

If you put your ear real close to the pipe you can hear all kinds of sounds: footsteps, squeaking doors, men arguing and even rats scurrying through the walls.

We settled on a very simple code. The first series of taps was an object like a door or a man. The next one was an action.

Two clangs was a man, probably Mr. Fur Cap. After the pause was an action. In this case one clang meant "walking" or "coming."

A rat was four clangs. We figured that out after we recognized the squeaking sound. If we heard a rat scurrying along, that would be *clang clang clang clang... clang*.

Ping tried to simplify the system by speeding up the clang sounds indicating that a fast series was supposed to be multiplied by itself: *clangclang* was supposed to be four clangs and *clangclang clang* was five, *clangclangclang* was nine, but doing the math made my head hurt. It was enough to keep track of what each number represented.

For really complicated objects that we couldn't hear in the walls, Ping came through with another clever idea: a way to send pictures...

Ping started by making a series like *clang clang clang clangclang clang clang... clang clangclang clangclang clangclang clangclang clangclang...* and so on. It was so complicated I had to scratch them into the wall with my spoon just to keep track.

It took me an hour to realize he'd sent me a picture of a stick figure man, kind of like the ones on my nephew's Atari. That clever Chinaman. If they ever give up that communist nonsense, watch out world.

Two days later we had a series of clangs for men, guns, doors, aircraft and even a map of the prison.

I started etching the words under my mat, so my jailers didn't find what looked like an escape plan—which it wasn't, because we were stuck on a tiny little rock covered with Russian special forces in the middle of the Siberian Sea.

This was just a way to entertain ourselves. And since Ping wasn't much for personal questions or games, building the clang-language was all there was to do between interrogation sessions—which I was getting fewer of since Ping showed up.

Clang clang clang... clang, Ping tapped. That meant men were coming and one of us was going to get worked over by Commander Ratface—Ping's name for the commander who first interrogated me.

I stared at my door, waiting to see if the boots stopped here or kept walking. I felt bad hoping that they were going to keep moving—because that meant they were going to pay a visit to Ping, and they always seemed to go a little rougher on him.

The key turned in the lock and the bald man, Jennings was his name, stood there with Ratface. Behind them was the short dark-haired sadist named Vostov they used to hold me down.

He walked into my cell, slipped an arm around my neck and put me in a chokehold. I didn't resist. I knew the routine by now, and so far it wasn't working out too well for either of us.

They'd ask me a question about my mission, I'd tell them about the color of Julie Conner's panties the first time she let me catch a glimpse of them and Vostov would squeeze my neck until I passed out.

He'd tried pain points, but discovered since the bailout there wasn't much more you could inflict on me.

In my five sessions over the last two days, I've managed to learn several things—probably more than they've learned from me.

These men are not expert torturers. This isn't even a prison. They probably never expected to have an American pilot here.

Also, I've come to realize they appear to be totally cut off from their superiors. On top of the storm that was raging across the region, the EMP that took out my radio also fried theirs.

"Captain Moore, why did your superiors send you to spy?"

"There were little blue flowers," I reply. "Tiny ones. She was sixteen and all I could think to myself was, did her bra

316

match as well? Was she even wearing one? Of course, I found out when we took that skinny-dip in the resa…"

Lights out.

When I come to I'm on the floor, looking up at Ratface. He's got a pistol pointed at my balls and is yelling at Jennings to translate something. Of course, if he spoke slower, I could do it myself, but I haven't let on that I speak any Ruskie.

"What do you know about the other airman?" asks Jennings.

"It was cold that day, but oh boy! It was even colder for Julie. I quickly forgot about those little blue flowers."

Ratface gun-whips me and I see stars.

"Are you aware of any others like the airman?"

"Lots," I reply, before reminding myself I need to be antagonizing them. "Lots of guys would have given anything to see Julie like I did that day. Man, oh man."

Jennings squats down next to me and holds out a hand, motioning Ratface to wait before striking me again.

"I know you think you're being clever, Captain Moore, but there's much more at stake than your parochial little geopolitical posturing."

"Did you defect because there was nobody left who wanted to listen to you?" I tilt my head toward Vostov, standing in the corner. "Comrade, could you choke me out again so I don't have to listen to this traitorous piece of garbage?"

This gets a reaction from Ratface who yells at Jennings. Clearly the defector has some kind of authority, because he's able to yell back at the Russian officer.

"Whose balls did you lick?" I say to Jennings.

"Amusing. My reasons for working with the Soviets are more complicated than politics. Suffice to say that I was interested in areas of scientific research that had fallen out of fashion in the West.

"Which brings me to the critical question that will decide if you live another twenty-four hours. What, if anything, do you know about the incident that occurred here?"

"If you thought Julie Conner's tits were something to look at, touching them was…"

Jennings, who had been the calm one up until now, slaps me across the face and yells to Vostov in Russian, "After we leave, beat him as much as you want."

Jennings and Ratface get up to leave. Vostov gives me a half smile, unaware that I know what's going to happen next… or is supposed to happen next.

I pull myself to a seated position on my mattress while Vostov shuts the door behind him. He's become so used to my not putting up a fight the poor bastard thinks he has the upper hand.

What he doesn't realize is that I took this mission prepared to die. I even had a suicide capsule in my flight suit. To other guys it was a joke. Not to me.

Every time I strapped on my pressure suit and squeezed into that tiny cockpit I knew there was a chance it was a one-way mission. I also knew that if I got caught behind enemy lines, my one and only duty was to make sure secrets that could cost American lives didn't fall into enemy hands.

Some guys struggle with this. Not me. I was ready to lay down my life without hesitation. I knew that back when I took that skinny-dip with Julie Conner. Billy, I said to myself, this is the best day of your life. Everything that comes after is just an afterthought.

Vostov cracks his ape-like knuckles and strides toward me.

He doesn't notice that my hands are in the space between the mattress and the wall where I keep the spoon I'd used to carve the code Ping and I created—the spoon I'd took the bowl off, so I could use it like a sharp pick to etch into the concrete.

Vostov holds my head against the wall, getting ready to punch me. As his arm rears back, I throw out my own fist, clenching my shiv, and hit him right in the kidney.

His eyes bug out as he tries to process what just happened. I stab him under the jaw in his neck and he stumbles backwards. The spoon handle is yanked from my fist as he falls against the other wall.

Warm blood starts gushing out over his fingers as he tries to close the wound.

I get to my feet, too filled with adrenaline to notice my own pain. Vostov makes flailing motions as he tries to stop me from rifling through his pockets for the key.

A blood-soaked hand clenches my face, but I swat it away. His heart just can't pump hard enough to keep him going.

My chances of escape are somewhere between zero and nonexistent—but it's not the plan. My plan is suicide—death by Russian Army.

When they put my star and no name on that memorial marker at CIA headquarters, I want it to be because I died trying to escape, not because I froze to death or spilled my guts so they would trade me back for some Soviet spy.

I find the key to the lock and get ready to burst into the hallway and fight the first man I see, maybe even getting his AK like Ping did and take out a few of them on the way.

Ping… would he want to get in on this suicide mission? Maybe he thinks his masters back in Beijing are willing to trade for him and it's not worth the risk. Should I even ask? Why not?

I tap a series of clangs, the one I use for me and the one for him, followed by "door" and "move."

There's a long pause—probably only five seconds, but it feels like a day. Then: *clangclang.*

Yes.

Then it gets weird. Ping taps something that seems to mean if I get him out, his friends will come get us.

Which doesn't make any sense, because the Chinese aren't about to invade Russia on the account of us.

But whatever. We'd both rather die on our feet than in here.

I head into the hallway, looking for a weapon—a spare AK-47, a pistol, anything—but all I can find is a wooden chair.

I take it and go down the flight of stairs to the level below me. There's a big elevator, but I'm sure it's been dead since the blackout.

At the bottom of the steps I spot a guard sitting in front of a gas lantern, his rifle by his side and his back to the wall near a massive door.

Since he's the only other person in this wing, I assume this is Ping's cell.

"I bring chair," I say in Russian so bad the soldier just stares at me, trying to figure out if I'm mildly retarded.

He doesn't know if I'm supposed to be in my cell or outside running errands. It doesn't matter after I grab the top rail and swing the edge of the seat into his face.

His nose shatters in a spray of blood and he falls out of his seat. Before I remove the massive metal beam holding Ping's door shut, I have to slide the unconscious man out of the way.

I sling his rifle over my shoulder then open the door to Ping's dark cell. The first thing that greets me is a pungent, almost acidic smell.

It's a big chamber and the light from the lantern barely makes it past the door frame. I pick it up and move closer.

"Ping? Um, *Clang*? You in there, pal?"

Clangclang

Yes.

My light falls onto some medical carts and equipment. There's a whole rack of scalpels covered in a yellowish fluid.

I push them out of the way and go toward the sound in the back of the room. "What the hell are they doing to you in here?"

There's a kneeling man with a hood over his head, his arms bound in chains, stretching from one side of the room to the other.

Even though he's on his knees, I can tell he's a big boy.

"How the hell did they fit you into a cockpit?"

He pulls at a chain attached to the metal pipe and clangs out a message: *Big plane.*

It must not have been a JZ-8. I set the lantern down on a cart and reach for Ping's hood.

"Sweet Mother of God!" I blurt out when I see his face. "You're not Chinese!"

It's like every creature I ever pulled out of the creek, all smashed into one nightmare. I'm too shocked to be frightened.

"Did they do this to you?" I ask, trying to comprehend how a man could have such a horror show for a face. Then I look around at his body and realize that everything is wrong. His skin has a sickly greenish-white hue. The musculature is all off and his hands aren't anything that evolved on God's green earth.

And those eyes—those tiny yellow-silver balls—they're just... alien.

Other pilots have told stories about picking up strange radar reflections at altitudes too high for planes. I've even heard of accounts of pursuits after phantoms. But those were just... stories.

Worry about the present, Billy.

I realize that battery acid smell is coming from him. I spot several oozing wounds with a greenish-yellow liquid dripping from them. It's not pus or infected—it's the kind of thing an eight-foot tall spider would leak if you poked it.

"Ping?" I say again.

Clangclang

Yes.

I grab my rifle and contemplate running for my life. Then I realize it isn't really worth much right now. And besides, a promise is a promise.

I fumble through Vostov's bloody keys and go over to the lock holding Ping to one wall.

"You're uh, not planning to invade us, are you?"

Ping just watches me. I'm not sure if he grasps the question.

I unlock his wrists and he stands upright.

Jesus.

My neck hurts staring up at him. He's at least seven foot tall. Definitely not Chinese.

His webbed fingers reach out and grab the AK-47. Moving almost too fast for me to see, he field-strips the gun, inspects the parts then puts it back together and pushes it into my chest, clearly not impressed.

He moves through the room, searching through the carts, then reaches up and yanks down the light fixture from the ceiling and begins to take it apart. I put on the guard's uniform and boots because I'm freezing my ass off. Ping doesn't seem to care.

"You making a ray gun or something?" I ask, looking at what he's doing, terrified of what it could be.

Ping creases the metal on the floor and bends the casing into something that looks like a huge machete.

He inspects the blade in the lantern light. It's crude but deadly.

"So how do you think we should go about this..." I start to ask, but Ping is already moving toward the door.

Fast.

Real fast.

I chase after him, doing my best to keep up, but he's already halfway down the upper hallway by the time I exit the steps.

Ping comes to a stop at the locked door that leads to the soldier barracks. I throw him the key ring.

He unlocks it then bursts into the other room before I can tell him to wait up and let the AK help us out.

It doesn't make a difference. By the time I'm in the barracks there are bodies everywhere. The soldiers who managed to get to their weapons fired indiscriminately, killing their own.

Ping is using a limp body as a shield and flinging cots left and right. I squeeze off a few rounds at men trying to shoot at Ping from a shielded position—hesitating only slightly at the thought that I'm firing on my own race. Yeah, well, they never should have asked Vostov to beat me to death.

Ping grabs a man and flings him across the room, his neck snapping as he slams into a concrete wall.

Blood and broken bodies litter the floor. And silence.

I survey the massacre. At least twenty men are dead—all in under two minutes.

Ping's blade is bent and covered in gore.

Footsteps come from the other hallway. I rush to the door, aim my AK down the corridor and start picking off soldiers as they race to the barracks to see what the commotion was about.

Catching them off guard, I manage to drop six of them before they return fire and I have to go back into the barracks.

Bullets streak through the door as I hear someone scream for reinforcements.

When I look back into the room for Ping, he's gone.

What the hell?

Something grabs me by the neck and I'm lifted off the ground.

It takes me a moment to realize that Ping has managed to climb into an airshaft—a miracle given his size—and pulled me inside.

He's already racing through the conduit like a greyhound by the time I orientate myself.

I give chase and find even more momentum when the tunnel starts to get barraged by automatic weapon fire.

A hole emerges inches from my knees and I spot a terrified soldier staring up at the shaft. He knows what just got loose. I'm not sure if I do, but I'm starting to get an idea.

I don't stop to tell him that he's not shooting at the monster.

The monster… or as the Russians would say: *monstr*. Same thing.

There's a cold blast of air as Ping kicks open a vent. He found a way out and is already running across the snow toward the edge of the facility.

A group of unfortunate soldiers come running around the corner from the opposite direction and Ping slashes through them, sending one man's head rolling across the snow.

Christ Almighty.

I try to step over a massive puddle of blood, keeping up with Ping.

There are lights coming from a rise just beyond us. Generators hum over the night air. They must have been able to scrounge enough parts to get them working.

Ping has finally stopped his locomotive pace and is lying on the edge of a hill looking down below.

I crawl on my belly until I'm next to him. I try not to stare. But it's hard.

Below us, Jennings and Commander Ratface are standing in a huge crater barking orders to men with welding torches and various tools as they try to disassemble the thing that's in the middle.

A goddamn spaceship—at least part of one. The other half looks smashed up.

There's a bunch of tarps strewn over the top so our satellites can't see what's underneath.

"I'm not rocket scientist, but I'm pretty sure that bird ain't going to fly again."

Ping grabs me by the back of the head and aims my nose toward the generator at the edge of the crater, points a terrifying finger at it, then at me.

"Want me to take out the generator?"

For the first time I hear him make a sound. It's a click... actually two of them. *Clickclick.*

Yes.

So, my newfound pal wants me to march down to the middle of the crater that's filled with all of the rest of the soldiers from the base and try to take out the generator?

I asked for a suicide mission, but I wasn't counting on it being actual suicide...

Then I remember that I'm wearing the uniform I stole from the guard back at the base. At least I'll be shot in the back as I flee, and not the front as I approach.

I slide down the hill and make my way to a gap at the farthest end from the spaceship.

At any moment, I assume some survivor from the base is going to come running here, telling them what happened. While it would seem logical that the Red Army soldiers here would then race back to help their comrades, I gather Commander Ratface and Jennings would decide it more important to protect the spacecraft.

I enter the caldera and get a better glimpse of the ship. What looks like the cockpit is almost completely smashed.

I have no idea how Ping could have survived that— *unless he wasn't inside.*

Wait? Is Ping like our demolition boys who make sure our airplanes and boats don't fall into the wrong hands?

I stop halfway to the generator. That would mean Ping intends to blow this whole thing up.

Something tells me anything capable of destroying that huge craft is going to leave a crater a lot larger than the one I'm standing inside.

How do I feel about that?

Hell, if it comes between the Russians getting ahold of this tech or not, then this suicide mission got a lot more purposeful.

"Captain Moore!" Jennings yells from across the crater.

I look up from the generator and see fifty commies staring back at me. I'd been trying to find an off switch with no luck.

"Put down your weapon!" Jennings screams as he runs toward me.

Guns are trained on my body from every direction.

I hold my AK-47 in front of me and act as if I'm going to set it on the ground. Instead, I squeeze the trigger, blasting rounds into the generator, and dive toward the frozen dirt.

The lights go out.

There are screams.

Lots of screams.

Bullets whiz through the air and bodies fall. Something hits me in the side, but that part of my body is already numb.

I don't move, deciding it's best to let Ping do his thing.

Suddenly there's a greenish glow from what remains of the cockpit and the silhouette of Ping—then he vanishes.

Dead soldiers are everywhere.

Two heads come rolling toward me: Jennings and Commander Ratface.

Ping has one hell of a sense of humor.

A big hand grabs me by the neck like a kitten and yanks me to my feet.

Ping is on the move *away* from the ship.

We enter the frozen tundra and my lungs are screaming from the freezing air. Ping doesn't stop moving.

"We're going to run out of island, pretty soon, pal."

Ping isn't deterred. I get a sense it's going to be a *very* big explosion.

We reach the edge of the small bay that looked like an ancient meteor crater from the surveillance photos.

I drop to my knees, exhausted. That's when I feel my own blood trickling out my side.

The commies got me.

"Ping, it was a good run," I say through halting breaths before falling on my back and staring up at the stars.

My vision begins to fade and I hear a splash.

"Swim for it, man. Never stop."

The last thing I see is the Aurora Borealis glowing like neon overhead. It's a beautiful thing. So much brighter than I've ever seen it.

Still not as beautiful as…

———

I remember lying there for an eternity, expecting to die. At some point I think I woke up again. There was a loud explosion—louder than anything I could even imagine.

Then I passed out again.

Strange smells.

Even stranger sounds.

And now I'm floating in the water. The stars are overhead again. Crickets are chirping and I can hear frogs croaking.

It's a beautiful symphony, just like the one we heard back in the reservoir—the day I found true love and I promised Julie Conner I'd marry her one day.

I raise my hand up and look at the wedding band, reminding myself that part wasn't a dream.

I tell myself I could lay here in perfect bliss, but my back starts to hurt. I roll over and realize I'm on the bank, only half in the water.

Ping is nowhere to be found. In fact, everything is different than I remember…

I get to my feet and look around me.

The chain-link fence.

The no trespassing signs.

My elation is quickly usurped by my frustration.

I'm thousands of miles away from my base—half a world away from where I ditched out of my plane.

And I'm standing in the middle of the backwoods of Alabama wearing a Russian Army uniform.

What am I going to tell my superiors?

Hell, what am I going to tell my wife?

BUFFALO JUMP

BY   WENDY   N.   WAGNER

The corn dolly sat beside the bottle of gun oil on Anderson's desk. He wiped his hands a second time, grinning. The town of Coyote Creek had hired him as their sheriff because he could shoot a can of tobacco off a fencepost a hundred yards away, because he could hoist a drunk miner over his shoulder without throwing out his back, and because he didn't let anybody scare him, not even if they were giving him the business end of a shotgun. Somehow they'd forgotten to ask if he had a softer side.

Assured that his hands were finally clean, he picked up his daughter's latest construction and tucked it in his breast pocket. He could give the dolly back to her when he stopped by the boarding house for lunch. Big Bess Sandford liked to tell the sheriff he spoiled his little girl, but as far as he could tell, there wasn't anything spoiled about his Mina. She helped Bess around the boarding house and could help her daddy out of his boots in under thirty seconds, which was pretty good for a kid with hands as small as hers. She'd knocked the socks off the school teacher at the start of school last week, too.

Anderson adjusted his battered hat and knocked his grin into the semblance of a stern expression. He had an hour or two of patrolling before he could sneak back to Bess's place, and he'd better look the part.

The door flew open, and Max Corbin, the grocer, launched himself inside. His tongue darted out the corners of his mouth and his eyes had gone two sizes too big. He opened his mouth to talk and settled for licking his lips again, a lizard cornered by a hawk.

"What is it?"

"Bunch of men at the tavern asking about you," Max managed. "Mean-looking."

Max's store had been robbed three times before the town hired Anderson. He knew what mean looked like.

"I'll take care of it." Anderson grabbed the box of shells out of the top drawer of his desk and shoved six of them in his pocket. If things got ugly, he wasn't likely to get a chance to reload, but he liked to be prepared. He hurried out of the jailhouse.

Coyote Creek wasn't the biggest town in southern Oregon, but it sat in the middle of enough successful mining towns to draw the attention of any number of bandits, rustlers, and hustlers. Farmers up in the Willamette Valley liked to brag about how peaceful and prosperous their state was. They didn't know squat about life down here on the Californian border.

He strode into the tavern and stopped in his tracks. The black-haired man leaning on the bar was mean-looking alright; Anderson didn't know anyone meaner. He'd been running away from him since he was twenty-two years old, and he'd prayed every night that Wallace McBurnie wouldn't find him.

"Why, boys, it looks like Johnny Anderson done went and grown up." McBurnie gave the dry bark that passed for his laugh. It usually meant he was about to hit somebody, and for the ten years Anderson had lived under McBurnie's thumb, Anderson had been the nearest punching bag.

"McBurnie." Anderson looked around the room. McBurnie's men came out of the corners, closing around Anderson in an ugly circle. He recognized a few of the faces: Ugly James, Fat Malone, Piss-Bucket Johnson. The other half-dozen or so were strangers. "You lost both the Lee brothers?"

"Big Lee got stabbed by a whore down in Virginia City, that cheap sumbitch. Wee Lee's serving ten years in Wasco for robbery. He never had the same touch with a safe that you did, Johnny."

Anderson felt a surge of anger. "You let Wee Lee break a safe on a job? Are you crazy? I told you that boy didn't have the hands for it."

McBurnie lit a cheroot, his eyes fixed on Anderson even as his nimble hands struck the match. He had a way of rooting a man into place with his blue eyes, so pale they were like chips of ice struck from some mountain glacier. He blew a long stream of smoke. "You did tell me. But I had high hopes I could train him up the way I trained you."

He lifted the cheroot to his mouth again, the little cigar held between the blackened stumps of the first two fingers

333

on his right hand. He could shoot like the devil himself with his left, but he could never train it up for safecracking. Anderson's own fingers gave a twitch.

"So why are you here?"

One of the gang spat a stream of chew onto the floor. McBurnie shot him a look, and the kid Indian quailed. He had a bruise on his jaw, no doubt from McBurnie's fist. McBurnie hated chewing tobacco.

"Do I need a reason to look for my adopted son?"

Anderson raised an eyebrow.

"I need a safecracker. I've got a big score out in Malheur County, and you're the only one who can handle the safe."

"I ain't opened a safe in six years, and I ain't ever going to open one again." Anderson's hand went to the butt of the revolver sitting on his hip.

McBurnie followed the move. His eyes crawled up to the star on Anderson's breast pocket. He smiled that smile of his, the ugliest Anderson had ever seen. "I'll just give you some time to think on that."

He beckoned to the kid Indian. The boy and the rest of the gang fell in step behind him. Their shoulders bumped into Anderson's as they passed, a long string of hard thuds. He stood his ground.

The door thumped softly behind the last of the thugs.

"Reckon they saw me pull out my shotgun," the bartender called.

"Reckon that was it, Lem," Anderson called back. But he had a bad feeling things weren't over. He patted his breast pocket. Patrolling be damned. He wanted to go give his little girl her corn dolly and a hug, right this second.

After a hasty lunch, he headed out to the Nielssen ranch. Lars Nielssen was his deputy, but Anderson would have wanted his advice even if he wasn't. Lars had given Anderson a job and a place to live when no one else would. He and his wife were the closest thing to family Anderson and Mina had, and he had taught Anderson what being a sheriff and a father really meant. Six years ago, Anderson would have just run away from Wallace McBurnie and Coyote Creek. Today, he was looking for backup.

He found Eva and Lars in their barn, reshoeing their old mare. With the help of their hired hands, the old couple ran three hundred head of cattle through the canyons and gullies of Coyote Creek. They were both tough as nails and smart as the critters they named the creek for.

It took a minute or two to explain the situation, and then Lars clapped him on the shoulder. "I'm here for you, son. You know that." He turned to Eva. "Beeves got to go down to the big field tomorrow. You think you and the boys can handle that?"

Eva had already taken the mare's foot between her knees, directing a flurry of half-English, half-Norwegian orders at Lars. The big man disappeared into the house and reappeared a moment later with his rifle and his going-to-town hat.

He gave Eva a brisk kiss, and Anderson helped him load up his gear. The two men worked in silence. Lars's stolid presence settled Anderson's jitters. They'd faced down worse trouble than one small gang. It didn't matter who led this one: Anderson and Lars were a good team. They could manage this.

He believed that right up to the moment they turned the

corner of Main Street and he saw Bess Sandford standing in the middle of the street with blood running down her face.

Anderson crouched behind the fallen cottonwood, studying the gang's camp on the sandy peninsula. It had taken all evening for Lars to track the devils down to this site. It was the perfect location: impossible to sneak up on, unless you could walk on water.

Now a dense thicket of brambles and the curve of the creek stood between him and the site. The rush of the creek's current covered up any but the loudest noises, but his very bones could hear Mina calling to him for help. The flickering campfire lit up the armed men at their posts. Beside the fire, he could see Mina huddled in a nest of saddle blankets. She looked so fragile, clutching her corn dolly to her chest with her tiny bound hands. Every fiber of Anderson's being ached for her.

He crept away from the creek to the little ravine where Lars hid, divvying up shells and checking over their weapons. "They're ready for an attack." Anderson picked up a handful of pebbles and began arranging them in a semblance of the gang's camp. "It's a good site, too—the way the creek bends, they've got water on three sides."

"There's no way to sneak up on 'em."

"No." Anderson rubbed his eyes. "Goddamn it! I keep trying to come up with something, but all I can think about is Mina tied up like that."

Behind them, a man shrieked.

Anderson jumped to his feet. "What the hell was that?"

A shot echoed off the hills. Men shouted. A horse

screamed. Lars tossed Anderson a rifle and ran past him. The big man could move.

Anderson ran after him, furtiveness forgotten in the chaos. A man smashed into him, screaming in pain and fear, knocking Anderson into the creek. Anderson splashed back onto the beach, his heart racing. Mina. Jesus God, what was going on in that camp?

A searing blue light flashed and the sudden stink of burned hair and flesh filled the air. Something pattered down on him, hot and sticky. It took him a second to recognize the hunk of flesh that struck his boot as a man's hand. He kicked it off and ran faster. He passed Lars grappling a tall man. There was no time to stop and help Lars. He had to get to Mina.

"Mina!" He couldn't hear his voice, but he could feel his anger and his fear scorching in his throat.

A stream of white light flashed past him. The smoke of his own burning hair assaulted his nostrils. But he only had eyes for one thing: his daughter, now clasped in Wallace McBurnie's arms.

The gang leader ran through the campfire, charging toward the creek. Anderson jumped over the stack of saddle blankets and stumbled over the motionless form of Fat Malone. He just caught himself as a giant hand closed around McBurnie and Mina.

"Mina! Mina!"

For a second the pair hung suspended in the grasp of the hand—no, not a hand, Anderson realized, his mind finally catching up with his senses, a *net*—and then they were wrenched through the air, skipping off the surface of the creek like a flat rock. In the darkness, a tremendous slashing accompanied them, and then they were gone, vanished into the night and woods beyond the creek.

Anderson dropped to his knees. "Mina," he whispered. "Oh, baby, I'll find you. I'll find you."

It took him fifteen minutes to find Lars in the devastation of the camp. He'd only been a boy during the Civil War, but he'd grown up hearing stories of what cannon-fire did to a man, and he could only imagine that whatever that blue flash was, it put a cannon to shame. No noise, no explosion: just pure carnage. Half the gang's horses had been reduced to scraps by it. Fat Malone had a horse hoof driven through his chest by the force of the blast.

Lars lay under the body of a tall man with the tooled boots of a dandy. Even in the dull glow of the dying fire, Anderson could see the neatly scorched circle on the back of the dandy's fringed leather jacket. It was as if a hot awl had punched right through the man's body, and when Anderson rolled away the dandy's corpse, he saw without surprise that the hole continued through Lars. The look of surprise on the deputy's face suggested death had been more surprising than painful. Anderson closed Lars's eyes.

Anderson's own insides felt hollow. He was alone. He had lost Lars. He had lost Mina. He knuckled his eyelids.

"Help."

Anderson went still, listening. The voice had been very small.

"Help me!"

He turned back toward the campfire, where a heap of supplies and what must have been a tent or two lay smoking. The heap shook, and a bag of coffee slid to the ground. Anderson began tossing aside saddlebags. A bottle of whiskey smashed as he flung it aside.

The kid Indian sat up. Blood ran down the side of his face. He clutched his head and hissed.

"You okay?"

The kid tried to nod, made a face. Up close, he wasn't quite as young as Anderson had first made him out to be— but he was maybe eighteen at the oldest. The kid looked around the stinking, blasted camp. "What happened?"

"I don't know."

"There was a light. The horses—" The kid stopped. He looked sick. "What the hell can do that kind of thing?"

"I don't know." Anderson turned a bag of beans onto its side and plopped down on it. The rush of energy fear had given him had burned out, and now the long tense day had caught up with him. It wouldn't be long until morning. He wanted nothing more than to close his eyes and sleep for a couple of hours, but he knew he couldn't. Mina was out there somewhere. He had to find her.

"You're the safecracker."

"Yeah."

The kid turned in a slow circle, studying the camp. He stooped beside the fire, studying something in the dirt. Whatever it was, he pocketed it. "Where's your little girl?"

"Something got her. Her and McBurnie. It took them across the creek." Anderson thought about standing up, kept sitting. "I've got to track them down."

"What do you know about tracking, city slicker?"

McBurnie must have told the gang about finding him on the streets of San Francisco and taking him in. He narrowed his eyes at the kid. "I know enough."

The kid snorted. "I heard you crashing through the brush over there, trying to hide behind that cottonwood. If you knew anything about tracking, you would have managed a little better than that."

"So you're a tracker."

The kid pulled a bag of tobacco out of his pocket. "No shit."

"Why didn't you turn me in when you saw me?"

The kid shrugged. He bit off a twist of chaw and began turning it between his front teeth like a knot of spruce gum.

Anderson studied him a moment or two. The kid was observant, that was for sure. Anderson had to admit to himself that without Lars's help, he was going to have a hard time finding where that net had taken McBurnie and Mina. He hadn't caught even a glimpse of the men behind the attack, hadn't heard any horses, hadn't seen anything. The only thing he could be sure of was the net—the net and some goddamn terrifying firepower.

"I want to hire you to help me track down my girl. Whatever your price is, I'll pay it."

The boy shot a string of spit into the campfire. "Hell, no. You see what those bastards did to this camp? You really want to have a run-in with men like that?"

"With a tracker like you, I won't have to have a run-in." Anderson got off his sack of beans and stood in front of the kid. "Those bastards have my little girl. I know you think that's wrong. Otherwise, you would have turned me in the second you saw me behind that cottonwood."

"Shit." The kid got to his feet. "It won't be cheap."

"How much?"

"Ten dollars."

"*How* much?"

"Ten dollars."

It would mean digging up his cache beneath Bess's sycamore, but that didn't matter. He'd been saving that money for Mina. If something happened to her, that silver may as well rot.

"It's a deal." Anderson put out his hand. "What's your name, son?"

The kid shifted his plug of chaw into his cheek. "Billy Novak. And I ain't your son, Sheriff. Let's keep this business only."

"All right, *Mr.* Novak. Get your gear and we'll go back to my camp for horses."

"Wait a second." Novak held out his hand. "You should have this."

The corn dolly sat on his palm, ash-streaked and crumpled, but still whole. Anderson felt a surge of gratitude.

"Thanks."

The kid grinned. "You're damn lucky to have me."

As the sun nosed up over the hills, Novak helped Anderson wrap Lars in the remnants of the gang's tents. There'd be time to bury him later, Anderson promised himself. He and the kid piled the gang's gear around the grisly bundle. He hoped it would be enough to keep the body safe from buzzards and vultures until he could take better care of it.

After that business, it was a relief to walk away from the camp. In the dark, it had been bad. In the cold light of dawn, it was worse. Every bit of sand and stone had been pelted with blood and meaty bits. The stink was impossible. Anderson's stomach, luckily empty, turned around itself. He changed course, hurrying toward the place where he'd left his horse.

"Wait," Novak whispered, holding Anderson back.

A body lay in the shallows. A big man, taller than Anderson and twice as wide. He clawed at the mud and then fell back, gasping.

Novak's eyes narrowed. "Piss-Bucket." His hand went to his cheek, where a second fresh bruise shone.

Anderson waded to the big man's side and grabbed the back of his collar. "Morning, Piss-Bucket." He hauled him a foot higher up the beach. He'd never liked Piss-Bucket Johnson, not even when they'd worked together. He hadn't recognized the fat man when he'd knocked Anderson into the creek last night, but he wasn't surprised he'd run away in the middle of a fight.

He glanced at Novak. The kid folded his arms against his chest, his face dark. Anderson remembered his own time in the gang. Piss-Bucket Johnson had his own way of making life hell for a teenaged boy.

Piss-Bucket groaned. Anderson worked his boot into the man's fleshy ribs and flipped him onto his back. The smell of burned meat overpowered Piss-Bucket's eponymous aroma. The remnants of his coat and shirt hung in rags off his scorched chest.

"What happened?"

Piss-Bucket's eyes shot open. His mouth opened and closed, fish-like, as he gasped in pain and fear. His burns were too severe for him to last much longer. Any other man, Anderson might have felt bad for.

"A ghost," Piss-Bucket gasped. "A ghost!"

"What's he saying?"

Anderson slapped the fat man's face. "What did you see, Johnson?"

"A ghost." Piss-Bucket's eyes fluttered, then widened again. "I saw a ghost wading through the crick. An invisible ghost, splashing around." He twitched, jerked.

"I didn't see anything," Novak mused. "Not a thing."

"A ghost!" Piss-Bucket went stiff and then his head fell back.

"Good riddance," Anderson said.

Novak drove his boot into the fat man's side. "Yeah."

They didn't say anything else until they were well away from the campsite and its horrors, the warm September sun drying the clothes they'd rinsed in the creek. Anderson kept slipping in and out of memory, the bad old days with the gang weaving into moments from Mina's childhood. He'd tried so hard to grow up and be a decent man for her, only to have his past come back and bite him in the ass.

"I didn't see anything," Novak said again. "I thought it was just the darkness, the explosion, the noise. But now I wonder about it."

"You're not saying Piss-Bucket was right about you being attacked by a ghost."

Novak shook his head. "No, of course not. If a spirit wanted revenge against McBurnie, it wouldn't have carried him off in a net."

Anderson couldn't argue with that logic.

"Plus, spirits don't leave footprints, and whoever's dragging that net definitely is."

"What?"

Novak pointed to the ground. "I haven't even had to get off my horse—that net is leaving more traces than a mama grizzly on a rampage. But that there is definitely a footprint."

Anderson pulled up his mare and dismounted. Novak joined him on the ground. "You sure it's a footprint?" He'd never seen a print like this in his life. No man's foot had ever been this shape. The toe area was far too wide, and the whole thing was nearly twice as long as Anderson's.

"Maybe it's some new kind of caulk boot?" Novak pointed out the strange indentations around the footprint, punctures in the earth like nothing so much as the imprint of four forward-pointing claws and one backward one.

Anderson raised an eyebrow.

"Hey, just trying to make sense of what I'm looking at." Novak gave the print one last look and then got back in his saddle. "I think it's headed into the next canyon."

"At least it's away from town and the mining camps." Anderson frowned. He knew that canyon all too well: he'd helped Lars move cattle through it every fall.

And Eva was bringing the herd there today.

The canyon followed the creek for two miles before it began to widen, the hills peeling back to let the sun play on the packed surface of the Nielssen's road. Novak kept his eyes on the ground, following the scuff marks the invisible attackers had left. Anderson had chafed at waiting for sunrise, but he knew even a good tracker would have lost the trail in the dark. If the invisible men had left the creek and gone into the hills, they would have just vanished.

Anderson opened the gate that marked the end of Lars

and Eva's property. The big field stretched out ahead of them, the most open stretch of ground for miles. Here the net holding McBurnie and Mina had cut a swathe even Anderson could follow.

A massive rumbling shook the ground, followed by a horrible clank and whine. Then the field went silent again.

"What the hell was that?" Anderson slammed the gate behind him and climbed back on his horse.

"Some kind of engine maybe? It doesn't sound like it's working very well." Novak patted his horse's neck. The mare was high stepping, its nostrils flared. Anderson had never seen the creature look so nervous. "I don't like it. The trail goes over to that side of the field and then just stops."

A white horse caught Anderson's eye. Its rider was pushing it hard. He recognized the diminutive figure in the saddle from her slight build and the blue scarf tying her hat on tight.

"John," Eva called out, still a good ways away. "Where's Lars?"

A quail shot up from the ground, startled by the horse, and she cut toward the edge of the field to avoid the beating wings. The flapping cut the air like gunfire, and just like that she was gone. No horse, no rider, just grass and sky. The quail soared away, tiny as a sparrow.

"Eva!" Anderson burst into a run. Had she fallen into a sinkhole? Had the ground simply swallowed her whole? "Eva!"

With a resounding clang, the top of his head hit something hard and he toppled backward into the grass. He lay still, his head spinning. His neck felt as if it had been stretched double.

"John, are you all right?" The woman knelt beside him, her craggy face worried. She held up three fingers. "How many fingers?"

"Four. No, damn it." He tried to sit up and let his head fall back again. "Three. What are you doing out here?"

"Looking over the field before we move the herd." As if in response, somewhere farther up the canyon a cow let out a bellow. "I've got Smokey and Gene rounding them up in the upper field."

Anderson winced. Here he was, laid out cold, and in a couple of hours, this field would be filled with cattle. He and Novak didn't have much time to search out where they'd lost the net and its owner.

The kid Indian's face filled his field of vision. "It's a ghost wagon."

"What the hell is this kid talking about? You're the one who hit your head, but he's the one talking crazy," Eva growled.

Anderson forced himself upright. He rubbed the side of his aching neck. "What do you mean, Novak?"

"Piss-Bucket called it a ghost, the thing that attacked us last night. Remember? And I didn't see anything. Not a thing."

"You two are looking for a ghost?" Eva looked from one to the other. "And where the hell is my husband?"

"Oh, Eva." Anderson reached for her wrinkled hand. He told her what happened during the night. His eyes filled up with salt. Lars was gone. His friend and deputy was really, really gone.

She pulled her hand out of his grasp and covered her face. For a moment, she was motionless. Then she brushed her cheeks dry. She gave a fierce sniff.

"I'm so sorry, Eva."

She shook her head. "There'll be time for that later. Your little girl is still out here somewhere. We've got to find her before something happens to her."

"I think I know where she is," Novak said.

Anderson had almost forgotten about him. He turned around to see the kid lying on his belly, his face close to the ground.

"The soil's dry enough it doesn't take much of a print, and the ghost was walking careful here. It wasn't dragging the net at this point." He pointed at something Anderson couldn't make out. "He stood here a moment, waiting for something." The kid sprang to his feet. "I can picture it."

"What?" Eva snapped.

"I spent some time on the docks when we were in 'Frisco," Novak said. He jumped back a few feet, nodding. He pointed to a patch of broken grass, then a gopher hill. "I'm sure you did, too, Anderson, back when you were a kid."

Anderson got to his feet. "Yeah. So? What's your point?"

"The ships put out a gangway so they can load up their cargo, right? Like a big tongue coming out of the ship."

Eva got up, running her hands along the air beside her, stroking something she could feel even if she couldn't see it. "A ghost gangway for a ghost wagon."

"Right!" Novak grinned at her. "I was doing the same thing, Mrs... erm..."

"You can call me 'Eva.'" She rounded a corner and the top half of her disappeared. "You can't see it, but you can feel it."

Anderson put out a tentative hand. "A ghost wagon." He stroked the side of the thing. A slippery kind of warmth bit at his palm. He could feel his nerves crackling in his skin, as if he'd touched a very tame form of lightning. "You're saying Mina and McBurnie got loaded up in this invisible ship like a load of beaver pelts."

"Yeah."

"We've got to get in there." The angry cow bellowed again. It sounded closer. Anderson smacked his hand against the invisible ship. They didn't have time for this shit.

Eva reappeared. "How? There's not exactly a door to knock on."

Novak grinned. "I might have an idea."

The back end of Eva's herd looked more formidable than Anderson remembered. The times he'd ridden beside Lars urging his cows into the big field, the work had seemed boring, frustrating, the mass of cattle a wall of balky, plodding flesh. Now Anderson saw them as Novak had described them: a wall, alright, but a wall that could pulp a man in its path. A wall that could break open anything, even a ghost wagon.

Novak grew up listening to stories about walls of flesh like that. His Shasta grandmother had married a Sioux miner who'd come down out of the Dakotas looking for gold in the rush of 1849. The great herds of buffalo dotting the Dakota plains dwarfed Eva's herd by a thousandfold. His grandfather had been only a boy when he'd helped process the massive meat harvests, but he'd never forgotten it, and now Novak wanted to repeat history.

"They call it a 'buffalo jump.' They'd just stampede the buffalo right off a cliff," he explained. "Like a waterfall of animals."

Eva had held up a hand. "Is this going to wipe out my herd? I'm counting on taking these to auction next week."

Novak shook his head. "You felt what the ghost wagon is like. Top heavy. When the beeves hit it, they'll knock it over. At the speed they'll be running, it ought to smash right open."

"What if that doesn't do anything?" Anderson asked. "Or what if Mina gets hurt?"

"You got a better idea?" Novak shot.

Anderson had to admit he didn't. Even right now, facing three hundred head of cattle, he couldn't think of anything.

He swiveled in his saddle. Novak stood beside a long, low heap of straw and wood that all but closed off this end of the field. He gave Anderson a nod and struck a match.

Everything was ready. Anderson pulled out his revolver and shot three times into the air, startling the animals nearby. Novak dropped the match into the straw.

The match hit the dry tinder and caught immediately. In less than a minute, flames began to run along the side of Novak's firewall. Anderson shot at the sky again, but it wasn't necessary. The cattle were already surging forward.

Anderson urged his horse forward. The pounding hooves vibrated his very bones. Eva's hired hands whooped and waved torches, encouraging the cows into the side of the field where the ghost wagon sat.

The terrible grinding and whining sound repeated itself, frightening the cows into a more desperate run. A blue crackling lit up the first wave of cattle.

For a second, Anderson hardly understood what he was seeing. Something had appeared where the invisible wagon ought to be, a vehicle twice the size of a Conestoga wagon with a smooth, arched back. But what dazzled his brain was the gigantic man emerging from the trap door in its roof. His hair—was it hair?—swirled around his strangely deformed face as he sighted down the ugliest rifle Anderson had ever seen.

Bolts of white light shot out at the first wave of cattle. A cow's skull burst. The animals screamed and ran even faster.

They hit the ghost wagon in a crash and shriek of metal and hooves. Anderson covered his ears, reeling at the sound.

The giant man—no, by God, that face couldn't belong to a man—appeared in the middle of the herd, firing lightning bolts like a god with a vendetta. Anderson's revolver was suddenly in his hand. The tusked monster's head was a hell of a lot bigger than a can of tobacco.

The revolver bucked in his grip and the thing dropped. The cows trampled on, headed for the open grass.

"Mina!" Anderson dug his heels into his horse's side. The river of cattle had flowed on by the ghost wagon, and he had to get inside.

He didn't bother tying his horse, he just jumped off, running right into the dark mouth of the wagon's hatch.

It was as if he'd entered the steaming mouth of hell. A low red light suffused the space, and a dense, acrid fog filled the air.

"What the hell is this?" Novak whispered. Anderson hadn't heard the scout catch up with him.

"Mina!" Anderson shouted.

Novak shook his arm. "Look." The kid pointed to a clear box lying at their feet. "That's a man's, ain't it?"

The raw meaty thing in the box took a moment to resolve into a familiar shape. If Anderson hadn't helped Lars with

the butchering, he might not have recognized the string of
knobby bones running into the still-bloody skull. How you
got a man's spine out of his body without disconnecting it
from his skull, Anderson didn't want to know.

"Anderson! That you? Help me!"

McBurnie's voice came from the other side of the strange
cargo hold. Novak kicked aside a pile of boxes full of more
bloody trophies, revealing a black crate made of some slick
material Anderson couldn't identify. A few narrow slits
revealed McBurnie huddled within. He pushed his fingers
out through one of the gaps, desperate for human touch.

"Is Mina in there?"

"I don't know what that thing did with her."

Anderson dropped to his knees. "Oh, God. Mina."

"Daddy?" A tiny figure popped out from a dark spot
in the wall—an open cabinet or a ventilation shaft, maybe.
"Daddy!"

Dirt coated every inch of his little girl, but when he
swept her into his arms, she felt whole. She trembled and
clung to him.

"Mina." The voice came from behind them.

Anderson spun around. The figure silhouetted in the
open hatch was far too large to be human. Novak reached
for his rifle.

"Mina," the thing repeated, its voice a perfect mimic of
Anderson's. It stepped inside but made no move toward
them. It took another step sideways, moving into the darkness
beyond the foggy cargo space. "Mina," it said yet again.

"Let's get the hell out of here," Anderson said.

"Wait! Don't leave me," McBurnie begged. His fingers
closed on the fabric of Novak's jeans.

Novak wrenched away. "I'm done with you, McBurnie, you murdering, kidnapping bully."

Anderson grabbed Novak's arm. "Let's go!"

The creature made some kind of sound as they passed it by, but they were moving too fast to understand if it was words or a threat or some bizarre alien call.

They burst into the sunshine, gasping for air. The hatch closed behind them. There was another horrible grinding, whining sound, and then a rushing whoosh. The ghost wagon vibrated and shook. Then it leaped into the air. It hovered for a moment, and then it streaked into the sky, a bird, a star, gone.

Eva walked toward them, her face streaked with smoke. "You all okay?"

Anderson nodded, not sure of his voice. Not sure of his eyes. What had he seen in there? What did that thing want with McBurnie? Why hadn't it hurt Mina? The whole day and night had the weird unreality of a nightmare.

Mina squeezed her arms tighter around his neck. "I knew you'd come for me, Daddy."

He tightened his grip on her. He'd changed his life to give her a better one, and his past had nearly gotten her killed. He wasn't sure if he deserved any of her faith, but at least he hadn't let her down. "I love you."

Novak looked from Eva to Anderson. "Either of you have any whiskey? Because I sure could use some."

Eva laughed and put her arm around the kid's shoulder. "You're all right, Novak."

"Yeah, but now I don't have a job."

Anderson looked up from kissing Mina's head. Eva was giving him a hard look.

He'd been just like Billy Novak once, a lost, scared kid looking for a better life. And Lars Nielssen had convinced the town of Coyote Creek to give him one.

"I'm down a deputy," he said. "And I could use someone who knows a thing or two about tracking."

Novak's mouth opened and closed, but no words came out. Anderson understood. It was a big jump from outlaw to law enforcement.

While the boy flapped, Anderson settled Mina onto his horse. "I brought something of yours."

He pulled the corn dolly out of his pocket and watched her cover it with kisses. The smile on her face could've touched the heart of any kind of monster. He glanced at the sky.

Any kind of monster.

DRUG WAR

BY BRYAN THOMAS SCHMIDT
AND HOLLY ROBERDS

Chirping birds, insects, animals, and bustling traffic mixed with the lilting of people chattering in Portuguese all around him. The smell of mangoes, pineapple, exotic fragrances, piss, and petrol filled his nose—the marks of big city life. Retired LAPD captain Mike Harrigan felt like he was in a different world until he stepped inside the modern convention center and heard a familiar voice.

"Weapons of the future! The best new technology! Load 'em up, blow 'em away!" It was a voice he hadn't heard in twenty-five years and never thought to hear again. Not since his time with the Los Angeles Police Department, a voice from a time of one of the biggest crises in his entire forty-year career. But here he was, in Rio de Janeiro, Brazil, of all places, and the former Fed, Garber, was standing right in front of him, under a bright neon sign that read: LEGENDS, INC.— Legendary Tech, Legendary Power.

After what they'd both barely survived in Los Angeles, all they'd seen, Harrigan was a burned-out ex-cop who occasionally got invited to speak at urban police conferences like this one, and Garber had moved on to selling weapons and high-tech destruction. Harrigan wondered which of them had learned the most from their experience with the alien bounty hunter.

Vendor booths lined both sides of the long entryway leading to exhibit halls, theatres, meeting rooms, and more of the Rio de Janeiro Convention Center. Crowds of cops, military types, private security, mercenaries, and more examined the wares.

As Garber hefted a long, sleek, heavy-looking weapon—a rifle of some sort with laser scope, attached grenade launcher, and two cartridge bays—a chubby, sunburned, flowery-shirted American tourist poster child and his shorter, round wife stopped and smiled.

"Awesome!" the man said. "Me and my Pebbles need something just like that there back in Texas!"

Garber smiled his best salesman smile. "Totally legal, folks. I can set you up today."

From behind the Americans, a tall woman with long black hair and seductively tan skin approached with her companion, a shorter, bulkier, older man with a well-developed paunch like Harrigan's. Both wore sidearms holstered at their belts, despite their three-piece brown suits, and as they turned, Harrigan spotted badges hanging from their belts: detectives.

"Amigo, what is that thing?" the woman asked in the lilting Brazilian accent that had grown so familiar.

"Ah, *policía*!" Garber said, smiling broadly as he met her eyes. "This is the answer to all your problems, officers—the LI547-B1, the only assault rifle you'll ever need once you own it."

"It looks heavy, like a monstrosity," her partner said, shaking his head. "You expect us to run with that?"

Garber grunted. "Why run when everyone else will? Once you whip out this baby, it's over. You can stop them from sixty yards away. Pow!" He chuckled. "Problem entering a building? One blast from the grenade and you can blow your own entryway right through a wall. Blam!" As he described it, Garber demonstrated each move by aiming the weapon and pretending to shoot, shaking it for emphasis at each explosion.

Harrigan rolled his eyes, and the two detectives exchanged a look.

"If it's even legal," the female said.

"Oh trust me. Down here, it's totally legal, or else I wouldn't be here," Garber said.

Her companion shook his head again. "It's insane, amigo. The department would never approve that."

"What if I told you they had?" Garber argued.

Just then the floor vibrated and Harrigan heard the distant thrum of a big explosion outside. As people around them muttered and exchanged looks, Harrigan and the two cops raced for the door simultaneously, the automatic glass doors opening wide in their path to emit distant screams and further explosions.

They stepped out onto the sidewalk and scanned the

area surrounding the Convention Center, their eyes finding a nearby hillside slum where smoke drifted into the deep blue sky, a few buildings in flames as people yelled and scattered down the perilously narrow, steep sidewalks and passages between shacks, trying to get away.

Garber ran up to join them then. "What the hell was that?"

"It's Cortado Centro," the male detective said as he squinted toward the hillside. "A favela, slum."

Another explosion rocked the hillside, debris, flames, and smoke flying outward to form a funnel.

"*Merda!* What is going on?" the female detective inquired.

"Holy shit!" Garber exclaimed, spotting something through his weapon's scope.

"What?" Harrigan asked.

Garber looked at him, recognition dawning in his eyes. "Harrigan? LAPD?"

"Retired two years now," Harrigan replied with a nod. "Garber?"

Garber grunted and handed him the weapon, pointing high on the hillside where a building burned.

Through the scope, Harrigan soon saw it too: a body hanging from a tree, human and bloody—it had been skinned head to toe. The sight was one that had haunted Harrigan's nightmares for twenty-five years. Ever since the Predator. He couldn't believe he was seeing it.

"It can't be," Harrigan muttered.

"You know it is," Garber replied.

"What?" the female detective asked anxiously.

"They're under attack," Garber said, taking his gun back. "Time to arm up." Garber turned back for the Convention Center. "Hang on! Let me get my stuff." He ran back inside.

"Attack? By what? This kind of thing happens with drug dealers a lot," the male detective said.

Harrigan shook his head. "Trust me. We've seen this before. We've gotta clear the area, lock it down!" Without further word, Harrigan was running off toward the burning slum and the two detectives followed.

"Lock it down from what?" the female detective called after him.

The three detectives stopped at a busy intersection, racing across as soon as there was an opening, the vehicles whizzing by with narrow misses just as they reached the other side. No one even seemed to have slowed at all.

"Jesus," Harrigan muttered as he felt the vibration of a speeding box truck racing by, the smell of petrol and sweat mixing with chemicals, piss, and other unpleasantries common to Rio's streets as he'd discovered.

"Who are you?" the female detective asked, looking at him as they ran.

"Mike Harrigan, former LAPD," Harrigan replied.

"Ana Rios and Rodrigo Villaça," the female said, motioning to her partner. "Metro Police, homicide."

Harrigan nodded a greeting as they continued running. "Nice to meet you."

"You wanna tell us what's going on?" Villaça asked.

They rushed onward, reaching the base of the hill, where screaming men, women, and children were rushing out of the makeshift buildings and walkways.

"A hunter, hunting humans," Harrigan said.

"What?" Rios replied. "A serial killer?"

"Yeah, kinda like that," Harrigan said. "And we'd better hope to God there's only one."

"*Rápido, rápido!*" Fernando cried to his neighbor's passel of kids, swatting their little behinds as they bolted away.

One of them breathlessly paused to glance up at Fernando, tears welling in his little seven-year-old eyes: "*Obrigado*, Fernando."

Their mother, Solange, was away when an explosion rocked the favela, upturning the table where Fernando and his grandmother were having lunch and their usual argument about how he was wasting his life. It started, of course, with the flamboyant blouse.

His grandmother chastised him in Portuguese while pulling pão de queijo out of the pathetic makeshift wood-burning oven. "You think you are special, Fernando?" She gestured to the blouse, adorned in colorful palm fronds, tropical plants, with a giant tiger's face smack dab at the center.

"I like it, it makes me feel fierce." Then when her back was turned, Fernando gave an obstinate shimmy in her direction.

Her head swiveled around to give him the stink eye. Grannies saw everything.

"You'll see, *Avó*," Fernando said, confidently. "I'm not destined for life in the favela, I am going to be a star." Licking the cherry gloss on his lips, he smiled. "I'll soon be acting alongside Brad Pitt and Ryan Gosling in major motion pictures."

She snorted derisively and settled her creaky bones into a rickety chair only to be catapulted out when the explosion hit.

Fernando blinked hard, finding himself splayed on the ground next to his grandmother, balls of pão de queijo bouncing and rolling around their heads.

Jumping to his feet, Fernando hauled his granny up and out of the shack. The streets were swarming with cariocas fleeing the favela. Smoke visibly rolled through the air.

It was too close.

Solange's kids called out from next door. They were trapped inside.

Grabbing a fleeing man, Fernando firmly transferred his granny's hand onto the man's arm, instructing him to get her out safely. With a grave nod, the man took off, dragging protesting grandma behind him while Fernando hastened to help the neighbor's kids.

Now that they were out, Fernando knew he needed to get his own fabulous unsinged butt out of there, too. That's when he saw the trio fighting against the flow of cariocas. They stuck out like a bad perm in a sea of salon-styled hair.

Policía. Two of them, along with an older black man, his face an arrangement of ferocious intensity. They were all armed and stalking further into the favela.

The woman *policía* shouted over the crowd to the black man: "If you are retired, what are you doing here at an arms conference, Harrigan?"

Harrigan shot her a glance. "If Los Angeles has taught me anything, Rios, it's that war can break out at anytime, anywhere, by anything. I'm all about being prepared."

Los Angeles! Fernando's heart thudded in a different fervor of excitement now. If he could just get to the City of Angels, he could be a star! Everyone who moved to Hollywood was instantly given opportunities and made into movie stars. Fernando looked closer but didn't recognize this Harrigan person, but maybe Fernando just hadn't seen his movies yet.

Harrigan stopped to squint up at the smoke plumes. "Are you sure we are going in the right direction? I feel like we are running in circles."

Fernando stepped directly in front of Harrigan, forcing him to stop, and grinned. "Yippee ki-yay, motherfucker!" He deepened his voice, despite his heavy accent: "He's the disease and we're the cure." He still had some work to do on his Stallone impression.

"Get out of my way," the cop growled. Pointing up at the smoke plumes, Fernando tried a new tactic. "You want to be there? You need my help. It's a honey brush in here."

The man called Harrigan gave Fernando a strange, uncomprehending look. The other two *polícia* slowed to a stop. "Honeycomb," the other *polícia* man corrected him.

"Come on, Villaça," the woman called Rios said to her partner. "We don't have time for this." They hurried past Fernando, but he refused to get out of Harrigan's way.

Seeing as Harrigan was about to slam him to the side if need be, Fernando spoke quickly. "They won't find it either. This place is a honeycomb." He used the correct phrase this time. "I help you get there fast, you help me get to the City of Angels."

Harrigan shook his head like he didn't have time for this, until he saw his two *polícia* friends double back, having taken the wrong way the first time.

"Take me there," Harrigan said through tightened teeth.

Hope blossomed in Fernando's chest and he couldn't help the smile spreading across his face. "And you'll get me to City of Angels?"

"Can we discuss this later?" Harrigan said as an explosion rocked a nearby shack and sent debris raining down on them. Fernando whirled around and led him to where the smoke billowed up, darkening the sky.

Hurrying up and down the winding paths of the favela past rusting housing units, Fernando was about to tell him they were close when another explosion hurled them to the ground.

Sputtering out puffs of sandy dirt, Fernando lifted his head and turned to see if his new buddy was okay. White sand was caked to the side of Harrigan's unhappy dark face.

Extending an arm, Fernando pointed just around the corner of the next building. "There."

Harrigan tried to jump to his feet quickly, but the way he moved and the wince on his face told Fernando he had creaky bones like Grandmother. Getting up with more ease to follow, Fernando smacked into Harrigan when he abruptly stopped. Peeking around him, Fernando saw what made him stop.

All hell had broken loose.

———

The slanted wood and clay roof next to him exploded as Harrigan followed the Brazilian up the winding narrow walkways through the favela. Pieces of clay, wood, dried palm leaves, and dirt rained down on their heads as they both ducked instinctually even while they kept running.

"*Merda!*" the Brazilian man muttered.

Then they rounded a corner and entered a small square and the man stopped cold, staring, his jaw dropped open. "*Mãe de Deus!*" he whispered.

Harrigan saw it too. A decapitated corpse lying in a heap, the head beside it on the cement covering the square, just a few feet from where they'd left the walkway. Blood was still pouring from the body and head, forming crimson pools. To the left, another body lay, stabbed through the chest with a gaping wound—a kind Harrigan had seen before: the Predator's spear. The decapitation had clearly happened from one of those computerized Frisbee-like discs they carried. Scorched marks smoked on the sides of buildings and a patch of cement between the two bodies—body laser. The stench of burnt concrete and blood now mixed with that of the urine, mud, sweat, and general uncleanliness of the favela.

A familiar clicking sound echoed from the distance. The creature. This shit was not happening again. Not while Harrigan could stop it. His memories of the last time had not faded one iota over the two decades since. If anything, they'd become more vivid. It was a situation he'd never thought he'd face again, and yet somehow he'd always known, always feared the aliens would be back. But this time he had an advantage: this time he knew what to do, and whatever it took, he'd do it.

Automatic weapons fire exploded above them—further up in the favela, tearing apart more roofs, trees, and more, followed by screams and yelling. These people are poor? Drug lords? He put a gentle hand on the Brazilian's shoulder, as the man stood frozen, staring at the bodies. "Hey, buddy. What's your name?"

No response.

Harrigan squeezed his shoulder. "Buddy!"

The Brazilian mumbled, "Fernando."

"Okay, Fernando, who's doing the shooting up there?"

"*Milícia*," Fernando said, still staring.

"Militia?" Harrigan asked. Poor slums with their own militia? Jesus Christ, what was going on down here.

Fernando shook his head and met Harrigan's eyes. "Drug lords, they run all the favelas."

Harrigan nodded. "Okay, well, we have to get up to where the Predator is. Can you still take me?"

Fernando stared back at the bodies and nodded.

"There's nothing we can do for them," Harrigan said, stepping toward the entrance to the continuation of the climbing walkway across the square. "Come on!" He motioned to Fernando.

Fernando crossed himself, like the traditional Catholic he was, then forced his eyes to Harrigan and hurried to join him resuming the climb.

They ducked under laundry lines, filled with linens and clothes, dodging through more small squares, climbing even as it sounded like the world was exploding above them. Fernando said nothing, he just led the way and Harrigan followed, weapon at the ready.

A few scared women and children rushed past them, headed down. At times, the passage was so narrow, either the runners or Harrigan and Fernando would have to stop, press themselves against a wall and wait for the others to pass. No one said anything; it was all in the eyes. As soon as they were clear, each party continued on their mission, racing as fast as they could.

And then, as they rounded a curve, plaster and wood exploded beside them as a stream of bullets struck a building then raked across the pathway. They halted, shrinking back against the wall and waiting, and Harrigan moved into the lead, motioning for Fernando to stay back as he moved cautiously, sliding along toward the corner to grab a peek.

There were four men armed with assault weapons—two AK-47s, and IMBEL IA2s, of local make—using what cover they could and yelling back and forth as they fired toward a rooftop a level or two higher.

Their bursts of automatic fire were met with streams from an invisible laser cannon exploding against buildings, cement, and other objects around them. The Predator was cloaked, but his red triangular targeting laser appeared and highlighted its targets, causing many to panic, confused. Who was the enemy assaulting them? They did their best to aim in the direction of the laser fire, but the Predator kept moving quickly, each burst coming from some new position, and the four men were hopelessly beaten, even if they couldn't accept that.

Then, one by one, they were hit, their chests highlighted by a red dot before the laser tore holes through them. From behind his cloak, the Predator laughed or clicked, and Harrigan heard the familiar sound of hydraulics as its laser cannons honed in on one target at a time. Occasionally branches would bend as the creature leapt between them or dust flew from clattering tiles, marking its movements. Each time, the survivors' fire became more and more desperate, as they sprayed the rooftops and surrounds, spinning, eyes desperately searching for the target. The first three screamed as they died, their chests smoking as they fell.

Their companion's panic grew with each fallen comrade, and then he was alone, and a thump came from behind him. The man whirled, aiming his IMBEL but then the Predator was on him, a spear slamming through his chest as he gasped, its tip poking out the front as blood flood. The man tried to stay on his feet, stumbling, even as his weapon fell.

Then his neck tore open as an invisible knife pulled across it and he collapsed.

"*Meu Deus!*" Fernando whispered from beside Harrigan, where he'd sneaked up to get a peek.

Then there was a shimmer and a buzz as the Predator uncloaked, his full ugly green spotted, dreadlocked mass appearing before them. The Predator bent to retrieve its treasures, quickly scalping the latest victim, and grabbing his weapon, as Harrigan flashed back to memories of his previous confrontations.

Fernando gasped loudly. "A monster! *Cristo Jesus!*"

The Predator chittered and whirled, alert and staring right toward them, even as its laser cannon's servos whirred and took aim.

"Get back!" Harrigan shouted, reaching back to pull Fernando behind the wall, even as he heard a whistle growing in volume, and the ground near the Predator's feet exploded.

"Take that, you son of a bitch!" Garber shouted and moved into view along a rooftop to the east, aiming a grenade launcher with laser sights, the red dot lighting up the Predator's chest.

And then the world exploded again as Garber and the Predator unleashed their hellfire on each other.

Harrigan grabbed Fernando and threw him to the ground as fire swallowed the air above them. Coughing from more concrete dust and thick smoke, Fernando mourned his blouse wasn't likely to survive this insanity.

When he tried to get up, Harrigan smacked him back down again. Carefully, Harrigan rose to a crouch to get a better view of the fight without losing his head. He stunk of sweat and fear, a scent Fernando had become intimately familiar with in the favela.

Except Fernando's fear dissipated as he stared up at the crouching retired *polícia*. His mouth dropped in a small 'o' as he took in the white dust smeared across Harrigan's face; his forehead glistened with sweat and blood, and a gun was clutched firmly at his side. He looked like an action movie star.

And action movie stars needed bigger guns. Lots of big guns.

Scooching back on the ground before getting up, Fernando then whistled at Harrigan. "Hey, you want more guns like crazy down there?"

Harrigan's head swiveled around to look at Fernando, but his gaze was unseeing, almost haunted. Fernando saw the monster too, but he could question reality and cry like a hysterical baby later. He sternly reminded himself the favela overflowed with hidden and not-so-hidden monsters. You learned quick not to stop and stare when you found one.

He locked eyes with the ex-cop. "Say hello to my little friend, eh?"

Harrigan's brow creased and his eyes flickered with understanding.

"*Rapido*, Harrigan," Fernando cried and took off running just as the building next to them shuddered violently. Laser bolts and gunshots flew overhead. Apparently, neither the monster nor the crazy guy below was dead, yet.

"Guns, yeah, yeah I'd like more guns," Harrigan said, still distracted but following Fernando now.

Daintily stepping over a couple of bloody decapitated

bodies and into a shack twice the size of any near it, Fernando raced around looking for weapons.

Harrigan watched, skeptically. "What makes you think there are guns in here?"

"Because," Fernando said exasperated, still not having found them, "the drug lord always has guns. Lots of guns." A flicker of an idea practically lit up over his head and Fernando ran to the small attached bathroom.

"Yoohoo," he called to Harrigan, pleasure evident in his voice.

Harrigan barely fit into the bathroom alongside Fernando. The rusted-out bathtub overflowed with guns. Big damn guns. AK-47s, Heckler & Koch MR762 models of various types, shotguns, even a few Uzis and other machine guns. Boxes of ammo shoved in stacks wherever they fit around them.

Harrigan greedily gathered up several AK-47s, two H&Ks and an Uzi, but nearly dropped them. Fernando followed his fixation to where the bloodless face was now revealed in the center of the tub. Someone was dead and buried under the guns.

Picking up a handgun, with his forefinger and his thumb, Fernando said, "Yeah, don't mind him. He was already here." Then he gingerly placed the gun back on the pile. "I'm a lover not a fighter."

Thoroughly strapped with semi-automatic weapons, pockets bursting with ammo, and a sawed-off shotgun slung over his shoulder, Harrigan started back for the warzone.

Fernando grabbed his arm to stop him, having second thoughts. "What if you die? How will I get to the City of Angels?"

"If either of us are going to get to the City of Angels,"

Harrigan jerked his head to the outside, "we'll have to go through hell first."

Fernando clapped excitedly. "Oh, I think I *have* seen your film."

Harrigan shook his head before running back, Fernando close on his heels. They found the big crazy one shooting a stream of fire out from a flamethrower. The Predator had thrown up some kind of invisible shielding but it weakened his own invisibility. Fernando gaped as large chunks of the alien flickered in and out of visibility.

The alien gave a high-pitched shriek of anger as it felt the heat of the firepower.

———

The top of the slum was exploding with gunfire, detonations, flying debris, and noise as Harrigan led Fernando back along a winding pathway, climbing, searching for a good location to get a bead on the deadly Predator. Men shouted, screamed, and bullets whizzed—filling the air.

"Come on, motherfucker! Is that the best you got?!" Garber shouted and sneered as he launched another grenade then sent a laser-guided stream of automatic fire in its wake straight toward where the alien had been crouching moments before. A wall exploded and fell, the roof caving in—no sign of the fast-moving foe. It was all too familiar, Harrigan's memory flashing back to images of Los Angeles—gang wars, the streets, Leon Cantrell, Danny Archuletta, Jerry Lambert, even his old Captain Pilgrim. Archuletta and Lambert had been killed by a Predator in LA years ago during Harrigan's last encounter with one. Now, countless others were adding to the Predator's body count.

In front of him, a wall exploded, a thatched roof caving in, accompanied by the screams of a woman and children, an infant crying. Harrigan fought the urge to run in and rescue them. It wasn't safe. He couldn't do anyone good buried in wreckage.

Drug dealers with grizzled faces bearing various stages of facial hair screamed in Portuguese, firing their AK-47s, Uzis, and sawed-off shotguns at the fast-eluding alien, now cloaked again in the barely visible vibrating haze, but Harrigan knew what to look for. His trained eyes multi-tasked, searching the mountainside for both an ideal sniper position and the alien foe at the same time.

There he is! Over in that palm tree, moving to a new position. He was tempted to call out but knew his warnings would be too late every time, if anyone even heard them over all the noise. Instead, he ran faster, dodging, ducking, and diving for cover whenever the explosions or bullets came too close. As long as he and Fernando stayed hidden and in shadows, as long as other aggressors took the alien's focus, they'd be safe. Predators targeted prey who fought back with only occasional innocents caught in the crossfire. They were about the sport of it, and killing unarmed innocents wasn't sporting on their planet either.

Like his foes, the Predator kept firing off a steady stream of laser fire, his red triangular laser sights the only indication of his location along with hand-thrown bombs of some sort. Occasionally, Harrigan thought he could pick out a familiar chittering chirp, but each time he turned to look, the beast had moved on.

"Look out!" Fernando shouted fruitlessly from behind Harrigan as the corner where Garber had just fired from exploded into a cloud of dust, debris, and orange and yellow flashes.

"Fuck me!" Garber yelled, but somehow he was still standing, face blackened when the smoke cleared, even as he raced for a new position.

"Holy God," Harrigan muttered as Fernando crossed himself.

"Up there," Fernando pointed, and Harrigan turned. It was actually a perfect spot—a partially shielded small balcony above one of the few semi-solid buildings on the hill—some sort of residence just north and around the bend from them.

Harrigan nodded. "Good eye. Thanks." And led the way.

As they rounded the bend, through a break between shanties and trees, Harrigan watched as the ground exploded at a drug dealer's feet and the man fell, screaming, his body shaking as red holes appeared up his legs, his AK-47 letting off a continuous stream as he fell.

The acrid smoke combined with burning thatch and stucco in a cloud that made Harrigan's eyes water as it passed over him. Behind him, Fernando squinted, and coughed. "I love the smell of gunfire in the morning," he quipped, clearly evoking the famous Robert Duvall line from *Apocalypse Now.*

"Napalm," Harrigan muttered as he climbed a stepped stone wall up toward the house with the balcony and headed for stairs leading up the side. "It was napalm."

"Ah," Fernando said. "Yes. I don't know what is napalm."

"Nasty shit," Harrigan replied. "I hope you never will."

The seven feet of steps led to a landing covered by thatched roofing and then another enclosed, winding staircase that led up to the short balcony. Harrigan examined his weapons and ammo as he climbed. He had to hit the Predator and hit it fast before the alien spotted his position. Surprise was key as much as focus and staying ahead of the alien.

As Harrigan set up his shot, three more drug dealers fell, chests and heads exploding from their deadly foe's precision targeting. Only one had a mouth left to scream as he fell and the three companions left standing were panicked, eyes wide and darting about like raving animals now—their attempts at returning fire a mere waste of bullets.

Harrigan looked around: Fernando had disappeared. Where was he? He shook it off—no time to worry about him now.

The rooftop where the Predator stood erupted with fire from a screaming Garber then and splotches of green appeared as the alien was apparently hit. Harrigan heard an alien scream.

Garber cackled. "Take that, you alien fuck!" Seconds later, his face froze as an alien missile finally found its mark and blew his legs apart. What was left of him screamed as he fell, and a red laser lit up his head just before it exploded.

Harrigan had the alien in his scope when it uncloaked, clearly intent on gathering trophies. It hopped down from its perch to the plaza and headed for the nearest fallen prey, chittering.

Harrigan's hand moved toward the trigger when the alien whirled and their eyes met. He saw recognition there, the alien muttering a strange word, "Ooman... Cetanu." Its shoulder cannon shifted, taking aim.

Harrigan jerked, his focus back to his scope, when he heard a strange yell—almost like a Southern Rebel yell but with faster syllables. Then below, someone began pelting the uncloaked alien with coconuts, pineapples, and... were those lemons or oranges? Shouting insults in Portuguese.

Then Fernando appeared, fruit strapped to bands on his body like ammo pouches, the Brazilian screaming as he ran. "Shoot him, maaaaaan!"

Harrigan couldn't believe his eyes.

———

Fernando was performing the role of his life, and though the audience was limited, he was going to play it out like his life depended on it. Which it did.

While Harrigan raced to high ground, Fernando observed all the other players in the show getting their heads blown off, splat. It didn't take long to do the math.

Fernando had survived many shootings and riots because when the screams started, civilians ran around in blind panic. Even at nine years of age, Fernando had recognized that those people made themselves targets, like a flock of birds prime for the shooting. While they flapped around, he would slip away unharmed amidst the raging melee.

His action hero was going to get blown up because there were no more birds left to distract the big bad. If Harrigan was blasted away, so would Fernando's hopes of surviving as well as his dreams of moving to the City of Angels.

Ducking away, he found an abandoned fruit cart. Nimbly, he used the nets from the cart to arm himself with coconuts, oranges, and whatever else until he resembled a fruit-strapped Rambo, then he rushed back into the battle, positioning himself opposite Harrigan to divide the monster's focus.

"Hey, you big ugly," Fernando taunted in Portuguese, chucking another coconut. "You look ridiculous in that net body suit! Don't you know that only looks good with boots and a miniskirt? Are you into bondage and domination or are you just not over the eighties?"

The monster cocked its head, and though its features were practically alien, its human eyes shone a disbelief that mirrored Harrigan's stunned face from where he was perched. As its shoulder laser cannon pivoted to aim at Fernando, he ran and screamed, "Shoot him, maaaaaan!"

A shot echoed. Fernando winced, resisting the urge to cover his ears and hit the deck. He kept his eyes open long enough to watch green goop spurt from the monster's left shoulder as Harrigan's bullet hit its mark.

Without wasting a second, the monster dropped and rolled, disappearing from sight as it vanished once more.

Still chucking fruits in the direction where the monster had disappeared, Fernando suddenly felt very exposed in the open space.

"Move your ass, Fernando!" Harrigan cried, already on his feet to find new cover.

With a surprised eek, Fernando ducked down an alleyway coming face to face with Harrigan a minute later, who reared up with surprise at Fernando's quick appearance.

"Honeycomb," Fernando explained again, panting with fear.

Harrigan barely slowed down. "He's bleeding which means he's leaving a trail."

Nodding, Fernando ignored his shaky knees and followed. Mustering all his confidence he added, "I wonder if the punk feels lucky?"

Harrigan threw him a strange glance as they raced towards the rooftop where they'd last spotted the creature.

"Like Clint Eastwood," Fernando added, insistently. "That is us. We are the Clints."

"Yeah, yeah, I get it." Harrigan grumbled, not wanting to play along. "We need to get to those guns down there." Harrigan pointed to where the crazy man had got himself blown to bloody bits.

"But," Fernando protested in a whine, "I already got you guns. You have all the guns."

"Not the right ones." Harrigan shook his head. "I got lucky. Garber almost got the upper hand, and we need the same kind of firepower."

With an exasperated sigh, Fernando grumbled as he turned around to backtrack down to where the firepower was. "I give you guns, but no, you want crazy man guns."

As they wound their way down the favela, they had to take care not to trip over the bodies. Half of the bodies were scalped and two skinless bodies swayed sickeningly overhead. Fernando daintily touched his lips, fighting his gorge. He'd never seen such indescribable evil.

"He isn't taking time to retrieve his trophies." Harrigan grimaced. "We've got him on the run."

Opting to stay back, Fernando pointed to the landing where Garber's intestines and fleshy bits littered the surrounding area like gory confetti.

Harrigan rushed ahead, shedding the guns Fernando cleverly found him before, opting for two large firearms, soaked in dead man's blood. From what Fernando could tell, it didn't look like those things shot bullets.

Screams resounded in the distance.

"Come with me if you want to be living," Fernando called to Harrigan, knowing exactly where the screams originated.

Harrigan shouted after Fernando, "If you want to live!"

Tossing a quick look back, Fernando said, "Of course I want to live! I want to go living in the City of Angels!"

Fernando didn't understand Harrigan's snort of anger, but whipped by shanties to the east side of the favela. Something wet dripped onto Fernando's head. Slowing to wipe it off, his eyes widened as he saw it was the same florescent green gloop that had jettisoned out of the creature.

Harrigan came to a full stop and looked up. "He's running the roofs."

"Do you know if this can wash?" Fernando asked, lip curling, dismayed to find the shoulder of his poor blouse had also been dripped on.

Harrigan didn't answer, he was busy trying to heft himself up onto the roof by gripping the edge and pulling himself up. The idea was better than its execution.

Shaking his head, Fernando critiqued his performance. "You're too old for that shit."

Sweating and shaking with exertion, Harrigan's head whipped around to shoot Fernando a nasty look. "Thanks," Harrigan reluctantly groused.

With a sigh, Fernando dragged over a nearby table, climbed on it where it was a medium step from there onto the rusting metal roof. Reaching down he gave Harrigan a hand up.

"Look." The cop pointed at the roof where the green blood visibly glowed and led towards the east end toward where Harrigan and the Rio detectives had entered the favela.

Running the roofs made for a fast trail though they had to take care where they stepped so not to fall through the rotting or rusted roofs.

"*Deus me ajude!*" Fernando muttered, praying as he ran.

They stopped abruptly when three roofs down, a ratty-looking carioca struggled in the creature's grasp; the carioca's handgun slid off the roof and away. The creature, no longer cloaked, cocked his arm back, jagged blades attached from his wrist jutting out past his hand, about to make the killing blow.

Fernando gasped, and the monster jerked around. Meeting eyes with pure evil itself, Fernando froze; even his heart seemed to stop. He barely registered the small cannon mounted on its shoulder redirecting aim at him.

"Fernando!" Harrigan yelled, prompting him to look down at his chest where three red laser dots were trained.

Harrigan pushed Fernando to the side with tremendous force at the same time a bright blue laser beam shot from the shoulder cannon. Fernando screamed as fire burned his left shoulder with such intensity he burst into tears, praying to God that he wasn't ready to die.

Smacking hard onto his back, somehow managing not to slide down and off its edge, Fernando saw Harrigan had propelled himself in the opposite direction avoiding the creature's shot.

Gasping, Fernando managed to get out, "Go ahead, make his day," hoping his action hero could save them.

A stream of bullets exploded from below and Harrigan heard voices shouting orders, even before he saw the Brazilian detectives, Rios and Villaça, firing their rifles as they directed other police and armed civilians to where the alien stood atop the roof.

Harrigan scrambled to his feet, after verifying that

Fernando was only shot in the shoulder—he'd live. At least, he had as good a shot as any of them did to get out alive.

The alien emitted a piercing growl as bullets struck its uninjured arm and shoulder, sending more glowing green blood trailing down its body. Sparks and electrical streaks ran across its armor, indicating something important had been damaged. It stabbed the captive carioca it still held firm in its grasp, even as it turned to run, hurling the corpse with its inhuman strength toward the firing humans to provide a distraction and block their aim. Bullets tore up the roof beneath its pounding feet as it ran.

Down below, a blonde, bulky tourist in a flowery shirt Harrigan recognized grabbed his short, round wife by the arm and yanked her away just as the carioca's corpse landed right where she'd been standing.

"Son of a bitch almost hit my Pebbles!" the man screamed and opened fire with an LI547-B1, one of the crazy futuristic cannons Garber had been demonstrating. The rooftop where the alien had once stood exploded, shattering clay tiles, stucco, and wood into flying splinters.

"*Calma, amigo!* We need to find him again," Rios called, shaking her head as her eyes and her partner's searched for the alien.

Harrigan used the distraction to pull Fernando back to his feet. "Get behind me," Harrigan instructed. "You want to go to the City of Angels right? Stay sharp."

"What is a Pebbles?" Fernando mumbled, still trying to wrap his mind around the idea he might live.

Below, two SWAT-type vans pulled up, lights flashing, and armed men with body armor poured out, setting up a firing line behind the two detectives.

"Do you see him?" Villaça called, spotting Harrigan.

Harrigan shook his head and cupped his mouth: "He can cloak! Stay ready! And shoot for the head and upper body!" If they hit him enough times there, the beast would falter, maybe even die. All it took was one good shot, Harrigan remembered from decades before. Back then it had taken a lot more but now they had much better weapons with computer targeting.

With a thumping crash, the Predator landed down below, mandibles flaring, and ran across another rooftop, struggling with its control panel as it went.

Harrigan suddenly realized the alien couldn't cloak. "There!" he yelled and aimed the grenade launcher he'd retrieved from Garber at the alien, letting the targeting system beep even as he shut off the safety and fingered the trigger. He launched two grenades at once, before taking off at a run again, Fernando staggering but close on his heels.

The Predator almost made it off the roof to another when the grenades hit, blowing up the ground beneath its feet. As it leaped into the air, trying to minimize damage, and whirled toward a nearby tree, trails of automatic gunfire flowed through the air all around it. Harrigan thought for sure it would be hit multiple times, but it landed with barely a grunt and glared back at him, then scanned the area below where the police and armed civilians had formed a line, assessing its options.

Harrigan lined it up in his sights again, preparing to use the second grenade launcher's contents. Automatic fire tore up the edges of the roof, but the Predator was at an angle where the police and civilians couldn't see much of it from the ground as their fire tore up the edges of the roof and the ceramic tiles and thatch, doing the alien no harm.

"That'n-da s' yin'tekai!" the Predator shouted, raising its chin in defiance, back arched, mandibles flared as it typed furiously on its wrist control.

"Oh shit!" Harrigan yelled, realizing what that meant. The bomb. It was arming the bomb. "Run!" he called to Fernando, even as he took off to put distance between himself and the alien.

Then the air shimmered ahead and four Predators appeared—spears in hand, eyes narrowed with determination, mandibles flaring—and marched toward him.

"Meu Deus! We die!" Fernando exclaimed, shrinking back and halting his steps, uncertain. He cradled his wounded arm, fear shining in his eyes.

The lead Predator stopped and locked eyes with Harrigan, saying, *"Na'tauk, ooman."* It raised its hand, holding a 3D cube of glass or some composite metal and aimed it at Harrigan.

Harrigan stopped running and prepared to dodge. Fuck. What was it—some new weapon?

Then the cube flashed and an image appeared—a picture of the Predator who'd been attacking the favela, his markings clear, bright, bold words in the alien tongue above and below. The layout resembled a wanted poster.

The lead alien nodded. *"Tarei hsan,"* it said and all three of the other Predators stared with contempt at their injured comrade, mandibles clicking rapidly as they emitted some kind of rumbling clicking—a form of laughter mixed with contempt, Harrigan thought.

The injured alien growled, staring at them with almost challenge for a moment, then lowering its head and eyes, as if in surrender. And the cube went dark again.

"Harrigan, get down!" Rios called as Harrigan looked back to see the police and civilian line redistributing themselves to positions where all four Predators were in range.

Harrigan turned and raised a hand. "No. Wait!" His eyes met Rios'.

"Are you crazy? There's more, we can take them," Villaça shouted.

But Rios suddenly understood and nodded to Harrigan. "Hold your fire!"

Harrigan sighed and turned back to the Predators, nodding. "He's all yours."

The Predator search party quickly surrounded their wounded comrade, stripping away his weapons and securing him with some sort of restraints then grabbing him by the arms to lift him. Two whirled him around and led him back toward where they'd appeared, up the hill near the remains of some shacks.

The lead Predator clicked, mandibles crossed, and nodded to Harrigan. It looked almost like respect. *"That'n-da s' yin'tekai,"* the alien said warmly, as with great respect.

"Thatinda yinteki," Harrigan did his best to repeat back and nodded.

With that, the lead alien raised a palm in salute, then whirled and followed its comrades, all four soon disappearing as if fading into a mist, only the air was filled with smoke and debris instead.

Harrigan turned back to Fernando. "You okay?"

Fernando nodded weakly, bleeding heavily but keeping conscious. "What happened?"

"He was wanted, a criminal," Harrigan explained.

"Wanted by us, for sure," Villaça said as he and Rios hurried up the hill to stand beside Harrigan and Fernando.

"His own will punish him in their way," Harrigan explained, realizing his understanding was more intuitive. He hadn't understood the words but somehow the meaning still reached him.

Rios glanced around them at what was left of the ruined favela. "What a mess," she said, shaking her head. "Think they'd fix this?"

Harrigan laughed. "I think the rest is up to us."

Fernando grinned, hopeful. "So now you take me to City of Angels?"

Harrigan grunted. "Are you sure you want to leave all this excitement behind?"

All three Brazilians laughed.

"Just a normal day in Rio, amigo," Fernando laughed, but it soon turned into a wet cough. He crossed himself.

"If only that was a lie," Rios added. Harrigan joined them then in laughing.

"Let's get you some help, hero," Harrigan said, clapping Fernando on his good shoulder as ambulances began joining the other vehicles at the base of the favela. Fernando beamed proudly and they all started down the hill together.

RECON

BY DAYTON WARD

QUẢNG TRỊ PROVINCE, VIETNAM—JANUARY 1968

Sergeant Daniel Roland ducked and sprinted to his left, bullets chewing into the mud behind him. He threw himself against the trunk of a wide tree, forcing himself to take slow, deliberate breaths. M16 and AK-47 rifle fire pierced the air around him, punctuated by the occasional bark of the shotgun carried by his team mate, John Coffren.

Cries of pain erupted from somewhere over Roland's shoulder, and he shifted his position for a better look. Voices to his right indicated where members of his team were reacting to the ambush, seeking whatever meager cover they could find. Two figures scrambled behind a fallen tree to his right, and he saw the barrel of Coffren's shotgun as the other man angled for another shot. A native of northern Maryland, the young Marine had been a shotgun aficionado his entire life and preferred it to an M16, which was fine with Roland. At close range, the Remington 870 in Coffren's hands could be devastating, and Charlie was plenty close.

"Roland! You okay?"

The shout from Coffren drew fire from the jungle somewhere to Roland's right. Pushing his soft-brimmed jungle hat farther back on his head, he aimed his M16 in that direction and emptied the rifle's magazine, uncertain as to whether his rounds were finding any targets. Feeling the weapon's bolt lock to the rear, he ducked back behind the tree.

"I'm good!" he shouted, dropping the spent mag and fishing a replacement from the pouch on his equipment harness. He jammed the new magazine home and chambered a round. Shifting his position for a better look, he scanned the bush in search of threats and gave thanks to the hillside at their backs. That would reduce the likelihood of ambushers slipping in behind them, and they'd already cleared the bunker hidden there, so no surprises would be coming from that direction. Still, Roland knew the longer the firefight dragged on, the better the chances of Charlie getting reinforcements.

The repeating metallic snap of an AK-47 on full auto erupted from the undergrowth somewhere very close, and Roland crouched lower as several rounds chewed into the other side of his tree.

"Scotty! How's about it?"

Rather than say anything, Lance Corporal Scott Pearson pushed himself to a kneeling position behind the fallen tree and fired his M79 at something Roland couldn't see. The hefty round of buckshot tore through the jungle foliage along with any soft bodies that happened to be in the way.

Now we're talking.

Hearing yells of alarm in the wake of the shot, Roland aimed his M16 toward the voices, unloading another magazine. Coffren added his shotgun and someone else, either Bill Leisner or the team's leader, Lieutenant Matthew Byrne, was firing their own rifle.

New cries and what sounded like terrified shrieks burst from the nearby jungle, followed by a wave of intense, sustained weapons fire. Roland hunkered down behind his tree, but after several seconds he realized none of the fire seemed aimed in their direction.

What the hell?

To his right, Coffren and Pearson rose from behind the massive log that was their makeshift shelter, aiming their weapons toward the source of the gunfire. Pearson let loose with another buckshot round from the M79. With practiced ease and confidence, Pearson dropped the spent shell from the grenade launcher, replacing it with another round in quick fashion while Coffren provided covering fire. Then Coffren recoiled, dropping to the ground as something bright and yellow-green tore through the underbrush and slammed into Pearson. There was time for Roland to register that the shot—whatever it was—passed completely through the other man before the grenadier lurched backward. Pearson's arms flailed as he fell to the ground.

"Scotty!"

Shouting toward his friend, Roland divided his attention between Pearson and Coffren, scanning the tree line, looking for the source of the shot, but saw nothing. Further back in the jungle, he still heard frantic cries and AK-47s firing as though in every direction.

Then, everything went quiet.

No gunfire, no voices, nothing. The abrupt, surreal change was enough to make Roland and Coffren exchange befuddled looks. Shrugging, Roland moved from behind the tree, his M16 leading the way. Coffren mimicked his team mate's actions while making his way to the fallen Pearson, who lay in an awkward sprawl, his rucksack arching his back. Beyond them, Roland saw Corporal Bill Leisner rise from where he'd been lying prone in a small depression. Damp mud and a few leaves clung to his dirty uniform.

"Where the hell did everybody go?" asked Leisner.

Unable to answer, Roland simply shook his head.

"Pearson's dead," reported Coffren, gesturing down to the body of their friend. "Don't ask me how."

That was obvious to Roland even from where he stood. The man's eyes were open in a fixed expression of shock, and the wound in the center of his chest, surrounded by blood and blackened skin and muscle tissue, was at least as big as his fist.

Cradling his M16, Leisner stepped around the other two Marines. "Where's Byrne?"

For the first time, Roland realized he hadn't seen or heard Lieutenant Byrne since the beginning of the skirmish.

"Sweep the area. Find him."

From his vantage point, camouflaged within the thick canopy of the tree branches high above the ground, Nk'mecci watched the final moments of the fierce skirmish taking place far below him. The two groups, one far outnumbered by the other, had ceased firing their weapons and the larger contingent moved deeper into the jungle, its numbers greatly reduced both as a consequence of the fight as well as his own influence. Heat signatures generated by the bodies of the combatants and picked up by his bio-mask's visual sensors told Nk'mecci that the smaller cluster of fighters now numbered three. They had survived the clash with their enemy on the ground, though two had fallen to him, along with several others from the larger group.

In truth, he could have taken all of the combatants with little effort, but there was no sport in that. Besides, a simple hunt was not the purpose of his visit. That might come later, provided the current circumstances didn't change to any significant degree.

He regarded the skull in his hand, still covered with blood and remnants of tissue from his quarry's body. Cleaning and polishing it prior to adding it to his small yet growing trophy collection would have to wait. Only with great reluctance did he set aside the skull, perching it atop a branch just above his head. As for the others he had taken, Nk'mecci disliked the notion of leaving them for the local animal life to consume. He would return for his trophies before departing this world, if at all possible.

With slow, deliberate movements, Nk'mecci checked the wounds he had sustained while on the ground. Removing his left hand from his side, he saw that the bleeding there was slowing. Despite his cloak, he was unable to avoid being injured by the humans' projectile weapons. Vital organs appeared to have been missed, but the injuries to his torso and leg still required attention, if for no other reason than to prevent infection. His leg injury would be simple to treat, if painful, but he would need to remove the projectile from his midsection. His movements might be hampered in the short term, though it was nothing he could not endure.

His equipment was another matter. The power cell for his cloak had also been hit, and now the shroud only operated in intermittent fashion. Continuing to use it in its damaged state might draw more attention than if he simply moved without it, so Nk'mecci opted to deactivate it. From this elevation, he could escape detection with greater ease, but attempting to stalk the humans would prove problematic. On the other hand, this new limitation would increase the challenge as he carried out his mission.

It was not Nk'mecci's first visit to this planet. Many cycles ago as a young, unblooded *Yautja*, he had accompanied his father and older sibling to hunt. The choice of location was altogether different in both terrain and temperature, and the indigenous weapons and technologies had been somewhat less advanced. As now, though, the humans tracked and killed during that previous hunt were caught up in the grips of their own conflict, albeit on a much larger scale in terms of numbers and the level of wanton violence and destruction. The hunting had been fruitful, with the three *Yautja* bringing back numerous trophies and other mementos to mark the occasion.

For this excursion, Nk'mecci traveled alone for the first time, as was customary for blooded hunters. Preliminary scouting reports of the escalating conflict on this world had drawn much interest, and many *Yautja* were clamoring for the chance to revisit such fertile hunting grounds. The opportunity offered by his clan to investigate this region of the planet was one he could not ignore, and to do so on his own would also be viewed as something of a test.

Based on the observations made since his arrival,

Nk'mecci concluded that while the invading force was better equipped and possessed armaments and vehicles not shared by its adversary, the combatants who seemed to be guardians of this region were defending it well. There were indications of influence and assistance by yet another contingent, which also wielded better weapons and technology, but their role appeared limited and confined to areas well away from here. Nk'mecci guessed that situation might change, depending on how long this conflict persisted. It would be fascinating to observe, he decided.

For now, the defending force seemed well-suited to the battle it faced. Nk'mecci guessed that a familiarity with the terrain was at the heart of the advantages these warriors enjoyed. While observing their movements, he discovered a network of underground tunnels and passages which seemed to be all but unknown to the invaders. The tactic was noteworthy, in that it allowed the defenders to transport personnel and materiel through the unforgiving jungle almost without detection and at speeds greater than their counterparts. It was not a true equalizer in the grand scheme of things, but it served to make things interesting.

As for the invaders, they appeared reliant on their superior weapons and equipment, almost to a fault. They infiltrated enemy areas of this vast, unrelenting jungle in small numbers, using their primitive airborne conveyances to transport combatants from secure locations to these remote areas. They moved with relative stealth, as though conducting reconnaissance of their own. Perhaps they were gathering information for later use by a larger force with a more conventional goal of securing territory and resources. This made sense from a strategic perspective, but only time would bear out such a theory; time Nk'mecci did not possess.

Below him, the humans from the smaller force were gathering around the remains of their comrades, doubtless attempting to deduce what had happened. It had been a simple matter for Nk'mecci to identify the leader of each group and remove them from the equation, allowing the remaining combatants to process and adjust to the change in status quo so that he could study their reactions. This activity was not a component of his mission parameters, but remained within the acceptable sphere of deviation. Such opportunity could not be forsaken, particularly if it provided valuable insights about the object of a hunt.

What would they do now?

Staring down at the corpse, it took Roland an extra moment to ensure himself that he was in fact looking at the remains of his patrol leader, Matthew Byrne.

The brass bracelet on the lieutenant's right wrist—a gift crafted from old shell casings by a Montagnard villager—was a better identifier for Byrne than the man's own face, which was all but unrecognizable owing to the complete lack of a skull. It, along with the entire spine, appeared to have been cut or pulled out by some measure of force. How was that even possible? Blood was everywhere, dark red and glistening after having drained from Byrne's body to stain his uniform and equipment. The stench of loosened bowels and bladder was almost overpowering, and Roland forced himself to breathe through his mouth. Reaching for the M16 lying on the ground next to the lieutenant's right hand, he inspected the weapon.

"He never got off the first shot." He ejected the full magazine, sticking it in the pocket of his drab green uniform blouse.

"The gooks did this?" asked Corporal Bill Leisner, who along with Roland served as one of the team's riflemen. Roland heard the uncertainty and fear in the other Marine's voice.

"Who else?" Even as he asked the question, Roland shook his head. "What I don't get is how. We were out of each other's line of sight for, what? A minute?"

Unable to look away from Byrne's mutilated form, he instead studied the extensive damage inflicted upon the lieutenant's body. John Coffren had been the one to find him, nearly twenty meters from where Roland was standing when the ambush came, along with the bizarre sequence of events accompanying it which resulted in the deaths of Scotty Pearson and, it seemed, Lieutenant Byrne.

"What I want to know is why they ran," said Coffren. "You heard them, right? Something spooked the shit out of them."

Roland nodded. In addition to Byrne's body, the team had found eight dead Viet Cong soldiers sprawled in the jungle. The positions of their bodies indicated not all of them had died as a result of the recon team's return fire during the attack. Four were killed some distance from where Leisner determined the ambush was set, and one of those had died in a manner similar to Pearson, with a massive wound punched through the center of his chest.

What the hell does that kind of damage?

"We can't stay here," said Coffren. "The pricks we didn't shoot will be back, and they'll have friends."

Glancing past the other Marine, Roland studied the bunker set into the side of the sloping hill. All but invisible in the thick jungle undergrowth, the hideaway was a shelter built from tree branches and other broad-leaf vegetation designed to let the structure blend into its surroundings. So effective was the bunker's camouflage that the recon team's point man, Leisner, almost tripped over the damned thing. It was an unexpected find, yielding nothing of use or potential value, although the ambush was enough to prove that Charlie must have known they would be here to investigate.

This was enough to make Roland nervous, especially in light of their mission to find any evidence of a prisoner of war camp somewhere in this stretch of the Quảng Trị Province's northern boundary. Rumors about such a camp had circulated off and on for months with nothing to back them up, and the issue was set aside as more pressing matters demanded the attention of recon teams. Things only heated up again when it became known that the son of a prominent United States senator was an Air Force pilot shot down somewhere near the demilitarized zone. If a POW camp existed in this area, it would be a logical place to take the pilot, assuming he was even still alive.

Familiar enough with the region, both from studying charts and photos as well as time spent surveying it on the ground and in the air, Roland was confident no camp was here. Regardless, orders were orders, and it had been with a degree of renewed urgency that his team was dispatched to investigate. Unlike typical Force Recon patrols, this outing was planned as a short hop and pop into the area, with a five-man team to keep things light, fast and mobile. Forty-eight hours on the ground after a near-dawn insertion to validate or refute the intel about the POW camp and then out, hopefully without attracting enemy attention.

The plan lasted the better part of thirty-six hours before going to shit, as Byrne and Pearson could testify.

"Remind me to cock-punch those S-2 assholes when we get back," said Coffren. "They said this place was supposed to be quiet."

Roland grunted in agreement. The team's pre-mission intelligence briefing indicated no significant enemy activity or movement in the area, an assertion which had gone up in smoke. Now, the question was to what degree that intel was incorrect.

"If those guys were part of a larger force," he said, "then we're in some right deep shit."

Coffren replied, "Neck deep, and with raging hemorrhoids." He was busying himself with finding room in his rucksack and pockets for the extra magazines he now held. Both he and Roland along with Leisner had divided the remaining ammunition carried by Byrne and Pearson. Coffren had taken the extra step of burying the dead men's weapons and other equipment that was of no further use.

"I think we got lucky," said Roland. "If they really knew we were coming and had time to plan, they'd have set up a larger ambush and cut us to shit."

The Viet Cong were notorious for their ambush tactics, which involved elaborate setups that took into account everything from weather to terrain, and involved recon and tracking activities which might take hours and even days to bring to fruition as they prepared to attack a targeted force. However, that did not rule out a smaller contingent performing its own recon patrol and simply taking advantage of time and opportunity to carry out its own ambush.

"Maybe we spooked them, but next time? They'll have

our asses. We need to get gone. *Now.*" Removing his boonie hat, Roland wiped sweat from his face. Even with the relatively cool January temperatures, the jungle was still hot and humid. "Too bad we can't call for a ride."

Despite Roland's misgivings, none of the team even carried a radio in accordance with their orders. Their mission called for such stealth that in the minds of those calling the shots back at HQ, even the risk of monitored communications carried too much risk. Of course, that ruled out calling for helicopter extraction ahead of the prearranged rendezvous time and location. Like the others, Roland had memorized that information rather than marking it on the map he carried in his pocket, in the event he was captured or killed and the map found by enemy soldiers. He knew he could navigate with his map and compass to the landing zone. They just had to get there by the scheduled time. If for some reason they failed to make that rendezvous, there was a backup time and LZ location. After that? They were screwed.

So, let's start hoofing.

"Guys," said Leisner, who was standing several yards away. "Check this out."

Strapping Pearson's M79 and bandolier of remaining grenades across his back, Roland moved with Coffren to join their companion. Roland was the first to see what had drawn the other Marine's attention. It was the body of yet another Vietnamese soldier, killed in a manner similar to Pearson and the other Cong. The corpse lay face down, with the muddy ground visible through the hole in its torso.

Coffren frowned. "One of you guys packing a rocket launcher you didn't tell me about?"

"He may have been the leader," said Roland, kneeling

next to the body and indicating the canvas satchel slung across its left shoulder. After verifying the bag wasn't booby-trapped, he removed it from the dead soldier and opened it. Papers comprised most of the contents, along with a pair of maps, which he handed to Leisner.

"Holy shit," said the other Marine after a minute studying the find. "This is a map of the province and the surrounding area. Look what's marked." The faster he talked, the more his distinctive Upper Midwest inflections asserted themselves.

Leaning for a closer look, Roland recognized several terrain features as well as Vietnamese and American military bases in proximity to the demilitarized zone. He couldn't help but note the lines drawn toward U.S.-controlled locations such as Đông Hà, Da Nang, and Quảng Trị City, along with numerous others across South Vietnam.

"What are these figures supposed to be?" asked Coffren.

Leisner shrugged. "I think it's code." The group's designated translator, he could speak and read Vietnamese, including several of the trickier dialects. After a moment, the Marine's eyes widened. "Damn. I think this might be an attack plan."

"Where?" asked Roland.

"Everywhere." Leisner stabbed the map. "This looks like a major offensive."

Coffren asked, "When?"

"Don't know. Nothing here indicates a date or time."

"Could it be for the attacks they just pulled?" The memories of the recent rocket and mortar assault on Quảng Trị Base and other American targets just days earlier, prior to their departure for this mission, were still fresh in Roland's mind.

Leisner shook his head. "This looks bigger than all of that. A *lot* bigger."

"We take it with us." Roland gestured with his satchel toward the map. "Somebody smarter than us can figure it out when we get back." He checked his watch. "We've got about twelve hours to make it to the LZ. Let's get the hell out of here."

The three humans were walking into a trap.

Lurking high above the jungle floor and using both the now fading darkness and the thick tree canopy for concealment, Nk'mecci watched the genesis of the attack as it evolved. The sensors in his bio-mask showed him the heat signatures of the twelve bodies maneuvering into position, well away from the narrow rail that wound through the undergrowth for some distance toward a larger, wider path used by ground vehicles. In another direction, he observed that the jungle gave way to a large, relatively clear area dominated by high grass. Based on his observation of the smaller group's progress through the region, Nk'mecci suspected that glade might well be a location designated for retrieval by one of their airborne vehicles.

With fascination, he observed this larger force's inspection of the area, working as if to anticipate the course being charted by the interlopers before assuming positions within the thick foliage. The group had decided on a straightforward arrangement of the individual combatants, with a portion of them directing their weapons toward the approach vector they expected their adversaries to utilize. The balance of the group was arrayed along what should be a flank, assuming the targets followed their current path through the undergrowth. It was a tactic not that dissimilar from schemes Nk'mecci utilized as a young, unblooded *Yautja* learning the ways of the hunt on the homeworld under his father's tutelage. Those schemes were designed to stalk and kill large game animals, though experience taught him they were useful against more intelligent quarry, as well. Such appeared to be the case here.

Nk'mecci shifted his position, adjusting his bio-mask's visual sensors to increase their magnification. The trio of invaders was now visible, unknowingly making their way toward the site of the coming ambush. He had trailed their progress throughout the previous day until they settled into a defensive position as darkness fell. Only then had he detected the presence of the enemy force. The three now were charting a course running parallel to the established jungle trail which allowed them to utilize the undergrowth for concealment. They were not charting a direct path for the glade, but their only logical reason for being in this area, based on their past behavior, was a rendezvous just after daylight. Though they moved with stealth and alertness, they appeared to have no idea what awaited them. If all went according to plan, the attackers would be able to take their prey with ease.

The ambush would be a slaughter.

———

Feeble, predawn sunlight filtered through the trees, providing the only illumination. It was sufficient for Roland to make out the ground ahead of him. Moving in a slow, deliberate fashion, he chose each step with care, stopping each time to listen and search for signs of danger. The telltale sounds of insects and even the odd bird filled the air, but otherwise the only thing he heard was his own breathing, which he fought to keep low and regular.

Almost there.

A nerve-wracking day spent traversing the jungle followed by a defensive watch to get them through the night had brought them to this point. If his read of the map and compass were correct, they were less than an hour from the primary extraction point. Sixty minutes and he and the others would be on the chopper, heading back to base.

It would feel like an eternity.

Unable to sleep, Roland spent the quiet hours trying to order his thoughts. There would be much to report upon their return, particularly about the strange weapons which had killed Byrne and Pearson. Were the Russians supplying some kind of new technology to the Cong? That didn't explain the dead Vietnamese soldiers, but the thing had come from somewhere. Who was responsible?

The spooks can figure it out.

Two short, low hisses from behind him made him pause in mid-step. The muted warning from John Coffren told him that the other Marine had heard or seen something. With agonizing slowness, Roland placed his foot back to the ground before lowering himself into a crouch. Once there, he shifted just enough to see Coffren. The lance corporal squatted five meters behind him, the barrel of his shotgun resting across his left forearm. Behind him and separated by a similar interval, Bill Leisner had dropped to one knee, his M16 up and ready. Coffren, his gaze focused on Roland, pointed toward his own eyes, then gestured toward the jungle ahead of them.

Enemy spotted.

Turning to look in the indicated direction, Roland scanned the jungle, searching for movement or anything which looked out of place; some shadow or shape that seemed not to belong. Though his eyes and ears told him nothing was there, every muscle and nerve ending signaled danger. Despite his best efforts, Roland felt his breathing quicken in anticipation, and his pulse now pounded in his ears. Staring into the gloom, he felt his right hand tightening around his M16's pistol grip.

Something's wrong, damn it!

The crack of a tree limb, perhaps thirty or forty meters away, was like a rifle shot ripping apart the silence around them. Roland jerked his head around to look for the source, catching sight of something moving among the high branches of a tall tree. A dark silhouette scrambled as though trying to keep from falling. Without thinking, Roland lifted his M16 and sighted down its barrel.

He was too late. Someone else fired first.

AK-47 fire from multiple points among the dense undergrowth tore apart the night air. Roland flattened himself on the ground, glancing behind him to see that Coffren and Leisner were following suit. Ahead of them, the gunfire continued, though now it was accompanied by... something else?

"Hear that?"

It was Coffren, his voice low. He pointed his shotgun toward the chaos. "It's the thing that killed Pearson. I'm sure of it."

Roland realized his friend was right. Flashes of green light, like tracer fire but larger and slower, were raining down from the trees. Each time one of the pulsing orbs struck they detonated like dynamite, and Roland saw a figure silhouetted by the blast.

"Ambush," said Leisner, who had crawled closer to his companions. "Jesus, we almost walked right into it."

Rifle fire concentrated on the tree that was the source of the odd light, and Roland saw the other, larger figure moving with speed and agility among the branches. Who the hell could move like that?

Shouts from somewhere else in the nearby bush, anxious voices yelling in Vietnamese, were accompanied by shots. This time, the rounds were coming in their direction, and Roland and the others flattened themselves on the ground.

"I think they know we're here," said Leisner.

Exchanging his rifle for the M79 slung across the top of his rucksack, Roland breached the weapon and exchanged the buckshot round for one of the high-explosive shells from the bandolier he'd taken off Scotty Pearson. Leisner was already firing his M16 into the brush, and Coffren added four shots from his Remington shotgun. Raising his head, Roland caught sight of two enemy soldiers crouching behind a fallen tree.

"Fire in the hole." He aimed the M79 and pulled the trigger. A second later the grenade struck the tree in front of the enemy soldiers and detonated. Roland saw both men fall back and out of sight. For the first time, he realized that all of the other shooting seemed to have stopped.

"How many?" he asked, dropping to a knee.

Coffren, bracing his left shoulder against a thick tree, fed new shells into his shotgun. "Ten or twelve at the start. No idea, now."

"Over there!" shouted Leisner, elevating his M16's

muzzle as though sighting on a target well above the ground.

Roland tracked the other man's aim in time to see the dark figure scrambling among the high branches. The thing was huge, far larger than a man, and crossing gaps between trees that were too far for any normal person to negotiate. Its size and agility were matched only by its speed, which was almost too fast to follow.

Coffren unloaded his shotgun while Leisner emptied another magazine from his M16. None of the rounds seemed to find their mark, as the shadowy figure lunged from branch to branch. Reloading the M79 with the buckshot round, Roland shifted his aim just as the thing stopped less than ten meters away, and he saw something on its left shoulder pivoting as though aiming in their direction.

"Look out!"

The warning came too late as a blob of green energy spat forth from the odd device, striking Leisner and driving him backward. Roland saw the bolt drill through the corporal's chest and chew into the damp, muddy ground behind him. Already dead, Leisner fell in a limp heap, his jungle hat falling from his head and revealing his open, unseeing eyes.

"No!"

Roland aimed the M79. Before he fired, he had time to note the figure's bizarre appearance—a helmet that covered its face and clothing that looked more like mesh covering a massive, muscled body. A belt and harness carried numerous items, none of which Roland recognized.

What the hell is it?

He pulled the trigger and the thing started to move but the grenade was faster. The expanding cloud of buckshot hit it full in the chest, knocking it from its perch and sending it crashing toward the ground.

Out of buckshot, Roland loaded the launcher with one of his remaining high-explosive rounds. He aimed the weapon where the thing had fallen. Was it still alive? Where had it come from? He started to advance, but stopped when he felt Coffren's hand on his shoulder.

"Listen!" his friend hissed, and pointed toward the sky. "Choppers."

The pain was severe, yet manageable.

Nk'mecci rolled onto his side, every movement a small agony as he took stock of his condition. The swarm of projectiles had inflicted several wounds across his torso and extremities. His bio-mask remained functional, allowing him to see the two remaining humans plunging deeper into the jungle. Judging by their movements, they were discarding stealth in exchange for speed while seeking escape. In the distance, Nk'mecci heard the familiar sound of human air vehicles, drawing closer with each passing moment.

He cursed his carelessness. Spotted by one of the soldiers lying in wait to ambush their adversaries, he was left with no choice but to neutralize the humans. What he had failed to anticipate was a tree branch that was insufficient to support his weight. Its breaking had drawn the attention of the entire party, and without his cloaking shroud, Nk'mecci was forced to protect himself. He had taken most of the ambush force, with the others killed by their adversaries. That his kills were born of necessity rather than sport was disappointing.

There were the three last remaining humans, but his chance to take them was fading.

They, at least, might provide one last challenge, but was he up to the task? A drug from his medi-kit provided a powerful stimulant and helped keep his pain at bay, but healing his wounds required the resources aboard his ship. Returning there would likely mean giving up this final chance to take trophies.

For a blooded hunter of any worth, there was only one choice.

Pulling the incendiary grenade's pin, Roland threw it toward the center of the glade. The grenade disappeared into the tall elephant grass and began spewing yellow smoke, the color designated as the signal for their extraction. Within seconds the cloud of smoke expanded and rose toward the sky.

"Here they come," said Coffren from where he crouched next to Roland in the tree line south of the clearing.

Roland felt the first rush of relief begin to wash over him as he watched the first Bell UH-1 helicopter appear over the nearby trees and make a circuit of the area, flying low and fast. Its side door was open and a gunner sat behind an M60 machine gun, aiming the weapon toward the ground as he searched for threats. If anything looked as though it might present a danger to the choppers, Roland knew the gunner would unleash the M60's fury upon the jungle below them.

"Get ready."

Wearing the M79 slung across his chest while he gripped his M16, Roland divided his attention between the trees behind them and the second Huey as it maneuvered into view. Unlike his companion, who had assumed an orbit above the landing zone to provide security, this chopper was making a rapid descent toward the clearing. Roland waited until the Huey was less than twenty feet above the ground to slap Coffren's back.

"Go!"

Both men sprinted from the tree line and into the open. Roland counted the seconds as the chopper dropped to hover mere feet above the ground. The action of its rotor blades flattened the grass, providing a clear approach for the two Marines as they closed the distance. All other sounds were drowned out by the Huey's engine, which the pilot was already revving in anticipation of takeoff.

Then Roland saw the bolt of green energy punch through Coffren, never hearing the bark of the strange weapon that killed him.

"John!"

Coffren, already dead, was falling to the ground as the Huey's gunner swung the barrel of his M60 to return fire, and Roland had to drop as a hellish torrent of bullets spat from the weapon toward something he couldn't see. Rolling away from Coffren's body, Roland twisted around and came up on one knee, aiming his M16 back toward the tree line, just as another green fireball streaked across the clearing. The shot was off, but still close enough to graze Roland's left shoulder. Molten heat exploded at the point of impact as he spun and dropped to the grass. The M16 fell from his hand and he landed hard on the grenade launcher that was still slung across his chest, gasping as he felt what had to be a rib crack.

He looked to the edge of the clearing in time to see the mysterious figure—the *thing*—emerging from the undergrowth forty or so meters away. Even from this distance, Roland saw yellowish-green fluid draining from multiple wounds in its chest and arms. Whatever it was, it certainly wasn't human. It was like a nightmare come to life.

The odd weapon mounted to the thing's shoulder swiveled to aim toward the sky. There was no time or chance for Roland to offer any warning before the weapon fired a stream of hellish green energy skyward. Three of the shots struck the chopper, including one that hit its engine compartment, and the Huey exploded in mid-air, ripping itself apart as it lost all flight and plummeted in a flaming heap to the ground. It disappeared into the trees north of the LZ where a second detonation released a roiling cloud of fire and smoke.

Behind him, Roland could just hear the remaining Huey's gunner, shouting above the roar of the engine.

"Come on, man! We've got to go!"

Without air cover, the chopper was in greater danger of attack by ambush from the trees. Its pilot would want to get the hell out of here, and Roland knew if he didn't move, he risked being abandoned.

Then the creature charged.

Not as fast as Roland had seen it move earlier, the thing was still able to dodge the Huey gunner's renewed string of M60 fire. It released a guttural roar that Roland heard even over the chopper's engine, weaving and dodging the machine gun's bullets with uncanny speed.

Roland ignored the gunner's shouts to get aboard, along with the pain from his shoulder and his injured rib. Every breath was like someone stabbing him in the side. Gritting his teeth, he lifted the M79. Without thinking or even really aiming, he pointed the grenade launcher at the creature and fired.

The round landed short, perhaps three meters in front of the thing, but when it detonated, the blast was enough to knock the creature off its feet. Muscled arms and legs flailed as the thing dropped to the ground, hidden by the elephant grass. The Huey gunner raked that area with the M60 as Roland turned and ran for the chopper's open door.

He stopped short as the other man was thrown backward by another of the green bolts, his body sailing through the open door on the helicopter's far side. In the cockpit, the pilot's expression turned to one of horror before the entire side of the canopy disappeared in a burst of fire and glass that was whirled about by the action of the Huey's rotor blades, and Roland fell to the grass to avoid being struck by shrapnel. A third round from the bizarre weapon ripped through the chopper's cockpit, killing its co-pilot while Roland could do nothing but watch.

A shadow fell across the grass in front of him, and Roland rolled over to see the creature standing above him. The thing was massive, its hands terminating with oversized claws which were not at all human. Its left arm hung limply at its side, and the same pale yellow-green fluid ran from dozens of wounds across its body. Even the strange helmet it wore to shield its face was marred, likely peppered with shrapnel from the grenade. Its breathing sounded as though it might be labored, and while it looked capable of killing him with little effort, Roland sensed no real malice from the creature. It was studying him, as though he were nothing more than a lab specimen, or even an insect.

"What the hell are you?"

Nk'mecci was dying.

His wounds from the explosive, coupled with the injuries already sustained, would prove fatal if left untreated. That much he had learned from his ship's automated medical equipment. Honor precluded him from using those same facilities to heal his failing body. While he had successfully completed his mission—the records of which would be returned to the homeworld with or without his being alive to accompany them—he had failed to carry out the hunt. One might argue that the exercise was unsanctioned, and therefore not subject to the rules and codes observed by all blooded *Yautja*. Nk'mecci chose not to exploit such a faithless interpretation of the rituals which had defined his people for uncounted generations.

He had failed. Therefore, his life was forfeit.

Sitting at the controls of his ship, Nk'mecci studied the flow of information being relayed to him through the vessel's network of scanners and recording devices. From orbit high above the lush blue-green world, he was able to watch the land battle currently underway in the section of continent he had left behind. If the data from the scans was accurate, the invading or occupying force with its superior weapons and equipment was currently enduring simultaneous armed incursions at numerous locations across the region. The attacking force, which seemed to call this land home, had launched a massive, multi-pronged offensive. It was a bold strategy, its scope rivaled only by its audacity and synchronicity. Nk'mecci suspected the targets of this attack would retaliate, bringing to bear all of their supposedly greater weapons and technology. The question was whether their spirit would be broken by this assault, or fueled by a need for vengeance. Regardless, it would be something to behold, though he would not live to see it. He cared not at all about which side might be the victor. It was the thrill of the conflict which drove him, as it did all true hunters.

All that remained for him was to verify that his ship would follow its programmed course home, and that the report of his mission was safeguarded until it could be studied. He was confident his findings would be greeted with much enthusiasm by those eager to partake of a new challenge here on this world which already had afforded so much in that regard.

This much was embodied by the skull sitting before him on the console. Despite his injuries, Nk'mecci had taken the time to ensure it was cleaned and polished, ready for display along with the rest of his collection. His prey deserved such respect, for this was a proper trophy, taken from the remaining human who had proven a worthy adversary. If Nk'mecci harbored any regrets, it was that he would never again partake of such rewarding contests. This prize, along with his report, would provide his clan with all the assurance and encouragement they needed to return to this world and relish in the sport it continued to offer.

Hunting here remains fruitful.

GAMEWORLD

BY JONATHAN MABERRY

1

"Who's ready to die?"

The words blasted out of the speakers and a thousand voices roared back in one huge, inarticulate bellow of bloodlust.

The club's owner, Sake Chiba, grinned like a ghoul. He was dressed in a glittering green suit with pinned-back collars and a pair of lizard-skin shoes that cost more than most soldiers made in a month. Hogarth Fix watched him from the competitor benches, shouting when the others shouted, screaming when they screamed.

"Who wants to see blood on this deck?" growled Chiba, pointing a stiff finger at the metal floor on which he stood. The pentangle was not padded or sprung, there were no mats. Only unforgiving steel and paint. All of the colors were bright whites and yellows so that blood would stand out. There was always blood. Most of it was red. Some of it was human. All of it was spilled for pay.

Fix sat at the end of the second row of fighters. He wasn't on tonight's card and, with any luck, wouldn't ever have to step into the pentangle. He was a good fighter, maybe as good as most of the men and women here, but men and women weren't the only things he might have to fight. In the Special Forces, they taught you how to win fights by any means necessary, including a hell of a lot of ruthless, no-compromise hand-to-hand; but they usually sent their operators in loaded down with guns, knives, and explosives. And wrapped in body armor.

Chiba wasn't about that.

Fighters wore spandex shorts. The women were allowed a sports bra. No cups, no pads. Tape on the hands, but no bite shields or Kevlar-4L, no spider-silk limb pads. None of that. Meat and muscle, blood and bone, and the advantages of knowledge and experience.

Against monsters.

Last night the title match featured a big Serbian kid who had served five tours with the Interglobal Soviet People's Army, and who had a win record in mixed martial arts matches on Earth of twenty-eight and one. Moose of a guy. Fix wouldn't have wanted to meet him in a dark alley with anything short of a shoulder-mounted rocket launcher. The Serbian went in as the odds-on favorite and if he had thrown down against any of the other guys on this bench he might have walked out. Instead they shoveled him into a body bag. The parts of him that the tiger hadn't eaten.

If you could call that cocksucker a tiger. Transgenics is a funny thing. The body was tiger, but the jaws hinged open like a snake and the neurotoxin sacs in his mouth were from a puffer fish. The Serb lasted longer than anyone would have guessed once Chiba trotted the beast out of its cage. Eighty-seven seconds. Everyone in the first six rows were speckled red.

That was how this worked. If the Serbian had beaten the tiger, or even lasted the full three minutes, he'd have pocketed enough cash to buy a farm on one of the terraformed moons. A good-sized farm, too. Maybe grow hashish for the crews of the long-range haulers. Instead the cleanup crew had collected enough of him for burial purposes, and his participation fee—a few thousand—went to his mother back on Earth. Fix wasn't sure what kind of message went with it. Probably airlock failure. That was always popular.

Sake Chiba was still whipping the crowd up for the next bout. He was a big man himself, a former sumo wrestler from New Osaka, who'd retired while he was still on top and invested half his money in promotion and the rest in technologies stocks. He was one of the new class of trillionaires who seemed unable to stop making money. His latest enterprise, *Gameworld*, was technically off the books, but people knew about it. Whispered about it. Bragged about having been there.

Chiba was why Hogarth Fix was here. Not the fights. Not the mutant monsters. Not this fucking crowd of bloodthirsty privileged dickheads who spent insane amounts of money to watch illegal matches.

Chiba.

If you wanted to bet on it, have sex with it, eat it, or kill it, Chiba could set it up. And because *Gameworld* was in "the rocks"—a part of the asteroid belt between Mars and Jupiter that had questionable territorial affiliation—he got away with it.

That was going to change, Fix promised himself. And when it did, Chiba was going to the mat and Fix was going to stroll off with enough money to make sure his kids never had to want for anything. Not ever again. Not after this.

Fix watched Chiba's eyes as he worked the crowd. The man fed on this. Not on the fun, not on the energy, maybe not even on the money. No, he was like a vampire. He fed on the adoration, and that's what this was. People *worshipped* him as the celebrity's celebrity.

"Do you want blood?" demanded Chiba.

People—some of whom were as rich as Chiba—were screaming hysterically, pumping their fists in the air, faces flushed red, eyes wild. One of them, the actress from London who was in those movies about the ice dancer on Europa, started the chant.

"Blood! Blood! Blood!"

The rest of the crowd took it up at once.

"Blood! Blood! Blood!"

Fix glanced around at his fellow competitors. Eighteen men, eleven women, one surgical hermaphrodite. Five of them had won several matches here. This wasn't the Roman circus, as one of them had told him during training. Sometimes it was human against human. Sometimes the fighters on this bench won out against the trans-G animals. Helga, the troll-like woman next to him, had broken the neck of an orangutan last Tuesday. She still had bandages over the stitches, but she'd won, and when the bandages came off she swore to go back onto the floor to "paint my name in the blood of anyone or anything they send out of the gate. Take that to the bank, newbie." That's what she'd told him.

The animals weren't the only things here that had paid a visit to their local Dr. Frankenstein. Helga's muscle mass had no origin in nature. The metal struts supporting the Mexican wrestler's back sure as hell weren't original packaging. But that wasn't something the *Gameworld* recruiters told guys like Fix. Not until they'd already signed on. Which meant that half the people on the competitor bleachers were as unenhanced as he was.

The Mexican had talked about it with him the other night. "They need someone to die out there," he said philosophically, "because people don't come all the way out here to watch us thumb wrestle. You don't pay these ticket prices to see two knuckle-draggers batter each other to a split decision. Fuck that. You got to have something dead on the floor by the end of the night. Chiba's got a reputation to keep up. But… screw it. Who wants to live forever, right?"

That was how it was.

Fix pretended to smile, faked his war chants, shook his fists, and felt his heart hammering against the inside of his chest. He had been a soldier for a lot of years, and a rough and tumble street kid before that. He'd killed with guns and knives and his own hands, and he'd walked off battlefields littered with fallen comrades. But he had never, not in all his life, been this scared.

2

They didn't call Fix's number that night.

Or the next.

Or the next.

"Don't worry," said Helga. "You'll get your shot, sweetie."

"Can't wait," he lied. He was sure he'd told bigger lies than that, but he couldn't remember when.

Life on *Gameworld* was strange. Long periods of calm and even some luxurious living, interspersed with intense workouts and shocking violence. Every day.

This was day sixteen for him. Most fighters, he learned, didn't get their first undercard match for a month or two. There was that much competition to be noticed as having fought for Chiba. They called the dormitory the Box of Scorpions, which was a name that everyone seemed to think was stupid and juvenile but no one could shake. It was mentioned in a lot of the press, and customers could even pay to bunk down with the fighters. A few—only the really tough ones or the abominably stupid ones—paid to train with the team. Everyone else was scared off by the wording of the personal injury waivers.

The fighters could choose to train at any time. Never against each other, of course. But Chiba seemed able to tap an endless supply of willing sparring partners. Fix spent a lot of time watching the other fighters train, studying their moves, gauging their skill, calculating how much was natural talent, how much was learned technique, and how much came from actual experience. That was one of his gifts, perhaps his most useful one. He could read people. He'd been able to do it growing up in the slums of Gary, Indiana, fighting for food money, fighting for money to keep his three younger sisters fed and dressed and healthy after their single mother rode a needle into the big black. It served him well, even against better fighters, when a judge suggested he box in a local gym or spend six months in juvie. It helped him when another judge suggested that the military might be a better calling than working a prison detail mining precious metals on an asteroid. And it had kept him alive all through his twelve years humping battle rattle around the solar system.

It had not, sadly, helped him figure out that his ex-wife had been sleeping with nearly everyone who had a dick, a pulse, and a good credit rating. That blindsided him as surely as she'd been blindsided by an autonomous-drive UPS glider. Life's a quirky bitch like that.

On a busy Friday morning he climbed into the sparring ring with a new training partner. A black guy with a shaved head and cat's eye implants that were supposed to psych people out. Fix rarely looked at an opponent's eyes. Bad fighters don't know where to look and good fighters use their eyes to fool you. As Fix and his sparring partner—Owl— began moving around, Fix watched the other guy's body.

They moved in a counter-clockwise circle, Owl moving forward with a rocking motion, shifting weight between front and back leg with a lot of springy tension.

He's either a jumper or kicker. Or both.

Owl tried a few experimental jabs to try and provoke a counterpunch from Fix. That was telling. When Owl jabbed there was nothing behind the blows. They were light and fast, but he wasn't even trying to hit. *Not a boxer,* Fix decided. A boxer who could kick moved differently than a kicker who could throw a punch. Boxers had pride in their jabs, and there was always something to them. There was often a momentary set of body mass to make sure all of the PSI went down the arm and into the other guy instead of the way this guy did it. When Fix blocked Owl's jabs the lack of weight

PREDATOR: IF IT BLEEDS

placement caused some of the force to recoil against his own mass, and Owl rocked back each time.

Fix filed that away.

Sometimes a good boxer will pivot, even on a jab. Not a lot, but just enough and at high speed to make sure there was some authority to even the lightest punch.

Couple more jabs and he's going to kick, thought Fix. *A low Thai kick to the thighs. Something to keep me from outpacing him.*

It was inevitable. Owl jabbed, jabbed, faked, jabbed, and then kicked. A Muay Thai shin kick. Very, very fast.

Fix evaded it because he saw it coming yesterday. He could have swept the man right there and then. He could also have J-stepped into him, checked the kick on his hip, and done some of what his old coach had called "neighborhood work"—a series of body blows designed to bruise the ribs so bad that breathing would take too much effort. Fighters who lose their wind lose their fights. Owl was good, but he wasn't good enough for *Gameworld.*

Some of the trainers and staff were wandering around, watching the sparring matches. Out of the corner of his eye, Fix saw Chiba come in, and that split second of inattention earned him a creditable front kick to the gut. Fix rode it backward, letting the kick spend its force as a push, and then he danced sideways and let Owl chase him until Fix caught his breath.

Owl seemed to think he was winning the fight because he charged after Fix with a series of mid-height kicks that would have done a lot of damage had any of them landed. Fix worked his way backward and around, not letting the kicks drive him to the edge of the ring but instead tapping the incoming legs and using the force of his taps to power sideways cuts and jags. The kicks were very fast and as Owl got more frustrated the kicks carried more power. Too much. Fast kicks using snap were okay for a flurry, but heavier smashing and thrusting kicks used more of the kicker's body mass to deliver them, and that drained energy. Fast. Owl was sweating heavily and the match clock said they'd been going for only two minutes.

Then Owl's frustration overwhelmed his common sense and he tried to close the deal with a huge, max-power spinning heel kick. Had it connected it would have knocked out Fix and everyone he was related to.

But it was too big a kick for a match like this. Fix could have gone out for a sandwich and a cup of coffee and been back before that spin brought Owl's heel anywhere near his intended target. The problem was Owl had committed so heavily to it that Fix was going to have to dent him to keep this from getting truly ugly.

Fuck.

He stepped in, chin tucked, shoulder hunched and checked the spin at its source by jamming hard against the thigh. It was where the spin was most vulnerable. And, because there was no other way of wrapping this up, he did some neighborhood work.

He could see the look of confusion and then understanding in Owl's eyes as the man realized how badly he had underestimated his opponent. Fix was in his late thirties and his hair was prematurely salt-and-pepper. Bad posture and scar tissue made him look like someone who'd been living the hard life. He looked older, slower and smaller than he actually was.

Owl went down to knees and palms, choking and

gagging and trying to breathe. Fix sighed and stepped back, feeling sorry for the man.

When he turned away he immediately stopped because Sake Chiba was standing ten feet behind him. The big sumo wrestler was smoking a fat Europan cigar and grinning.

"What's your name?" he asked.

3

They were in Chiba's office, which was the size of most hotel lobbies, seated on opposite sides of a huge hardwood desk that must have cost a fortune to ship all the way out here, where everything was plastic or metal. One wall was filled with shelves crammed with trophies and awards from Chiba's days as a pro wrestler. The opposite wall was a massive glass aquarium in which transgenically-designed mermaids swam. There were harsh laws about human-animal hybridization, but Fix thought that the upper halves of each mermaid was a real adolescent girl. There was a vague look of self-aware horror in the oversized eyes of the swimming creatures. It was appalling.

Behind the desk was a wall safe with a massive steel door and a complex locking mechanism set with several kinds of biometric scanners. Fix longed to raid that safe, but there was no chance in the universe that he'd ever even glimpse what was inside. More than he'd ever need in ten lifetimes. Shit, even if that vault was stacked floor to ceiling with currency it couldn't be more than a drop of piss to someone like Chiba. The man was worth—according to the financial news—six point six trillion dollars. His beer money would pay every bill Fix would ever have and still leave enough to buy Texas.

Chiba waved him to a seat and poured them both a good

knock of gin over frozen cherries.

"That was a very interesting exhibition," said Chiba as he settled into his own massive chair.

"Just a sparring match, sir. Owl's got some nice moves. Made me work for it."

Chiba grinned. "Bullshit. I saw eleven separate times where you could have hurt him and you didn't. I could *see* that you didn't. Not until he gave you no choice."

Fix sipped his drink, said nothing. Waited.

"Why not?" asked Chiba.

"Just a sparring match," Fix repeated.

"Ah," said Chiba, brightening. "You didn't want to go all out because there were no stakes."

"That's part of it, sure."

"Let me guess the rest. There were other fighters in the room. You didn't want to school them on how you really fight."

Fix nodded. "That's about it, boss."

Chiba swallowed half his drink and sat crunching a cherry, his eyes studying Fix. "You're ex-army?"

"Yes. Been out for a while now."

"Special Forces, as I understand it."

"Sure."

"Where did you see action?"

"Here and there. Lot's been going on around the system. Mostly by the time they sent us in things had either gone to hell or cooled down. The movies they make glamorize it, but we didn't do anything too crazy."

"Oh? It's my understanding you were a team leader when SpecOps breached the prison ship after it had been taken over by the inmates."

Fix said nothing. The records of that mission were sealed. No one outside of the military high command should be able to read that file.

Chiba continued, "Then there was the Rubio Cartel on Mars that got wiped out virtually overnight. And the rescue of the ambassador and her entire staff. A twelve-man team goes in and saves the lives of eighty-six people in a hot zone. One hundred and seventeen hostiles dead. Shall I go on?"

"Guess you don't have to."

The big man nodded. "And now you're here."

"Now I'm here."

"And why is that, Mr. Fix?"

"If you know everything about me, then you already know why I'm here."

"Fair enough," conceded Chiba. "You have three kids. Your wife is dead and you are sinking in debt. Your youngest—is her name Daisy?"

"Daisy," said Fix hoarsely.

"Daisy. She has cancer. Your health coverage doesn't begin to stretch far enough to cover the medical bills. Not if you can get her into the new treatment program in Stockholm. You could never hope to beg, borrow or steal that much money."

Fix said nothing.

"So, while I can understand what might have made you look in my direction—I am known as a generous employer and fight purses *will* stretch far enough to provide for your family—why risk it? You can't earn enough money if you're dead."

"Actually," said Fix, "I can."

"Life insurance policy?"

"Yeah. With an off-world danger clause. The way I figure it, either I earn enough and bring the cash home, or I die trying and my estate planner and lawyer make sure Daisy and the other kids are taken care of. As long as I fight, I can't really lose."

"You're not afraid of dying?"

Fix was prepared to lie, because he lied a lot. He didn't give Chiba a lie in answer to that question.

"Of course I am. But I'm a lot more afraid of failing my kids."

Chiba finished his drink and poured another, then he sat back and studied Fix for a long, quiet time. A slow smile formed on his face. "I'm not sure I can remember the last time I was impressed by personal integrity."

"Um... thanks?"

"But I like you. I like the moves I saw downstairs. I like the fire I see in your eyes. And I even like the fear I see there. Ruthless fighters are a dime a dozen. They're entertaining in the short term but boring overall. You, on the other hand, might be something else. You're not fighting because you hate everyone, or because you're dead inside. No, you're fighting for love. Not sure I've ever seen that before. Certainly not on *Gameworld*."

Fix sipped his drink. His pulse had suddenly jumped.

"I want to offer you a fight," said Chiba.

"Okay," Fix said neutrally. "Kind of why I'm here, though, isn't it?"

"I'm not talking about a brawl with one of the lunkheads in the Box of Scorpions. No... I have a special card coming up and I've been looking for exactly the right fighter for it."

"Why is that me?"

"Because I like what I saw today, and I like what I've seen in your military record. You are that rare kind of counter-fighter that is a kind of scientist of combat. It's there in the after-action reports from your SpecOps missions and it was evident in the way you fought Owl. You analyze, you deconstruct and assess, and then you adjust your own fighting style accordingly. That's an old samurai skill, and it's very much the way I used to fight. It's why I won so many times. It's why I'm good in business, because I study my opponents and can anticipate what they will do, how they'll move, *when* they'll act."

Fix studied Chiba over the rim of his class as he took a micro-sip. "If you're talking about asking me to fight a grizzly or some shit, then I don't see that as a real career opportunity for me. I trip and fall out of an airlock and the insurance company will still pay off to my kids. I don't need to be humiliated in some stunt match."

"Stunt match?" echoed Chiba, mildly miffed. Then he shrugged. "Sure, okay, you got me on that. The rubes love them, though."

"I'm not a rube."

"No," agreed Chiba, "but that's really not the kind of fight I have in mind. No bears, no tigers, no growth-enhanced centipedes. And... I don't think I want to waste you on mouth-breathers like Helga or the other idiots you've been bunking with."

"Who's that leave?"

"Not who," said Chiba, beaming at him. "It's really more of a *what*."

GAMEWORLD

4

"What in the *hell* is that thing?"

Chiba and Fix stood on a catwalk above the lighted rim of a containment tank. The tank was circular and thirty feet deep with smooth walls and a floor covered with straw and piles of dark green matter that stank like shit. Fix realized it probably *was* shit, despite the color. There were bones and pieces of torn meat scattered around the pit. No bed, no furniture.

A single figure stood in the center of the pit, staring up at them.

"I have no idea," said Chiba happily.

"How can you not know? You made it, didn't you? Or your pet scientists?"

Chiba shook his head. "No, I told you, this isn't one of my genetic toys. Quite frankly none of us know what this thing is. And isn't that wonderful?"

"Is it… is it… human?" stammered Fix.

Chiba pointed down at the creature. "Human? That? You tell me."

The thing was vaguely manlike, in that it had two arms and two legs, a muscular torso, a head and two eyes. Beyond that any resemblance to humanity faltered and died. It stood a little over six feet tall and its limbs were packed with dense, corded muscle. It had skin as pale and mottled as a mushroom. The hands were hideous, with long clawed fingers ending in wicked claws. Fix couldn't see its face because it wore a helmet of strange design, but braided hair hung like dreadlocks down to its shoulders. The only clothing it wore was a pair of trunks made from dark brown leather and some kind of netting that covered its limbs and massive chest. Some of the netting was torn, Fix could see, and there were green lines, like scars, crisscrossing its body, and from a few of these thin lines a more luminous green oozed.

Chiba noticed him looking at that and said, "Blood. My science guys are having orgasms trying to figure out its chemistry. It's nothing they've ever seen, which makes them all very, very happy. They're badgering me about whether they'll be able to publish. Which, of course, they won't." He grinned. "Possession of an alien life form is illegal. Even way out here in the rocks. It's one of the few things all governments agree on."

"'Alien'...?"

"It was discovered in the wreckage of a crashed ship on the dwarf planet Ceres," said Chiba. "They're terraforming Ceres, you know, doing a nice job of it, too. They've found a lot of wonderful mineral deposits and a lot of water ice. More than the surveyors said to expect. But they never expected to find anything as remarkable as this."

"This is incredible. God, how come everyone doesn't know about this? This changes... shit, it changes everything."

"Sure, I could sell it to a government or a museum and make a quick billion. But, let's be real, that is very small change compared to what I can make with this thing in my stable of fighters."

Fix shook his head. "If you put this... *thing*... on a title card everyone's going to know about it."

Chiba snorted. "Oh, I have that covered. We can bounce a video signal out to the rim, jog it around a bit and then send it back as if it comes from somewhere outside of anyone's territory. Our signal boosters are on military grade stealth

GAMEWORLD

satellite pods with EMP and explosive failsafes. Trust me, Mr. Fix, I've been doing this for a long time."

Fix nodded. Someone as rich as Chiba had more than technology on his side. He could afford to bribe, threaten or own key people in the agencies that were supposed to regulate or arrest people like him.

They stared down into the pit.

"My people tell me that you will need at least a million to pay for your daughter's treatment over the next few years. And you'll need half of that to settle debts and care for your other kids. Round it up for inflation and you need two million. Does that sound fair?"

Fix cleared his throat. "Yeah."

"If you can last three minutes with our friend down there I will pay you nine million."

Fix wheeled around. "*What?*"

"That is three million per minute. But here's the kicker, my friend, I want you both alive at the end. Hurt it, break it, I don't care, but I need it alive because my molecular biologists have a lot of fun things planned with its DNA."

"What kind of fighter is it? I mean, does it have special skills?"

"It has training," said Chiba. "It moves like a warrior. It's incredibly strong and fast, it has excellent reflexes, and it is definitely a killer."

"Meaning...?"

"Even badly injured and starving it managed to kill seven members of the crew of eleven on the salvage ship that found it. And since I acquired it, I've done a few experiments."

"With people?"

"Not at first. Animals. A cougar, a mountain gorilla. Like

427

that. People came later. Came... and went. Our friend down there seems to enjoy extreme combat. It's one of his most endearing qualities."

"Has anyone come close to beating it?"

Chiba shrugged. "In exosuits with military-grade shock rods, yes. Otherwise... well, we're on the wrong side of the learning curve with him. His injuries are mostly healed, except for a few recent scrapes from our ongoing tests. It's worth nine million to me to put him in a ring with a fighter with your skill set. Someone who can use his brains as well as his fists. Nine million is nothing to me, but it's everything to your family, Mr. Fix, and that makes this a fair contract. You were ready to throw your life away against transgenic animals or bio-enhanced fighters. This is single combat of the most basic kind. No weapons, no armor. Only whatever natural gifts you both bring onto the pentangle. This will be the most important fight in the history of... well... fighting. This will *be* history. And win or lose, you're going to be the most famous warrior in the solar system. So... do we have a deal?"

The creature in the pit raised its head as if it could understand Chiba's words. The lenses on the helmet prevented Fix from seeing its eyes, but he knew if he could there would be nothing there but hatred. He knew that his own eyes were probably filled with different emotions. Need. Desperation.

And fear.

"Yeah," he murmured. "Yeah, I'm in."

5

The prep work for the event took weeks.

During that time Chiba provided Fix with the best

trainers, the best sports medicine people, the best food and every luxury Fix might want. Fix turned down the prostitutes and the AI sexbots. He trained and trained, and recorded long videos for each of his kids to try and tell him the things a father would. He repeatedly requested the chance to view any video files of the "tests" conducted with the creature that involved combat, whether against humans or animals. Chiba refused on the grounds that it would "pollute the integrity of the event."

With each day Fix felt his tension growing. He slept badly and had to eat antacids by the handful to keep from throwing up his guts. The doctors gave him shots of vitamins and they monitored his health, often offering sleeping pills, dream gas, or medical sex therapy, but Fix bulled through without any of that. This was going to be tough enough without his brain being fogged. After a while, though, he forced himself to try and get more sleep, to meditate, to eat a saner diet of protein-rich foods.

The weeks melted down to days and then hours.

On the morning of the bout, Hogarth Fix woke from a terrible dream of running through a jungle being hunted by something that he could not see. Something that filled the air with flashes of red that tore through flesh and bone and stone and trees. He ran past the bodies of every soldier he had ever known, and although many had died on worlds or moons far away from *Gameworld*, their bodies were all in the dream, freshly killed, slaughtered, skinned, hung up like deer carcasses after a hunt. The invisible thing pursued him all the way into a trap—a cave filled with the skulls and spines of all of those dead. A mountain of them. Fix fell to his knees and looked around at the walls, seeing trophies

PREDATOR: IF IT BLEEDS

hung there. The skulls of the great hunting cats, cave bears, elephants, alligators. And more—dinosaurs and other creatures Fix had only ever seen in museums. All dead. All conquered. He sank to his knees.

A sound made him turn, and behind him, in the cave's mouth, a massive form was appearing out of nowhere. At first there was only a shimmer and then *it* appeared. Monstrously tall, massively built, heavily armored. Dreadlocks whipped back and forth as the creature looked around its trophy room. It was much bigger than the thing in the pit. Impossibly tall. It raised one arm, fist closed, and a set of three wicked metal blades sprang from sheaths built into the gauntlets. There were smears of fresh blood on those blades. Fix looked down at his own stomach and saw that his shirt and flesh were torn. His guts slid out and flopped wetly to the ground between his knees.

Fix screamed himself awake.

In a happy, chirpy voice the AI system said, "Good morning, Hogarth. It's fight day. Would you like scrambled eggs and coffee?"

6

Fight day.

There had been a lot of matches at *Gameworld* since Fix agreed to this fight. Humans against humans, humans against transgenic animals, teams against teams. Fix had watched them all, trying to prepare his mind for this. As if that was even possible.

He was going to fight an alien.

Yeah, history.

Shit.

He stood in a shower hot enough to boil a lobster. He lost it in there, too. Weeping and pounding his fist on the wall.

Chiba called him a warrior. Sure. Fix had known a lot of them. Only the fools went into battle without fear, and they were usually the first ones to fall. Most good soldiers were like him. Professional, yes; capable, to be sure; but human. They hid their fear because fear is both personal and contagious. They carved religious symbols into their gear. They wore religious medals or good luck charms. They wrote out death letters. Some took pictures of their loved ones with them; others refused to even name their wives or husbands or children for fear it would jinx them. Some took confession and others let hot showers wash their tears away in hopes that it cleansed them of excess fear.

Then they got ready for war.

With Hogarth Fix the ritual was all about being quiet. He toweled off and dressed in fighting trunks. He said nothing at all to the corner man who wrapped the tapes around his hands. Before the match he sat on a stool in the locker room, not praying, not thinking, just letting a silence fill him inside. He meditated, drifting right below the surface of wakefulness while his preconceptions dropped like pebbles to the bottom of his pool of awareness. When he heard the game bell, Fix stood and looked into the mirror, into the eyes of the scarred and ugly man who stared back at him. Into dead eyes that told him nothing and would betray nothing to his opponent. There was no hate in those eyes. No judgment, no anger. There was nothing, not even a mirror for the enemy to see his own strengths and weaknesses.

He stood up, turned, and walked out to the war.

7

The crowd was enormous. Every seat was taken and there were people standing in the aisles and crowding the balconies. The bleachers for the fighters were filled with past champions, each of them wearing their victory belts and sashes. Fix saw their eyes, saw the resentment, let it slide off of him. He knew that there were better fighters among them. Stronger, younger, faster, more talented. That was what it was. Chiba had picked him. Over the last few weeks Fix had gone through the agony of doubt, wondering if Chiba could be trusted, wondering if the promoter had picked him as an appetizer, intending Fix to be killed in order to show how tough the alien was. Probably. That was okay. Chiba still wanted a good fight. A long fight. Only record-keepers and trivia freaks ever really wanted a fight to end in the shortest time. Fans wanted to see the competitors fight it out all the way to the final bell. They wanted to *see* something.

They wanted a war.

That's what Chiba had to want, too. A big, showy fight that commentators could dissect on news programs all over the solar system. A fight that would show human ingenuity and skill against something beyond all human experience, but which would end with the human—with Fix—dead on the deck. Dead or crippled, but the loser either way. That way the ticket or logon price for the next bout would be higher, and there would be no end to the list of fighters who would want to be the one who not only fought an alien, but defeated it. A victory by the next guy was the only possible bigger fight news.

Chiba walked into the center of the pentangle in a blood-red sequined suit, his massive bulk seeming to fill the place. There was a lot of yelling, a lot of rabble rousing. The din became one vast homogenous roar, like white noise turned high. Fix tuned it out. It was irrelevant and therefore a distraction, if he allowed it to be such.

When his name was called, he walked out onto the floor and did what he was expected to do. He raised his arms and danced on the balls of his feet, turning this way and that, grinning like an ape so that every camera could get a good shot. Looking mean. Acting the part.

"And facing our champion, Hogarth Fix, today is a new fighter. New to *Gameworld*, new to the pentangle, new to our kind of fighting," bellowed Chiba, and a pregnant hush dropped heavily over the chamber. "I can guarantee you, my friends, that this is a fight like nothing you've ever seen. Like nothing *anyone's* ever seen. You are about to witness a fight between one of the toughest men who I've had the privilege to know and an opponent so strange, so rare, so new that none of us know what's going to happen in the next three minutes. I don't know his name but once you take a look at him you'll understand why we all call him the *Nightmare Kid*!"

With that a section of the pentangle floor hissed open and a big metal cylinder rose into sight. It was opaque and painted with images from a couple hundred years' worth of horror stories. The cylinder turned slowly so everyone could see. Bug-eyed aliens, lumbering moon-beasts, spiders from Mars, space invaders, bat-winged monstrosities, and more. The creatures of books, comics, and film. Fix recognized some of them and others he didn't.

Then the revolving cylinder dropped back down, revealing the figure of the hideous creature standing there, wrists and ankles secured by heavy shackles attached to retractable steel cables. The monster was dressed in black trunks now, but the torn netting was still there. And now he wore no helmet.

Fix could feel a cold hand of terror reach past his professional calm and clamp icy fingers around his heart. That face.

Dear god, that *face*.

It was every bit the nightmare promised by its nickname. Not even vaguely human, with spiked mandibles that were like some parasitic monster, or a spider, or a crustacean. It hissed at the crowd, and the spiked corners of its lips peeled back to reveal sharp, deadly teeth.

There was one long, lingering moment when all sound in the room suddenly died as the people stared at the thing. This wasn't a publicity stunt and it wasn't transgenics, and everyone seemed to grasp that all at once.

And then the crowd went absolutely wild.

Forty guards with shock rods came trotting out of a side corridor and surrounded the pentangle. The creature turned its head to watch them and there was hatred and something else in its eyes. Not fear, Fix thought, but a wariness. The kind that comes from experience. It remembered those shock rods and seemed to understand the odds against it. Forty big men in full riot gear. A moment later a ceiling vent opened and a turbo-cannon dropped into sight, its laser sight finding and locking onto the Nightmare Kid. The creature looked down at the spot where the laser sight hovered and then he looked at Chiba, who stood a few yards away.

"That's right, you little cockroach," murmured Chiba in a voice only Fix and the creature could hear. "You try any of your tricks and you'll get worse than you got downstairs."

The crowd had gone insane. Local and long-range cameras swiveled into position. A senior tech gave Chiba the thumbs up. "All of the subscribers are logged in, boss. We are live from Neptune to Mother Earth."

Chiba returned the nod and amped up the wattage on his grin.

"Are you ready for blood?" he roared to the crowd.

Their response shook the whole place. Everyone was cheering, even the fighters on the bench.

"Then let's put three minutes on the clock," bellowed Chiba, and a large digital display showed the time in seconds. It was a more dramatic countdown. Two hundred and forty.

Chiba stepped off of the pentangle and took position behind six of the biggest guards.

"Shackles off!" he yelled and the bonds disengaged on ankles and wrists and were whipped out of sight beneath the floor, which closed over them.

The monster stood his ground, looking around, cautious, adjusting what he had experienced so far to what was happening now. Fix could understand it and even follow the obvious logic. He had been captured, overpowered, poked and prodded, been given opportunities to fight and had won each time. Maybe Chiba had tried to tame him with the shock rods and other tools. If so, Fix did not believe it had been a successful attempt. Now it was in a protected enclosure with another possible enemy. Even if it did not know what *Gameworld* was, it could put two and two together. This was a fight.

It turned toward Fix.

On impulse, Fix raised his left arm, fist clenched. It was a salute but also a test.

The creature considered him, then it, too, raised its arm. Fix saw a tiny twitch of its right shoulder before it raised its left. That was very interesting. Did that mean it was right-handed? Did it mean that it was conditioned to salute, and to do it with its right? If so, why did it use its left? In straight imitation?

Maybe.

Fix was right-handed, too.

Chiba yelled out the Japanese word to begin, "*Hajime!*"

The clock started. The crowd roared.

The creature instantly shifted its stance, feet wide, knees bent, body leaning forward, the muscles of chest and shoulders and biceps tensing. Making a show of it as it let out a terrifying, challenging roar.

The movement was tribal and ritualistic.

And telling.

Then it attacked.

The monster was fast. Good lord it was fast. For all its size and bulk, it seemed to turn into a blur as it came straight at him, claws slashing toward Fix's throat.

The claws cut only air though.

Fix saw the muscles tense in the creature's thighs and calves, read the coiled power, knew the lunge was coming. Nothing moves without some kind of tell. Not even the greatest fighters in history. The body is an interconnected series of tightly meshed ligaments and muscles, bones and moveable flesh. When one part of the body moves there is always a compensating flex or shift. The best fighters can minimize this so that they appear to go from zero to full speed without any intermediate process of acceleration. Fix was good at that.

He was even better at reading it.

The Nightmare Kid tore through the spot where Fix
had been, but Fix was moving with light, quick steps on an
oblique angle. He moved like a fencer, like a tennis player,
his weight balanced on the springy balls of his feet, knees
bent to act like shock absorbers, everything else loose so as
not to drain energy.

The alien whipped around and tried it again, relying on
his speed and greater reach to end the fight quickly.

The tips of those nails brushed across Fix's hip and there
was a sudden flash of heat. The monster was faster even than
he looked, and those nails were scalpel sharp. The creature
howled in triumph, owning the moment of first blood. He
reared back and bellowed at the crowd.

Fix darted in and to the right and punched him on the
outside of the thigh, driving a corkscrew knuckle punch at
the juncture of two big muscles. The creature hissed and
dropped to one knee but slashed again to chase Fix away
from a combination off of that hit.

The crowd screamed.

The Nightmare Kid got back to his feet, chest heaving.
Was he angry that his moment of triumph had been spoiled?
Fix thought so. Interesting. Very interesting.

The creature leaped at him, getting great height and
distance for his bulk, and Fix had to twist away from him,
but once more those claws drew lines of fire, this time along
Fix's upper back.

Fix immediately countered with a sideways lunge and
punch, hitting exactly the same spot. Harder. The creature's
knee hit the deck and it launched again from there, trying
to slash its opponent's legs out. Fix slap-parried the thing's
wrists and hit him with two fast left jabs in the side of the face.

That became the rhythm. The monster tried a dozen different angles of attack, relying on its enormous power, speed, and reach, each time trying to deliver a crippling blow. Each time Fix read the thing's body language and moved with the attack. Those claws, though, found him time and again. Never deeply, but enough to hurt. Fix had to force the pain and the fear that it brought back down to the bottom of his pond of mental stillness.

Each time the Nightmare Kid attacked, though, Fix counterattacked with a left-hand punch, often striking the same spot on the monster's leg. The monster was starting to limp, but it was clearly no slave to pain. It seemed to eat the pain and use it to fuel another attack, and another. If it was tiring, it did not show.

The clock said one hundred and two.

It felt like hours.

Out of the corner of his eye, Fix saw an aide hand a small communicator to Chiba, who covered one ear and listened. Fix saw Chiba's brows knit with some kind of consternation. There was no time to observe more, though, because the alien nearly killed him with a double high slash followed by a savage kick that Fix almost, but not quite, evaded. Instead the kick propelled him into the air, and the monster dove forward to be under him when he fell. A nice trick. Like a cat might do.

Fix tucked and turned and came down feet first, stamping down onto the monster's arms and missing the claws by inches. Fix pitched forward and rolled, came out of it without rising and spun on the floor, sweeping the monster as it charged after. The Nightmare Kid fell hard and lay stunned, but Fix wasn't fooled. The landing wasn't hard enough to do that much damage. It was a trick and Fix wasn't buying. Instead he backed up and began circling, waiting for the creature to stop playing and rise.

It did, but when it was halfway up Fix attacked, punching it once more in the leg, pivoting backward off the impact so that he was chest to back with it, and then laying into the thing with some hardcore neighborhood work. He drove solid punches into kidneys—if it had kidneys—ribs, under the shoulder blades, into the vulnerable soft spots below the armpits. He worked it fast and hard, torquing his body for maximum power and then bailing fast by skipping backward.

The creature went down onto both knees and for a moment it looked like it was truly dazed.

But it got back to its feet once more and began stalking Fix.

There was something different in its eyes now. Fix wanted to call it a loss of confidence, but that was probably only partly true. It had the muscle and stamina to win this. Fix was breathing heavy and there was still a million years to the end of those three goddamn minutes. Fix was bleeding from a dozen shallow cuts. The alien didn't even look bruised.

It limped, though. There was that.

Seventy-three seconds on the clock.

Christ. Might as well be forever.

Chiba was on the far side of the pentangle and Fix frowned as he saw the big man moving away, heading toward his private elevator, his six men surrounding him. Some of the crowd were looking at Chiba, others were talking on private communicators. More than half the crowd was no longer looking at the fight.

The Nightmare Kid did not seem to notice any of this. Instead he lunged in again and this time his claws tore into

Fix's left forearm, detonating white-hot agony. Fix kicked it in the knee and backpedaled to safety. His arm was hurt, the fingers sluggish, blood welling thickly from two deep cuts.

With a howl of pure animal joy, the monster came at him, driving in toward Fix's left side, confident that its opponent was crippled.

Fix knew that there was a time for playing the game Chiba wanted him to play, and there was a time to fight for his life. For his kids.

He accepted the rush and then shifted left, pivoting to kick at the monster's knee, but then launching a series of blows with his right. With his dominant, much faster right. He'd underused it all through the fight, training the monster to regard him as a left-dominant counter-fighter. Schooling it for this moment.

The creature was tough but it was also strangely naïve. It bought the fiction and had built its strategy around it. And now Fix made him pay for that lack of perception.

As the Nightmare Kid slashed, Fix leaned out of the strike path and hammered its forearm with two punishing blows to the point where the muscles stretched thinnest behind the wrist. Then he stamped on its foot, grinding hard to break bones, then he headbutted it, accepting a deep cut on his own forehead to break one of the mandibles. He grabbed with his bad left hand, needing only a marginal grip, and hit the monster with a series of brutal, full-speed snap punches to throat, groin, eyes, throat, heart, throat, temple, and throat. Then he sidestepped, cocked his right leg, and heel-kicked the same point on the thigh he'd been hammering since the fight started. The creature went down and Fix shifted behind him and was one micro-second away from grabbing its head to try and snap the thing's neck when the wall behind the fighters' bleachers exploded.

The force plucked Fix and the Nightmare Kid up and hurled them into the audience, chased by a storm cloud of flaming debris and bleeding body parts. Fix hit two people in the face and heard necks snap as he fell.

He landed badly and lay there, nearly unconscious, blinking through blood and smoke and madness, taking in what happened next in haphazard images.

There were flashes of red lightning. Or... laser pulse blasts? Something like that. Fix fought for consciousness. People screamed and fell. When a red blast caught someone, they simply flew apart. Customers trampled each other, clawing and fighting, kicking, and biting to escape.

Someone yelled, "It's the police!"

But that was stupid. It was wrong. Hurt as he was, Fix knew that. The police used machine guns and lead bullets, even out here. And they used high-intensity gas guns for microgravity EVA fights. Who the hell used pulse guns outside of deep-sea mining?

———

Chiba was banging on the button for his private elevator, his face pale with panic, eyes wide. He had a pistol in his hand. His guards were battering at the crowd, using the shock rods to keep them away from the elevator door.

Some of the fighters—those few who had survived the explosion—had grabbed chairs, fallen shock rods or anything else they could grab and were crowding toward whatever had breached the wall. Fix saw them fall.

One.

By one.

By one.

One of them—Helga, the trollish woman—had a big commando knife, God only knew where she'd gotten it, and with a furious battlefield shriek dove into the smoke.

A moment later she came out again.

But Fix could not at first understand what he was seeing.

Helga hung writhing in the air, her body torn and bloody, dangling in the smoke like a puppet on broken strings.

And then *it* emerged.

Just like in his dream, a thing appeared out of nowhere. There was a shimmer in the troubled air and suddenly a form took shape. Monstrous, unnatural, armed, and armored. It held Helga up and now Fix could see that three steel claws had been thrust entirely through her body and the bloody tips stood out from between her shoulder blades. The creature wore the same kind of helmet that the Nightmare Kid had worn when Fix first saw him. The pale flesh of its body was covered in the same netting, but instead of a simple pair of trunks it wore complex armor, hung and fitted with exotic weapons. Knives and guns and other things Fix could not begin to identify.

The monster was huge. Much bigger than the creature Fix had fought. At least a foot taller and half again as broad in the shoulders. The brute peered at Helga, seeming to take note of her musculature, her scars. It made a series of weird clicks, sounds nearly lost beneath the screaming, and then it flung Helga away. Her dying screams chased her across the pentangle and she landed with a bone-breaking thud five feet from where Fix lay, the knife still in her hand, its blade smeared with green.

Fix tried to get up, tried to reach for that blade.

Then a shape pushed itself up from beneath a pile of debris and corpses. The Nightmare Kid, bleeding bright green blood, wild-eyed, furious. It looked down at Fix and hissed at him, the three remaining mandible spikes twitching, claws flexing. It took one threatening step toward its enemy and then it stopped and wheeled, looking first toward the much larger killer who was now tearing into the remaining fighters, and then at Chiba, who was crowding into the elevator with his men. The door wouldn't close, though, because of all the people trying to claw their way in.

The Nightmare Kid howled in fury, and all of its rage, all of its hatred shifted from Fix to Chiba. It bolted toward the elevator, slashing people apart even as they fought to get out of its way.

Fix struggled to his feet just as the smaller of the two monsters smashed its way through the crowd and into the elevator. The doors closed behind it and Fix had a brief view of electronic flashes from the shock rods and a spray of bright red blood.

The larger monster was killing its way across the floor. The remaining guards rallied and attacked it with shock rods, and for a moment they seemed to drive it back, though at the cost of many of their own lives.

And in a moment of sudden crystal clarity, Fix put the pieces to all of this together.

The nickname Chiba had given to the alien—the Nightmare Kid—might have been more apt than he knew. From the size of the newcomer, and the superb combat skills *it* demonstrated, and the comparatively smaller size and more naïve skills of the Nightmare Kid, Fix realized that he had been fighting just that. A kid. A younger, less experienced, less dangerous version of the true nightmare that was slaughtering the most skilled fighters in the solar system. This creature—mother or father—had come looking for its kid. It had attacked a whole space station full of people to protect its own.

And now that kid was fighting for its life, either in the elevator or in Chiba's office. Fighting against armed killers and the brutish champion sumo wrestler. The kid was outnumbered, outgunned, and—because of the last few seconds of the fight—injured.

Before he knew he was going to do it, Fix was up and running, his fatigue forgotten, his pain channeled into some other part of his brain. He grabbed the knife and used it to cut his way to the elevator controls. The customers, already hurt and shocked and frightened by the last onslaught, and by what was happening in the area, gave way, cursing and weeping. And dying.

The elevator opened and Fix stepped inside and punched the button for the office. The walls of the lift were smeared with human and alien blood, and three of the six security men lay in broken heaps on the floor.

Below, even through the doors and distance, he could hear the frustrated roar of the thing's parent. Had it seen its child escape? Was it losing this fight to save it?

No way to tell.

Then the elevator shuddered as something struck the frame. A blast or a fist?

The door pinged open and Fix jumped out and to one side, narrowly evading the swing of a shock rod. He ducked low and cut high and the guard sagged back as blood erupted from his upper thigh and groin.

Across the room Chiba was fighting the Nightmare Kid.

Fighting, and winning. The young alien had taken a lot of damage in the elevator fight and was barely able to stand, and Chiba, for all his size, was a champion and a killer. He battered the alien with one after the other of devastating blows. Even so, the kid kept fighting. It was clear it was never going to stop fighting. Maybe it was the thing's nature, maybe its culture. Whatever. It was losing the fight that would kill it, but it was going to make Chiba earn that victory.

The two remaining guards were torn—help their boss or stop Fix?

They split the difference. One of them rushed over and jabbed the Nightmare Kid with his shock rod, which made the creature stagger down to hands and knees. Chiba used that moment to lunge toward a gun safe bolted to the wall and begin punching a code.

The other guard rushed at Fix, jabbing with the shock rod as he circled for the best angle. Fix had no armor and a metal knife. Not good odds against a professional with an electric weapon. They dueled and darted and Fix saw his moment. The guard tried for a long reach, leaning into it with too much weight on his lead leg. Fix collapsed beneath the glowing end of the rod and stamped out at the man's shin. The guard fell hard and Fix caught him, rolled with him, rolled atop him, and drove the point of the knife through the guard's right eye socket.

He looked up to see Chiba whip the door of the safe open and pull out a heavy caliber navy automatic. He leveled the weapon at Fix and pulled the trigger.

At the exact moment the elevator door exploded inward. Fix, sprawled on the floor, felt the steel door whistle overhead and saw it smash Chiba's desk to pieces.

Then the larger alien jumped out of the shattered elevator shaft. It was covered with bleeding cuts and one eye was swollen shut. Some of its weapons were smashed and melted from multiple impacts of the shock rods. Its hands and chest and thighs were soaked with bright red human blood.

Chiba shoved the remaining guard toward the alien, wrapped a powerful arm around the smaller alien's throat and jammed the barrel against the Nightmare Kid's head.

"No!" roared the sumo champion.

The moment froze.

The big alien stood there, panting with exertion and pain, glaring at the humans in the room. The smaller alien hissed but did not struggle to break free.

The guard gaped in naked terror, his confidence in his shock rod gone.

Fix was on the floor, ten feet from Chiba, two feet from the guard, six yards from the big alien.

He read the scene, read the moment. He understood because understanding the nuances of combat was who and what he was.

He had kids at home that he knew he would never see again. The insurance was there, though. They would be taken care of. It hurt so bad to think that he would never see them again, but at least he hadn't failed them.

So he did what any father would do.

He swept the foot of the remaining guard and while every eye went to that man falling, Fix threw his knife.

He did not throw it at the guard, or at the big alien, or at Chiba, who was too well hidden behind his inhuman shield.

No, he threw the knife to the Nightmare Kid.

The young alien caught it, twisted, biting down on the

gun arm of the distracted Chiba and then turning more and using that knife. Using it with the ferocity of a warrior; using it with the precision of a butcher.

No, of a hunter.

Gutting, ending, emptying, destroying.

Chiba tried to scream but there was not enough of his throat left for that. There was no air in his ruptured lungs. There was nothing left of him or for him, and the alien stepped aside to let the heavy body fall.

The guard flung his weapon away, got to his knees and begged for mercy that was not his. Fix slapped away the pleading hands and chopped him across the throat.

Then he fell back onto the floor, spent. Nearly gone.

The big alien crossed the room in a few long strides. He stepped over Fix without even looking at him, grabbed the younger alien, slapped him hard across the mouth, once, twice, hitting him so hard the lights flickered in the Nightmare Kid's eyes. Then the big alien gave the younger one a single, fierce hug and shoved him roughly away, adding one more slap for emphasis.

The younger alien staggered, swayed, but stayed on his feet. He held the bloody knife up and hissed. The bigger alien looked at it, at the blood, and nodded.

Fix watched in horrified fascination as the younger alien rolled Chiba onto his stomach, slit him from crown to anus, tore open the fatty flesh and with a savage grunt tore the entire spine and skull out of the sumo champion's body. It was disgusting and it was terrifying. The Nightmare Kid stood there, panting, admiring his trophy. Then they turned and looked down at Fix.

There was absolutely nothing Fix could do. He had barely

outfought the younger one and the adult was so far beyond his skill as to be absurd. This was where he, too, would die.

The big alien studied Fix for a long time. It looked over his head at what was left of Chiba, then at the knife its child held, and at the trophy, then back to Fix.

It gave him a single, small nod.

After a moment, Fix returned the nod.

Warrior to warrior. Parent to parent.

He lay there and watched the aliens move to the elevator shaft and then jump down to where the sound of screams could still be heard.

It took Fix a long time to get to his feet.

It took him nearly an hour to figure out how to open Chiba's safe. As it turned out it was a biometric scan. A full palm print was all it took, and the aliens had left Chiba's hands nicely intact.

He stood for even longer in front of the open safe.

Smiling.

AUTHOR BIOGRAPHIES

BRYAN THOMAS SCHMIDT (Editor and Co-Author "Drug War") is a Hugo-nominated editor and author. His anthologies include *Shattered Shields* with Jennifer Brozek, *Mission: Tomorrow, Galactic Games, Little Green Men—Attack!* with Robin Wayne Bailey, Joe Ledger: *Unstoppable* with Jonathan Maberry, *Monster Hunter Files* with Larry Correia, *Infinite Stars*, and *Predator: If It Bleeds*. His debut novel, *The Worker Prince*, achieved Honorable Mention on Barnes & Noble's Year's Best SF of 2011. It is followed by two sequels in the *Saga of Davi Rhii* space opera trilogy. His short fiction includes stories in *The X-Files, Predator*, Larry Correia's *Monster Hunter International*, Joe Ledger, and Decipher's *WARS*, along with original fiction. He also edited *The Martian* by Andy Weir, amongst other novels. His work has been published by St. Martin's Press, Titan Books, Baen, and more. He lives in Ottawa, KS. Find him online as BryanThomasS at both Twitter and Facebook or via his website and blog at www.bryanthomasschmidt.net.

TIM LEBBON ("Devil Dogs") is a *New York Times* bestselling writer with over thirty novels published to date, as well as dozens of novellas and hundreds of short stories. Recent releases include *The Silence*, *The Hunt*, *The Family Man*, and *The Rage War* trilogy (licensed *Alien* and *Predator* novels). Forthcoming novels include the *Relics* trilogy and *Blood of the Four* (with Christopher Golden). He has won four British Fantasy Awards, a Bram Stoker Award, and a Scribe Award, and been shortlisted for World Fantasy and Shirley Jackson awards. A movie of his story *Pay the Ghost*, starring Nicolas Cage, was released in 2015, and other projects in development include *My Haunted House*, *Playtime* (with Stephen Volk), and *Exorcising Angels* (with Simon Clark). Find out more: www.timlebbon.net.

JEREMY ROBINSON (aka: Jeremy Bishop and Jeremiah Knight, "Stonewall's Last Stand") is the international bestselling author of more than fifty thriller, horror, science fiction, fantasy and action-adventure novels and novellas including *Apocalypse Machine*, *Hunger*, *Island 731*, *SecondWorld*, and the Jack Sigler thriller series, which is currently in development to be released as a major motion picture. His bestselling kaiju novels, *Project Nemesis* and *Island 731*, have been adapted as comic book series from American Gothic Press/Famous Monsters of Filmland. His novels have been translated into thirteen languages. He lives in New Hampshire with his wife and three children. For the latest news about his novels, comics, movies and TV projects, and the Beware of Monsters podcast, discussing all things monstrous, visit www.bewareofmonsters.com.

Prior to working full-time as a freelance writer, **STEVE PERRY** ("Rematch") worked as a swimming instructor, lifeguard, assembler of toys, clerk in a hotel gift shop and car rental agency, aluminum salesman, martial art instructor, private detective, and physician's assistant.

Perry has written sixty-odd novels and scores of short stories. He has written books in the *Star Wars*, *Aliens*, *Predator*, *Indiana Jones*, and *Conan* universes. He was a collaborator on the *New York Times* bestselling *Tom Clancy's Net Force* series. Other writing credits include articles, reviews, and essays, animated teleplays, and several unproduced movie scripts. One of his teleplays for *Batman: The Animated Series* was an Emmy Award nominee for Outstanding Writing.

He is a practitioner of the Indonesian martial art pentjak silat, and plays blues and geezer rock on the tenor ukulele.

WESTON OCHSE ("May Blood Pave My Way Home") is a former intelligence officer and special operations soldier who has engaged enemy combatants, terrorists, narco smugglers, and human traffickers. His personal war stories include performing humanitarian operations over Bangladesh, being deployed to Afghanistan, and a near miss being cannibalized in Papua New Guinea. His fiction and non-fiction has been praised by *USA Today*, *The Atlantic*, *New York Post*, *Financial Times* (London), and *Publishers Weekly*. The American Library Association labeled him one of the Major Horror Authors of the 21st Century. His work has also won the Bram Stoker Award, been nominated for the Pushcart Prize, and won multiple New Mexico-Arizona Book Awards. A writer of more than 26 books in multiple genres, his military supernatural series SEAL Team 666 has been optioned to be a movie starring Dwayne Johnson. His military sci-fi series, which starts with *Grunt Life*, has been praised for its PTSD-positive depiction of soldiers at peace and at war.

PETER J. WACKS ("Storm Blood") is a cross-genre writer and world traveler. In his spare time he enjoys Scotch, beer, swords, magic, and absurdist philosophy. Over the course of his life he has worked across the creative fields, and in the pursuit of character research has done side jobs ranging from I.T. break-fix to private detective. You can find him online on both Twitter and Facebook, where he occasionally pops in to crack jokes about the state of the world. Or if you just want to stalk him a little you can go to www.peterjwacks.net.

DAVID BOOP ("Storm Blood") is a Denver-based author. He's also an award-winning essayist and screenwriter. Before turning to fiction, he worked as a DJ, film critic, journalist, and actor. As Editor-in-Chief at IntraDenver.net, David's team covered Columbine, making them the first Internet-only newspaper at such an event. They won an award for excellence from the CPA for their design and coverage.

His debut novel, the sci-fi/noir *She Murdered Me with Science*, returned from WordFire Press after a seven-year hiatus. Additionally, David edited the anthology *Straight Outta Tombstone* for Baen. Predominately a weird western author, he's published short fiction in horror, fantasy, mystery, and media tie-ins with *The Green Hornet* and *Veronica Mars*. His RPG work includes *Flash Gordon* and *Deadlands: Noir* for Savage Worlds.

He's a single dad, part-time temp worker, and believer. His hobbies include film noir, anime, and the Blues. Find out more on his fanpage: www.facebook.com/dboop.updates or Twitter: @david_boop.

JENNIFER BROZEK ("Last Report of the KSS Psychopomp") is a Hugo Award nominated editor and a Bram Stoker Award nominated author. She has worked in the publishing industry since 2004. With the number of edited anthologies, novels, RPG books, and nonfiction books under her belt, Jennifer is often considered a Renaissance woman, but she prefers to be known as a wordslinger and optimist. When she is not writing her heart out, she is gallivanting around the Pacific Northwest in its wonderfully mercurial weather. Read more about her at www.jenniferbrozek.com or follow her on Twitter: @JenniferBrozek.

S. D. PERRY ("Skeld's Keep") writes novelizations and tie-ins for love and money; she has worked in the shared universes of *Star Trek*, *Resident Evil*, and *Aliens*, among others, and in her spare time reads and writes horror. S. D. lives in Portland, Oregon, with her husband and two children.

KEVIN J. ANDERSON ("Indigenous Species") is the author of 140 novels, 55 of which have appeared on national or international bestseller lists; he has over 23 million books in print in thirty languages. Anderson has co-authored fourteen books in the *Dune* saga with Brian Herbert; he and Herbert have also written an original SF trilogy, *Hellhole*. Anderson's popular epic space opera series *The Saga of Seven Suns*, as well as its sequel trilogy *The Saga of Shadows*, are among his most ambitious works. He has also written a sweeping fantasy trilogy, *Terra Incognita*, accompanied by two rock CDs (which he wrote and produced). He has written two steampunk novels, *Clockwork Angels* and *Clockwork Lives*, with legendary Rush drummer and lyricist Neil Peart. He also created the popular humorous horror series *Dan Shamble, Zombie P.I.*, and has written eight high-tech thrillers with Colonel Doug Beason.

He holds a physics/astronomy degree and spent 14 years

working as a technical writer for the Lawrence Livermore National Laboratory. He is now the publisher of Colorado-based WordFire Press. He and his wife, bestselling author Rebecca Moesta, have lived in Colorado for 20 years; Anderson has climbed all of the mountains over 14,000 ft in the state, and he has also hiked the 500-mile Colorado Trail.

MIRA GRANT ("Blood And Sand") lives and writes in the Pacific Northwest, where her home overlooks a large swamp filled with frogs. Truly the best of all possible worlds. When not writing as herself, Mira writes under the name Seanan McGuire, and releases a truly daunting number of books and stories during the average year. She regularly claims to be the vanguard of an invading race of alien plant people; any time spent with her will make this surprisingly credible. Mira shares her home with two enormous blue cats, a lizard, some very odd bugs, and a daunting number of books about dead things. She loves horrible diseases, and is not always a good dinner companion. Keep up with Mira at www.seananmcguire.com, or on Twitter at @seananmcguire. Mira would very much like to show you what lurks behind the corn, but for some reason, the editors won't let her.

JOHN SHIRLEY ("Tin Warrior") is the author of numerous novels and books of short stories including the Bram Stoker Award winning collection *Black Butterflies*. His novels include *Bleak History*, *A Splendid Chaos*, *BioShock: Rapture*, *Predator: Forever Midnight*, *Halo: Broken Circle*, and *Black Glass*.

LARRY CORREIA ("Three Sparks") is the *New York Times* bestselling author of the *Monster Hunter International* series, the

Grimnoir Chronicles, the *Saga of the Forgotten Warrior*, the *Dead Six* thrillers with Mike Kupari, *The Adventures of Tom Stranger Interdimensional Insurance Agent*, novels set in the *Warmachine* universe, and a whole lot of short fiction. Before becoming an author, Larry was an accountant, a gun dealer, and a firearms instructor. Larry lives in Yard Moose Mountain, Utah, with his very patient wife and children.

ANDREW MAYNE ("The Pilot") is the author of the ITW Award-nominated *Jessica Blackwood* series and star of A&E's magic reality show *Don't Trust Andrew Mayne*.

A life-long nerd, **WENDY N. WAGNER** ("Buffalo Jump") is also a writer and Hugo-winning editor. Her novels include *An Oath of Dogs* and the *Pathfinder* tie-in adventures *Skinwalkers* and *Starspawn*. Her short fiction has appeared in over thirty venues, including *Cthulhu's Daughters*, *Shattered Shields*, and *The Way of the Wizard*. An avid tabletop gamer and gardener, she lives in Portland, Oregon, with her very understanding family.

HOLLY ROBERDS (Co-author "Drug War") is a science fiction and romance writer who lives in Colorado. Always juggling five jobs at any one time, Holly has worked for a private investigator among other things. Holly enjoys bunnies, books, and booze, but not necessarily in that order.

DAYTON WARD ("Recon") is a *New York Times* bestselling author or co-author of more than twenty novels, often working with his best friend, Kevin Dilmore. His short fiction has appeared in more than twenty anthologies, and he's written for various magazines including *Kansas City Voices*, *Famous Monsters of*

Filmland, Star Trek, and *Star Trek Communicator*, as well as the websites Tor.com, StarTrek.com, and Syfy.com. Dayton lives with his wife and two daughters in Kansas City. Visit him on the web at http://www.daytonward.com.

JONATHAN MABERRY ("Gameworld") is a *New York Times* bestselling suspense novelist, five-time Bram Stoker Award winner, and comic book writer. His books include the *Joe Ledger* thrillers, *The Nightsiders, Dead of Night, The X-Files Origins: Devil's Advocate,* as well as standalone novels in multiple genres. His YA space travel novel, *Mars One,* is in development for film; and his *Monk Addison* short stories and *V-Wars* shared world vampire apocalypse series are being developed for TV. He is the editor of many anthologies including *The X-Files, Aliens: Bug Hunt, Nights of the Living Dead* (co-edited with zombie genre creator George A. Romero). His comics include *Captain America,* the Bram Stoker Award-winning *Bad Blood, Black Panther, Punisher, Marvel Zombies Return,* and more. His *Rot & Ruin* novels were included in *Booklist's* Ten Best Horror Novels for Young Adults. His first novel, *Ghost Road Blues,* was named by *Complex* one of the 25 Best Horror Novels of the New Millennium. A board game version of *V-Wars: A Game of Blood and Betrayal* was based on his novels and comics. He was a featured expert on the History Channel's *Zombies: A Living History* and *True Monsters.* He is one third of the very popular and mildly weird *Three Guys with Beards* podcast. Jonathan lives in Del Mar, California with his wife, Sara Jo. www.jonathanmaberry.com.

For more fantastic fiction, author events, exclusive excerpts,
competitions, limited editions and more

VISIT OUR WEBSITE
titanbooks.com

LIKE US ON FACEBOOK
facebook.com/titanbooks

FOLLOW US ON TWITTER
@TitanBooks

EMAIL US
readerfeedback@titanemail.com